PRAISE FOR J. DIRTY DEEDS SERIES

BAD FOR YOU

"*Bad for You* is a distinctive blend of passionate romance, heartrending story and hopeful message, and it left me a satisfied mess with a big smile on my face...A beautiful romance that is a testament to acceptance, love and second chances."

—*USA Today*, Happy Ever After

"If you're a fan of tortured bad boy heroes with hearts of gold who fall head over heels for their one true love, then you are going to absolutely adore this book!"

—Aestas Book Blog

HIT THE SPOT

"An intense, passionate game of wills that will have you speeding through the pages to find out what happens next."

—S. C. Stephens, #1 *New York Times* bestselling author

"Sinfully sexy and surprisingly sweet, from the first page you will fall in love with Jamie and Tori's story."

—Jay Crownover, *New York Times* bestselling author

"A perfect balance of laugh-out-loud funny and crazy sexy, *Hit the Spot* is an alpha romance brimming with sassy banter that you won't want to miss!"

—Meghan March, *New York Times* bestselling author

DOWN
TOO
DEEP

DOWN TOO DEEP

J. DANIELS

FOREVER

New York Boston

Cover design by M80 Design
Cover copyright © 2019 by Hachette Book Group, Inc.

Forever
Hachette Book Group
1290 Avenue of the Americas, New York, NY 10104
read-forever.com
twitter.com/readforeverpub

First edition: October 2019

Forever is an imprint of Grand Central Publishing. The Forever name and logo are trademarks of Hachette Book Group, Inc.

The publisher is not responsible for websites (or their content) that are not owned by the publisher.

The Hachette Speakers Bureau provides a wide range of authors for speaking events. To find out more, go to www.hachettespeakersbureau.com or call (866) 376-6591.

Library of Congress Cataloging-in-Publication Data

Names: Daniels, J., author.
Title: Down too deep / J. Daniels.
Description: First edition. | New York : Forever, 2019.
Identifiers: LCCN 2019009315 | ISBN 9781538743478 (trade pbk.) | ISBN 9781549115035 (audio download) | ISBN 9781538743485 (ebook)
Subjects: | GSAFD: Love stories.
Classification: LCC PS3604.A533 D69 2019 | DDC 813/.6—dc23
LC record available at https://lccn.loc.gov/2019009315

ISBNs: 978-1-5387-4347-8 (trade paperback), 978-1-5387-4348-5 (ebook)

Printed in the United States of America

LSC-C

10 9 8 7 6 5 4 3 2 1

For my brother, Craig.
A great man and an even better father.

chapter one

NATHAN

Wake up, Nathan."

My phone vibrated against the dark oak of the bar, pulling me out of the memory I frequently lost myself in. I blinked the room into focus, palmed the device, and slid my thumb across the screen as I took a generous sip of whiskey.

Get your ass home

My father's text read as an order and was meant to be taken as one. It was also a message I'd been expecting for a long fucking time. I was shocked it hadn't come sooner.

He was finally stepping in. The man who never bit his tongue around me had been unusually tolerant of my shit the past twenty-two months. But now he'd reached his limit—or, more likely, my mother had. She'd never say anything to me directly, of course. She would see my guilt and cave, allowing this to drag on indefinitely. Her only option was my father.

He was the better choice anyway. She knew I always listened to him. At least, I did before, back when we actually spoke to each other.

I pushed off the stool I'd been occupying for the past two hours and drained the remainder of my drink, dug the wallet out of my back pocket, and dropped two twenties on the bar, catching Levi's attention.

We weren't friends. I didn't know the guy outside of this building. But when you frequent the same bar nearly every night, you pick up a few names.

"Thanks, man. I'll see ya tomorrow." Levi swiped the money off the wood and wiped the bar down with a rag.

"No," I said, palming my phone and reading the text again. I met Levi's gaze. "You won't."

* * *

"We've raised our children, Nathan. Your mother and I are too old for this. We're supposed to be enjoying our retirement, but we haven't been able to do that, now, have we?" My father's voice echoed off the vaulted ceiling of my family room and loomed over me like thunderclouds.

He wasn't screaming. He didn't need to. His voice carried no matter what volume he used, and truth be told, he could've whispered this shit to me and I would've heard it as loud as I was hearing it now.

The truth was deafening.

"Now, we love that little girl—you know we do—and this is breaking your mother's heart, but I can't take this shit anymore. I've kept my mouth shut for long enough. You have a responsibility, Nathan. Marley needs you. Hell, she's *needed you*, and you are goddamned lucky she hasn't been damaged by this already. You can thank your mother for that—the beautiful angel that she is. She's put her life on hold for nearly two years while you've been doing everything except what you need to be doing, and—are you even listening to me right now, Nathan? *Nathan*." He grabbed my shoulder and shook me.

I barely reacted, slowly tipping my head back to peer up at him where he stood. I couldn't get angry. I'd seen this coming.

"I'm listening," I told him.

2

"Good. Because this ends now." He braced his hand on the back of the chair I was sitting in and bent closer, getting in my face.

My father was a big man. A former college linebacker who didn't look like he was pushing sixty-five. Two years ago, I would've shifted in my seat having him this close to me. Now I didn't even blink.

"We're giving you through Memorial Day, and then I'm taking that woman on a much-deserved vacation far away from here, and when we get home, we're going back to being grandparents who *visit* with their grandchildren. Our child-rearing days are over, son. It's time you step up. There is absolutely no reason why you should be at that restaurant as much as you are. This is long overdue."

Shock overwhelmed me. I felt my teeth clench as my back went rigid against the leather cushion. "You're giving me six days? That's not enough time for me to line something up."

"We've given you almost two years. I think that's more than enough time."

"Be reasonable."

"Reasonable?" His eyes narrowed. "How about you be the man I raised, because I don't even know who the hell I'm looking at anymore. I can smell the alcohol on you, Nathan. You're lucky I didn't call you on this shit a long time ago."

"Why didn't you?"

I was getting bold. There was a time I'd never take issue with anything my father did or the way he decided to do it. Right now, I didn't even care if he hit me. I had checked out.

"I don't question how a man needs to grieve his wife," he answered without pause. "That's something I don't have experience with, and I pray to God I never will. But life moves on, son, and you gotta move with it. The drinking stops now. That won't give you what you're looking for. There's no changing what happened."

"Do you think I don't know that?"

"I don't know what the hell you're thinking anymore. You've shut us all out."

"And dropping this bomb on me is your way of getting me to open up?" I asked.

Movement caught my eye as my mother entered the room from the kitchen, balancing my daughter on her hip. Dad straightened up as Mom wiped at her nose with a tissue. She'd been crying. I could still see the tears in her eyes.

"This is a joke," I said to my father. "I need more time."

"You should've hired help already, Nathan."

"And you expect me to find someone in six days? What am I supposed to do with her?" I tipped my head in Marley's direction. She was resting her head on my mother's shoulder. She looked nearly asleep. "I still have to work. It's my restaurant, Dad. Who's going to watch her?"

My father shrugged like he didn't give a fuck about my problems anymore and folded his arms across his chest. "You're a parent, son. Sometimes you just gotta figure it out as you go along. We don't always have the answers."

"You're not even going to help me out until I find a sitter or something?"

"Vacation's already booked. We won't be here."

My leg began to bounce.

I stared up at him, waiting for sympathy to call his bluff and back down his demand, but he was unyielding. Panic tightened the wall of my chest. I felt like I couldn't breathe.

"I don't know how to do this," I whispered.

Not even that unusual admission changed his demeanor. He remained eerily still. My mother was another story. She immediately shuffled closer, most likely wanting to comfort me or give in and call this off. Her thirty-year-old son was breaking down for the first time in front of her, but she didn't make it two steps before Dad held her back with his hand raised, keeping his eyes on me.

"You'll figure it out," he said.

"Dad, please..." I was willing to beg. I would've done anything in that moment to have their help a little longer.

How could I do this by myself?

"Nathan." My father bent down and squeezed my shoulder. "You will figure it out." He spoke with confidence. He was certain, not doubting me at all, and I wanted that to ease my mind, if only a little, but it couldn't.

I knew I'd fail at this.

After goodbyes were said, I paced my house from end to end, trying to calm Marley, who began screaming the second the door latched shut.

My daughter wanted my parents, not me. She barely knew me.

Her cries were deafening. She squirmed in my arms and pushed against my chest with more strength than a two-year-old should have. Her tears wet my neck and soaked into my shirt.

I kept walking. I didn't know what else to do. She was typically already asleep by the time I got home at night. I didn't know what soothed her.

My parents ignored my calls. *You'll figure it out.* Guess that advice was going into effect immediately. I was on my own with this.

I lapped the family room thirty-eight times that night. An hour later, the house was finally quiet.

After laying Marley in her crib, I collapsed on my bed, fully dressed. I didn't even bother taking off my shoes.

"Wake up, Nathan."

I opened my eyes and turned my head on the pillow. The bedroom was dark.

I was alone.

chapter two

JENNA

"Which animal do you think I should get on my face, Mama? A butterfly or a cat?"

Olivia, my daughter, studied her sun-kissed cheeks in the mirror above the sink as she washed her hands in the Whitecaps women's restroom.

We were here for the Memorial Day carnival the restaurant was hosting, and Olivia had made it known how badly she wanted her face painted the second we arrived. Especially after she discovered Sydney was running that booth. Olivia adored my brother's girlfriend.

"I think you'd look beautiful with either one," I answered, handing her a paper towel when she finished up and walked over to me. "Which one did you want first? That's probably the one you want the most."

"A butterfly."

"Then ask Syd for a butterfly."

"But what if I change my mind and she's already painted a wing? I'll be *doomed* if that happens. Cats don't have wings." Face reddening in distress, Olivia huffed and shook her head like this decision was eating her up inside. Her bright blue glasses slid down her nose.

I fixed them for her, smiling. "Do both, then."

Her eyes widened in hope-filled wonder. "I can do that?"

"Why not? You have two cheeks, don't you?"

She thought on this plan, her gaze briefly drifting to the floor. Then she nodded quickly, looking up at me. "I *totally* have two cheeks. I can be a cat butterfly! I bet nobody else will think of that. I'll be the only one and everyone will think I'm *so cool*, right?"

"Oh, absolutely. You'll be the coolest girl here."

Olivia pumped her fists into the air, hooting and hollering as she bounced on her toes. "This is the best idea *ever!*"

I followed her out the door, both of us giggling. When I noticed my son and Olivia's twin brother, Oliver, was nowhere to be seen inside the restaurant, I assumed he really *did* need to use the restroom, even though he'd assured me he hadn't.

"Oliver?" I called out, holding the men's room door open.

There was a wall separating anyone doing their business and the spot where I was standing, so I couldn't see anything. Thank God.

"Yeah?" he answered.

"Mama, can I go? I want Syd to get started on my face." Olivia jumped from one foot to the other and tugged on the two dark braids hanging past her shoulders. Her flip-flops smacked against the tile.

"Go ahead, but stay with Syd."

Even though my children were eight years old and knew better than to wander off, it was ingrained in me to remind them.

I waited until Olivia made it to the front of the restaurant before I turned back to the men's room. "Is anyone else in there, Oliver?"

"Just a man."

"Okay. And what's he doing?"

"Really?" a deep voice answered.

I ignored it, which was what I typically did in situations like this, and pressed on. "Oliver?"

"He's going to the bathroom, Mom."

"What else would I be doing in here?" the guy said.

I rolled my eyes at his tone, feeling completely justified in my questioning, and leaned my back against the door, getting comfortable just in case my son was nowhere near finished.

"Do you want to get your face painted like your sister? I bet Syd could do something cool, like a shark or something."

Water flushed. I heard the faucet kick on—someone was washing their hands.

"No. I wanna do the dunking booth. That looks fun."

"Do you think you can dunk Uncle Brian?"

"I *know* I can dunk him." Oliver's voiced raced with excitement.

I smiled, picturing my older brother doing anything he could to make sure Oliver could drop him into the water. Brian always went above and beyond with my kids. He was the main reason we'd moved to Dogwood Beach three years ago, leaving Denver, my old life, and our parents behind. We'd lived with him for a while until I found my apartment, and in those few months, Brian and my kids became inseparable.

We were incredibly lucky to have him in our lives. And I frequently made sure he knew that.

I lost some of the smile I was wearing when the man with the eye-roll tone moved out from behind the wall to exit the restroom. He had thick dark brown hair that was styled short, wore black-rimmed glasses, and had a tall, *really tall*, lean build, with a good amount of muscle putting stress on the button-up shirt he was wearing. I stared at the outline of his biceps a little longer than I meant to as I flattened my back against the door, allowing him room to pass.

"Excuse me," I offered politely.

His eyebrows shot up. "Do you always hold conversations like that in men's rooms?"

"If my son is in one of them, then yes," I answered, pairing my response with a fake smile. I didn't owe this guy anything. "Either that, or I'm coming in there and making sure nobody's doing anything they shouldn't be doing. You can never be too careful—creeps are everywhere."

The man's gaze hardened as he looked back at me over his shoulder, like what I'd just said offended him. What did he care? I hadn't actually walked in on him.

When he reached the door with the word "Manager" written in bold white, he stepped inside the office, disappearing out of view.

"Shit," I whispered. Eyes pinching shut, I dropped my head back and groaned low in my throat.

I felt bad. I knew that man. Well, I knew *of* that man. I'd never met him, obviously. But I'd heard stories about Sydney's boss, who didn't just manage Whitecaps. He was the owner. All the girls who worked here spoke highly of him. I was good friends with most of them and had heard talk about this guy. In fact, they appreciated him so much, the girls had come up with the carnival idea for today as a way of boosting summer sales for the restaurant and giving back to a man they all very much liked.

And you just alluded to his place of business as being a possible hangout for child predators. Way to go, Jenna.

I wanted to apologize, or at least explain myself. I could also sprinkle in some heavy compliments. Even though we'd eaten here only once before, I thought Whitecaps was a really nice restaurant. I could embellish a little and say it was one we fre-quented. He'd never know the truth.

Oliver finished up and stepped out of the bathroom as I thought on this plan, showing the same amount of excitement his sister had about the carnival, his voice carrying through the restaurant animatedly. And evidently, a little on the loud side.

Just as I was about to head toward the office, the door latched shut.

Okay. Someone didn't want to be bothered.

"How many tickets can we get, Mom?" Oliver asked. "Please say enough to do all the games. The games look *so cool.* They got a ring toss and the one where you gotta knock over the cans. I better warm up my arm."

I smiled, fixing his glasses for him when the windmill motion he did nearly knocked them off his nose. His excitement prompted a better idea. I'd show my support for Whitecaps while giving my kids a day packed full of memories. A face-to-face with the owner could wait for another time.

chapter three

JENNA

Two Weeks Later

Looking forward to tonight. Are you sure I can't pick you up?

Me too! I'll meet you there. I need to drop off my kids at my brother's house. He's watching them for me.

Oh.

I didn't know you had kids.

I frowned reading the texts. Did this guy not read my profile? I'd mentioned being a mom. Should I have bolded that information?

Forcing myself to stay positive, I typed my response. Maybe this guy still had potential. That *Oh* didn't necessarily mean anything.

Yep. Two of them. Is 6:30 still a good time?

I'm really not looking for anything serious.

Translation: The thought of getting tied down to someone with kids disinterests me. This will only be a one-time fuck.

Disappointment came on swift, even though I should've known better. Every other guy I'd interacted with on CupidMatch.com had been a letdown, and seemingly only after sex. Nothing real or sustainable. It was my own fault for having any expectations here. But I was beginning to realize hope was a difficult emotion to turn off.

I believed in love. Why wouldn't I have faith in it?

Not that I had any personal experience with it in terms of a relationship. I hadn't been in love yet. Not real love. Crush-love, yes. The two voices booming from the living room were a testament to that. They were also the reason why I wasn't as practiced in dating as other twenty-seven-year-olds. Being a mom took priority. But I tried to grab a date as often as I could. And even though the men of Dogwood Beach were turning out to be more frustrating than anything, I still put myself out there.

I was, however, beginning to regret the dating app route. That really wasn't working out for me. And unless I became a different person, one who was looking for a meaningless hookup and nothing more, it *wouldn't* work out for me.

I finished applying my mascara, then stood from my vanity stool as I typed out my response to this guy. A response that might not have been necessary, but just in case, I needed him knowing—I was no longer interested.

I'm going to have to cancel tonight. Thanks anyway.

By the time I walked down the short hallway that opened up to the living room, that app had been deleted off my phone.

"Uno out!" Olivia shrieked. She threw her playing cards down on the coffee table and pumped her fists into the air. "Whoop, whoop!"

"Aw, man! I was so close to winning." Oliver collapsed sideways onto the sofa and punched the cushion. "I want a rematch, Livvy! You *always* win."

"We can play tonight at Uncle Brian's. I'll pack the cards in my bag."

"Good idea."

"What if we did something else *besides* going over to Uncle Brian's tonight?" I asked, stopping behind the sofa.

Olivia peered up at me. "But what about your date?"

"I don't have a date anymore."

"Why not?"

"I just don't. I decided to cancel."

"But you were really excited, Mama."

"I know, baby, but sometimes things just don't work out the way we want them to."

Olivia glowered, reaching into the back pocket of her shorts. She pulled out a pen and a small notepad, flipped it open to a page, and violently crossed something out.

"What's that? What are you doing?" I tried to see what Olivia had marked off, but she closed the pad before I caught sight of it.

"I had high hopes for him," she mumbled. She tucked her notepad away after sliding the pen through the rings. Then she took a seat on the coffee table and pouted.

I fought a smile. My daughter was a hopeless romantic as well. I wondered if she was becoming a little too invested in my personal life.

"What are we gonna do if we don't go over to Uncle Brian's?" Oliver asked, rolling to his back so he could see me above him.

"Well, I thought since today is your first official day of summer break, we should probably celebrate somehow." I paused for dramatic effect, looking between the two of them. "And I am pretty hungry…"

"Can we go out to eat?" Olivia sprang to a standing position and held her breath. Her eyes doubled in size.

"Mom, can we?" Oliver asked, scrambling to his knees. "Please? Please!"

I knew this would make up for the change of plans. Even though my children loved going over to my brother's house almost more than anything, they were practically addicts when it came to restaurant food. There was something about ordering off a menu. And because I kept us on a strict budget—a necessity since I was a single parent of two very active children who were always involved in some sort of extracurricular activity—I didn't allow meals out very often.

"Get your shoes on," I gave as my answer.

"Whoop!" Olivia punched the air. She fell into a fit of laughter when her brother stood up and shook his butt. The two of them high-fived, then raced each other for the front door, where their shoes were stacked against the wall.

"Can we go to Whitecaps?" Oliver asked.

"Sure. Wherever you guys want to go."

"I want a burger. They got the best burgers." He pushed his heel into his shoe and stomped the floor. "You know I'm right, Mom."

"I want a burger too," Olivia said, tying her laces.

I quickly shot a text to my brother, letting him know he was off the hook in terms of babysitting duty, and then I grabbed my keys and purse off the small table by the door. A large antique mirror hung above it on the wall. I checked my reflection while the kids finished getting ready.

I hadn't changed for my date yet, so I wasn't wearing anything fancy. Just a favorite pair of jean shorts and a soft yellow flowy top that had the shoulders cut out and billowed at my waist. But my hair and makeup looked more done up than usual. My long brown locks were loosely curled, making the caramel highlights my friend Shay had given me a few weeks ago stand out a bit more. I was wearing foundation instead of my typical tinted moisturizer, but kept my skin looking dewy since I'd skipped the powder. My eyes were lined black. Lips shiny with gloss.

"You would've looked real pretty for your date, Mama," Olivia announced, coming to stand beside me.

I smiled down at her and cupped her cheek, which was flushed from exertion. "Not as pretty as you."

"Are you sad?"

"Not one bit. I get to go on a date with you two now." I winked at her when she grinned big, and then I ruffled Oliver's dark hair when he got beside his sister. "And have the best burgers in Dogwood Beach."

"Oh yeah!" Oliver hollered, adjusting his glasses when they slid down his nose. "Let's go. I'm starving."

The kids rushed outside when I opened the door. I followed, grinning as I watched them sprint to the car and pile inside it. Their unrestrained excitement was infectious, and I realized halfway to the restaurant how much truth had been in the answer I'd given Olivia.

My children always made the best dates.

* * *

The oceanfront restaurant was busy, typical for a Saturday night, I was sure. The kids didn't mind the thirty-five-minute wait

15

though, and spent it playing I Spy on the wraparound porch while I stared out at the ocean.

I braced my elbows on the railing and watched the waves crash through a break in the dunes. The June air warmed my shoulders.

I loved the beach. I couldn't imagine living anywhere but here now.

Olivia chose our car for the second time in a row and stumped Oliver, who called her a cheat and demanded a rematch. When it was her turn to guess, Oliver started with the same description—I spy with my little eye something silver—and I had to bite my cheek to stop myself from laughing.

It was precious, how well they got along. I had a feeling even if they weren't twins they would've been this close.

Kali, one of the waitresses I was friends with, stepped outside and called our name, then led us to an open booth by the window. The kids sat across from me, both up on their knees, and immediately got started on the children's menu coloring activity.

"Can we get soda, Mom? You know, since we're celebrating."

"I think we can do that."

Oliver's grin took up his entire face. He leaned closer to his sister, who remained focused on her drawing. "You hear that? I'm getting a Dr Pepper."

"Me too."

"No. You get something else. Then we'll swap and get double the soda."

"Okay. Good idea."

I studied the menu, humming along to the Twenty-One Pilots song playing overhead.

"Hey, it's my favorite Savages." Tori walked up to our booth, flashing a smile at the kids. Our last name was Savage. She shot me a questioning look. *Date?* she mouthed.

I gave her a thumbs-down.

Tori shook her head in disapproval and mouthed, *Seriously?*

I'd become good friends with Tori after my brother got together with Sydney a little over a year ago. Tori and Syd were best friends. And now Tori was engaged to Brian's friend Jamie, whom I'd known most of my life.

"Oh well. On to the next guy," Tori mumbled, giving me a cheeky smile.

She knew how hard I was looking.

"We're here celebrating," Olivia shared, her crayon stilling so she could lift her head and look up at Tori. "School's out!"

"Oh yeah, that's right." Tori turned to me. "Don't you get off for the summer too?"

"Yep. Three months with my babies."

I was eternally grateful for that job perk.

The attorneys at Price & Price LLC, the law firm where I worked as a paralegal, had offered me the option to work from home three years ago when I was first hired. I'd expressed concern about summer hours and affordable childcare, anticipating the worst and hoping for nothing. I'd thought for sure I'd be stuck working forty-hour weeks in the office and shelling out my entire paycheck to cover daycare. But they were impressed with my résumé and willing to work something out.

Unless I could somehow get paid to stay at home with my kids full-time, I was never leaving that job.

"*Mom.*" Oliver groaned. "We're eight now. We're not babies."

"You'll always be my babies, no matter how old you are." I reached across the table and pinched his cheek.

"That's weird." He huffed, shaking his head.

Tori giggled, poising her pen to write on the ticket book in her hand. "Do you guys know what you want, or do you need a minute?" She looked from me to the twins.

"We're ready," Olivia answered.

I perused the menu while the kids rattled off their orders, thinking I wanted a burger but making sure of it. Everything listed looked delicious. It was hard to pick just one thing. I knew Stitch, the cook and Shay's man, killed it in the kitchen. Everything he brought over to Sunday dinners at Syd and Brian's house tasted amazing.

Movement near the back of the restaurant caught my attention. I leaned to the side to watch a little girl—a tiny thing, barely two years old if I were to guess—walk between the booths lining the window and the tables spread out in the middle of the room.

She was seriously adorable. Big blue eyes looking all around her. A head full of blond ringlet curls. With the cutest little summer dress stopping at her knees. She was also barefoot.

Huh. That was a little odd.

"Hi." I cooed, smiling and waving as she stumbled closer.

Her mouth stretched into a toothy grin.

"Mo Mo, you're *killing me*, babe." Tori set her pen and ticket book on the table and scooped up the little cutie, propping her on her hip. "What did I tell you? You can't be coming out here."

"Oh, do you know her?" I asked, grinning at the girl. "Hi! Yeah, I'm talking about you, sweetheart." I gave her little knee a gentle squeeze, and she giggled.

God. Seriously cute.

"She's Nate's," Tori answered.

I followed her gaze to the manager's office door, which was open just enough for a tiny body to slip through.

"His parents can't watch her anymore or something, so he's been bringing her here with him, and that is not working out, let me tell you," Tori said. "The other day, she made it all the way into the kitchen before anyone saw her. Thank God Stitch grabbed her before she could put her hand on the grill."

I gasped. "Oh my God. You're not kidding." I pictured the worst happening and felt my stomach tighten and twist.

"I don't know what he's doing," Tori mumbled with sadness shining in her eyes.

I remembered hearing that Nate was widowed, and pain pulsed inside my heart. For him and his daughter. I glanced at the office door again.

"Excuse me? Can we get the check over here?"

"Shoot." Tori looked behind her and smiled politely at the man who'd spoken. "I'll be right there, sir." Then she met my eyes again. "Let me take her back to Nate and get that guy's check, and then I'll be back over to take your order, Jenna."

"Here, I'll do it." I reached for the little girl as I slid out of the booth. "I can take her to him."

"Are you sure?"

"Absolutely." I had an apology to deliver anyway. What better time than now? "What's her name? Mo?"

"It's Marley. I just call her Mo." Tori passed her off to me and gave my forearm a squeeze. "Thanks, Jenna."

"No problem." I put my attention on the little peanut I was holding, and the bluest eyes I'd ever seen. "Hi, pretty girl. Hi, Marley." I spoke softly to her, trailing my fingertips down her arm to her hand. She squeezed my thumb.

"Hi," she said, her voice husky and soft.

Holy Lord. I could eat this girl up.

"Mama, she's *so cute*!" Olivia tickled her feet and Marley giggled.

"She's breathtaking." I tucked a bundle of blond curls behind her ear while Marley plucked at the chain I wore around my neck. "I'm going to take her back to her daddy. You two stay here, okay? I'll just be a couple minutes."

"Okay," Olivia answered. Oliver leaned over his drawing and kept coloring.

"Oliver?"

"Yeah, Mom. Got it."

I made my way to the back of the restaurant.

"Where are your shoes?" I asked Marley as I walked between tables, dropping my head close to hers. Her soft hair tickled my nose. "You need shoes. The floor is dirty."

"No, no shush. *No* shush."

"Mm. Does somebody like the word 'no'?"

"No, no, no. No!" Her voice grew louder and broke with a giggle.

"You're cute even when you're talking back. How's that possible?" I asked her, shifting Marley to my right side when I reached the manager's door. I knocked on it even though it was partially open already and peered inside the office.

Toys littered the floor. Blankets. A crib mattress. It looked more like a nursery than a workspace. There was even one of those round gated play yards in the corner of the room with one of the sides unlatched and open.

I guessed that was how Marley had made her great escape.

"Hi. Remember me?"

Nate was seated at his desk, concentrating hard on one of the papers in front of him. He lifted his head when I spoke. Recognition narrowed his gaze. "Men's room, right?"

"Good memory."

"You're hard to forget."

20

My back straightened. *Whoa. What? Is Tori's boss hitting on me?*

Not that I would object. This guy was crazy attractive. I'd be thrilled if he was hitting on me. I'd be surprised too. I didn't think I'd made a good first impression that day.

Nate cocked his brow, as if to read my confusion. "I've never been asked what I'm doing while I'm in there."

Ah, right. Now that comment made more sense. "Well, now if it happens again, it won't be weird," I joked, smiling.

His gaze lowered to my mouth, held for a breath, then fell away. "Did you need something?" he asked, putting his attention back on the paper.

He was busy. That was clear. I should probably get to the reason why I was bothering him so he could get back to work.

"A couple of things," I said, pushing the door open further and moving inside the room. I sidestepped a few stuffed animals. "First, I believe this belongs to you."

Nate looked up again, saw Marley in my arms, and cursed, rushing to his feet. "God, how do you keep getting out?" He rounded the desk and took her from me.

"They're like little escape artists at this age."

Marley pushed against Nate's chest and squirmed in his arms, fighting his hold immediately. When she started whining and going red in the face, he sat her in the play yard, closing the latch so she couldn't walk out. He dropped a handful of alphabet blocks in her lap to occupy her.

"Sorry if she bothered you," he said, returning to his seat.

"She didn't bother me. She's adorable. I miss that age."

Nate's brows ticked up as if he couldn't understand my response.

"I also wanted to apologize for the other day," I began, moving closer. "I don't know if what I said insulted you, about creeps being everywhere. I know it sounded like I was alluding to them being *here*, and I didn't mean it like that. Ever since my son turned eight, he's been adamant about not going into the women's room with me, and I just…well, you get it. You're a parent."

Nate stared at me, his face expressionless.

Okay, maybe he didn't get it yet.

"It's just hard to turn off the side of me that panics whenever I don't have eyes on my kid," I explained. "Your restaurant is really nice. I'm sure perverts don't gather here."

His mouth twitched. "That's a relief to hear. Putting security in the men's room might've caused some alarm." Leaning back in his chair, he adjusted his glasses and looked ready to say something else, but turned his head when Marley started whining again.

She was standing at the gate now, gripping it and giving it a good shake.

I watched Nate get to his feet and drop nearly every toy she had into the play yard. He spoke under his breath, too low for me to hear, but I could tell from his tone how exasperated he felt.

Marley kept whining. She stomped her foot and shook her head at him when he held out a stuffed giraffe. He swapped it out for a book, turning to a page and pointing at one of the pictures. She wasn't interested. Marley fell back onto her butt as tears hit her cheeks. Her legs kicked against the floor with fury.

Nate pinched his eyes shut, ran a hand through his hair, and looked down at her. He appeared lost, and possibly on the brink of a meltdown himself.

He was overwhelmed; that was clear.

"Has she eaten dinner? Maybe she's hungry," I said, walking over to the play yard. On instinct, I bent over the gate and held out my arms. I wanted to soothe her somehow. I at least wanted to try. I hated seeing this sweet thing so upset.

Marley immediately stood up and came to me. When I got her on my hip, she settled down and played with the chain around my neck again.

"I don't know what she is," Nate replied. He held up his glasses and rubbed at his eyes. "I guess she could be hungry."

"If you want, I can take her out there and she can eat with us. It's just me and my kids."

"Really?"

"Sure. What does she like off the menu?"

He looked at Marley, thinking hard on that question. "Normal two-year-old stuff?" Our gazes met. I saw the embarrassment in his eyes before he looked down and away. "Sorry. I really don't know what she likes. I haven't spent much time with her." He gripped the back of his neck, mumbling, "I'm sure that's obvious right now."

His shame was palpable.

Something about the way Nate spoke, the humiliation in his voice, the rejection—he *wanted* to know his daughter. He wanted to have the answer to any question I could ask him about her, and he didn't know how.

Impulse loosened my tongue and pushed the words out of my mouth before I had the chance to really think on them. Although, even if I had paused, I wasn't sure I wouldn't have spoken my next words.

Everything inside me that made me who I was wanted to help him.

"Tori mentioned something about your sitter situation changing?"

His gaze came up.

"I know you don't know me, but I could watch her for you. I work from home during the summer..."

"Are you serious?" he asked on a rush, his shoulders pulling back as he stood taller.

"Yeah. I wouldn't mind. Honestly, I'd probably really enjoy it. I love kids."

"Yes."

A laugh bubbled in my throat. I waited for his expression to relax and shift out of serious. It didn't.

"Oh, okay. Um...well, if you need references or anything, you can ask any of the girls about me. Sydney is practically my sister-in-law. She's dating my brother, Brian. I'm sure you've seen him around here. And I hang out with Tori, Shay, and Kali all the time. You can trust me with your daughter."

"Okay," he said easily.

I wanted to smile at him—I was happy to do this for Nate. But I couldn't help wondering how desperate he might've been feeling. He wasn't hesitating at all to accept my offer, or even taking a minute to consider it. I felt sad for him. Nate clearly wanted to do better by his daughter. He couldn't even tell me what she liked to eat.

I began to wish I could've offered my assistance sooner. Everyone needed help sometimes. I knew that from experience.

"Did you want to watch her at your place?" he asked, cutting into my thoughts.

"I should probably watch her at yours. My apartment isn't really toddler proofed anymore." Lucky for me, I could take my work anywhere, and frequently did in the summer. Parks. The beach. Playgrounds. I worked on the go so my kids could *stay* on the go.

"That works for me. Whatever you need."

"Great." I smiled at him, gave that smile to Marley, who was playing with my earrings now—she was so girlie, I loved it—then turned back to Nate. "Okay, I'll get her fed so she's not a little grouch-bucket anymore, and then I guess if you want to go ahead and give me your address, I'll see you Monday?"

His face fell. "You can't start tomorrow?"

"Oh, do you…?" I paused, realizing today was Saturday. He obviously needed help on the weekends too. "No, tomorrow works. I can do tomorrow."

Breath left him loudly, as if he'd been holding it in.

"It's just temporary," he said, moving over to the desk and jotting something down on a Post-it. "I won't need every day covered for long. Just until I hire someone to help me out in here. I'll be able to cut back my hours once I do that."

"No problem," I answered, meaning that.

I obviously hadn't anticipated this becoming an everyday thing, but even if it would've been a permanent summer gig, I didn't think I'd have any issues. My kids went along with anything. They were easygoing. And I was more than comfortable around toddlers. I'd handled two at once before.

Plus, I *wanted* to spend time with Marley. God, who wouldn't? She was absolutely adorable.

Nate tore the note loose and walked it over to me. "Here's my address. I'm only ten minutes from here. If you could be at my house by eight thirty, that would be great."

"Sure. That works." I tucked the Post-it into the back pocket of my shorts, boosting Marley on my hip when I was finished. "Does she have any allergies to anything, or can I feed her whatever she'll eat?"

"No allergies. I do know that."

"Okay, great." I smiled at Marley. "Do you want to go eat? Are you hungry?"

"Eat!" Her legs kicked out excitedly.

I began to turn away with her but stopped. "Oh." My hand shot out. "I'm Jenna, by the way. Sorry."

"Nathan."

His grip engulfed mine. This guy could probably palm a basketball, no problem. *Wow. What a weird thing to think, Jenna.*

I cleared my throat as we separated, checked the floor behind me for toys, and then backed up toward the door. "Okay. I'll get her fed and let you get some work done."

"Thank you. I…" He closed his mouth with a pained expression, as if he was afraid to speak or even hear his next words. His Adam's apple bobbed heavily in his throat.

I froze.

I wanted to hug him, or at least promise everything would be okay. He looked like he desperately needed to hear that. And the desire to do more than what I was offering already stole my breath.

"I really appreciate this. Thank you," he said quietly.

Before I made this awkward and actually initiated an embrace, I settled on an honest "anytime" while holding in the *anything* that wanted to follow.

I'd help Nathan however I could.

chapter four

NATHAN

I didn't deserve her help. I didn't deserve help from anyone anymore. Taking care of Marley was my responsibility. It *should* fall on me.

But *fuck*, I didn't know what the hell I was doing. And whatever I *was* doing wasn't working.

I was pretty sure my daughter hated me.

Not that I could blame Marley. What had I ever done for her? If she thought I was a dick for letting her mother die...yeah, I deserved that. Sadie's suicide was my fault. I should've helped her and I didn't. I left Marley without a mother, and then I completely checked out as a father. I couldn't stand myself for it.

Every word I spoke to her tasted like regret. I wanted those twenty-two months back. I wanted to fix this, to be better.

God, I needed to be better.

The last two weeks had been a nightmare. I'd tried getting Marley in at every day care in Dogwood Beach, but everything was booked solid for the summer. Every babysitter Care.com had to offer in my area already had a job lined up. All of them. The only option left was to bring her to work with me.

I was fucked. Between Marley sneaking out and getting into shit and her constant screaming whenever she actually remained in my office, someone was close to calling the cops. I had prepared myself for that *and* for unemployment. One or the other was happening. I couldn't see this working out any other way.

Then Jenna walked in and saved my ass. That entire conversation felt like a dream. I didn't know this woman at all, and she was offering me the lifeline I desperately needed.

Jesus Christ, I could've kissed her. Did she have any idea what she was giving me? A day later and I was still shocked by her kindness.

I pushed my arm through the sleeve of my shirt and fixed my collar. Just as I checked my watch to note it was nearly eight thirty, the doorbell rang. I'd been half convinced our conversation *had* been a dream. A part of me hadn't expected her to show up.

God, this woman is a saint.

I rushed downstairs and paused in the buttoning of my shirt to open the door.

Jenna stood on the porch with two young kids flanking her. I recognized the boy from the restaurant on Memorial Day. That was definitely the strangest conversation I've had to date. Based on the tight, uncomfortable smile he was giving me, I'd guess he felt the same way about it. The little girl, on the other hand, couldn't have been grinning at me any bigger.

"Morning," Jenna said. Her eyes fell to my open shirt and she frowned. "Sorry. Are we early?"

"No. No, you're perfect. Come in." I stepped back and held the door open. The little girl moved inside first, tipping her head back further when she stopped in front of me.

"Hello." Her voice was soft and a little shy.

"Hey." I gave her a polite nod.

She stared up at me and kept grinning.

"Olivia, scoot over, baby."

Hearing that request, the girl stepped over and got beside me.

The duffle bag she was carrying hit the floor at her feet with a *thud*. The boy came inside next. His mouth dropped open as he peered around the room.

"Whoa. Your house is *huge*. Mom, this is almost as big as Uncle Jamie's house." The boy looked up at me then, his hand gripping the strap at his shoulder. His bag appeared to be just as full. "His house has, like, twelve rooms. How many rooms you got here?"

I smirked. "Not twelve."

"How come?"

"Oliver, that's...a little rude," Jenna scolded. She shuffled him over, stepping inside now herself, and offered me an apologetic smile after I closed the door. "Sorry. No filter."

"That's okay," I answered. Honestly, her kids could say or do whatever they wanted. No way was I asking her to leave.

"So, these are my two. You've sort of already met Oliver." Jenna stood behind him and squeezed his shoulders while he kept gazing around the room. "And that's Olivia. She's very excited to be here, if you couldn't already tell."

I looked down at the grinning face beside me, smiled politely back, and watched her eyes widen behind bright blue frames. When she dropped down and started digging through her bag, I turned back to Jenna and asked, "How close in age are they?"

They were the same height. Had the same glasses. Same color hair and chocolate-brown eyes. They could've been...

"They're twins," she answered.

"*Jesus*. And you're still sane?"

Jenna shrugged and laughed lightly, tucking her hair behind her ear. I could see freckles on her nose and cheeks and the flush as it colored her skin just now. I didn't think she was wearing any makeup at all. Still, even without it, I would've turned my head.

Awareness paused my breath. I blinked and looked away. When was the last time I noticed a woman's looks? Nearly two years. That answer was simple.

"How about I show you around?" I asked, checking my watch once more, then getting back to the shirt buttons I still needed to fasten. "I got a little time."

"Sure. Where's Marley?"

"In her room." Away from me, which was where she preferred.

"Mom, can we go out on the deck?" Oliver asked.

Jenna looked to me and waited.

"Yeah, have at it," I told him.

Oliver took off immediately, calling out for his sister to follow him.

Olivia peered up from the notepad she was writing in. "How old are you?" she asked.

"Thirty."

She looked from me to Jenna, then back to me briefly before putting her attention on the notepad again. "That's perfect," she mumbled, jotting something down, my age possibly.

My brow furrowed. *Is she worried she'll have to ask for it again?*

"Olivia, go with your brother, please." Jenna shuffled forward and spun her daughter around. Then she picked up the duffle and carried it over to the couch, dropping it there, along with the messenger bag she was wearing cross-bodied. The sleeve of her top slipped in the process, revealing a small butterfly tattoo on the back of her left shoulder. Jenna reached up to fix her shirt, peering back at me when she was finished.

Our gazes locked. I quickly cut my eyes away, putting my attention on Olivia.

The little girl moved fast through the family room, weaving in between the furniture as she finished taking notes and pausing only when she reached the open slider that led outside to the deck.

"Whoa! We can see the ocean, Ollie!" she yelled. The glass door slid closed behind her, cutting off her brother's animated response.

"Can we go get Marley?" Jenna asked. "Is she awake yet?"

"Yeah, she's been awake." I led Jenna through the family room and into the kitchen.

"Your house is really nice."

I glanced over my shoulder and watched as she ran her hand over the long marble island. She gazed in wonder at the row of cabinets mounted on the wall.

"It's not twelve rooms nice," I joked.

"Your kitchen is beautiful. Do you cook a lot?"

"No. My wife did."

Her bottom lip caught between her teeth and her gaze fell away. Just by her expression, I could tell she knew about Sadie. She'd probably heard about it from one of the girls. She'd said they were friends.

We ascended the stairs in silence.

"Bathroom," I said, pointing at the first door on the left at the top of the stairs. "This is Marley's room." I stopped at the door across the hall and twisted the knob, pushing it open halfway before I met resistance. "What the...?" I leaned inside to figure out what the obstruction was but didn't need to. Marley crawled around the door. "*Shit*." I pushed it open further and glared at the empty crib.

"Good morning, pretty girl." Jenna bent down and scooped Marley up. "Have you been playing in here all by yourself?"

Marley giggled.

"She must've climbed out of her crib." I pinched the bridge

of my nose as the threat of a migraine pulsed beneath my scalp. What the fuck? *Really?* "She hasn't done that yet. I thought I had more time before I had to worry about this. How the hell am I supposed to keep her in here now?" I gestured inside the room.

I'll never be able to close my eyes again.

"Is the mattress lowered all the way?"

My brows lifted at Jenna's question. *Fuck. Is it?*

I walked over to the crib and examined the notches on the inside rails. Then, kneeling beside it, I looked under the mattress and grinned at the sight. I had one level remaining.

"Thank God." I dropped my head back and sighed in relief.

Jenna laughed from the hallway. "Not ready for a big-girl bed yet?"

"No. Never." Not if it meant Marley getting around at night. She'd leave me for sure. I stood up and headed out of the room. "Let me grab an Allen wrench and take care of this before I go."

"She hasn't eaten yet, has she?"

"No, not yet."

"Okay. I'll take her downstairs while you do that."

"Great."

Jenna went one way and I went the other.

I grabbed the small toolbox I kept under the sink in the master bath. After lowering the mattress and fixing the bedding, which Marley had pulled out of the crib and spread out around the room, I finished getting ready. Tie on, I slid my glasses into place and headed back downstairs.

The kids were seated at the kitchen table. Oliver and Olivia had their bags in front of them, rifling through each other's while they carried on conversation. Marley was in her booster seat. She was watching the other two, completely engrossed in what they were doing, while Jenna stood beside the chair, feeding her bites of waffle.

I finished rolling up my sleeve to match the other one as I moved around the island, stopping at the Keurig and powering it on. I grabbed the travel mug out of the cabinet and loaded up a K-Cup. The smell of coffee permeated the air.

"You wear glasses too?" Olivia asked, her voice pitching higher.

I turned my head and watched as she flipped that notepad open again.

She whispered, "Oh my gosh," not waiting for a response and obviously not needing one before she clicked her pen and scribbled something down.

What the hell is she always taking notes about?

Jenna set the plate on the table after feeding Marley another bite and walked to the end of the island, where she had a spiral notebook open to a blank page. "Is there anything I need to know? Medications she takes or a nap schedule she follows?"

I shook my head and blew across the mug. "No medications. A nap schedule? Like, she's going down every day at the same time?" I chuckled. "That's hilarious. I usually just let her go until she drops. It's easier than fighting with her."

Jenna's brows lifted. She appeared to be holding in a laugh. "Oh, well, you know, kids like routines. They actually thrive on them. Plus, it'll just make your life easier. So, if it's okay with you, I'll probably get her on some sort of schedule."

"Works for me. Honestly, whatever you want to do. You're basically saving my life here."

She smiled and shrugged off the comment, as if everything she was doing for me was nothing, and God, it wasn't. That couldn't have been further from the truth.

"We haven't talked about compensation yet," I said. "If it's fair to you, and please be honest with me, I'm willing to pay you two hundred to two-fifty a day for this, depending on how long you're here."

Her lips slowly parted. "That's…more than fair. You don't need to pay me that much."

"I priced daycare in this area. I know how much it costs."

"It doesn't cost two hundred dollars a day. I've priced it too."

"No, but you're doing more for me than a daycare would. They wouldn't keep her on weekends."

She tilted her head, thinking on this. "Okay, but still, that's a lot of money…"

"I wouldn't feel right paying anything less," I told her, hoping to shut down any further argument. "She's a lot of work, Jenna. It isn't like she's just going to sit still for you. Not to mention how last minute this is. Please, let me do this the right way. I won't be able to sleep at night if I feel like I'm cheating you."

Her smile came on softly. "Okay."

"And anything you buy for her—food or whatever—just save the receipts and I'll pay you back."

"I'll do that." She picked up the pen lying across the notebook and held it out to me. "Do you want to write your number down? In case I have any questions or need to get in touch with you."

I stuck the lid on the mug and set it aside, then took the pen from her and stepped closer.

"I haven't given my number to a woman in eleven years," I confessed without any fucking thought *at all*. My hand froze inches from the paper.

Why the hell did I share that information? Maybe she didn't hear it…

I looked up. Green eyes stared back at me, widened with full awareness.

I cleared my throat and wrote my number down so fast, it was barely legible. "Can you read that?"

"Yep."

"Great." I dropped the pen and pushed the notebook away, exchanging it for the mug and stepping back. "I should get going." Before I revealed anything else completely irrelevant.

She offered me an easy smile, as if I hadn't just made this awkward as fuck. "Should I feed her dinner too?" she asked. "What time were you planning on getting back?"

"I never make it home for dinner."

"Oh." She frowned. "Okay."

Shit. Is that too late for her? "Is that a problem?" I asked. "Like I said before, it's only temporary. I won't be working late once I get someone in there."

I wondered if she could hear the panic in my voice or see it written all over my face—I was certain it was there—because Jenna recovered so quickly, I wouldn't have known how she initially reacted to hearing how late I was going to be unless I'd been watching her the way I was doing.

"No, that's fine. Don't worry about it." Her smile was carefree.

"Are you sure?"

"Yeah, I'll make dinner. It's really not a problem." She spun around when Marley started whining for more waffles. "Seriously, Nathan. We'll be fine."

"All right, great." Relief lightened my limbs. Noting the time on the stove, I felt around my pockets, making sure I had my keys, cell, and wallet. "I need to head out," I announced. "If you need anything, just call me."

Jenna looked up at me, holding on to the grin she was giving my daughter. "I will. Have a great day."

"Thanks again for this."

"It's nothing, really."

"It's not nothing. It's…the farthest from nothing. Trust me." I adjusted my glasses and smiled at her. "I'll win this argument. Don't even try it."

She fought a grin, then mimed zipping her lips.

I was nearly to the door when Jenna called out, stopping me from retreating any further. I turned and watched her rush into the room with Marley on her hip.

"Wait! She didn't say goodbye."

I almost laughed. I didn't believe my daughter cared one way or the other about giving me any send-offs, but then I wondered if maybe I should've been the one giving them to her.

Why didn't I? Shit.

Jenna stopped in front of me, smiled, and coaxed Marley with a "Tell Daddy buh-bye."

Marley blinked at me with the same eyes as her mother. "Buh-bye, Daddy."

"Give him a kiss."

I stared at Jenna. "I don't think—" My next words got caught in my throat when Marley leaned forward, no hesitation whatsoever, reaching out with one arm and gripping my neck. I pitched closer and bent lower, so fast I nearly knocked into them. Sticky syrup lips smacked on my cheek and smeared. Jenna offered an "oops" as they pulled away and winced like this would bother me, but fuck, I didn't even care if my daughter got syrup all over my shirt. How could this bother me? It couldn't.

"Bye, sweetheart," I said to Marley, then looked at Jenna. My heart pounded against my ribs. "Thank you."

She gave me a smile before she turned away and left the room.

* * *

It was just after ten by the time I made it back home that night.

I could've stayed at Whitecaps later. Truth be told, I could've worked all night if I knew Jenna would've been okay with it—I had a lot to catch up on. I'd barely gotten anything accomplished the last two weeks. But I couldn't ask this woman for more. I worried if I was already asking too much.

The entire bottom floor of the house was lit up when I pulled into the driveway.

I sat in my truck after cutting the engine, dropping my head against the seat and staring through the windshield. My breathing slowed.

I wasn't used to it looking like people were home. Not anymore. My mother would always wait up for me, but typically, she'd keep most of the lights off and read in the family room next to one of the small table lamps. The house would always be quiet every time I'd step inside.

It's strange—the things you don't realize you miss.

As I was walking toward the house, the front door opened and Jenna stepped outside.

"Hey," I called out.

"Hey." She frowned as I approached, crossing her arms below her chest. "You really need to let me know if you're planning to be this late, Nathan."

Brow furrowed, I joined her on the porch. "Shit. Did something happen? Is Marley okay?"

"Of course. If something had happened, I would've called you." Her frown deepened as she stared up at me underneath the light. "I'm sorry you thought something was wrong just now. I would always call you if it involved Marley. I didn't tonight because...well, I didn't want to bother you at work with this, but it is something we should talk about."

"Okay." I nodded, encouraging her to continue.

"You said you wouldn't be home for dinner. I just assumed that meant you'd be a little later than that. Not *this* late. It's after ten. Is this typical for you?"

"Until I can get someone else in there, it will be." I sighed as I pushed a hand through my hair. "Is this too late? Do I need to make other arrangements?" Fuck. Where would I even begin to look for someone?

"I'm not saying I can't stay. I'm just…" Jenna dropped her arms. "I have kids too, Nathan. I don't mind staying this late and neither do they, but you need to communicate with me."

She was right. I honestly hadn't thought to clarify what time I'd be home, and I wasn't sure why I hadn't. Maybe I just assumed it wouldn't be an issue, and if it was, she would've called me. That was my mistake.

"I'm sorry," I said. "I should've given you a heads-up."

"I should've made you specify earlier, but—"

"No, this is on me. I should've told you, Jenna. And I should've made sure you were okay with it before I left this morning. This won't happen again."

She blinked up at me, a soft smile pulling at her lips. "Thank you."

"Of course."

Jenna hooked her thumb at the door. "Shall we?"

I gestured for her to head inside. "After you."

The TV was tuned to some cartoon channel Jenna's kids were watching. Both of them popped their heads up from the sofa when we entered the house.

"Nate!" Oliver sprang from the couch and spun around, wincing when Jenna hushed him and mumbling an, "oh, right," when she corrected his greeting. "Sorry," he told her before looking over at me again. "Um, I mean, Mr. Nate, you played football?" He rushed over to the bookcase along the far wall and picked up one of the picture frames, holding it out to show me.

I closed the door and moved farther into the room, stopping at the end of the sofa.

"You can call me Nate," I said, feeling bad for the kid. He obviously knew what he wanted to call me. And what the hell did I care?

"Cool." Oliver smiled and looked at Jenna. "Hear that, Mom? We can call him Nate. He just said we could."

"I heard him. I'm right here." Jenna laughed softly as she moved to the other sofa. She began to pack up her bag, stacking papers together and tucking them inside the large pocket.

"Hi, Nate." Olivia waved from her seat.

"Hey."

Her smile stretched into a grin. "Hi," she repeated, a little softer this time.

My chest moved with a laugh. She was cute.

"I just wanted to make sure you heard, Mom." Oliver met my gaze again and gestured at the picture in his hand. "Football? You played?"

"Yeah. All the way through college."

"What position?"

"Quarterback."

His eyes went round. "What? No way!"

"*Oliver*," Jenna scolded, hushing him again. "Marley is asleep."

"No way," he repeated on a whisper. "I want to be quarterback too, but my coach said my arm isn't strong enough. I'm fast though. I made four starts at running back last season. My coach said I did really good. That might be my position. But I don't want to *not* try to be quarterback. That's my dream spot." He

39

glanced at the picture, then slowly tilted his head back to look up at me. "I really hope I get over six foot. You have to be tall to be a quarterback. How tall are you?"

"Yeah, how tall are you?" Olivia pressed from her spot on the sofa. She had that notepad open in her lap now and a pen ready.

Her and the notes. *What is with that?*

I loosened my tie and popped the top button of my shirt, answering, "I'm six four."

"Wow," Olivia whispered.

Oliver gaped at me. "Could we play catch sometime? Like, are you busy *right now*? 'Cause I'm not busy. I have the whole night free."

I chuckled, gearing to answer with an obvious, "Maybe another time," when Jenna stood from the love seat and walked over to him.

"Oliver, it's way too late. You wouldn't even be able to see anything out there." She took the frame out of his hand and placed it back on the bookshelf, then grabbed his shoulders and spun him in the direction of the kitchen. "Go get your stuff packed up, please. Olivia, you too."

Olivia shot up and ran after her brother.

"Sorry." Jenna laughed a little and reached up, pulling the pencil out of the knot on top of her head. Her hair tumbled over her shoulders. It was dark brown with hints of gold near the ends and straight, not wavy like it was that day in my office. I watched her run her fingers through the ends. It looked soft.

I blinked. *It looked soft? Why the fuck did I think that?*

"Here." I tugged my wallet out of my back pocket and pulled out some cash, handing it over.

I needed to pay her. Truth be told though, I also knew there was a good chance she'd quit fixing her hair if she was holding money. And I apparently needed her to stop drawing my attention to it.

"Thanks." Jenna folded the bills together. Her hands stayed lowered.

Perfect.

"How was Marley?" I asked. "Did she give you any problems?"

"Oh my God, no. Not at all. She's so good."

"She went to bed okay for you?"

"Yep. No issues." Jenna giggled when I shook my head, completely stunned. "I'm used to putting two kids to bed at once though, so one is a piece of cake for me." She walked over to the love seat, slipping the money and her pencil into the outside pocket of her bag, then drew the strap over her head. The movement raised the hem of her shirt, revealing tanned skin above the tattered waistband of her cutoffs.

Jenna was a petite woman, which put her a helluva lot shorter than me. But she was all legs in those shorts. They were small and frayed along the edges. A bit uneven. I wondered if she'd taken scissors to a pair of jeans and made them herself. I wondered if she had freckles on other parts of her skin.

When she kicked her sandals away from the sofa to slip them on, an action that might require her bending over, I quickly looked away before I began *wondering* anything else.

Jesus. Get a fucking grip, Nathan.

"I made ziti for dinner. There's leftovers in the fridge if you're hungry."

I looked at her then. *I had stuff around here to make ziti?* "Did you go to the store?" I asked.

"No. I couldn't. You didn't leave me a car seat."

I cursed under my breath and gripped my hair. "Sorry." She

smiled at me. "I didn't even think about that. My parents have their own, so it's never something I worry about."

"It's okay. You had everything I needed for dinner. Ziti only takes a few ingredients." Her expression tightened as she straightened up, hands curling around the strap across her body. "I didn't even think about feeding us when I asked if I should feed Marley. I'm sorry. I should've asked first."

"Jenna, you can eat my food," I said, holding her gaze. "If I haven't made it abundantly clear already, you're saving my ass here. You can do whatever you want. I'm not going to have a problem with anything you do. Same with your kids. I promise."

"Don't tell them that," she warned, smiling at me and then giving that smile to Oliver and Olivia when their quick footsteps padded into the room. "Are you guys ready?"

"Yep," they answered in unison.

"I stuck a paper on your fridge with a few notes about Marley," Jenna said, pausing on the porch while her kids raced to the car. "Just stuff for me to remember. If you think of anything, feel free to add it."

"I doubt I have anything, but okay." I held the edge of the door and pressed my shoulder into the frame. Oliver's and Olivia's voices carried out into the night. The house was still and silent behind me.

I fucking hated it.

"I'll give you a car seat tomorrow. And a key," I told Jenna.

"Great. Same time?"

"Yeah, if you can."

"I can." She smiled big and bright at me under the light. Jenna didn't look a bit exhausted from spending the day chasing after Marley and her two kids. She appeared eager for tomorrow, to do this all over again.

Where the hell had this woman come from?

After they drove off, I locked up and headed into the kitchen, wanting some of that ziti she had made. I didn't care how late it was. I'd skipped dinner earlier so I could keep working. I looked over the paper stuck to the front of the fridge while my plate heated in the microwave.

Marley's Likes:

Hide & Seek
Stories—let her read to you. It's cute!
Coloring
Playing house (kitchen set)
Music—loves to dance!
Walking on the beach

Dislikes:

Shoes

Nap—put her down around 12:30

*Rock her to sleep.

The microwave had stopped sometime during my third read-through, and the only thing I could hear now was my slow, even breathing. Jenna told me she'd written this down for her to re-member, and yeah, that was possibly the only thing motivating her to do this. She didn't know my daughter. Having a list like this would make things easier on her until Marley became more familiar. But my own daughter wasn't even familiar to *me*. And Jenna knew that.

This list wasn't just for her.

I pulled the paper down and memorized it while I ate.

chapter five

JENNA

Go slow, Ollie!" Olivia said, her voice tight with panic.

"I am. I am." Oliver forced out a deep breath, cracked his knuckles, then cautiously reached for the Jenga block he'd chosen after a two-minute in-depth strategic discussion with his twin.

Olivia bit at her nails and fought the urge to bounce as she stood beside him. "Oh my gosh," she whispered.

"Watch. Watch him." I spoke quietly in Marley's ear and pointed at the ongoing game.

She stood between my legs while I sat on the sofa, my arms around her so she wouldn't lurch forward. And, boy, she wanted to lurch. Marley loved collecting the Jenga blocks. She was currently hoarding three.

"I'm so stressed," Olivia said, pressing her hands to her cheeks.

I smiled into Marley's hair. There was a lot riding on this game. Their Jenga tower stood taller than it ever had before. I'd already been instructed to take multiple photos of it, just in case this was it.

All eyes were on Oliver as he pinched the block between his thumb and first finger and slowly eased it away. The tower held strong for a breath, then another, and I thought we were in the

44

clear, but then it swayed to the right and tipped fast, sending the blocks crashing to the large oak coffee table. A few spilled over to the floor.

"Oh no!" Olivia shrieked, while Oliver dropped to his knees and pulled at his hair.

"No! I knew I should've picked the other block! I *ruined* it!"

Hearing her brother's distress, Olivia wiped her face clean of reaction and placed her hand on his shoulder. "It's okay, Ollie," she said, her voice sweet and unconcerned. "I think it would've fallen no matter which block you took."

"Don't be so hard on yourself, Oliver," I added when he punched his thigh and growled until his face burned red. "That was a really good game. You should be proud of yourself."

"It could've been better though. We were so close to beating it. I should've worked from the other side." He squeezed his eyes shut, nostrils flaring with his heavy breaths.

Marley wiggled out of my hold and picked up two more blocks, adding to the three in her grasp. She held them out for Oliver to take.

"O'ver, here. Here, go."

Warmth spread through my chest. I loved how she said his name.

Oliver opened his eyes and took the blocks from Marley. "Thanks," he grumbled.

"More, O'ver. Look. I get dem." She spun around and grabbed another handful of blocks, carrying them over to him, repeating this until Oliver couldn't stay mad or disappointed anymore because his lap overflowed. When Marley tried stacking the blocks on his shoulders, his head, Oliver laughed at her.

"Okay, stop. That's enough, Marley." He shook the blocks off and got to his feet.

Marley lunged at him and giggled, wrapping her arms around his leg.

"She's *so cute*," Olivia said, grinning at the two of them.

"Mom." Oliver groaned as he tried squirming out of Marley's grasp. "She's doing it again. Why does she keep doing this?"

"Because she likes you, Oliver."

"Well…I like her too, but…" He carefully backed around the chair and through the room, trying to dislodge himself, but Marley stayed with him. "This is getting ridiculous!"

Olivia and I shared a laugh.

It was day five of watching Marley, and her attachment to Oliver was getting stronger by the minute. She loved playing with Olivia as well, especially when my daughter brought over her accessories kit. The two of them would giggle and whisper together as Olivia put every clip and barrette she had in Marley's hair, styling her like we were going somewhere fancy.

But Marley's bond with Oliver was different. She watched him constantly and had to be sitting near him no matter what he was doing. It was sweet. And even though Oliver complained, I suspected he didn't mind the attention as much as he wanted us to believe. He never minded it from his sister.

The timer on the oven buzzed from the kitchen.

I stood from the sofa, picked up the blocks at my feet and set them on the coffee table as I moved around it, announcing, "Lunchtime." I smiled at Marley when she craned her neck to look back at me. She was still holding tight to Oliver, who had momentarily given up on escaping. "Are you ready to eat some pizza?" I asked her.

Marley's eyes lit up. She released her hold then and moved to rush at me, but spun around and ran after Oliver instead when he bolted for the kitchen.

"O'ver! O'ver!"

"Oh my gosh. I'm *right here.* Jeez!"

Nathan's house had an open floor plan, so I could see into the kitchen without any obstructions as I crossed the family room. I watched Oliver pick Marley up and sit her in the booster seat, get her buckled, and then rethink his own seating choice, pulling out the chair beside her and planting himself in it instead of the open spot next to Olivia, which was where he typically sat.

He shrugged when he saw me notice. "She's just going to whine if I don't sit right here. You know I'm right, Mom."

"I didn't say anything," I replied, head turned toward the oven so he couldn't see my smile.

After making sure the homemade pizzas were finished cooking, I handed out slices of double pepperoni to Oliver and Olivia and then cut up a slice of extra cheese for Marley, plating one for myself. Marley had made it known how she felt about pepperoni earlier when the four of us were garnishing the pies. Half of the pack had ended up on the floor.

"Oliver, slow down, please," I said, watching my son nearly hit crust on his first taste. "You're going to choke."

His cheek puffed out with his bite, and he spoke on a mouthful. "It's just really good, Mom."

"It's *so good,*" Olivia echoed, smacking her lips, then licking them. "Super yummy. Just like the ones we make at Uncle Brian's."

Syd had introduced my kids to make-your-own-pizza nights after she and my brother babysat a few times. Both Olivia and Oliver raved about the recipes. And because of that, we never ordered out pizza anymore.

"S'per yummy," Marley echoed. She giggled around her bite while her eyes stayed glued to Oliver's every move.

"Wash your hands before you grab your iPads, please," I told the twins when they were finished up with their slices.

They nearly knocked each other over rushing to the bathroom on the other side of the family room, excited for iPads after going all day without them. I typically limited their screen time during the summer, but I'd been restricting it even more than usual and allowing it only during Marley's naps. My kids had enough to occupy them here.

Nathan didn't just have a beautiful, spacious home on the inside. The outside was equally amazing. His front yard had plenty of room to run, and he had a basketball hoop mounted above the garage and an air hockey table set up in there. On top of that, his house was beachfront. Stepping off his deck, you hit sand. And within a short walk between dunes, your toes dipped into the ocean.

Children were meant to spend summers outdoors in my opinion. Being on the fifth level at my apartment complex, we didn't even have a blade of grass to call our own. My kids were loving every second of being here.

I pulled a baby wipe out of the pack I kept on the counter and walked over to Marley, who was still in her booster seat and currently occupying herself by smearing pizza sauce all over her hands.

"Okay, girlfriend. Are you ready for a nap?" I asked, pausing in my wipe-down of her. She looked seriously cute and so stinking happy right now, I wanted Nathan to see it. I tugged the phone out of my pocket and snapped a picture of Marley, prompting her to smile big and giggling at her when she delivered. I attached the picture to a text.

Your girl loves pizza!

This wasn't the first picture I'd sent Nathan. I hadn't needed to text him with any questions or for any other reason yet, but I had sent him multiple candid shots of Marley and a few short videos. Sometimes he'd text back with a *thank you*. Sometimes he wouldn't, and I'd assume he'd been too busy at work to reply. But even if he didn't respond to any of the pictures I'd sent, I still knew how much he wanted me to send them.

His desire to know his daughter was written all over his face. And the way he'd look at her before he left for work and ask about her day when he got home…how he made an effort even though he appeared so unsure, which, God, was the most important thing he could ever do—Nathan was trying so hard. I could see it.

I slipped my phone away and reached for Marley's messy hands. "Let's get you ready for your nap."

Marley squealed, "No, no nap!" But she didn't fight me, and she yawned while I cleaned off her face. Halfway up the stairs, her head hit my shoulder.

The nursery was sweetly decorated in pinks and soft grays, adorned with alphabet artwork and snapshots of Marley growing up, and it always smelled like lavender. I was convinced the scent was infused in the paint. I loved being in here with her. She had one of those growth charts with penciled dashes, molds of her hand- and footprints, a quilt with her name stitched on it hanging on the wall, and toys, of course. Her room was filled with love. With memories. But there was one thing missing, and not just in Marley's bedroom. It was missing throughout the entire house. I couldn't find any pictures of her mother anywhere, and I didn't understand why.

As I rocked Marley to sleep in the chair beside her crib, I looked at the clues around the room. The collage on the wall with a missing eight by ten and the empty spaces on the hutch.

Why weren't there pictures? Did Nathan hate his wife? Did he not want Marley to remember her mother? The questions grew louder in my mind and became impossible to push aside. On day three, I told myself this wasn't any of my business. On day four, I sang to Marley while I rocked so I wouldn't hear myself think. Today, I did both and nothing worked. I knew I couldn't ignore this anymore.

Marley was asleep by the third repeat of "You Are My Sunshine." I laid her in the crib and had Tori's contact information pulled up on my phone before I'd stepped out into the hallway. Halfway down the stairs, the call connected.

"Hey, Jenna."

"Hey." Surprise lightened my voice. "I figured I'd just leave you a message. You're not at work?"

"No. I'm off today. I'm headed to Wax to load up on graphic tees. I need some more sleep shirts."

Wax was the surf shop my brother and Jamie, Tori's fiancé, owned together.

"Oh, cool. I need to get over there. Oliver has been bugging me for clothes."

I stepped into the kitchen and moved down the counter, stopping where the baby monitor was plugged in. I slid my thumb over the volume dial until it was the loudest it could go.

"So, what's up?" Tori asked. "How's babysitting going?"

"Good! Really good. Marley is so sweet."

"It's really nice of you to help Nate out like this."

"It's nothing. I enjoy being here." I wasn't seeing this as a job. I wanted to spend time with Marley. "Speaking of being here, um, I had a question I'm not sure you know the answer to, but I figured you'd be a good person to ask before I took this any further."

"Shoot."

"It's about Nathan...I, uh..." I paused when Tori made a pleased sound through the phone. "What's that for? What are you doing?"

"Nothing," she answered, an obvious smile in her voice. "What is it you'd like to ask about *Nathan?*"

"Why are you saying his name like that?"

"Because *you're* saying his name like that." She giggled. "I've never heard anyone call him *Nathan.* I call him Nate. Syd calls him Nate. Shay—"

"Well, he introduced himself to me as Nathan, so...I don't know, I thought that's what he wanted me to call him." Why was this a big deal? This wasn't a big deal.

"Okay." Tori was smiling so big right now, I could practically hear it. "He's hot, isn't he? I always thought he was hot."

"Uh, yeah...he's hot. Definitely."

"What all do you think is hot about him?"

"I don't know. *Everything.* His face...Have you seen his jaw-line? I'm pretty sure that thing could *literally* cut me in half."

Tori burst out laughing.

Like a fog lifting, I became hyperaware of the strange direction this conversation had taken. *What are we doing?*

"Can I ask you my question now? I actually did call for a reason."

"Yes, sorry. Go ahead."

"Does Nathan hate his wife?" The question left my mouth so quickly, it shocked me to hear it. My heart began to race. "He doesn't have any pictures of her anywhere in his house," I elaborated when Tori remained silent. "None."

Tori breathed softly in my ear. "I don't know the answer to that question, Jenna. I don't *think* he does, but I've never asked

51

him about Sadie. I don't really want to, you know? I only ever see Nate at work, and that's not really something I'd want to bring up there."

"Of course," I replied, shifting on my feet. My back pressed against the edge of the marble counter. "This isn't any of my business. I don't know why I'm even curious."

"You're curious for Marley. I get that."

I nodded as if she could see me. "I know Nathan wants to have a relationship with her, and I'm trying to help him with that. I just don't know if he wants his wife included. I feel like I should know."

"You should."

"I'm not sure I can talk to him about this. I feel like maybe I'm overstepping."

"The worst he could do is get angry at you for asking…"

I thought for a moment. "I don't know."

"I think you should ask."

"You just said you wouldn't talk to him about his wife."

"Yeah, when I'm at work. I'm not taking care of his kid every day like you are."

She had a point.

"Jenna, you're asking for Marley. I think Nate will understand that. You wouldn't be wrong for doing it."

I bit my lip and looked out into the family room, where Oliver and Olivia sat close on the couch, quietly playing their iPads.

My thoughts drifted to Derek—their father—and I tried harder than I ever have before. I tried hating him for a solid second when he deserved to feel that for the rest of his life, and I couldn't do it.

My decision was incredibly easy to make.

I still had reservations and God, was I nervous—I didn't want to upset Nathan in any way—but a bigger part of me needed to know how he felt, because I didn't think he could ever have the relationship he wanted to have with Marley if he hated his wife for what she did. I was speculating postpartum depression. I didn't know the specifics about Sadie's death. Maybe I was way off, but even if I was…

"Okay," I told Tori. "I'll ask him."

* * *

I was in the kitchen wiping off the table when the front door opened.

I listened to Olivia fire a series of questions at Nathan the second he stepped inside the house, a habit she had developed.

"Do you like board games, Nate?"

"Can you build your own campfire?"

"How do you feel about s'mores?"

I wasn't sure if he was up for answering her tonight, and I didn't wait to find out.

After sweeping the crumbs into my hand, I lifted my head and informed her, "Olivia, if you'd like a little more iPad time, I'll allow it right now."

She gasped and turned on her heel, sprinting for the outlet beside the television console, where her iPad was charging. I needed her occupied for the conversation I was about to have. And now Nathan could move throughout his house without answering fifty questions.

Two birds, one stone.

Although, possibly not necessary. Because when he entered the kitchen, Nathan didn't appear to be a bit annoyed by my daughter or even on the edge of irritation. His smile was subtle, as if he was tired, but already there when I glanced over at him after dumping the crumbs into the trash can by the fridge. I wondered if he had been wearing that smile for Olivia too.

"Hey," he greeted me, stopping at the edge of the island. He hadn't worn a tie today, and the top button of his shirt was already undone.

Never in my life had I focused on a man's neck this much before. But God, I couldn't help it. If Nathan owned any turtlenecks, they needed to be burned immediately.

"Hey," I returned, brushing my hands off over the bin.

"Where's your other one?"

"What's that?" I watched him hook a thumb over his shoulder in Olivia's direction and realized he meant Oliver, who was typically always with his sister. "Oh, he had a Scout meeting tonight. And then he has a sleepover with his friend. They're going to drop him off here tomorrow."

"Boy Scouts?"

"Yep. Did you ever do that?"

He shook his head.

"Oliver likes it, unless it's football season, and then he wants nothing to do with it. Football becomes his life."

"I can appreciate that," he replied, his cheek twitching. "How was Marley today?"

"Awesome, as usual. We were going to go to the playground, but since it rained, we did Play-doh instead. She loved it."

I walked down the island, moving closer to Nathan. I was already smiling because talking about Marley with him always made me happy, but when he asked, "Your day was good too, then? Did you get a lot of work done?" I fought to keep my mouth from stretching any wider.

This was the second time Nathan had asked about me after

54

inquiring about his daughter. Yesterday, he'd gestured at my bag and questioned what I did for a living. He'd seemed genuinely interested. We'd talked for a good ten minutes about my job and how I felt about it.

It was nice. And this was nice too. He didn't need to ask about me.

"I did. And my day was good. If the kids are good, I'm good." I stopped beside him at the corner of the island. "What about you? How was your day?"

"Productive."

"That's how you like it, then? You don't miss having to keep an eye out at all times for two-year-old escape artists?"

"What eye? She spent more time out of my office than in it. I can't imagine how you dealt with two at that age."

I shrugged, answering, "It's the only normal I know."

A look of understanding washed over his face. He dug some cash out of his wallet and handed it over. As I was sliding the money into the front pocket of my shorts, he checked the time on his watch.

Shit. I still needed to ask him about the pictures, and he was clearly gearing up to walk me to the door. Another nice thing he always did.

"Can I talk to you about something?" I asked.

His expression grew tense. "Is it about you watching her for me? I know I'm asking a lot. You're here all the time..."

"No. Everything is fine with watching her."

"The ad for the assistant manager position just went live today. It shouldn't be much longer."

"Okay. I mean, it'll be great when you can cut down on your hours because that'll mean you get to spend more time with her, but I'm good. We're good—my kids love being here."

Nathan visibly relaxed. He pushed his hand through his hair. "Thank God. I think I'd lose my mind if you stopped coming over."

My stomach tightened.

I knew he was speaking in terms of watching Marley and *only* that, but still, I couldn't help it. I smiled up at him, and when he smiled back in that subtle, sleepy way he did after working a long day, I momentarily forgot what we were talking about and just kept smiling.

Nathan had the brownest eyes I'd ever seen and a day's worth of stubble covering his jaw, which always made men more attractive even when you thought *there is no way this guy could get any more attractive*, which was something I was beginning to think every time I looked at him. His lips were full and his hair was a little messy now, like he'd just taken a helmet off. I began to wonder what he would look like playing football.

"You were going to talk to me about something?" he probed after only a second or two, I hoped.

How long was I staring?

I cleared my throat. "Yes, I...um..." I slid even closer, not wanting Olivia to hear. "If I'm overstepping by asking about this, please tell me. It won't hurt my feelings."

His brows furrowed. "Okay."

"You don't have any pictures up anywhere of your wife. Is there a reason for that?" The words left my mouth in a one-breath rush. I basically vomited them all over Nathan. And when he reacted by setting his glasses on the counter and rubbing harshly at his face with both hands, I panicked and attempted to backpedal.

"I'm sorry. I'm only asking because... Well, I shouldn't even *be* asking. It's not any of my business. I wasn't, like, looking for photos. It was just something I noticed and I didn't know what I should do if Marley were to ask me about her—"

His gaze snapped to mine. "Has she?"

"No." I quickly shook my head. "No, not yet."

Nathan sighed and looked down at the counter, then slid his glasses back into place.

"She probably won't, and that's my fault," he revealed, shame lowering his voice. He stepped away, crossing the room and pausing at the fridge to peer back at me. "You coming?"

"Yep," I answered immediately, my feet shifting fast.

I had no idea where we were going or why Nathan wanted me to follow him, but it didn't matter and I didn't ask. I ascended the stairs right behind him.

There were five rooms on the second floor, two of which I'd been inside. The other three remained closed. I had assumed they were all bedrooms.

"You said you're friends with Tori and them, so I'm sure you know what happened to my wife," Nathan said, passing the bathroom and Marley's nursery. "Did one of them tell you?"

"They mentioned how she died, yes."

"I was upset at first, of course—my wife was dead. I found her. Then, almost immediately, I got really fucking angry." He stopped at one of the closed doors.

I felt like I couldn't breathe. "You found her?"

Nathan looked down at me, hand on the knob, not turning.

"I didn't know that," I quickly said. "I really don't know much about what happened…hardly anything. I—"

"She took a bottle of pills while I was at work. I found her in the bathroom."

Breath left my body. I suddenly felt dizzy.

"God, Nathan, I'm so sorry." Instinctually, I reached out and

57

wrapped my hand around his wrist, nearly touching his hand, but then I second-guessed my action and swiftly pulled back. "Sorry. I'm sorry."

His eyes narrowed slightly and his gaze intensified, as if he were examining me. Then he looked away and pushed the door open, stepping inside the room. I followed behind him.

It was a bedroom, although I could barely see the bed. Boxes were everywhere—on the floor, covering the bare mattress, stacked high beside the dresser. None of them labeled and all of them overflowing.

"Like I said, I got angry after Sadie died. This is all her stuff. There are pictures in one of these boxes." Nathan rubbed at his neck, a short, deep chuckle leaving him. "I think I knew I didn't have any fucking right being mad at her, and that's why I kept everything instead of getting rid of it. Even her clothes." He gestured at a box with a shirtsleeve hanging out over the side. "I kept everything. I shut it up in here so I wouldn't have to look at it."

I moved beside him, looked around the room once more, and then stared at his profile, waiting. I knew he had more to tell me. He didn't make me wait long.

"She never told me she was depressed," he shared. "I didn't even know she was taking medication until I found the empty bottle. Apparently, she started going to a therapist right after Marley was born. I was angry with her for not telling me."

"Are you still angry with her?"

"No," he answered immediately, meeting my gaze.

Relief filled me, not just for Marley but for Nathan as well. I didn't know much about depression, or mental illness for that matter, but I did know one thing. And I needed to make sure he knew it too.

"I think there's this stigma attached to depression, where

the person can feel ashamed or embarrassed, and maybe that's why they suffer alone. Not that they should feel that way. They just do."

"She tried to tell me." His voice grew quiet. "In a way, she did. I just didn't listen to her." His jaw twitched, as if he was clenching his teeth or grinding them. He looked out at the boxes again. "I didn't realize it at first. I know now. I've *known*, and this shit is still in here. I've avoided everything because I'm terrified to deal with it. I don't know how to deal with it."

His vulnerability drew me nearer. I stepped closer, fingers knotting together at my stomach so I wouldn't reach out. The urge to hold on to him again overwhelmed me, but I didn't know if I could do that. I didn't know if I should. I considered us friends at this point. Or at the very least friendly. If I needed comfort and Nathan offered it, I wouldn't think it was strange or wrong. So why was I holding back with him? I shouldn't. Still, I did. I kept hesitating. But I wouldn't stand there and remain silent. I knew how I felt about this, and I wanted him to know it too.

"You're dealing with it now, right? You're changing your schedule so you can spend more time with Marley—"

"After avoiding her for most of her life," he interrupted. Our eyes met. "I checked out, Jenna. You see how much I'm gone— I've done that for nearly two years."

"There's no rule book on how you should grieve, Nathan. You did it the right way for you."

"How was *this* the right way?"

"You made sure Marley was taken care of. She had your parents, right? She's a very loved little girl. I can tell. You cared enough to make sure she was getting that when not all fathers go to those lengths. Some don't even ask about their kids. I understand being angry or ashamed about how long you took to get here, but you're here now. And that's going to be what matters to Marley."

Nathan's chest heaved with slow, heavy breaths. He didn't speak, and I wondered if he was waiting for more, for something else to reassure him. I thought about his humiliation when I asked about the pictures, about the boxes still being in here. How he couldn't answer every question I had about Marley yet.

I knew what he was waiting for.

I quit fighting and second-guessing and finally reached out, squeezing that same spot on his wrist I'd touched before.

"You're not too late. Not for any of this," I said.

He blinked hard after I spoke, dropping his head.

"I promise, Nathan. You aren't."

"I want that to be true," he nearly whispered.

"I know. And that's another thing that's going to matter. Not all fathers would be worried they'd missed their chance."

Nathan looked at me then. His eyes searched my face. "Sounds like you're speaking from experience."

I swallowed hard. I didn't want to talk about Derek, not now. This wasn't about him. So I pulled my hand back and shrugged, playing it down.

"I don't know what to tell Marley about Sadie." His voice was pained. "If she asks about her, what am I supposed to say?"

"You could tell her how much Sadie loved her," I suggested. "And you could always share *your* memories. I think Marley would love to hear anything you want to share."

His throat rolled with a swallow. He suddenly looked over-whelmed with worry. "Yeah, but what about...you know, what happened. What am I supposed to say about that?"

"Nathan, I think you'll know when it's the right time to talk to Marley about that. And I also think you'll know exactly what to say. But if you don't, there's always help. You could go see a therapist together. There's grief counseling for families. You and Marley...you share this loss. This is something you can help each other get through."

He looked away, silent for a moment, then met my eyes again. "Do you think she remembers her mom?"

"How old was she when...?"

"Two months."

"I don't." I paused, shaking my head. *God, she was so young.* "I really don't know. I'd like to think she does."

"Yeah...me too." Nathan smiled weakly and rubbed at the back of his neck. "Thank you for saying all of that. I needed to hear it."

"You don't need to thank me."

"Still..." He seemed to think carefully about his next words, dropping his arm. "Why do I always feel better after talking to you?"

I smiled softly. That was nice to hear. "Well, we're usually talking about Marley, so..."

"Is that it?" he asked.

Nathan stepped away, peering back at me briefly before he put his focus on one of the boxes on the floor in front of the bed. He began to rifle through it.

I willed my fast-beating heart to slow.

Was that it? It was, right? Before he asked that question I would've thought *yes*, without a doubt. But now, if *he* was questioning it, I wasn't sure how to answer.

"I don't know what to do with some of this stuff," he said, moving on to the next box. "Like her clothes? What do I do with them?"

"You could donate them," I suggested. "I think you'll want to keep some of her things for Marley for when she gets older. Or you could keep everything and let her decide what she wants. I don't think there's a wrong way to do this."

Nathan nodded lightly, considering that. He shifted two more boxes out of the way, flipped back the flap of another, and then heaved it off the floor.

"Here," he said, returning to my side. He held the box at waist level and plucked a framed picture out of it, holding it out for me to take.

It was a photo from their wedding.

Nathan stood behind Sadie on a large dance floor, his arms around her waist and his smile half hidden as he spoke in her ear. A man held a microphone a few feet away. His toast must've included a joke or two. Sadie was caught mid-laugh by the photographer.

"Oh my God." I brought my hand up to my mouth and smiled against my fingers as I studied the picture. "Marley looks *just* like her. Wow." Same hair. Same smile. Eyes that sparkled the prettiest blue. I looked up at Nathan. "She's beautiful."

Nathan took the frame from me when I held it out and studied it for a moment before placing it back in the box. He tipped his head toward the door, and I took the cue.

"I'll start on the rest of the boxes tomorrow," he shared, following me out into the hallway.

We were nearly at the stairs when soft crying stopped us both.

"Shit," he whispered.

"It's okay." I pushed the nursery door open and moved quickly to the crib.

I could see clearly with help from the hallway light and the glow from the moon shining through the window. Marley was on her knees, gripping the rails and peering between them. Tears wet her cheeks.

I scooped her up and brought her against my chest, where she rubbed her face against my shirt. I patted her back and hummed softly, knowing how to calm her since I'd done it several times before. When I turned my head, I saw Nathan watching us from the doorway.

"Come here," I whispered, waving Nathan into the room. Marley was already settling down again. He set the box next to the changing table and got beside me. "She's almost asleep." I shifted Marley off my chest and went to pass her over, but Nathan took a step back. I fought a smile. "Take her. Here."

"What are you doing?" he whispered back.

"I'm giving her to you so you can put her to sleep."

"But you're doing such a good job with it." He gestured at his daughter. "And look at her. She likes you."

I cocked my head.

"*You* do it. She's going to start screaming if you give her to me, Jenna."

"I don't think she will. And I need to go use the bathroom anyway…"

His gaze hardened immediately. "Oh my God. *Liar.*"

I dropped my head and laughed quietly into my shoulder. Nathan smiled.

"I'll be right here. Come on," I encouraged, stepping beside the rocking chair. "Sit down. I'll pass her to you."

Hands gripping his hips, he stared at me for another breath before he finally caved and stepped forward, mumbling incoherent words of protest.

"Fine. You want to see a kid freak out in two seconds?" Nathan took a seat in the chair and gathered Marley against his chest when I bent down and handed her over. He froze stiff when she stirred, then glared up at me with an unmistakable *I told you so* expression.

"Rock her," I suggested. "And rub her back. She likes that."

Keeping his eyes on me, Nathan pitched forward slowly, gaining momentum. His back remained rigid against the wood.

I whispered in his ear, "They can sense fear. Relax."

"How am I supposed to relax? Look at her."

On cue, Marley squirmed and stretched her legs like she wanted to stand. She was waking up.

I put my hand on top of Nathan's and coaxed him to rub her back. My other hand gripped the chair and rocked it.

"You're too nervous right now. If you calm down, she'll calm down."

Nathan cursed under his breath. He dropped his head back against the wood and forced his breaths to slow, an action that required a lot of effort, I could tell. We rocked together. My hand remained on top of his, moving us in gentle circles. When Marley cooed and snuggled closer, his gaze snapped to mine.

I grinned and whispered, "See?" I stepped back. "Keep going."

Nathan stared at the top of Marley's head as he rocked her. It was as if he was witnessing something he'd never seen before. I watched them from the doorway as minutes passed.

I knew she was asleep now. And I wasn't sure if Nathan had any intention of putting Marley in her crib anytime soon, but I wasn't going to suggest it. They were both more than content where they were.

And God, it was such a beautiful moment.

"I'm going to go," I said quietly.

Honestly, I could've kept watching them, they were so sweet

together, but it was getting really late. If Olivia wasn't already passed out on the couch, I was sure she was close to it.

Nathan looked over at me and nodded. "Thank you."

"You're welcome." I turned and moved out into the hallway.

"Hey, Jenna?"

When I filled the doorway again, he spoke.

"Tell Olivia…Monopoly only and I'm cutthroat at it, yes to the campfires, and what kind of a monster doesn't like s'mores?"

I smiled so big my cheeks hurt.

He smiled back, and then he offered a quiet, "Good night," before he put his attention on the little girl in his arms.

chapter six

NATHAN

Seated at my desk, I glared at the weekly food order I needed to review while attempting to ignore lyrics to a song I swore was playing on repeat today. Jesus Christ, this had to have been the twentieth time I'd heard it. Did this station have it out for me or something? What the fuck was going on?

Not that I hated this song. It was all right. And to be honest, up until very, very recently, it wouldn't have bothered me hearing it this much. I would've been able to block it out. I never paid much attention to the music while I was here. I was too busy. But today? Today I was having major difficulty keeping my focus. Fuck this song "Closer" and whoever the hell was singing it. This dipshit wasn't doing me any favors. I didn't need any reminders about shoulder tattoos.

Recently I had become *very* aware of them.

I adjusted my glasses and kept reading. I was almost ready to sign off on this. Then I could send over the order and move on to something else. When I was halfway down the page, marking a reminder to myself, the chorus started playing again.

My pencil hit the desk. I closed my eyes and groaned, fingers digging into my temples. I was contemplating tearing the speaker off the wall and cutting the wires when my office door swung open.

Tori rushed inside, face contorted in rage. She pushed the

door closed behind her, then stormed forward, looking ready to tear my head off.

"Seriously, Nate? You didn't even *think* to consider me? What the hell?" She stopped on the other side of the desk, stuck her hands on her hips, and glared. "I'm offended."

I kept rubbing my temples. "Care to fill me in?" I asked dryly, glancing up at her. "I'm not really in the mood to guess what you're talking about."

"The assistant manager position. I saw the ad."

"And?"

Her mouth dropped open. I watched her attitude slip away as her hands fell from her hips.

Either she was remembering the authority I had to fire her for talking to me the way she was doing or she was rethinking this approach altogether on her own. I wasn't sure which. But Tori's next words to me came without a trace of boldness.

"I want the job. I think I'd be perfect for it."

I leaned back in my seat, caught my head in my hand, and regarded her.

I didn't have a problem being perfectly honest with Tori right now. She helped me out a lot, doing extra work like managing schedules and securing coverage when it was needed. Tori wasn't just my top waitress. Her duties went beyond that, and we both knew it. I relied on her. I also knew how qualified she was, and the fact that I hadn't considered her for the position was solely my error.

"You're right. You would be perfect for it. And I'm sorry I didn't come to you straightaway. That was my mistake. My head's been...all over the place lately. No excuse though."

Shock widened her gaze. Her mouth worked speechlessly for a moment before she rushed out an, "It's fine. Not a big deal."

I bit back a smile. "Big deal or not, I know how much you do for this company already, Tori, and I appreciate it. The carnival was a huge success. I'm already seeing an increase in revenue. I have you to thank for that."

"Well, it was a collective effort."

"I know it was your idea. Take the compliment."

"Okay, sure."

I chuckled softly, and Tori smiled. "You read the job description?"

"Yes."

"So, you know what I'm asking of you . . . aside from maintaining company standards, you'll be supervising service operations and the service team, managing food costs, overseeing stock and contacting suppliers—"

"I know," she interrupted. "I'm good with all of it. I'd like to do more, to be honest."

I cocked my brow.

"You didn't mention anything about marketing, and I have a lot of experience in that. I'd like to advertise a little better than what we're already doing. I think it'll be received well. People love coming here, but word of mouth only does so much."

"What are you thinking?"

"Billboards. We at least need one off Coastal Highway. It's shocking we don't have one already. People will see it when they're driving to the beach." She tapped her chin, thinking. "We definitely need a Facebook page. I can handle that. Oh, and I could see if we could partner up with Wax Surf Shop. I'm sure Jamie won't mind. You know him, right? We're engaged." She quickly flashed the giant rock on her finger. "He's one of the owners. Along with Syd's guy. Anyway, they could have coupons at the register for free appetizers or something. We could put their stickers on the surfboards out front as a trade-off."

I thought on her ideas, specifically the last one.

"Syd's guy, as in Jenna's brother?" I asked.

It would take me a lifetime to repay Jenna for everything she was doing for me. This could be a good place to start. She spoke about her brother a lot. I knew they were close. Anything I did for him, she'd most likely appreciate as well.

A slow smile twisted across Tori's mouth. "Yep, that's him. So, you know, it'll be nice building up their business too."

"I agree."

"Great!" Tori bounced on her toes and clapped. She was beaming at me now. "When do you want me to start? Today?"

I laughed. "Uh—"

"Actually, let me just…" Tori slipped her phone out of her apron. Her thumb moved vigorously over the screen. "If Lauren can come in and cover for me, I can start right now. I could even close for you tonight. You've been here all day and I just got here." She lifted her gaze from the screen to peer around the room. "Mm. Should we get another desk? I guess we could share the one. We both won't need to be here at the same time. The whole point of you hiring someone is to cut your hours back, right?"

I stared at her, blinking.

"What? I'm excited."

"I can tell," I said, chuckling softly. I sat forward, smoothing my tie, and planted my elbows on the desk. "Should we talk salary first before you start decorating?"

"I'm good with the amount advertised." She smiled as her phone beeped, then looked down to read the text, sharing, "Lauren is available," while she typed a quick response.

"I guess you can have her come in, then."

"Already done." Tori slipped her phone away and grinned at me.

I shook my head, smiling. *This is fucking nuts.* Leave it to Tori to run this interview and basically hire herself.

"All right, just let me know when she gets here. You'll need to fill out a few forms for payroll. I'll get them ready for you." I opened the desk drawer with the file folders and retrieved the one for new hires. "You'll also need to hire your replacement."

"Oh, I know just the person for the job. My future sister in-law is moving here. She'll be looking for work."

"Great. Get her in."

"Awesome. Thanks, Nate."

"No, thank *you.*" I met her eyes again. "It'll be nice to get out of here tonight before ten."

Her mouth lifted in the corner. "How's everything going with Jenna, by the way?"

"Great. She's incredible."

I immediately began picking apart my wording as soon as it left my mouth—it somehow felt like an understatement. *What is greater than "incredible"? "Saintly" might work.* I watched Tori's smile brighten knowingly as I tried thinking of a more suitable word.

"What?"

"Nothing." She backed away slowly. "She *is* incredible, isn't she?"

"That's what I said."

"She's really pretty too."

I cleared my throat and looked down, picking up my pencil and sliding the food order in front of me again.

Don't respond, Nathan. Just act like you didn't hear that.

"Thank you, Tori. You can go now."

Tori's quiet laughter followed her as she stepped out of the office.

The song changed overhead—another Top 40 nightmare. Some tool sang about loving the shape of a woman.

"Hey, Tori?"

"Yes?" Just her head popped around the doorframe. She was still smiling.

I pointed at the mounted speaker on the wall. "Pick another station."

* * *

It was just after seven when I left work that night. I couldn't remember the last time I got off while it was still daylight out. Even before Sadie died, I worked long hours. I typically always closed. It felt strange leaving Whitecaps when I did and even stranger pulling into my driveway without the use of headlights. But I couldn't deny it, it felt good too.

I *wanted* to be here.

I pushed the front door open and stepped inside the house, expecting to hear the commotion I was becoming familiar with—and wishing for when I didn't have it. Instead, the house was quiet.

The TV wasn't on. There was no laughter coming from upstairs or quick footsteps against the floor. Olivia wasn't firing random questions at me. If I hadn't parked next to Jenna's car, I wouldn't think anyone was home right now.

After securing the door, I crossed the room and pushed the slider open, stepping out onto the deck. They had to be outside.

I'd hear someone if they were upstairs. Even when Jenna asked her kids to be quiet so they didn't wake up Marley, I could still pinpoint their exact location in the house—something she always apologized for when it was never needed. I thought it was funny. Oliver had a particularly difficult time keeping his voice down. Especially when he got on the topic of football.

71

I moved outside and crossed the deck, stepping up to the railing. My hands curled around the worn wood as I peered out past the dunes.

The sun was beginning to set. The sand glowed orange and yellow where the water touched it, giving the appearance of colored glass. I watched Oliver run in when the tide threatened to wet his feet. He sprinted over to the sandcastle Olivia was hard at work on and passed off a bucket. Jenna was crouched beside Marley a few feet away, pointing to something in her hand.

I'd never had an opportunity to watch them all together. Typically, Jenna and her kids left within fifteen minutes of me getting home. I never had time to *spend time*, and now I was realizing how much I wanted that. I liked her kids. They were amusing as hell. And Jenna... Yeah, no point in denying it. I liked her too. That admission was easy and becoming really fucking obvious—at least to me. I was pretty sure Tori had an idea, considering our conversation today. What exactly *liking her* meant, I wasn't sure. I didn't pick apart what the hell I was feeling. Who knew if I was even ready to do that? But I wouldn't pass up the chance I was being given right now. I knew that for a fact.

I toed off my shoes and socks before descending the stairs. I didn't even consider changing out of my work clothes. A part of me worried Jenna was close to bringing the kids inside, and I wouldn't risk missing out on this.

The shaded sand was cool beneath my feet as I walked down the path. My presence went unnoticed until I stepped out from between the dunes. Olivia's head came up first. She smiled big and pushed to her feet, towering over her castle.

"Nate!" she squealed. "Mama, look, it's Nate!"

I smiled at her, then passed that smile over to Jenna when she peered back at me over her shoulder.

Her face lit up with surprise. She spun Marley around, getting her attention off the ocean, and pointed in my direction. "Look who it is!" Jenna sounded just as happy about me being here right now as I was.

I couldn't deny how hearing that made me feel. Compression pinched in the center of my chest. Then that pressure spread out and filled my lungs, making it damn near impossible to breathe when Marley looked right at me and grinned.

My daughter was always honest with her reaction. She was also mostly indifferent to having me around. If she ever smiled at me before, I was damn near positive it had been by accident.

There was nothing accidental about the way she was looking at me right now.

"Hey, Nate!" Oliver yelled from down the beach, spotting me when I reached the sandcastle.

I held my hand up for him to see, and getting that, he started making his way over.

"Daddy, wook! Wook dis seashell." Marley reached her arm out, showing off the shell between her fingertips.

I couldn't get to her fast enough.

"Let me see what you got," I said, crouching beside her and Jenna. Marley let me hold the shell, then passed me a handful more after digging around in the bucket at her feet. On the third handful, I joked, "Baby, did you leave any on the beach?"

"We've been busy. Someone loves digging in the sand," Jenna said.

Marley dumped the bucket over, squealing in delight at the little mess she made, then lost interest in the shells altogether when Olivia called out for her to help with the castle. She rushed past me.

"How come you're home so early?" Jenna asked, collecting

the shells in the bucket again, something I was certain she was doing for my daughter without being asked to do it.

I gave her a hand with it, dumping what I was already holding into the bucket and then moving on to the ones sticking in the sand.

"I hired Tori for the assistant manager position. She basically kicked me out of my office."

"What?" Jenna smiled big. "That's great news! Well, not about getting kicked out of your own office."

"I didn't mind. I'm here, aren't I?"

Her green eyes went soft. "Mm. True. So, I guess your hours are going to be changing in a couple weeks, then?"

"Starting tomorrow," I answered.

Jenna's smile faltered the slightest bit. "Oh. That soon?"

I figured the reason for her surprise and quickly explained, "Tori doesn't really need to go through any training. She knows the restaurant. She's more than qualified. I'll work shorter days through Tuesday with her just to make sure she's good on her own. Wednesday I'm planning on being off."

Marley giggled, and I turned my head to watch her dump a bucket of sand onto Olivia's foot. The girls laughed together. Then Marley bent down to repeat the action after receiving encouragement from Olivia.

When I looked at Jenna again, she was back to smiling, looking nothing but happy for me.

"That's really great, Nathan," she said.

I nodded, agreeing with her. I couldn't believe my luck. I'd worried it would take weeks to fill that position, something I hadn't shared with Jenna. The fact that she wasn't pulling out of watching Marley for me before I *did* hire someone was a fucking miracle.

"Hey, Nate!" Oliver skidded to a stop beside me.

"What's up?"

"Nothing. You wanna play catch now?" He tossed a football into the air.

"Oliver, he just got home," Jenna said, getting to her feet now that all the shells were picked up.

She was wearing white shorts that sat low on her hips. Her top was a simple pale-blue tee with a pocket on her breast. It gathered at her waist and held with a knot, and I knew with every shift of her body, teasing hints of her stomach would peek out. A stomach I was currently eye level with.

I pushed to my feet before it seemed like I was waiting out an opportunity like that.

"Maybe another night. I'm sure Nathan wants to relax a little," Jenna added, looking to me for confirmation.

"No, it's cool. I'm always down for playing catch." I tugged at the knot in my tie, getting it loose enough to remove.

Oliver's smile took up his entire face. He tossed the ball into the air again. "You hear that, Mom? Nate just said he's down for it."

"Of course I heard him. I'm right here." Jenna laughed.

"Cool. Just making sure you know." Oliver spun around and took off running, putting space between us.

"Thank you," Jenna said, her eyes heavy with gratitude. "He's been dying to do this ever since he found out you played football. This really means a lot to him."

"Yeah, no problem. I'm happy to do it."

I meant that in more ways than one. Aside from making Oliver happy by obliging his request, this was another thing I could do for Jenna. Her joy ran parallel with her kids'. She'd said it before—if they were good, she was good.

I knew how much this would mean to her.

I untucked my shirt and worked from the collar down, getting it unbuttoned so I could slip it off. Not that I gave a shit about messing up my clothes right now. I just needed range of motion to throw. I had a white tee on underneath, and I untucked that as well before I lifted my head.

Jenna was staring hard at my shoulders, chest, and abs, her gaze moving all over me and *fuck* if her eyes weren't heavy with something else right now.

"Nate! You ready?" Oliver yelled.

I watched Jenna suck in a breath like she was startled. Her gaze snapped up to mine and widened in panic as heat burned like fire across her cheeks. Her reaction was instant. She was obviously embarrassed, and before I could even attempt to make this less awkward for her by saying I didn't mind her looking at me like that, she shot her hand out and grabbed the shirt and tie I was still holding.

"Here, I can—"

"Yeah, thanks." I released my hold on the garments when she tugged, and she quickly stepped away.

Jenna set my clothes aside, then knelt between Marley and Olivia, who were both working on the sandcastle now. They were focused on that and nothing else around them. And suddenly, so was Jenna. She helped Marley fill a bucket with sand and smiled easily at Olivia.

That did just happen, right? She was definitely staring at me . . .

"Nate!"

"Yeah!" After setting the bucket of shells aside so I didn't knock them over, I looked down the beach and raised my hand, signaling for Oliver to throw.

He grinned, excitement pouring out of him, and didn't waste any time putting the ball into the air, and even though there wasn't a ton of distance between us, he still got it to me without much of an effort. That impressed me.

"Your coach doesn't know what he's talking about! You've got an arm!" I hollered, spinning the ball in my hand.

I didn't think it was possible, considering how pleased he looked already just from getting the opportunity to play right now, but somehow Oliver became the happiest kid I'd ever seen.

"I'm trying out for quarterback next season!" he shouted.

"You should!"

We tossed the ball around for a while, gaining an audience pretty soon after I gave Oliver that ego boost. On my second throw, Jenna cheered for him after he made the catch. When he made me run for it, whipping the ball toward the ocean, I noticed Jenna watching me on my jog back in and held my arms out to encourage applause.

A laugh burst out of her. "Woo!" she yelled, hands cupping her mouth.

"I see how it is. He gets a cheerleader and I don't?"

"I'll cheer for you!" Olivia bounced on her toes and punched the air. "Go Nate! Go Nate! You're the best! Whoop! Whoop!"

I chuckled. "Thank you, sweetheart."

Olivia immediately began to challenge my earlier assessment of her brother being the happiest kid to walk the earth when her grin amped up to full potential. She pushed her glasses higher up on her nose, then tipped her chin up proudly, like hearing my appreciation meant something big and important to her.

Jenna's smile was soft when I looked at her again. Until I winked, which was something I *don't do*. Not once before. I wasn't a guy who winked at women—what a prick move. But when those full lips of hers parted like a heavy, heart-pounding breath was leaving her, I became the guy who winked.

If it got a reaction like that, I'd wink so much around this woman, people would think there was something wrong with me. *Holy sh—*

"Nate, I'm going long!" Oliver yelled, turning my head.

I adjusted my grip on the ball, cocked my arm back, and launched it. The ball sailed into the air and hit the sand a good ten feet past his outstretched arms.

"What was that?" he hollered, laughing at me.

"Sorry!" I winced. *Your mother is distracting as shit.*

"Didn't you play in college?" Jenna taunted.

I slowly turned my head at that bold-ass question, and when our eyes locked, Jenna giggled shamelessly, looking a little too proud of herself.

Oh, I don't think so. "Come on," I said, jogging over to her.

Her eyes went wide. "Come on, what?"

"You want to see how I played in college? Let's go." I stopped in front of her, grabbed her hands, and gently eased her to her feet.

"This requires my participation?" She pulled out of my grip to brush the sand off her legs.

I smiled down at her. "I need *someone* defending me."

"Me?"

"You or Olivia. Although that hardly seems fair. A beast like her—she'd lay me out."

Jenna laughed hard, tipping her head back, then playfully gave me a shove. "Okay. You're on," she teased, looking over her shoulder. "Olivia, make sure Marley stays with you, okay?"

"Okay!"

Jenna's expression wiped clean of amusement as she gathered her hair off her neck and secured it using the tie around her wrist. When she grabbed hold of her ankle behind her, giving her leg a good stretch, I crossed my arms over my chest and fought a grin.

"I'm fast," she shared.

"Me too."

"Bet I'm faster."

"Okay, shorty. What's the wager? Aside from bragging rights..."

Her gaze narrowed. "I'm not *that* short."

"You're *very* short."

"I'm five three and a half."

"Yeah, that's short."

"It's average-ish."

"*Ish?*"

"I'm on the cusp of being average," she explained.

I smirked. "That's cute."

"Are you making fun of me?"

"I just said you were cute. If anything, I gave you a compliment."

Her eyes blinked wider. "Well...you're *not* cute. So there." She stuck her tongue out at me and hastily stepped away, calling out for Oliver to join us.

I quickly caught up to her. "I'm glad you don't think I'm *cute*," I said low in her ear before I brushed past. I gestured for the ball, and once I had it, I glanced back at Jenna.

She stood frozen in the sand, clearly trying to figure out what the hell I meant. I didn't necessarily mean anything. I could clear up any confusion she had and say I was simply joking around with her...

Or, since I wasn't confident that's all I was doing, I could keep my mouth shut.

"What's going on?" Oliver asked when he reached me. Sweat

beaded on his forehead and his cheeks were flushed. "I can keep going. I'm not tired yet."

"Good. We're going to play a little touch. I'll start out as quarterback, and then we'll switch. Your mom is on defense."

"What!" Oliver gaped at Jenna when she stepped up beside me. "Mom, really? This is awesome!" He punched the air. "We never get to play like this."

"Give me your glasses, please." She took the blue frames from Oliver and then mine when I held them out.

"Are you sure you don't need these to see?" she teased.

"I gotta give you *some* advantage. If I'm partially blind, you might have a shot."

Jenna rolled her eyes and smiled. She set our glasses aside with my clothes and said something to the girls, who were both still hard at work on the castle.

I brought Oliver into a huddle.

"What's the plan?" he whispered. "I mean, obviously it's boys against girls."

"Obviously. We rule, they drool."

"Yeah...I'm eight. I don't really say that anymore."

"Cool. Me either. I never say that."

"So, what am I doing?"

"Just run. I can put the ball wherever I want—I'll get it to you."

He cocked a brow.

"What?"

"You mean, just like the *last time* I ran for it?"

The kid had a point. "It's been six years since I've played," I argued. "Cut me some slack."

That excuse was a bald-faced lie. But Oliver couldn't know the real reason I overthrew.

Jenna walked back over to us. "Talking strategies?"

I gave Oliver's shoulder a squeeze, then released him. "Like we need any. Right, O?" I held out my fist and he bumped it.

Jenna looked between the two of us, arms crossed under her chest, appearing amused as hell. *"O?"*

"What, Mom? It's cool," Oliver scoffed.

"Yeah, shorty. Don't hate," I added with a smirk.

Smile teasing her lips, she held up her hands in surrender. "Not hating."

"Let's do this!" Oliver tossed me the ball. We spread out on the beach.

After taking my instruction, Oliver slid out to my right so he was playing wide receiver. He was excited—it was a position he hadn't played before and one I was confident he'd excel at. He didn't have any problem catching the ball. As long as I put it somewhere near him.

I slid my fingers between the laces and faced off against Jenna, who was crouched down, hands on her knees and expression cold. She looked cute as hell.

"Is that your game face?" I asked, smiling.

"Yep."

"I like it."

Her gaze sharpened. "Don't try to distract me."

"Is that what I'm doing?" I dropped down and held the ball out in front of me like I was taking a hike. Then I tipped my head toward Oliver. "Do you think he's having fun?"

Jenna smiled then, all soft and sweet. "Yes. Thank you again for this."

"Are *you* having fun?"

"Yes."

"Good. Hut! Hut! Hike!"

Even with the count, I still caught her off guard. Jenna shrieked and lunged forward, stumbling a little as I shuffled back.

I faked left, spun, and cut right, anticipating Oliver's run, and put the ball into the air before Jenna could touch me.

Oliver caught it and kept running like he was headed for the end zone.

"Ugh!" Jenna pushed against my chest as I grabbed on to her hips, slowing her so we wouldn't collide. We were both laughing. "I almost had you!" she said, hands gliding to biceps and holding there.

My fingers slid over warm, smooth skin. Her shirt had ridden up during the sprint or it had shifted when I'd grabbed her. I wasn't sure. But now I held on to bare hips, the shape of them fitting just fucking right in my hands, and it took every ounce of willpower I had not to hold on longer than necessary, which was solely decided by her. The second Jenna dropped her arms, I dropped mine.

"That was *awesome!*" Oliver hurried back over and tossed me the ball. "Let's go again!"

We repeated the play. Oliver broke across the middle. I stayed just out of Jenna's reach, put the ball into the air, and spun around, hands gripping hips while hers braced on my chest, then slid over to squeeze my biceps as we slowed. Oliver caught the ball and took off running.

Jenna was laughing.

I was laughing.

We touched for only two, three seconds before she pulled away and forced me to do the same. Most guys would want more than that. Some would've tried for a different play, hoping for an outcome that allowed for longer contact, hands in other places. I didn't want to change a damn thing. I'd run this play all night.

"It's my turn to throw!" Oliver announced on his jog back in, excited for the opportunity to switch.

I could feel Jenna's touch fading from my arms. I almost knew the curve of her waist. I wanted more of those two, three seconds. Just a few more passes...

Oliver stood at our mock line of scrimmage, loosening his arm up, and grinned at me when I asked, "What's your number going to be when you're quarterback?"

I let him call the plays the rest of the night.

* * *

Marley was still awake when Jenna and her kids left.

I almost asked for help putting her to bed. I thought Jenna was close to offering it before she told me good night, but neither one of us said the words. She was confident I could handle this on my own—that was clear—and strangely enough, I was too. And that was solely because of Jenna.

After getting Marley ready for bed, I sat in the chair with her beside the crib, held her against my chest as I rocked, and rubbed her back as if another hand were still on top of mine, coaxing me to move. Within seconds, Marley was breathing slowly and nearly asleep. I pressed my mouth into her freshly bathed hair and thought back to a memory.

"Your mom rocked you in this chair," I told Marley, keeping my voice soft. "She loved sitting here with you... She loved you so much, Marley. I'm going to make sure you know her. I promise, okay?"

I looked into the sleeping face of my daughter, then I let my head fall back against the wood and stared at the picture of Sadie on the wall, making silent promises to her too.

chapter seven

JENNA

My gaze drifted from the documents I was reviewing to the phone beside me on the couch, taunting me.

Although the whole out-of-sight, out-of-mind thing hadn't worked very well either. Up until twenty minutes ago, my phone had been in my bedroom charging and I'd still thought about texting Nathan every five minutes or so. I was incredibly distracted today.

It was Wednesday, his first full day home with Marley. I was happy Nathan was getting to spend more time with his daughter, but I couldn't deny how *off* I was feeling myself.

I missed her. I'd spent ten straight days with Marley, bonding with her and watching Oliver and Olivia do the same. We'd fallen into a routine together. A routine I loved. And it didn't matter how prepared I could've been for this time apart. Even though I'd see her bright and early in the morning and we'd have most of Saturday together as well, I still couldn't shake this feeling. I was practically crawling in my skin. I'd never wanted to send a text so badly before in my life.

Just one. What was the big deal? One text to see how it was going. And possibly a follow-up asking Nathan if he needed any help today. That would be it though.

No. I jerked my hand back before it curled around the device. *Don't do it. Don't do it. Just let them be.*

"It's so quiet in here," Olivia said, peering up from her iPad to look around the living room. She sighed dramatically and dropped her head against the cushion.

"Way too quiet," Oliver echoed. His gaze remained laser-focused on his DS screen.

My mouth twitched. It appeared I wasn't the only one missing our new normal.

"Do you guys want to play Jenga?" I suggested. That game was noisy enough.

"No," they answered in unison.

"Do you want to go outside? I can work outside."

"There's nothing to do." Oliver hit a button on his device and then turned his head to look at me. "It's not like at Nate's house, Mom. We can do everything there. We got the beach. We can play basketball…"

"Kickball," Olivia added excitedly. "Remember when we played kickball the other day, Ollie? That was *awesome*."

"I can take you guys to the park if you want to play kickball," I said.

"It won't be the same." Olivia pouted, sinking lower onto the couch.

"How about a board game? I can play with you…"

Two heads shook in synced twin-rhythm.

Olivia shuffled closer to her brother until they shared the same cushion and whispered loud enough for me to hear, "What do you think Marley's doing right now?"

I grinned at my lap.

Oliver snorted. "Probably being *crazy*. I bet she's running around. Wait." He sat up, narrowed his eyes at the clock on the wall, and then slumped backward again. "She's asleep. It's her nap time."

"Oh, yeah, I knew that," Olivia returned.

"She should wake up soon. *Then* she's gonna want to eat. You know I'm right, Livvy."

"Do you guys want a snack?" I asked.

"No," Oliver answered, while his sister said, "I'm not hungry."

I wasn't really hungry either, but getting something to eat would occupy my mind. Obviously, work wasn't doing it for me. Maybe it was time I took a break.

"I think I'll make myself a little something," I announced, stacking the documents together and setting them on the coffee table as I slid to the edge of the cushion. Just as I pushed to my feet, the phone beeped with an incoming message. I palmed it and flipped it over on my walk to the kitchen. The name on the screen briefly halted my steps. It was the CupidMatch guy. I'd deleted the app but forgot to erase him from my contacts.

Wanted to see if you were free this weekend to meet up. I'd like to see you.

I momentarily questioned why this guy would even think I was still interested in getting together—I'd thought I made it clear the other night—until I scrolled back and read the last message I'd sent him. I'd only backed out of our previous date, telling him something had come up. I hadn't mentioned not wanting to reschedule for another time.

Nothing had changed for me. I still felt the same way.

Just as I was about to respond, another text came through across the screen. This one took immediate precedence over Hookup Guy and possibly anyone else who could be texting me right now.

She's figured out the power she has over me. Took her a whole 5 minutes. I'm not proud.

I pulled out a chair at the table and took a seat, grinning as I typed my response.

Have you bought her a pony yet?

I will if she asks for one. Jesus Christ I hope she doesn't.

She's heard the word NO before.

Not today. I want her to like me.

I frowned at the screen. *God, did he really not know?*

She'll love you even if you tell her NO. I promise.

She'll love you no matter what.

Can I call you?

Of course.

I sat forward and braced for panic, answering on the first ring. "Hey, is everything okay?"

Nathan's chuckle was low and deep in my ear. "Yeah. Why would something be wrong?"

"Oh, uh...I don't know. I just assumed, since you asked to call me..."

"There's nothing wrong. I just wanted to talk to you."

"Oh." A fluttering sensation warmed my stomach.

He just wanted to talk to me. And I just wanted to talk to him. I didn't need a reason either.

"I'm sorry." I pressed my back against the seat again. "I didn't mean I was expecting something to be wrong or anything."

"That's good to know."

"I've been wanting to talk to you all day, actually."

He was silent for a breath. "Really?"

"Yeah, I've been dying to know how your day was going with Marley. How is it?"

He cleared his throat before answering, "Fine. Good. I think...It's not like she's said or anything. I'd actually kill for some reassurance right now."

I smiled. "I'm sure she's having the best time with you."

"Well, I'm basically letting her get away with murder today. You should see some of the shit I've allowed."

Laughing, I tucked my hair behind my ear and stretched out my legs until my bare feet were propped up on the seat beside me.

"What are you doing?" he asked.

I bit my lip. God, I liked how he asked about me. I liked it way too much.

"Nothing right now," I answered. "I'm trying to come up with something for the kids to do. They're pretty bored."

"You could bring them over here if you want."

Yes, I almost answered, not needing even a moment to think of a response. I wanted to spend time together so badly. And I knew the kids would jump at the chance to go. But I couldn't do that. It was Nathan's day to be with Marley.

"No, that's okay. Thank you though," I said. "I'm sure they'll occupy themselves somehow. Maybe I'll take them out for ice cream or something."

"Oh yeah? Where?"

I smiled against the phone.

Nathan laughed when I remained silent. "Is it obvious I'm fishing?"

"A little."

"Well, it's not like you own taking your kids to get ice cream, Jenna. I was planning on doing that anyway."

"Oh really?" I giggled. "What a coincidence, then. Were you planning on going to the Arctic Circle? Because that's where we like to go."

"I wouldn't think of going anywhere else. That's our favorite spot."

"Huh. Ours too."

"It's just been a while for us. Where is that one again?"

I was full-on grinning now. My cheeks were beginning to ache. "You know, by the Putt-Putt course and the old drive-in..."

"Right. Yeah, that's the one we go to. When are you planning on being there?"

I glanced at the clock on the oven. "Probably an hour. You?"

"I'm just waiting for Marley to wake up."

"Which should be in about thirty, forty minutes, if she went to bed at twelve thirty..."

"She did." I could hear the smile in his voice. I wished I could see it. "Marley's really looking forward to getting ice cream today."

"Oliver and Olivia too. They...can't wait. It's basically all they've talked about."

Holy *crap*, I was flirting hard with this guy. I was certain my face was bloodred.

"We can't wait for *what?*" Oliver asked, sneaking up beside me. He stood at my shoulder and stared curiously at the phone.

I jerked upright, dropping my feet to the floor. "To get ice cream," I blurted out. "You know, 'cause we're going in, like, an hour. I told you."

"We're getting ice cream? Cool! I didn't know that!"

"I want to get ice cream too!" Olivia hollered from the couch. "Great idea, Mama!"

Nathan laughed in my ear.

"I should go," I said quickly. I needed to disconnect this call before Oliver happened to mention how flushed my face had gotten at just the mention of dessert.

Nathan did not need to hear that.

* * *

"Nate! Hey, Mom, it's Nate and Marley!" Olivia waved out the back window as I pulled into the gravel lot surrounding Arctic Circle. She'd spotted them right away.

"Hey, guys!" Oliver yelled, leaning over as far as his seat belt allowed so he could wave at them too.

I parked in a space on the side of the building, not finding any open ones out front. The kids fled the car as soon as I slowed to a stop, leaving their doors wide open, they were so excited. I'd typically call them back for that, but I understood their eagerness. I hadn't mentioned anything about meeting up with Nathan today. I thought a surprise would be fun. After cutting the engine, I flipped the visor down and checked my appearance in the mirror.

My cheeks were flushed. My freckles more noticeable than usual, thanks to the recent sun I'd gotten on my face. I hated how prominent they became in the summertime. Freckles were cute on kids, my kids especially, who were both blessed with them. What adult wanted freckles? I didn't. I was suddenly kicking myself for not applying any makeup before I left the house.

Why the hell didn't I?

"Mom! Are you coming?"

I quickly finger-combed the ends of my hair before flipping the visor back up. Then I grabbed my wristlet off the passenger seat and slipped my hand through the strap so it dangled. I exited the car, hand on the door ready to shut it but freezing dead-cold when I locked eyes with Nathan over the roof.

Two things halted me.

First, it became very clear that I'd had an audience while I was clearly making a fuss over how I looked for this.

Everyone was gathered no more than ten feet away, watching me. Waiting. And while it wasn't something I'd typically mind if this had been an obvious date, this *wasn't* an obvious date. It wasn't anything, really. I wasn't sure whether I should care how I looked right now or not. I didn't want Nathan thinking I was seeing this as something it wasn't. What if he acted weird with me now?

The second thing freezing me up: I was completely unprepared for casual Nathan.

I was used to seeing him in work clothes. Slacks and button-up shirts. The occasional tie. Today he was wearing a worn, light-gray T-shirt and loose black running shorts, sneakers instead of dress shoes, no glasses, and a backward hat.

A backward hat? Are you kidding me? I had a *major thing* for boys in backward hats. They always drew my eye, especially in college. And now I could very easily picture Nathan in college.

He looked younger. Relaxed. He was smiling right at me, not at all acting weird...

I quickly closed all the doors and stepped up onto the patio.

"Mom, how crazy is this?" Oliver asked. "Did you know Nate was going to be here?"

I shook my head, smiling as I walked over. "Small world, right?"

Nathan grinned. He was holding Marley, who was playing peekaboo with Olivia over his shoulder. Both of the girls were giggling.

"Shorty," Nathan said when I stopped in front of him. I rolled my eyes at the nickname as he looked all over my face. "Nice freckles."

Oh God. I scrunched up my nose. "Yeah, right." I laughed.

"What?"

I rubbed at my cheeks, like that action was actually going to erase them or something. "They're so noticeable right now."

"I know. I'm noticing them." He smiled at me.

I stared back, not smiling and not at all knowing what to say in response. I didn't want him noticing my freckles, did I? Now I wasn't so sure.

Olivia moved away, most likely in search of her brother, who'd run around the building when I reached the group, and Marley turned her head and finally spotted me. Immediately, her little arms reached out as her body tipped forward, trying to get closer.

"Jenna!" she squealed.

"Hi, pretty girl. I missed you." I kissed her smiling cheek as I hugged her, then shifted her weight to the crook of my arm. "Oh my goodness, look at your outfit." I rubbed the tulle of her dress-up skirt between my fingers. It was light blue and sparkled in the sun. Underneath it, she wore a yellow polka-dot bathing suit. There were streaks of sunscreen on her shoulders and chest. "You look so fancy. Did you dress yourself today?"

"Daddy, no shush," she said, leaning over to grab at her sandal. She tugged at the strap with a grunt.

"Yeah, that was a battle," Nathan said. "I thought I was going to have to tape them to her feet."

I got Marley's attention on the necklace I was wearing. I knew she liked playing with it.

"Let's leave those on. You might want to walk around a little."

Distracted, Marley plucked at the gold chain. It was then I noticed her hot-pink fingers.

"And you painted your nails today. *Wow.*" I giggled.

The polish coated her nails and most of the skin around them. Drops had dripped onto the underside of her fingers as well.

"Yeah, that was me."

I looked up at Nathan, laughing when he showed me the splashes of polish on his own hand. "First time?" I asked.

"Is it that obvious?"

"Only a little."

"This stuff is like tar. I've been picking it off for two hours." He scratched at the side of his hand.

"Hey, we're up!" Oliver yelled, peering around the side of the building. He waved us over, saying, "Come on, guys. It's our turn."

Nathan stepped back and held his arm out for me to go ahead. When I made it over to the window, Oliver ordered his soft-serve chocolate cone with sprinkles and Olivia did the same. They always mimicked each other. I ordered a small vanilla in a cup. Just as I was slipping my wristlet off my hand to pay, Nathan stepped up behind the kids.

"I got it," he said, pulling out his wallet.

I smiled at him. "Thank you." That was nice of him to treat us.

He told the young girl working that we were all together and ordered himself a medium chocolate with sprinkles.

"Guys." I tipped my head at Nathan once I had Oliver's and Olivia's attention off their cones.

"Thanks, Nate," they said in unison.

"Yeah, no problem." Nathan paid for our order, then tucked his wallet away before grabbing both our cups.

"Are you ready to eat some ice cream?" I asked Marley as I followed behind the twins to the picnic tables in the grass.

She nodded slowly. "Wif spinkles."

Oliver and Olivia sat across from each other at the end of a vacant table. I put Marley on her feet, figuring she'd want to sit beside Nathan since he had her ice cream, and took a seat on Oliver's side. Then I slid down when Marley squeezed herself in between us.

"O'ver, you got spinkles too?" Marley asked.

Oliver sighed and scooted to the very edge of the bench, putting some space between them. "Yes. I have sprinkles."

Marley jumped down, eliminated that space he'd just created, then climbed on the bench again. She sat backward, swinging her legs in the air, and watched him lick his cone like it was the most interesting thing she'd ever witnessed.

"O'ver, I have some?"

"*Mom.*" He groaned.

"Marley, come over here if you want your ice cream." Nathan sat down across from me so he was straddling the bench and facing Olivia. He handed over my cup, then spooned a bite of chocolate soft serve, holding it over the table. "Do you want this?"

Marley jumped down and ran around the table. She let Nathan feed her a bite, chewed it up, and started the retreat back over to Oliver, but changed her mind halfway and went back for more. Nathan took bites for himself in between hers. I thought it was cute how they shared.

And how he'd let her dress herself today.

And painting her nails...that wasn't only cute. It was really, really sweet.

We were all mainly quiet while we ate, most of the noise coming from Marley when she'd ask for another bite and Olivia when she'd comment on how adorable Marley's little voice was. I got up and grabbed a stack of napkins when my kids were finished, and then I cleaned Marley off before she took off running after Oliver. Olivia led the way. The three of them chased one another in the grass, jumping over wishing flowers.

"I went through the rest of the boxes today. That's where I got the polish," Nathan told me when it was just us seated. He waited until I looked over at him before continuing. "I'm keeping a lot of it. I just... I feel like Marley should have a say in what stays. She might want all of it. I don't know."

I nodded. "I think it's better to keep it than regret getting rid of stuff if she asks for it later on. You might not be able to get it back."

"That's what I was thinking. I moved everything to the basement for now." He dropped his spoon into the empty cup, wiped at his mouth, then adjusted the hat, pulling it off and resituating it backward.

"You look so different today," I said.

He stared at me. "Different how?"

"Like snuggly." My eyes widened as amusement flared in his. "I mean, cuddly. *Comfy.* Comfy... not any other word I just said. I meant comfy." I cleared my throat, turned away, and watched Marley chase Oliver in a circle. Nathan laughed.

"Oh my God," I whispered, shaking my head at myself. I slowly looked over at him again, hiding half of my face behind my hand. I peered at him between my fingers. "Leave me alone."

"I don't think I've ever been called snuggly before." He slowly grinned. "Or cuddly."

"I meant *comfy.*" I let my hand fall to the wood. "You know, casual. You always wear business clothes. Give me a break. The hat is really throwing me right now."

"What's wrong with my hat?"

"There's nothing wrong with your hat." *That's the problem.*

"Then why is it throwing you?"

"I'm just not used to seeing you in one. You look like you're in a frat or something."

"Well, I *was* in a frat. Is that a bad thing?"

Goddamn it. I did not need that visual. I was struggling enough as it was. "A bad thing? *No.* Nononono. God, no..."

When laughter burst out of Nathan's mouth, I pinched my lips shut and trapped any further response I was about to give. *Dear God, bury me right here.* I needed to get a handle on myself. I needed to quit picturing Nathan at college.

"So, is that a no, then, Jenna?" he teased.

My phone beeped from my wristlet. *Thank you, distraction. Way to be hella late though.*

Before offering up unnecessary confirmation, I capitalized on this interruption, tugging my purse in front of me and pulling out my cell. It was another text from CupidMatch guy.

Shit. I'd forgotten to write him back earlier.

Whats up? You free this weekend?

My thumbs moved swiftly over the screen. I wanted to be done with this.

Sorry. I'm not really interested anymore. Take care.

I sent my response, then lifted my head and risked a glance at Nathan.

He was looking out at the kids now, mouth twitching as their adorable laughter filled the air. I wanted to sit here and watch him observe them for hours. The way he studied them like being given the opportunity to do so *meant something*...I knew how sweet our kids looked playing together. I wanted him familiar with it too, and I wanted to witness the moment this became a memory for him.

"They get along really well," he said.

I nodded, set my phone on the wood, and peered over at the three of them. "They do. I love watching them together."

"Marley asked about them today."

"Aw, really?" We locked eyes, and Nathan nodded. "Mine were wondering what she was doing right before you and I spoke on the phone. Oliver knew it was her nap time. It was really sweet."

"Marley asked about you too."

My heart melted hearing that.

"I missed her so much today," I revealed, laughing a little at myself. "You'd think I hadn't seen her in weeks. I don't know what I'm going to do when summer is over."

Nathan held my eyes for a moment, then looked down at the wood. He picked at the edge of a splintering piece. "You could always come around. I'm sure she'll want to see you."

"I'd really like that." I smiled at him when he glanced up, then palmed my phone again when it beeped. I flipped it over and slid my thumb across the screen to open up the conversation. "One second," I told him.

"Sure."

A picture of a dick downloaded instantly, along with the caption Still not interested?

"Oh my God! What the—" I turned my phone facedown on the table and trapped a curse inside my mouth. "*Oh my God,*" I repeated through clenched teeth, covering my face with both hands.

"You okay?" Nathan asked.

I shook my head, pulled my hands back to look at him, and immediately began fanning my face. I felt like I was burning up.

"No, I am *not* okay. I just…" *How do I explain this?* God, I didn't even want to. I covered my face again and lowered my head, groaning against my palms.

What the hell? This is so weird and embarrassing!

I felt the table move underneath me and seconds later, Nathan's hold on my wrist.

"Hey." He pulled my hands away from my face and forced me to look at him.

We were sitting so close now, our hips almost touched.

"What's going on? You're freaking out."

"I am freaked out. That's *exactly* what I am." I grabbed my phone and held it against my stomach so he couldn't see the screen. "This…*jerk* just sent me a picture of his, you know, *without* me asking for it. He just sent it."

Nathan's brows raised. "He sent you a dick pic?"

"*Yes.* And I would never ask for something like that. Never. My God, what if my kids were standing right here? They're next to me all the time when I'm doing stuff on my phone." I rushed in a deep breath. I could feel myself shaking. "They could've seen that, Nathan. Who sends stuff like that? What if Olivia had seen that text?" My stomach turned over and knotted at the thought. "Oh my God," I mumbled.

Nathan reacted to that possibility as well. His nostrils flared, and the sharp angle of his jaw twitched. I could suddenly hear his breaths.

"Who is this guy?" he asked. "Do you know him?"

I shook my head, then tipped it side to side. "Sort of. Not really." I winced. "God, this is not something I've told people about."

Nathan's expression wiped clean of reaction. "I have absolutely no idea where this conversation is going."

That made me laugh a little. "It's not, like, weird or anything. I met him on a dating app. We were supposed to go out the other day, until he found out I had kids and expressed how he wasn't looking for anything besides a hookup. I backed out immediately. Then he asked me out again today for this weekend, and I just told him a minute ago I wasn't interested anymore. The dick pic was to change my mind."

Nathan held out his hand.

I realized what he was asking for and blinked at him. I didn't move. "You...want to see it?" I asked slowly.

"That is the last thing I want, trust me." He gestured for the phone again, and when I handed it over, he stood with it and moved away from the seating area until there wasn't anyone within twenty feet of him. With his back to me, Nathan pressed the phone to his ear.

Is he calling that guy? Holy shit. What was he going to say?

Oliver ran over to me, asking, "Mom, can we play Putt-Putt? We all want to play. Even Marley."

"Um, we'll have to see," I answered, keeping my eyes on Nathan. I squinted at the back of his head and listened as best as I could, but he was too far away to hear.

"See *what?*" Oliver questioned.

"I don't know what their plans are after this."

"Oh, okay. Let us know when you find out. We're playing chase." Oliver hurried away again.

I watched Nathan grip the back of his neck, then pull the phone away from his ear and end the call. He stalked back over to the table, looking more like a pissed-off frat boy now than the playful one I just ate ice cream with.

His face was hard, shoulders drawn back. He appeared larger somehow.

"Here. He shouldn't contact you anymore, but I would still block his number." He returned my phone, then sat backward on the bench seat next to me. There was more space between us now.

I secretly hated it.

"Good thinking," I said.

I pulled up my settings and prevented this loser from sending me anything else. Then I went to my messages and erased our entire conversation.

"God, I can't believe he did that. What a creep."

Nathan was pitched forward, elbows resting on his knees as he watched the kids run around the field. He turned his head to look at me after I put my phone away.

"What did you say to him?" I asked.

His shoulders jerked. "I just told him off. Then I made it really fucking clear you weren't interested. I don't think he'll have the balls to send you anything else, but I feel better knowing he can't."

I smiled, liking how he cared about this. He didn't have to. "Thank you for doing that."

"You don't need to thank me." Nathan cracked his knuckles and stared out at the kids again. Just as I turned my head to do the same, he asked, "Are you still on that dating app?"

"God, no." I laughed. "I was striking out big-time on that thing. I'm done with it."

"You're done with dating?"

Our gazes locked when I looked over at him again. His dark eyes were serious.

"No, I mean, the app...I erased it."

Oliver rushed over before anything else could be said about dating apps, dating, Nathan's views on the subject...Was he even open to dating yet? I had no idea and was robbed of the opportunity to ask. My son was currently hollering in my face.

"Mom!" Oliver panted his breaths and pushed his glasses up his nose when they started sliding down. "Did you ask Nate yet?"

"No, not yet," I answered, bringing my leg over the bench seat so I was sitting sideways, making it easier to see everyone better. I tugged on the hem of my shorts.

"Ask me what?" Nathan picked Marley up when she ran over.

She stood on his thighs and giggled at Oliver as he leaned out of her grasp.

"We want to play Putt-Putt," Oliver announced, bobbing and weaving Marley's hands. "Mom said she wasn't sure what your plans were after ice cream."

"It's also Nathan's day with Marley, so if he wants to do something with just her, like Putt-Putt, we're going to go."

Olivia stood in front of Nathan and pouted as if she'd just heard the worst news of her life. Her braids looked messy now from playing.

"Can't this be *our* day, all five of us?" she asked, peering up at him.

"Olivia," I warned. Wow. Way to lay on the guilt trip.

"Please, Nate!" Oliver begged. "You want to spend time with us too, right?"

"Oliver, you shouldn't ask someone a question like that. You're putting them on the spot." I stood then, slipping my hand through the strap of my wristlet.

"Smart kid," Nathan said, getting to his feet as well. He shifted Marley to his left arm. Then he ruffled Oliver's hair and looked between him and his sister, asking, "So, what's the plan? Are we playing teams or what?"

Olivia's face lit up. "Yes! I want to be on your team!" she shrieked.

"Me too!" Oliver punched the air. He tugged on his sister's hand. "Come on, Livvy, let's go pick our colors."

They took off in a sprint, crossing the gravel lot after looking both ways for cars. The Putt-Putt course shared parking with the Arctic Circle, so I didn't mind them running ahead. I could see them even when they reached the small, hutlike building where you paid for your game and received your ball and putter.

Marley reached out for me as the three of us moved away from the table and followed behind the twins. I situated her on my hip.

"Are you sure this is okay?" I asked Nathan. We stepped off the curb together. The gravel popped beneath our feet. "I feel like we're invading your time with her. I'd hate to do that, Nathan."

He smirked as he stared ahead. "Jenna, if I didn't want to hang out with you and your kids, I wouldn't have called you. Or texted you, which was just my lead-in to call."

My stomach clenched. I suddenly became hyperaware of every pulsing beat of my heart.

"And if it wasn't obvious already, we never had plans to come here today. I was lying." He looked at me then, adding with sincerity in his voice, "I'm sure this is okay."

I pressed my lips to baby-soft hair, hiding the smile I couldn't help. Then I playfully narrowed my eyes at him.

"What?"

"Is this really your favorite spot to get ice cream?" I asked.

He looked ahead, mouth twitching.

I never got a response.

chapter eight

NATHAN

One Week Later

W*ake up, Nathan."*
     I opened my eyes and blinked into the darkness of my bedroom. Labored breaths left me, and my heart was pounding. I knew it was early, yet I was already wide awake and restless. I always was when I woke from a dream. From that dream...

Turning my head on the pillow, I reached for my glasses and slipped them on. I stared at the alarm clock on the nightstand until the fluorescent numbers came into focus: 4:27 a.m.

I still had another hour until I'd be forced to get up. I was opening at the restaurant today. I supposed I could go downstairs and work out now instead of waiting, but I found myself stretching for my phone instead. The screen glowed above me as I studied Jenna's number. My thumb hovered over the icon to call.

I wanted to talk to her. Exercise cleared my head, but my conversations with Jenna stilled that gnawing ache inside me, among other things. I liked talking to her. Even if I didn't tell her about my last memory of Sadie and the guilt I had over it, I knew I'd feel better simply listening to her voice. I could imagine our dialogue.

She'd ask about Marley, because she always did. She'd wonder if my daughter was awake yet and how her night had gone. Did she go to bed for me okay and *It's easy, isn't it? Once you're comfortable with her, she's comfortable with you.* She'd have excitement in her voice. My bond with Marley affected Jenna profoundly. It was pure and selfless and went beyond contentment for us. I wanted to know what exactly it meant to her, but before I could ask, she would wonder about me.

Maybe she would think something was wrong since I was calling her so early. I was sure she'd be able to tell without me saying a word, because she had this uncanny ability to read my discomfort. She did it that first day in my office. She'd do it now.

The call would connect, and Jenna would ask if I was okay. She'd wonder if it was Sadie, and if I told her *Yes...how did you know?* She would say something I needed to hear.

But I didn't want to wake her. Jenna would try to hide her sleep-heavy voice from me. She wouldn't want me to feel bad for reaching out, but I would. I didn't want to talk to her about this anyway. I didn't want to talk to anyone about it. I closed out of her contact info and pulled up my texts, reading the message I'd ignored yesterday out of habit.

July 4th 4:00. Hope to see you and Marley.

I dialed the number instead of responding. The call connected on the third ring.

"This can't be Nathan Bell calling me right now. I must still be asleep. I *should* still be asleep, you rude motherfucker. Do you have any idea what time it is?"

I chuckled and sat up, swinging my legs over the edge of the bed. "Hey, man. I..." My tongue froze inside my mouth. I scrambled for words. They sounded foreign to me.

What the hell was I supposed to say to my best friend after shutting him out for nearly two years?

I ran a hand through my hair, clearing my throat. "Hey, man," I repeated. It seemed like a good place to start.

"It's good to hear from you. Even if it is early as shit."

I chuckled.

"You all right?"

"Yeah...sorry. I know I should've called sooner."

"Don't worry about it."

He was giving me a pass. One I didn't deserve.

"No, I know it's been too long...I've been meaning to reach out."

"Seriously, man. I could go ten years without speaking to you, and it wouldn't change a damn thing."

My mouth twitched. "You're wrong, Davis."

"How am I wrong?"

"Ten years? You'd be bawling your fucking eyes out right now if I put that much time between calls. Admit it."

He was silent for a moment, and then he broke into quiet laughter. "Bastard."

I stood from the bed and swiped the switch on the wall, illuminating the room in soft light. Then I slouched into a nearby chair. The leather was cool against my back.

"All kidding aside, it'd be messed up if I pushed it any longer."

His response was immediate. "I'd understand it."

"You shouldn't have to."

"Look, man, we're cool. I get it. We *all* get it."

He was referring to the rest of my old teammates. A handful of us remained close after graduation though Davis was the only one who was persistent in trying to stay in touch with me. The rest of them had given up after a year.

"None of us knows what you went through, obviously," he continued. "But we all loved Sadie."

"Yeah, I know."

"How are you? What's going on? I get updates from your dad. I know the restaurant is doing well."

That revelation shook my head. "He never told me he spoke to you."

"It wasn't like I called all the time. Just every few months or so. I think it helped him, talking about you to someone. He was worried."

"Yeah." I picked at the leather seam on the armrest. "I need to get over there and see him and my mom. I'm doing better. I just... I wouldn't deal with it before. I am now. Slowly, I'm getting through it."

"That's awesome, man. I'm glad to hear that. How's Marley?"

I smiled. "Good. Getting big. I'm biased, but she's really fucking cute. You should see her."

"What about on the Fourth? Are you coming or what?"

I immediately thought about Jenna and the twins. I knew what to expect at Davis's party. I used to go to them every year. He went all out on the Fourth. Oliver and Olivia would have a blast. I could picture their faces watching the fireworks. Marley's too. I'd never taken her to see them before. I wanted to. I wanted this memory for us.

"I keep it kid friendly," Davis shared, misreading my hesitation. "Everyone brings their families now. Marley would have fun, trust me."

"No, I'm sure she would," I agreed. "I was thinking about inviting this woman who's been watching Marley for me. She has two kids. Marley's really gotten close with them. I know she'd like it if they came. Do you mind if they tag along?"

"Hell no. Bring them. More the merrier and shit."

"Thanks, man. I appreciate it."

"Don't thank me, Nate. I'm just glad to hear you're coming."

Head rolling to the side, I peered out the window at the ocean. Sunlight burned across the horizon, painting the water in streaks of light.

"It's going to be weird being there without Sadie," I said.

"I understand that."

"Or maybe it won't. Maybe I'll be fine...Is that fucked up? I'm not sure which is worse."

"You know what? Let's just play it out. If you're not feeling it and you need to go, no one is gonna say shit. Do what's best for you and Marley. Or if you're fine, which is how I think Sadie would want you to be, no one is gonna say shit about that either."

"I don't give a fuck about what anyone would say. That's not it."

"Then what's the problem?"

I sighed and sat forward, hunching over in the chair. I rubbed at my face. "Nothing...I don't know. It's early."

"No fucking shit, you bastard. You're the one who woke me up." We laughed together.

"Maybe it'll just be what it is, man," Davis offered, no trace of humor in his voice anymore. "Not wrong or fine without her. Just new, you know? Different..."

I considered this. Different wasn't bad—I was living it. This new normal...life without Sadie. I didn't hate it. I didn't want it either, and if I'd had a choice I'd never have asked for this, but it didn't feel wrong anymore. It just simply was.

Maybe Davis was right.

"Damn." He sounded impressed.

"What?"

"I just got real profound before five a.m. That does not typically happen."

I smirked. "Is this your way of saying you'd like a wake-up call every day? I could arrange that."

"If you call me again this early, I'll drive the two hours instead of answering and beat the shit out of you."

I chuckled. I was already feeling better. "It's good to talk to you, man," I said, meaning it. I missed this.

"I know. I'm a fucking delight."

I shook my head and stood, crossing the room to my dresser. I pulled out a T-shirt and a pair of shorts. "All right. I'll let you get back to your beauty sleep."

"See you on the Fourth?"

"Yeah, I'll be there."

"Good. Later, man." The call disconnected.

As I sat on the edge of the bed, tying my sneakers, a text came through.

Call anytime. I'll answer.

* * *

I got home that night just after seven, but instead of the laughter and animated voices I was used to hearing when I stepped up onto the porch, I heard yelling. Someone was clearly upset.

It was Oliver. That much was clear. I couldn't make out what he was saying though. Jenna's voice was raised too, just not as loud as Oliver's.

I pushed the door open and stepped inside the house.

"It's not fair!" Oliver screamed. "You don't get it, Mom! You just don't!" Tears ran down his reddened face. He was standing in front of the couch in his Boy Scout uniform, facing off with Jenna, who was cradling Marley against her chest a few feet away. My daughter was whining and burying her face in Jenna's shirt. Olivia was on the love seat, slouched over and covering her ears.

"Oliver, please calm down," Jenna said, glancing over at me and mouthing, *I'm sorry*, as I stepped farther into the room after securing the door. She turned back to Oliver. "We can talk about this later when you're not so upset."

"No!" He stomped his foot. "No, Mom! I don't want to talk about this later . . . Nothing's going to change! I'm not going!"

"Okay, fine, you don't have to go . . . Nobody is making you go, baby."

"What's going on?" I asked, rounding the couch and stepping up beside Jenna. I took Marley from her, holding my daughter against my chest, then looked to Oliver just as more tears rolled down his cheeks.

I'd never seen him upset before. He was always happy.

"You okay, bud?" I asked him.

Oliver looked at me. His lip started quivering a second before he slapped his hands over his face and sobbed so hard, he nearly folded in on himself. His little shoulders jerked in distress.

Jenna moved closer, reaching out for him. "Oh, baby . . . I'm sorry."

"I want to go," he whimpered. "I want to go so bad, Mom. This isn't fair . . . " He sniffled, lifting his head to peer up at her. Before Jenna could touch him, he jerked back and twisted out of reach, shouting, "Stop! Just leave me alone!"

Jenna straightened up and drew her hand against her chest.

Oliver scrambled onto the love seat with his sister, lying sideways with his back to us and curling himself into a ball. He cried into the armrest while Olivia patted his hip. She was crying now too.

"I'm so sorry," Jenna whispered, turning away from them to face me. She had tears in her eyes now.

I rubbed Marley's back and gestured for Jenna to follow me into the kitchen. "Come on. Let's talk."

She glanced back at her kids. "Can we go outside?" she asked, halting me at the slider.

"Yeah, of course." I pulled the door open and followed her onto the deck. The evening sun dipped toward the horizon.

Jenna stepped up to the railing and looked below us. Her hands curled around the wood. "I just didn't want them hearing," she explained when I got beside her. She offered me a sad smile.

"What happened?"

"I'm sorry he was yelling like that in your house."

"Jenna, I don't care. He can yell wherever he wants." I stepped closer. "What happened? Why is he so upset?"

Marley had settled down now and was rubbing her face against my shirt. She'd be asleep soon. I could tell she was tired. I pressed my lips to her hair and patted her back, watching Jenna gaze out at the ocean.

"Oliver's Boy Scout troop has this father/son campout every year," she began, her voice sad and small. "It's really cool. They do all these special bonding activities—fishing, canoeing, build your own campfire, stuff like that. For the past two years, my brother has gone with him...I didn't want Oliver missing out. Brian offered to go again this year, but Oliver doesn't want him to go. Apparently, the other kids have been making fun of him. They know Brian isn't his dad." She shook her head. "I had no idea they were doing that. I can only imagine what they said."

"Kids can be assholes," I offered, jaw clenching through my speech. I began to wonder what all was said to him myself. I didn't like knowing they'd upset him.

"Oliver is pretty tough. He's had kids picking on him before for different things, but nothing bothers him like this...This isn't like being made fun of for wearing glasses."

I waited, just kept watching her...I wanted to ask. I wanted to know—honestly, I had been curious about this for a while.

"Jenna." She peered over at me. "Where is their dad?"

"Denver," she answered. "Unless he's moved. I wouldn't know. We haven't spoken in seven years."

"He doesn't talk to them?"

"No." She turned her head toward the slider. "He never has."

I stood taller. Anger pulsed through me, straining the muscles in my shoulders and neck. Her response caught me off guard. I didn't know what I'd been expecting...a father who only checked in occasionally due to obligations or one who had passed away? Those excuses I could wrap my head around. Not this. I couldn't understand this. Even if you weren't on good terms with your kids' mother...This dick never spoke to Oliver and Olivia? Not even once? Why the fuck not?

"Um, okay, long story short," she began, looking down and away.

"Give me all of it," I said. Our eyes locked. "For me to understand this, I'm going to need to hear all of it...if you don't mind."

I added that last bit on a rush when it dawned on me how personal this conversation was about to become and how invading this might feel to Jenna. I was practically ordering her to share this with me. I sounded desperate to hear it.

Truth be told, what I was feeling wasn't far off. This information felt strangely vital.

Jenna nodded lightly. "We, uh, met in college. Freshman year...he was in my psych class. I had a *huge* crush on him." She rolled her eyes at herself.

"Is that embarrassing to admit?"

"Well, the feelings weren't exactly mutual."

"Was this an online course?"

"No. We met three times a week." Two lines formed between her brows. "Why?"

Because that would be the only explanation I'd understand. This jerk-off would have to be blind not to feel something for you.

"Nothing." I shifted Marley so her head lay on my shoulder. Her body was deadweight. "Go on."

Jenna gazed out at the ocean again. "There was this party. We hooked up...Three weeks later I found out I was pregnant."

I blinked. "Jesus. You were—"

"Eighteen," she answered for me. "Nineteen when I delivered. The pregnancy was shocking enough. We'd used a condom. I mean, I know there's still risks, but it wasn't like we were reckless. When I found out I was having twins, I almost hit the floor."

"I can imagine."

"I was so excited though." She looked over at me and smiled. Her long hair blew behind her shoulder. "Straightaway just so incredibly excited. I didn't regret anything. I wasn't even nervous. I couldn't wait to be a mom." Her smile faded to something softer, a little dejected. "I never saw that night with Derek as just a hookup. I wanted something more. I'd hoped for more. He didn't. I knew that. I never thought having kids with him would change his mind about me. I never once thought that. I only cared about them." She tipped her head at the slider. "I wanted Derek in their lives for them, not for me. I could see us making it work...co-parenting. Splitting custody. I thought he'd be excited about them. He wasn't. He asked me to get an abortion."

My shoulders drew back. Jenna noticed my reaction and nodded as if she knew I needed her to confirm what I'd just heard, because I was certain I'd misunderstood.

"I told him I wouldn't do that. I wanted them, with or without his involvement." She tucked a strand of hair behind her ear. "My parents were supportive of my decision, which was a huge relief. My brother was too. Though he wanted to kill Derek. I had to beg him not to fly out to Denver and hunt him down. I'm pretty positive he made a few phone calls. Derek would tense up if I'd mention Brian for whatever reason."

"I like your brother."

A soft laugh pushed past her lips. Her gaze lowered to the rail. "It's strange...I knew how Derek felt. I never doubted his decision, not even the day I went into labor. I didn't call him. I didn't tell him I was having them that day, but the moment I saw Oliver and Olivia, the *second* I looked at them...I knew if he saw them too, he'd change his mind. I was sure. I was in love with them after a glance. He just needed to see them...so, I texted him a picture. I told him what room I was in...that they were healthy. I told him their names."

"He didn't show up, did he?"

Jenna shook her head. "He never even wrote me back."

I cursed under my breath. Then I flexed my jaw. It was beginning to ache. "Okay. Then what?"

I suddenly wanted Jenna to rush through the rest of the details and possibly spare me the worst. I was two seconds away from getting in touch with her brother and getting this motherfucker's number for myself. I had my own calls to make. He thought he was tense before? I'd give a new definition to the word.

Jenna turned sideways to face me. "Then nothing for a while." She tucked more hair behind her ear. The breeze off the water was cool and swirled around us. "I dropped out of college and eventually moved back in with my parents. I left Derek alone. I still thought he'd reach out...He didn't. I went almost a year before I gave in to my parents' demands and considered hitting him up for child support. I didn't want him getting served. If he was bitter about it, we'd never get along again. I knew that. I thought we could talk. I still had hope—if Derek saw them in person, he'd change his mind. Again, I was sure. I just loved them so much. How could he not, you know? I sent him an invitation to their first birthday party, thinking we could go from there."

She shook her head, her gaze falling to Marley, who was sound asleep on my shoulder.

"He got in touch with me, finally, after that. Derek wanted to relinquish his parental rights. In order for that to happen, I had to approve it. So I did..."

"You never made him pay child support?"

"Not a cent."

"Why the hell not?"

"He wasn't giving up his rights to get out of paying. He couldn't." She looked at me then. "Derek never even knew I was considering going to court about that. I never said a word. He was giving up his rights because he didn't want anything to do with them. He never did. I just didn't believe him until he took it that far."

I pulled in a deep breath and released it slowly. "I don't know, Jenna. I would've still made him pay."

"It hurt me when he did that," she whispered. Tears welled up in her eyes again. They beaded on her lashes. "More than anything...more than when he asked me to abort them, and I

114

can't explain to you why. Maybe it was because he'd seen pictures of them and knew they existed, and I couldn't understand how he could still want nothing to do with them. I looked at my children *once* and I would've done anything to know them. I was with them every day, all day long, and when I started taking classes again and had to leave them for two, three hours at the most, I missed them so badly, I considered dropping out again. I considered it every time I went to class. Derek knew they existed and he still chose not to meet them, and when he contacted me that day, I realized nothing was going to change. I didn't want to fight with him for child support. I didn't want to send him invitations to parties every year and see the look on my kids' faces when their father didn't bother showing up. I thought they'd be better off without him instead of being constantly rejected, and ninety-five percent of the time, they are. They're great. You see them. You know. They're the happiest kids."

She blinked, sending a stream of tears down her cheeks. Her chest shuddered.

"But then there's that other five percent of the time when I can't be both parents, and it doesn't matter that they have an uncle who would do anything for them because he's not their dad. Olivia doesn't want to take Brian to the daddy/daughter dance, but she does, and even though she's smiling in their pictures, she'll cry herself to sleep that night. And it kills me...I want to hate Derek so badly, Nathan, and I can't. I won't say a bad word about him, because *what if*—I won't be able to take it back. Oliver and Olivia wouldn't understand. They want their father to *want them*. That's it!"

She wiped away tears as more continued to fall.

"Everyone thinks I'm crazy, and I might be. I don't know! I ignore my parents, who think I should write him off, and my

115

brother, who can't believe I'm still holding out for something...I ignore everyone, and I don't hate him. My son is *devastated* right now, but I don't hate Derek. I can't. I..." Jenna whimpered, cupping her mouth with her hand, and began to cry harder.

I reached out without a word, wrapped my arm around her small shoulders, and drew her against me. For a moment I feared I'd pulled Jenna a little too roughly and held my breath. My desperation to do this felt like its own living, breathing force, completely separate from me and out of my control. But Jenna didn't seem to mind what I'd done.

She molded to the left side of my body. Her face turned into my chest. Her hand gripped the waist of my shirt. She fit against me with urgency, but was still cautious of Marley, who was sound asleep, head on my shoulder and body limp. When my daughter stirred in a dream, Jenna turned her head away and slid an inch along my ribs. I closed my eyes, mouth pressed to her hair, and simply held her. It was a miracle I'd waited as long as I had. The second I'd seen her tears, I'd wanted to do this...

No, the second I'd stepped outside with her, or walked in the front door. Pick one—they were all true.

I forced myself to relax as much as I could. My grip around her body felt severe, and my fucking heart hurt. Screw calling this guy. I wanted to drag him here by his neck, bleeding and bruised. I wanted him begging for forgiveness. He didn't deserve to know them. He didn't deserve to fucking live another second.

After a minute, two at the most, Jenna had calmed down enough her body was no longer shaking. I couldn't hear her agony. Only the quiet hiccups in her breath.

"I'd let him see them," she said, her voice floating up my shoulder. She was still facing the ocean. "I would let Derek know them if he ever reaches out, but I swear to God...if he gets their hopes up just to hurt them further..." Her head shook. She whimpered and pulled at my shirt, needing more of it to hold on to.

"You'll protect them. You won't let that happen," I said. My next words spilled out of my mouth, and they were loaded. "Fuck, *I* won't let that happen."

Jenna's breath caught. We both went perfectly still, until she leaned back enough to peer up at me. She didn't say a word. Neither did I—I'd said enough.

This arrangement we had was on a deadline. The end of summer would be the end of *this*, me coming home to Jenna and her kids, seeing them practically every day, spending time together, knowing them as well as I did...It couldn't last. Jenna would return to work at her office and Marley would go to daycare. I already had one lined up. We wouldn't be in each other's lives like we were now and we both knew that, so what was I saying?

I caught a tear as it rolled down Jenna's cheek, wiping it away with my thumb. I expected her to question what the hell I was doing and to press for clarification on my promise to her and the kids, but she didn't. She closed her eyes and leaned into my hand, and I couldn't remember ever wanting to kiss someone so badly before. Not even Sadie.

That revelation paralyzed me. I suddenly couldn't breathe.

When Jenna pulled back and stepped away, pausing to ask if I was coming inside, I was grateful for the prompt. Without it, I wasn't sure I'd move. And when she didn't hustle her kids out the front door and instead cued up a movie on Netflix for them, I felt life in my limbs again. Blood warmed in my veins and rushed beneath my skin. Another revelation...

I didn't want them to leave.

Jenna sat on the couch and beckoned her kids to join her.

They flanked her side, Oliver settling into the crook of her arm and Olivia gripping her hand. Everyone's tears were gone.

Olivia smiled up at me like she always did and patted the cushion beside her. Again, I was grateful for the gesture. Why the hell I couldn't move all of a sudden without encouragement, I didn't know. But I knew I'd been waiting for it. I repositioned Marley so she was cradled in my arms and took a seat beside Olivia. When she scooted closer, eliminating the space I'd left on the cushion between us, and threw her bare feet up over my leg, I smiled at the TV.

Halfway through *Guardians of the Galaxy*, I stopped fighting the urge to look over at Jenna. Sensing the attention, she turned her head to me and smiled.

"Are you doing anything yet on the Fourth?" I asked, keeping my voice low.

"I don't think so."

"A friend of mine has this huge party every year. He's right on the beach... His house is ridiculous. Huge pool with a water slide." I smiled down at Olivia when that piqued her interest. Round eyes blinked behind her glasses. I looked at Jenna again. "Private fireworks show. DJ. Tons of food..."

"Sounds fun," she said.

"Do you want to go with me?"

"*I* do," Olivia answered just as Oliver sat forward to peer back at his mother.

"I want to go," he said. His hair was sticking up wildly from Jenna's fingers. "Mom, can we? That sounds cool."

"Sure." Jenna kissed the top of his head when he settled back against her. Then she looked over at me again.

I hadn't turned away. It took me half a movie to cave in to watching her, and now I wasn't sure I wanted to stop.

chapter nine

JENNA

I giggled, hand covering my mouth, as I scrolled through the four pictures of Marley Nathan had sent me an hour ago. In the first two, she was buried in the sand with only her head sticking out, the biggest smile on her face and Nathan's sunglasses shielding her eyes. In the second pair, she had Nathan's hat on sideways and was chasing after bubbles, trying to pop them.

"Earth to Jenna." My brother's voice tickled my ear.

"Mm? What? I'm listening." I stuffed my phone into my purse and grinned at Brian, who stood on the other side of the counter at Wax Surf Shop, arms folded over his broad chest and green eyes bright. He looked amused. "Did you say something?" I asked.

Brian smirked, glanced across the store where Oliver and Olivia were currently checking out boards along the far wall, verifying they were still well out of eavesdropping territory, before Brian turned back to me and said, "You tell me you're not doin' this guy and I'm callin' bullshit."

"*Brian*," I snapped, glancing over at the kids out of habit before I continued. "I'm not...*doin'* Nathan. God, why would you say that? I'm looking at pictures of his daughter."

His face was expressionless.

"What?"

"Getting defensive about it, I see."

Oh my God. "I was looking at pictures of his daughter! Here!" I stuffed my hand into my purse and palmed my phone but decided against whipping it out as proof.

Aside from the collection of pictures we'd sent each other, there was a good amount of texts between Nathan and me. Friendly texts...maybe a little flirting on my part—I wasn't sure how obvious though. But still, I knew Brian would read into our messages.

"You know what?" I crossed my arms under my chest and cocked out my hip. "I'm not doing this. I was smiling at pictures of an adorable little girl, who I'm allowed to smile at, by the way, and if you can't take my word on that, then that's your problem." I huffed out a breath. My face was suddenly hot, but I fought the urge to fan it. Maybe Brian wouldn't notice my flush.

Slowly, he smiled.

Crap. He was totally noticing.

"Stop, okay?" I pleaded, my voice losing its edge. I felt myself shrink an inch. "You're making this into something it isn't."

"Am I?"

"What do you want me to say? That I *like him*?"

Brian cocked a brow.

"Fine, okay, I like him...as a *friend*, because that's what we are. And yes, he's attractive. I'm attracted to him." *God, who wouldn't be?* "But we're friends. Nothing else has happened. I'm not sure it will." I held my arms out. "Happy now?"

I left off two minor details I wasn't sure were worth mentioning. Our ice cream/Putt-Putt get-together with the kids (date?) and three nights ago when Nathan held me while I cried over Derek (that promise he made...what was that?). My brother wasn't asking for particulars. I wasn't even sure any of that information was relevant. So why share it?

"Syd talks," Brian said. "You know this..."

"Yes. And?"

I adored my future sister-in-law, but was there nothing sacred between girlfriends? I had no idea what my brother was about to reveal. My weekly chats with Sydney covered a lot of bases.

I knew I mentioned Nathan here and there. She still picked up shifts at the restaurant, even though she worked full-time at the hospital now. She knew Nate. Of course we chatted about him. Though I couldn't for the life of me remember anything specific we'd discussed.

"You spend your days off with him," my brother began.

"Not today." I gestured around the room. "Obviously. Not every day off."

"Most."

I shrugged. Was this the best he had? Please. So what if Nathan and I hung out when he wasn't working? Our kids got along great.

"Spending the Fourth with him too," Brian added.

"He invited me and the kids to a party. So, what?"

"You typically spend it with me..."

I frowned. My arms fell to my sides. "Shit," I whispered. "I'm sorry, Brian. I didn't even think."

"Jen, I don't care. Take the kids. I'm just sayin', he's gettin' you for holidays now too?"

"It's a family holiday."

Brian's face lit up.

"I meant it's not a romantic one. Jeez! It's not like I'm spending Valentine's Day with him."

Why was this a big deal? I wasn't seeing the point he was trying to make.

My brother stared at me, considering my explanation. Then he cracked his neck from side to side like he was gearing up for a fight or to argue this until he was the only one left standing. That could take hours. I wouldn't go down easily. My argument was solid, for the most part, but God, I didn't want to talk about this anymore. What was the point? Nothing had happened between us. Nathan and I *were* friends. I hadn't lied about that. And I didn't want to dissect our situation any further, because I knew I'd look for things.

I'd put meaning into glances. I'd misinterpret. Or worse, I'd *hope*, more than I was already doing. I needed to stop this now.

"You know why I'm watching his daughter for him, right?" I asked, stepping closer to the counter. "Did Syd tell you?"

Brian lifted his chin. "Sad shit. I feel for the guy."

"No, I mean...well, yes, of course, it's sad. It's heartbreaking what happened." Pain knotted in the center of my chest. I hated even thinking about this. "And I might've offered to help just knowing about his wife, but it was more than that, Brian. You should see him with his daughter. He didn't really know Marley at all when I stepped in, and it hurt him. He cares so much about her, and that meant something to me. To see that? Watching a father actually *want* to be a father..." I paused and looked over at the twins.

Oliver laughed at his sister when she stood on a board and pretended to ride a wave. She hopped off to switch places with him, and they high-fived each other. I smiled watching them, then turned back just in time to catch my brother admiring the scene as well. When his gaze slid over to me again, it had gentled considerably.

Interrogation over, thank God.

He scratched at the stubble on his jaw, then tipped his head at the twins. "Still *no* on the campout?"

I felt my shoulders sag and shook my head. "No. I think he just wants to skip it this year."

"Let me know if he changes his mind."

"Of course. And thank you for offering to take him."

"Jenna." My brother's tone hardened. "Fuck Derek. I'll do it every year."

I blinked back tears and picked at the edge of the counter. I had the best brother, and my children had the best uncle. There was no match for Brian. Our happiness meant everything to him. And his was just as important to me. I hoped he knew that.

My head flew up. "Hey, shouldn't we be planning a wedding or something? Syd's divorce is final soon, right?"

That was the only reason why my brother wasn't married already. I knew he was counting down the seconds until a judge allowed them to wed. Syd too. She glowed at the mention of becoming a Savage.

Brian slowly grinned. "I should probably propose first."

"*Please.*" I giggled. "You guys have been planning on getting married since last summer. You're engaged. Time to make it official."

A wily look lifted the corner of his mouth. He was planning something, but before I could inquire further, the front door chimed, causing me to turn my head.

Jamie drifted into the shop, head thrown back as he laughed loudly. He wore a pair of board shorts and no shirt. His hair was saltwater damp, curling against his neck and with pieces sticking to his forehead.

If my brother's best friend and business partner ever looked like he hadn't just gotten out of the ocean, I'd fear we were under nuclear attack. Jamie was a champion surfer. He lived in the water. Growing up, he and Brian used to compete together all the time. Now my brother did it more as a hobby. Not Jamie though. He was always out to win.

"Choke!" Jamie held the door open for someone and grinned at Brian. "This motherf—"

"Jamie!" I glared at him while hooking a thumb over my shoulder in the general direction of my kids. "Little ears. Watch it."

Brows lifting, he smiled at me, a fifty-fifty mix of remorse and entertainment. The latter was permanent. It was a rare thing to see Jamie McCade serious about something.

"My bad, Jenna. Didn't know you were stoppin' in today." Jamie moved aside and released the door as another man stepped in behind him.

He was wearing board shorts as well but had pulled on a T-shirt that did absolutely nothing to hide his build, which mimicked Jamie's. Long, sinewy muscle with some bulk to his arms. His short blond hair was wet and would've curled had it been longer. It was in the genes.

I recognized him instantly. This was Jamie's older brother... *Travis, maybe?* I searched my memory for a name. I hadn't seen him in at least twelve years, but I could've gone twenty and I would've known exactly who this was. The similarity to his brother was uncanny. He was Jamie, grown-up and settled down.

"Sorry. I didn't know I had to announce my visits," I said. I gave Jamie a teasing look, which he immediately shot back. We joked around a lot. He was basically another brother to me.

"You don't. But it ain't like you've been comin' around here lately." Jamie stepped up to the counter and leaned on his elbow, facing me. He cocked his head in challenge.

"I've just been really busy," I shot back.

"I heard." A mischievous smile spread on his lips, popping out his signature dimples.

Ugh. Apparently, Tori had been sharing information as well. *Great*. Whatever happened to girl code? Was that even a thing anymore? I prepared myself for another hard-core grilling, but Jamie cut me some slack and didn't press further as his brother got up beside him.

"You remember Travis, right, Jenna? The brother with *zero* talent on the water..."

Travis side-eyed Jamie. "Where'd you get your PhD from again?"

"The University of Suck My—"

I lurched forward and slapped a hand over Jamie's mouth while directing at his brother, "Hi! Hello...I uh, sort of remember you. It's been a while."

Jamie grumbled and jerked back. "I wasn't going to say it."

Brian, Travis, and I all responded with different versions of "Yeah, right."

The four of us started laughing.

Travis gripped my hand and shook it as he searched my face. He smiled, revealing yet another similarity to his younger brother. Travis had dimples as well.

I felt my breath catch. God, the McCade grin game was strong as fuck.

"You were fourteen or fifteen the last time I saw you, right?" Travis asked, releasing me.

I thought back. "Mm, probably fifteen. We moved to Denver that year."

"Gross, Travis. You noticed Jenna when she was fifteen? You were twenty-three." Jamie winked at me.

Most women would've reacted somehow to being on the receiving end of so much as a look from Jamie McCade, but I remained completely unaffected. I didn't even blush.

I thought about Nathan winking at me...

He did it and my brain melted.

"How was it out there?" Brian cut in, directing that question at Jamie. The two of them fell into conversation about currents and wave height.

I looked to Travis and found him already watching me. His eyes were crystal blue. He smiled when I smiled. Sheesh, he was attractive. I felt heat rising up my neck.

"So, are you living here now?" he asked. "Or are you just visiting from Denver?"

"No, we're here now. Me and my kids." I pointed over my shoulder at the noise behind me. Olivia giggled on cue, and Travis's grin brightened. "My parents stayed out in Denver, though. What about you? Are you still local?" Growing up, we all had lived in Emerald Isle, a town about an hour down the coast.

"I'm up in Durham. Just visiting for the weekend."

"That's nice. Do you surf too?"

Travis had been off at college when Jamie and Brian were just kids, thirteen years old and entering competitions every weekend.

"I have. It's just been a while." He winced and pushed a hand through his hair. "I don't get to do it that much. I stay pretty busy."

"Excuses, excuses," Jamie muttered, straightening up to throw his arm around his brother's shoulders. They were both tall, practically the same height. Travis had maybe half an inch on Jamie.

"Put a scalpel in my hand, and I'll figure it out on the first go. Probably win trophies for that too."

"Is everything a competition to you?" Brian asked.

Jamie looked disrespected. *"Yes."*

Scalpel? "Wait, are you a doctor?" I asked Travis.

He nodded lightly.

His modest admission was almost laughable. Whereas his brother would've stood taller while he bragged on his accomplishments, Travis was quiet and shy about it. Jamie would've shared this information straightaway. He would've tagged it along with his greeting, or gone as far as to introduce himself as Dr. McCade. I wasn't sure Travis would've revealed this information without being goaded first. Interesting.

"That's really great," I said. "Good for you."

"Yes, good for him," Jamie repeated, sounding bored. "And good for me. I killed it today."

Travis sighed and shrugged out of his brother's hold. "I need to get going," he said, patting Jamie on the back, then leaning over and extending his hand to Brian. "Take care, man."

"See you around."

When they separated, Travis turned to me and reached for my hand again. He squeezed it gently.

"It was really good to see you, Jenna," he said. His tone dropped lower and held meaning.

"Yeah." My voice squeaked. I quickly cleared it and smiled at him. "You too."

When the door closed behind Travis, I turned back to Brian and Jamie, who were both staring at me.

I gathered my hair over one shoulder and picked at the ends. "What?" I asked.

Jamie smirked, then slowly looked over at Brian as he resumed leaning on his elbow. "You got a problem with me givin' it to him?"

"Not my business," Brian mumbled.

"What are you both talking about?" I asked.

"Travis gettin' your number from me." Jamie cocked his head and grinned.

I scoffed. They thought Travis was going to ask for my number? From that one interaction? We barely said anything. "Um, okay."

"First the daddy and now my big bro? Damn, Jenna. You're gonna need to start beatin' them off with a stick."

"Ew." I slapped Jamie's arm as he buckled over with laughter. "Don't call him that! That's *so weird*."

God, delete this conversation from my memory. I never wanted to hear that reference again.

"What?" Jamie straightened up and frowned. "Why's *big bro* weird? Oh, you mean *daddy*...Do you call him that?" He chuckled.

"Man, shut up," Brian growled.

"You're ridiculous. Guys! We're going!" I reached for the bag of tees Oliver had picked out. As I slid the bag off the counter, I noticed a stack of Whitecaps coupons beside the register. They advertised for one free appetizer. "What a great idea," I said, pointing at the pile.

"Your man didn't mention that to you?" Jamie asked.

My man? Why was I still here? *Move, Jenna!*

Grunting, I spun around and gestured for my kids. I was suddenly in a rush to leave, but I wouldn't let that on. Maybe we had plans? Maybe I had work to do? Nobody knew our schedule today but me.

"Where are we going?" Olivia asked, walking over. Oliver was right behind her.

"Home. I don't know. We have stuff to do." I herded the two of them toward the door, smiling over my shoulder at the guys. "See ya!"

"Whose home you goin' to, Jenna? Yours?" Jamie asked. "Maybe play another game of touch?"

"Ooh, Mom, can we?" Oliver was beaming. "Are we going to Nate's?"

"I wanna go to Nate's!" Olivia shrieked. "I love it there!"

I ignored my easily excitable children and narrowed my eyes at Jamie's smirk before getting us the hell out of there.

I was right. Girl code was so dead.

* * *

Later that night, I was snuggled up with the kids on the couch when my phone beeped from across the room with an incoming text. I squeezed out from beneath Oliver and Olivia and moved into the kitchen, swiping my phone off the table.

Hey it's Travis. Can I call you?

My stomach flip-flopped. *So he did ask for my number...*

"Mom, should we pause it?" Oliver asked.

"No. You can keep watching. I'll be there in a minute." I stepped further into the kitchen as I typed my response.

Yes

My phone rang immediately. I answered on the first ring.

"Hey." I kept my voice soft and faced away from the kids so I didn't disturb their movie.

"Hey, how are you?"

"I'm good. How are you?"

"Good." There was chatter around Travis until I thought I heard a door close. His surroundings quieted down after that. "Sorry. I'm at work and only have a minute. I'd rather talk than text."

"That's okay. I can talk."

"It was really good seeing you today, Jenna."

I felt my face heat. "It was good seeing you too. It's been a long time."

"Well, hopefully we won't go that long between visits again, which is why I'm calling." He cleared his throat. "I wasn't sure what your situation was and my brother said he didn't know, but if you aren't seeing anyone right now, I'd love to take you out sometime."

My thoughts immediately went to Nathan. I couldn't help it.

What was my situation? I didn't have one, right?

Nathan and I were friends. I hadn't lied when I'd explained things to Brian earlier. Nothing else had happened yet. I wasn't sure it ever would, even though I wanted it to. And I liked Travis. If Nathan wasn't in the picture, I wouldn't hesitate at all. I wasn't sure I had any reason to now. Why shouldn't I go out on a date? I wanted to...

"That sounds great," I said, answering how I wanted to answer. "I'd love to go out with you."

"Work is pretty crazy for me right now, but I can take some time after the holiday. I'll reach out to you after the Fourth and we'll set something up."

"Perfect."

"Great." I could hear the smile in his voice. "I gotta get back to work. I'll talk to you soon, Jenna."

"Okay." I was smiling now too. "Bye, Travis."

chapter ten

NATHAN

Jenna had the kids waiting outside and ready to go when I got home on the Fourth.

I'd only worked a half day, closing up around one and letting everyone off for the night. My staff was appreciative of that. The girls especially. Shay and Kali both stopped in my office several times to express their gratitude. I figured everyone had plans to celebrate, and my staff worked hard for me. I didn't mind giving them off for this.

Davis's house was two hours away, and I knew we'd hit traffic. I always had before. To save some time, I changed in my office before I left. Then I sent Jenna a text, letting her know when I was on my way.

Oliver and Olivia jumped off the porch and took off running through the grass when I pulled into the driveway. They both had their duffle bags with them, Oliver's slung over his shoulder and Olivia's dragging by her feet. Jenna was close behind, carrying Marley.

The four of them looked like a walking advertisement for the holiday, straight out of a catalog, wearing red, white, and blue, with matching Americana aviators shielding their eyes. Even Marley. Her glasses took up most of her face. It was cute.

"Here, Nate! We got you a pair too." Olivia stopped in front of me when I got out of the truck. She thrust a pair of aviators into my hand and encouraged, "Put them on!"

"All right." I bumped fists with Oliver before he climbed in the back seat. Then I swapped the sunglasses for the ones I was wearing, letting my prescription pair hang from the collar of my shirt. The stars and stripes tint were surprisingly easy to see through. "What do you think? Do they look good?" I asked Olivia.

She nodded quickly. "Can you keep them on so we match?"

"Sure."

Olivia grinned and stepped up beside me, grabbing hold of my hand. I thought she was going to give it a squeeze and let go, a way of thanking me for obliging her request, but she held on. I didn't mind it. Lately, she was showing me affection in one way or another every time we were together. Making sure she sat beside me or resting her feet in my lap. Both of Jenna's kids have been warm with me from the beginning. It was oddly comforting.

"Olivia, baby, we need to get going. Get in the truck." Jenna smiled at her daughter, who took that encouragement and ran around to the passenger side.

Marley reached out for me with one hand, holding her glasses on her face with the other. "Daddy, we go swinnin'?"

"Yeah, baby." I took her from Jenna and held her in the crook of my elbow, kissing her cheek. She smelled like sunscreen and citrus. "Are you ready?"

Marley hugged my neck. "Swinnin' in the pool?"

"Yep." I smiled at Jenna. "Thanks for the glasses."

"Sure. If you need the other ones to drive, Olivia will understand."

"I think I'll be all right. Mine are mainly for seeing."

Laughter tore out of her throat. She was wearing a sleeveless navy-blue top and jean shorts with flag patchwork on the pockets. Her bathing suit was on underneath. The white strings tied under her hair.

Jenna had curves in everything she wore, but they were even more noticeable today. Her top hugged her waist and the shape of her breasts and dipped low enough to show a hint of cleavage.

Obviously, she was planning on swimming at this party. Even if she hadn't been wearing her bathing suit already, I would've assumed the same. Maybe I should've considered this earlier instead of waiting until right fucking now. *Jesus*. I needed more than a couple of hours to prepare myself for the image of Jenna without her top on.

She wasn't small in the chest by any standards. Jenna would spill out of my hands. Easily. That top was modest. There was way more cleavage to come.

"Let me grab the bags," Jenna said.

"I got it." I moved past her and crossed the yard to the porch.

There were two bags by the door, Marley's diaper bag and a large tote stuffed with beach towels and pool toys. Two pairs of goggles sat on top.

I carried the bags to the truck, stepping up to the side Oliver was in. There was plenty of room for the bags beneath the kids' feet, which was a good thing. I didn't have a cap on the bed, and I didn't feel right making Jenna keep everything up front with her. My gym bag was already up there.

"Check it out, Nate!" Oliver had his duffle on his lap. He unzipped it and pulled out a football. "I'm bringing this in case we wanna play."

God, he was going to freak out. I couldn't wait.

"Sounds good, bud." I leaned over him and got Marley buckled in her seat. Olivia was on the other side, and she helped me slip Marley's arm through the strap closest to her. Then she smiled at me and pointed at her glasses.

"They're cool, right?" she asked.

"The coolest. We should get a picture of all of us," I suggested, knowing Olivia would get a kick out of that.

With a gasp, she tore through the duffle she had balancing on her legs and whipped out a bright pink Fujifilm camera. "With this!" she shouted. "Mama, can you take it?"

I closed the back door and got in the driver's seat.

Jenna fiddled with the camera, pressing a button on the front and making sure it was turned on. "I'm not sure my arms are long enough to get everyone," she said.

"Here. I got it." I took the camera from her and held it over the dash, aiming over my right shoulder. My thumb slid to the exposure button. "Ready?"

"Wait! Marley, smile like this...these two fingers. Okay, we're ready!" Olivia giggled.

I took the shot. The film pushed out. It was half the size of regular Polaroid film, and rainbow colored along the edges.

"This is cool," I said, admiring the camera after passing Jenna the photo. I hadn't messed around with one of these before. I was familiar with the older-style Polaroids.

"I got it for my birthday," Olivia shared. "I got regular film too. But I like the rainbow film the most. You can take another picture if you want."

"I'll take some at the party, okay?"

"Of us in the pool!"

"Aw, it turned out so good. Look." Jenna held the picture over the center console. "You got everyone in the shot."

I looked down at the photo and smiled. The kids were

squished together in the back seat, grinning big and holding up peace signs. Even Marley. Both of her hands were raised and positioned in front of her. Jenna was angled toward me. We were both smiling. Everyone matched in glasses and patriotic attire. Even the solid red T-shirt I wore complemented the group. Jenna was right. It had turned out good. Nobody was cut out of the picture. I'd been half expecting that. What the fuck did I know about taking selfies?

"Too bad there's only the one. I probably won't get another shot like that." I handed Olivia her camera. Then I pulled the seat belt across my chest, adding, "I would've liked a copy."

"Mm." Jenna tugged her phone out of her back pocket. She pulled up the camera mode and took a picture of the print. "Problem solved," she said, flashing me a grin. "I'll text it to you."

"Great. Thanks."

"Let me see it!" Olivia shrieked.

Jenna passed the photo over her shoulder as I backed us out of the driveway.

"Aw," Olivia cooed, her voice pitching higher. Then, barely above a whisper, she added, "We look like a family."

My foot nearly slipped off the brake.

"Uh…s-some music, maybe? That'll be nice for the ride." Jenna reached for the volume on the radio as I shifted into drive and hit the gas. Music filled the cab, which she quickly adjusted so it became unbalanced and spilled more into the back seat. Her fingers trembled as they hovered over the screen.

"It's okay," I said.

"Sorry." She settled on a station, pressed her back against the leather, and finally looked over at me. Her face was red, the flush creeping up behind her aviators. The lenses shielded the highest points of her cheeks. "She's just...She's never said that before. I'm so sorry. I'll talk to her."

"It's fine. You don't need to."

"She can't say stuff like that."

"Well, she's not wrong in thinking it." I glanced at the road again, turning us out of the development and heading in the direction of the freeway.

Jenna was silent beside me.

What was I saying? I needed to clarify that.

"I mean, you know..." I looked over at her again and gestured at my face. "The glasses."

"Right. Of course." She pulled hers off and folded them in her lap. Her gaze was shy and dropped away.

Christ, come on. This doesn't need to be weird.

"What are you doing?" I asked, smirking at the road. "I believe it's been requested that we match today."

"Huh?"

"The *glasses*...They're a requirement, Jenna. How could you?"

"Oh." Laughter feathered through her voice. "I didn't realize I was under obligation. So sorry." She slipped the aviators back on and sat forward to smile at me. "Will you be keeping yours on in the pool?"

"I'm never taking them off. I was asked to wear them, very sweetly, I might add." I glanced at her. A chuckle shook my chest. *Again?*

"What?"

"Nothing. I just winked at you."

"Oh, really?" Jenna was grinning now. "I'm sorry I missed that. Too bad for that pledge you just made."

"Yes. Too bad for that." I shook my head at the road.

"It's fine. You'll just have to tell me every time you wink."

Jenna's quiet laughter tickled my ear. I was quick to join in.

This doesn't need to be weird, I thought. And then immediately, *It isn't. Not even this—flirting.*

Should it be?

I quickly shoved that question out of my head. It was one I couldn't answer.

On the way, we talked about our favorite fireworks and played an interesting game of I Spy. Oliver and Olivia kept choosing the same object—my red shirt—and laughing at each other. They laughed even harder when Marley adorably tried to play. She didn't quite understand the concept of the game and kept repeating everyone's guesses. It took us a little over two hours to get to the house. I'd evaded Oliver's questioning as best I could during the drive, keeping my responses vague.

We're going to my friend's house, an old buddy of mine from college. Did I say his house was ridiculous? It's not that big.

I wanted this to be a surprise for him. For everyone. He'd know exactly where we were soon enough.

"Whoa." Jenna leaned forward in her seat and gazed out the windshield as I parked us in the sloped driveway that circled an obnoxious, four-tiered fountain.

That's new, I mused.

Jenna slowly peered over at me. "Who is your friend?"

I laughed and cut the engine, throwing my door open. "You guys ready?"

The twins chanted in exuberance as they climbed out of the truck. Marley giggled and squealed, grinning against my neck when I plucked her out of her seat.

"Daddy, go swinnin'?" she asked.

"Yeah, baby. We're going swimming."

Jenna insisted on carrying the diaper bag, scooping it up while I was reaching in the front seat for my hat. I slipped it on backward.

"What? My arms are free," she said, catching the look I gave her before I turned to shut the door.

I slid the beach tote up my arm. "I can handle all the bags."

"Nope. I want this or her, and she seems to be very content right where she is." Jenna smiled and stepped closer, tickling Marley's belly. "You like that, don't you? You like it when Dad—dy," she stammered. Then her mouth slammed shut and she quickly spun away.

I chuckled. "You all right?"

"Fine." She grinned at me over her shoulder, no longer flustered.

Did I imagine her reaction? Huh. Okay. Maybe that was nothing.

Even though Davis always had an open-door policy with me, I still rang the bell when I stepped up onto the porch. It *had* been two years. Plus, I knew the impact it would have if he...

Davis flung the door open and grinned. "S'up? You made it!"

"Hey, man." We passed on handshakes and settled for hugs, slapping each other's backs loudly.

Davis attempted to pluck Marley out of my arms once I stepped inside the house, but she burrowed against me and whined.

"She's shy," I explained.

"It's cool. I get it." He looked down at Olivia and then at Jenna when she walked in behind her daughter. His brows lifted. "Well, hi there."

"Hi," Olivia squeaked, stepping closer to my leg.

I reached down and placed my hand on her back, thinking

she was nervous. Strange man. New environment. I understood her reserve.

Olivia peered up at me and smiled easily.

"Davis, this is Jenna and her daughter, Olivia," I said.

"Nice to meet you guys."

"Your house is beautiful." Jenna shoved her glasses to the top of her head and blinked widely at her surroundings. "Thank you so much for having us."

"No, thank *you* for coming." Davis slid his gaze to me and shot me a look. *Are you fucking kidding me? You have so much to explain.*

I shook my head and braced for the interrogation of a lifetime. *What is wrong with me?* I could've predicted this shit. But had I prepared for it? Of course not. Just like the looming bikini reveal. I was wide open for this.

"Oliver, are you coming inside?" Jenna asked.

Stepping over, I looked back at Oliver and saw him frozen on the porch.

Eyes round above his aviators, which were now near the tip of his nose. Mouth gaped open. Shoulders dropped. His duffle sliding down his arm.

I grinned into Marley's hair.

"You're Dave Davis!" he screamed, slapping his cheeks. "Oh my God! I am not here right now. I am not at your house...Mom! Somebody pinch me!"

Everyone started laughing, except Oliver. He was still in shock, and scrambled into the house, nearly face-planting on his way in. He hoisted his duffle against his stomach and started digging through it.

"You brought a fan? God, I love you." Davis slapped my shoulder.

Jenna smiled at him. "I'm sorry...Nathan didn't tell us who

you were. And I—I'm still not sure who you are." She winced. "Sorry. Should I know?"

I threw my head back and laughed. Davis looked ready to punch me.

"Oh, please. The *fountain*. You need a good hit to your ego."

"Hey, it's pretty," he argued.

"Mom, really? This is *Dave Davis*. Starting tight end for Carolina. First-round draft pick!" Oliver shook his head. "Oh my God, this is embarrassing...How can you *not know*? How are we even related?"

Laughter shook my chest.

Jenna blushed hard and bit her lip, looking to Davis then. "I don't watch a lot of sports," she explained.

"It's cool." Davis stood tall and smirked. "I'll make sure you know all about me before you leave."

"I wouldn't doubt that," I threw out.

Oliver let his duffle hit the floor after retrieving his football out of it. He stepped around Olivia. "Could you sign this, Mr. Davis?"

Davis took the ball. "Sure. You got a pen?"

"Uh..." Oliver looked absolutely panicked. "N-no. Sorry."

"Don't worry about it, kid. I got tons of pens. Come on." Davis moved around us to close the door. Then he led the way through the foyer toward the back of the house.

The twins followed quickly behind him after Oliver retrieved his duffle. They spoke closely, their voices racing with excitement. Jenna flanked my side.

"Just some friend you went to college with?" she whispered.

I peered down at her and grinned. She elbowed me, shaking her head, and we laughed together.

Once we reached the back of the house, the room opened up.

Music poured in through open French doors. Guests filtered in and out, adults and kids, wearing swimsuits and carrying plates of food. Oliver and Olivia pointed outside and whispered with each other. They bounced on their feet and high-fived. It was so fucking cute. Jenna called them over to the kitchen, where Davis retrieved a Sharpie out of a drawer. He bit the cap between his teeth and signed the ball for Oliver. Then he tossed it to him across the counter, saying, "There you go, kid."

Oliver stared at the signature. "Wow," he whispered, lifting his head. He pushed the glasses up his nose. "Thank you, Mr. Davis."

"Just Davis. That's what my friends call me. We're friends now, right?"

Oliver nodded fast and hugged the ball. "Y-yes, sir. We're friends." Then he looked at me and mouthed, *Oh my God.*

When Jenna instructed him to put the ball away for now, he hesitated until she tagged on a warning of accidentally dropping it in the pool and smearing the signature. That got him moving.

"You guys wanna head outside?" Davis asked. "The party's already started."

"Sure. Sounds good." Jenna slid her smile over to me, then giggled at Olivia, who shook her hips to the music.

"I love this song!" Olivia shrieked.

We padded outside, stepping onto the large, covered patio. There were a few tables set up there for shaded seating, along with coolers filled with ice and beverages. The patio opened up to a lavish outdoor kitchen, which overlooked the pool. Everything was made of stone and marble. Two grills flanked a large swim-up bar. I knew Davis got a lot of use out of his setup, but he wasn't cooking anything today. The food was catered, and there was plenty of it. Ladles stuck out of rectangular, aluminum tins, with fuel canisters beneath them to keep everything warm. The pans covered the island.

I was prompted to ask the kids if they wanted anything to eat yet, but their attention was solely on the pool. I wasn't even sure they'd noticed anything else. I couldn't blame them. It was fucking excessive, but nice. I understood the appeal.

The pool was freeform, with three rock waterfalls, a spa Jacuzzi, and a giant custom slide built into a boulder. There were hidden caves under the falls with lagoon lighting, springs every ten feet or so along the perimeter, and one of those infinity edges. It was like an oasis built right onto the beach.

I stepped up behind the twins. "What do you guys think?"

"It's pretty sick, right?" Davis asked, joining me.

Oliver turned his head and gaped at us. "Are you *kidding*? How are we even here?"

I chuckled.

"This is awesome!" Olivia yelled, pumping her fists into the air. She tugged on Jenna's arm. "Can we get in now? Can we!"

"Sure!" Jenna looked at me and mouthed, *Wow*, a breathless laugh leaving her. Then she pointed to a group of unattended lounge chairs near the Jacuzzi. "Let's go put our stuff down over there. We need to get sunscreen on."

"Want to take her with you?" I asked, gripping Marley under her arms. "I'm going to catch up with Davis for a minute."

"Of course. Oliver, get that tote from Nathan, please."

I passed Marley off, then the tote, after testing the weight of it. "It's heavy," I told Oliver.

"I'm strong." He quickly flexed as proof, making sure Davis saw his muscle, then situated the duffle on one shoulder and heaved the pool tote over the other. He followed behind Jenna and the girls.

I watched closely as they passed the DJ, gauging their reactions. There were a lot of kids here, different ages too, so the music wasn't too loud. I wanted to make sure they weren't bothered by it, Marley especially. But none of them seemed to mind the noise. Oliver and Olivia were racing to the chairs, and Marley giggled at something Jenna was saying, her feet kicking excitedly.

"Well, well, well," Davis drawled.

I pulled my arms across my chest and stared ahead. "Here we go. Let's hear it."

"I was expecting Mary fucking Poppins, you bastard." He laughed, bumping elbows with me. "Not the bombshell girl next door. Jesus Christ."

"I told you I was bringing the woman who's been watching Marley for me. Any assumptions you made are your own fault."

Davis took a step forward and spun around, putting his back to the pool. "Nathan Bell, are you *banging* the babysitter?"

My gaze slid to his. "Come on, man."

"Come on *what*? You did not just bring her today so your kids could hang out. Don't lie to me."

"There's nothing going on."

He cocked his head.

I shrugged. "Nothing has happened. That's the truth. We're friends. She's watching Marley for me. We hang out—*all of us*—not just me and Jenna. What do you want? There's nothing else to say."

"Fine. You're friends. Love the matching outfits, by the way. Do you do *all* your shopping together now?"

"Oh, fuck you."

"You want something more to happen, Nate. Admit it."

I didn't answer that, mainly because I *couldn't* answer that. I hadn't allowed myself to admit to anything I was feeling. I knew I stared too long and found excuses to be around her. I sent texts that pushed the boundaries of friendship. I acted, though I didn't acknowledge. I knew what acknowledging this would mean.

"You're hesitating." Davis narrowed his eyes. He was being serious now, a rare thing to witness. "Why? It's been almost two years."

"I know how long it's been." My tone became sharp. I felt a muscle in my jaw jump. "What are you saying? Two years...Shit, that's the cutoff mark, right? Time to move on."

Davis sighed through his nose. "I don't think there's moving on. I think there's living. There's no right or wrong here, Nate. There's no judgment either. And fuck you for thinking there would be—you're my best friend. However you continue, for you *and* for Marley, I'd back your decision. Hell, I backed it when you refused to talk to me. Are you forgetting that?"

"No, of course not." I lifted the aviators and scrubbed at my face. "Fuck, man, it's just...I don't know what's right to do here."

"So do what you want. Nobody can tell you what you should be doing. Even if, God forbid, I ended up going through the same thing...what's right for me might not be right for you. Stop thinking and fucking move, man. You're always going to find a reason not to do something if you're looking for it. My suggestion?"

"Sure."

"Quit looking."

My mind opened up and grabbed at his logic. He was right.

The clarity had always been there, lingering quietly. Maybe I would've been able to work through this on my own in another month or so. Maybe not. I wasn't sure I'd take any opportunities without being given permission first. It was the entire reason I hesitated.

"So, are we ready to admit how we feel yet? Dr. Davis has other things to do."

I chuckled through a "shut up," then slid my attention over his shoulder when Olivia squealed. Davis stepped aside and turned to watch as well, just as Olivia dumped into the pool off the slide. Oliver was quick to follow.

I smiled when they emerged from the water with their goggles on, giggling. They looked so fucking happy to be here.

"Cute kids," he said.

"Yeah, they are."

"Jesus." Davis made a noise deep in his throat and cursed under his breath. I followed his gaze to the lounge chairs.

Marley sat on one with pool toys in her lap. She had streaks of lotion on her face and arms and was holding a bottle of sunscreen while bopping her shoulders to the music. And standing beside her...

Oh, holy fuck.

Jenna had stripped out of her top and shorts and was now wearing nothing besides a red, white, and blue bikini. Blue with white stars on one breast and red with white stripes on the other. The bottoms were solid white.

Again, preparation could've gone a long way here in terms of how I was going to react to this moment. It also could've done jack shit for me, because I wasn't sure my imagination had any idea what it was up against—the real thing I was currently staring at.

Davis was right; Jenna was a bombshell. And that was fully clothed. In a bathing suit, she was sin personified. Soft curves and strong, shapely thighs. A tiny waist. Plump breasts.

She was a goddess straight out of my filthiest daydreams.

I watched her with rapt focus as she rubbed sunscreen on her shoulders and wiggled her hands beneath the strings to apply it to her neck and chest. When her fingers disappeared into her cleavage, I stifled a moan and pinched my eyes shut.

"God bless America." Davis slapped my shoulder blade. I glared ahead. A hearty chuckle left him. "What a country, am I right?"

I stepped over and forced his hand to drop. I tried to look away from her—I couldn't. I kept my eyes on Jenna, on her hands as they moved down her stomach and curled around her hips to her back.

Goddamn, her body.

"Where's that admission at?" Davis asked. "Tip of your tongue? Or are you still hesitating…?"

I exhaled through my nose, ignoring him. Who the fuck said I had to admit to anything? Acknowledging to myself was a big enough step, and here I was, acknowledging.

I knew exactly who I wanted.

"How about I give you a little nudge?"

I blinked at his question. "What?" Dragging my gaze off the most alluring sunscreen application I'd ever witnessed, I watched Davis step out from underneath the patio and walk around the pool. "What are you doing!" I hollered.

He grinned at me over his shoulder. "No feelings, right? I'm not crossing any lines here."

My gaze hardened as his meaning and motives became clear. I took a step, then another, trailing him. "*Davis*," I growled. My pace quickened.

"Unless you wanna tell me to back off, I don't see why I can't—"

I gripped his shoulder and shoved him into the water.

chapter eleven

JENNA

Commotion had me lifting my head. I looked from Nathan to his friend as he pushed out of the water and sat on the edge of the pool. He was laughing and fully clothed.

"Message received!" Davis hollered, stripping off his soaking-wet shirt and wringing it out.

"Did he fall in?" I asked Nathan when he stopped in front of me.

"Huh? Oh…yeah." He glanced over his shoulder. "Actually, no, I pushed him in." Nathan shrugged, a smile teasing his lips. He began to stare at me, chest heaving.

Is he looking at my swimsuit? With those glasses on, I couldn't tell.

"Hey," he said.

"Hey yourself." I laughed, dropping my glasses down so I no longer needed to squint in the sun. "You're not going to push *me* in, are you?"

"Now, why would I do that?"

"I don't know. Why did you push your friend in?"

"Because he was coming over here to hit on you."

I swallowed. *Whoa…what?* Was he saying what I thought he was saying?

"Oh, yeah?" I asked, needing confirmation more than I needed to know *exactly* where Nathan was looking right now.

"Yeah," he answered.

"And that's not something he should be doing because he's...married?"

Wow. I was seriously reaching. But I wasn't sure Nathan would elaborate unless I pried for more. And I needed so much more than what he'd already given me. What was he saying here?

Nathan didn't answer my question. Instead he slid off his hat and both pairs of glasses, dropping them onto the chair beside Marley. Then he reached over his shoulder and pulled off his shirt.

My eyes lowered and locked on.

He was half naked. Holy God, he was half naked. I'd never seen him without a shirt on before.

Was he speaking now? Was he giving me the answer I wanted? I had no idea.

Nathan's body...He was such a liar. He'd told Oliver it had been six years since he'd played football, yet he was built like he'd never given it up.

His muscles were defined, thick in his shoulders and biceps but not bulky. He had a lean, long, sculpted torso, abs without flexing, and narrow hips. I followed the dusting of hair below his navel to his swim shorts. They hung low, at least two, three inches below his waist.

I squinted, studying.

No, three inches for sure. Thank God for these glasses. I could openly stare without anyone knowing. Nathan had no idea.

"So, nothing to say to that?"

My head jerked up. "Huh? Nothing to say to what? Did you say something?"

"I answered your question..."

Oh shit. What good were these glasses if I couldn't properly maintain conversation? I'd totally been had. Time to guess.

"Um, right. So, he's married, then?"

"No. I said he's *not* married."

"Oh." My voice came out breathy. "Well, you know...it's hard to hear you. With the music..." *And your body.* What a distraction.

Wait. Waitwaitwait.

Okay, so Davis wasn't married. He was coming over here to hit on me. And knowing that, Nathan pushed him into the pool?

My heartbeat accelerated.

I stared into Nathan's eyes, waiting for him to answer the unspoken question that hung in the air between us, but he didn't. He wouldn't say a word. He simply looked at me.

When Rihanna cut off mid-song and "A Groovy Kind of Love" began playing, a laugh pushed past my lips.

What the...?

Nathan frowned, his dark brows pinching together. Both of us turned to look over at the DJ booth.

Davis stood behind it, arms drawn across his bare chest and hair sticking up wildly from the pool. He smiled directly at us.

"Jesus," Nathan muttered, putting his back to his friend. He shook his head.

"Kind of an odd song to play right now." I giggled. "Is he a big Phil Collins fan or something?"

"Don't pay attention to him. He's taken a lot of blows to the head."

Bold laughter cut through the air. "Nudge!" Davis yelled.

Nathan cursed under his breath, then bent down and swapped the bottle of sunscreen Marley was holding for a pool toy, keeping her occupied. "Let's get in the pool," he said, moving urgently. He squirted lotion onto his palm and smeared it over his chest and shoulders. When his hand grazed his abs, I gulped in a breath and bit my tongue.

Lord, yes, get him under the water.

Nathan dropped the bottle onto a beach towel and scooped up Marley while I gathered my hair off my neck and secured it into a messy bun. Imagine Dragons was playing now. Some of the crowd sang along. Others cheered, grateful for the song change. We walked side by side to the pool, silent, neither of us bringing up the previous conversation.

I couldn't forget it though. It ate away at my mind.

I waved at Oliver and Olivia as they waited behind a row of kids for the slide. My two couldn't stop smiling.

"They're having so much fun," I said.

"Yeah." Nathan's face was tense when I peered over at him. When he halted at the stairs, I did the same. "Jenna, I need you to ask me."

"Ask you what?"

"Why it matters if Davis isn't married." He turned his head, eyes boring into mine.

I was still wearing my glasses, but Nathan wasn't. And even though his pledge to keep them on was one of the sweetest gestures anyone had ever done for Olivia, I was grateful for the break. I would've missed how carefully he was staring at me right now if he'd been wearing them.

"Um..." My hand tensed around the metal rail. "Okay, why does it matter?"

"Because I don't want him hitting on you," Nathan said. "And if anyone else tries something, they're getting shoved in the pool too. I don't care who it is."

I smiled immediately. It was purely reactional—I couldn't

help it. Nathan was telling me what I'd been hoping to hear. The reason I would've begged for. He didn't want his friend hitting on me because...Well, we weren't there yet. Okay. But we were getting somewhere.

This was a *good thing*. I wanted Nathan smiling now too. But even after that admission, he still looked so serious and unsure.

"What if they're already in the pool?" I teased, entering the water one step at a time. I watched him over my shoulder.

Nathan's mouth twitched. He waded in until the water reached his waist. "Then I guess I'm tossing them out of it." We circled each other with Marley between us, smacking at the water and giggling at herself.

"Nathan."

He stared at me over the top of her head. "Jenna."

My cheeks were on fire. I could feel it. "I don't have much upper-body strength, but I'll try to do the same if Davis hits on you."

His mouth stretched into a grin.

There it is, I thought. God, this man should always be smiling.

"I never thought I'd say this," Nathan began. "But now I'm actually hoping that happens. I'd love to see that."

"Right? Me too."

We laughed together.

Oliver and Olivia joined us after their turn on the slide and begged Nathan to play with them. After passing Marley off to me, he tossed Olivia across the pool and then guided Oliver into a backflip when it was his turn. Nathan could lift my kids above his head, no problem. *Damn, he is strong*. They sailed through the air. Olivia climbed on his shoulders and pumped her arms to the music, which stayed fast-paced. I hummed "A Groovy Kind of Love" while I guided Marley around the perimeter. I couldn't get that song out of my head.

We swam until the kids complained about being starved for food. Then we dried off and made our plates.

We chose a table in the shade and ate hot dogs and chicken wings, macaroni salad for Nathan and myself, and chips for the kids. Marley sawed on an ear of corn. Nathan said it was her first time having that. She loved it. Halfway into our meal, I watched Oliver stuff his mouth, his eyes on the game of catch that had begun on the beach between Davis and two other men.

"Oliver, you have plenty of time to play with them." I reached across the table and touched his wrist, grabbing his attention. "Slow down please. Take smaller bites."

"Sorry, Mom." His words were muffled. Bits of hot dog bun shot out of his mouth, making his sister giggle. "Oops," he mumbled, scooping up the mess. He glanced across the table at Nathan, who sat beside me. Marley was in his lap.

"We'll go out there as soon as we're done," Nathan said, forking macaroni noodles. "They'll still be playing. Trust me."

"Cool." Oliver resumed watching the game, appearing more at ease. His next bite was half the size of his previous one.

I knew my son was worried he'd miss this unbelievable opportunity—throwing around with a professional football player. I was surprised Oliver hadn't faked being full and fled the table already. I knew how anxious he was to get out there. But I hadn't expected Nathan to read Oliver the way I had. Maybe I should've? He'd eaten with us before. He knew Oliver needed the occasional *slow down* reminder, even without a pending activity hurrying him along.

A thought bloomed inside my head. Nathan was becoming familiar with my kids. I hid my smile behind a napkin.

While the boys played catch, Marley, Olivia, and I got ready for the fireworks show.

I pulled on my tank and shorts, and then I took the girls inside and got them changed in the bathroom. I hadn't packed clothes for myself, but I was dry enough. I hadn't gone completely under the water. My top had barely gotten wet.

When we made it back outside, I laid out their swimsuits to dry, along with our towels, then grabbed one of the picnic blankets Davis had provided from the basket labeled TAKE ONE.

Once we stepped off the tiled patio, Olivia and Marley ran ahead, kicking up sand and waving at the boys. I wasn't sure where the fireworks were going to be set off. I'd simply been told *the beach*. Well, Davis seemed to own a massive stretch of it. I couldn't see another house for miles.

I glanced around. It was beautiful here. Colored lanterns were strung up between posts. Tiki torches were lit. There was even a bonfire going.

I spread the blanket out near a group of others already set up and smiled at the families. Everyone was eating Popsicles.

"Help yourselves!" a woman said, pointing to her cooler.

"Awesome. Thank you!" I grabbed five, returned to our blanket, and sank to my knees just as the girls rushed over, holding hands.

"I think the fireworks are gonna start soon," Olivia said, her eyes lighting up when I held out a Popsicle. She dropped to her butt and tore the wrapper off. Her nose wrinkled. "Gross, green. Marley, do you like lime?"

Marley collapsed next to Olivia on the blanket and leaned over, licking the Popsicle my daughter held out. She hummed in delight.

Olivia giggled. "Guess that's a yes!"

"Here, Olivia. I think this is cherry." I passed her another one.

After confirming the flavor, Olivia put her back to me and

scooted to the edge of the blanket, digging her feet in the sand. Marley did the same. I opened another cherry and was halfway finished with it when the boys wrapped up their game. Oliver rushed over to us while Nathan jogged to the house.

"Mom, you know what Davis said?" my son asked, his cheeks flushed and a light sheen of sweat on his forehead. "He said he'll get us tickets to a game! And we can go on the field and stuff. He *actually* said that!"

"Cool!" Olivia squealed.

"Wow. I hope you thanked him for offering that."

"I did. I thanked him a bunch of times. You can ask Nate." Oliver collapsed onto his knees and caught his breath. "Oh, Popsicles." He licked his lips.

"Do you want to get changed?" I asked.

"No. I'm dry." He pulled the wrapper off a lemon-flavored one and bit the end.

Nathan returned to the blanket with a set of noise-canceling headphones for Marley. He must've gotten them out of the truck, because I didn't remember seeing them in the diaper bag. He'd also changed out of his swim trunks and was wearing his T-shirt again and a pair of gray basketball shorts. His hat was back on. I grinned when he slid the aviators into place. Olivia giggled at him and held up her thumbs.

"The sun isn't really out anymore," I whispered when Nathan sank down onto the blanket beside me. "Can you even see through those things?"

"I can see *you*," he said, voice serious.

I pressed back onto my heels. Despite the chill of the Popsicle, my chest and stomach warmed, delicious heat spreading through me.

God, is there a better feeling than this?

I smiled, knowing he could see it, and passed Nathan his Popsicle.

The kids spun around, and the five of us chatted until Davis announced a two-minute warning until showtime. Then he took off running down the beach.

Oliver and Olivia jumped to their feet and chanted their excitement, along with a few other kids around us. Marley crawled between Nathan's legs and scrambled into his lap. She yawned and rubbed at her eyes, her little body slumped sideways against him.

"Your mommy loved fireworks," Nathan told her before sliding the headphones over her ears. He kissed her head.

I smiled warmly at them and asked, "Has she seen them before?"

"No. And the last ones I saw were before she was born."

I reached out and rubbed Marley's leg, just below where Nathan held her. "I bet she's going to love them. My kids did at this age."

"Yeah?" His hand slid lower and bumped mine. Then his thumb rubbed over my knuckles.

My breath caught. I slowly lifted my head and stared at Nathan, at those sunglasses with the ridiculous tint I couldn't see through. But it wouldn't have mattered.

Tint or no tint, I knew he was looking right at me.

His thumb moved slowly, back and forth, back and forth, then grazed between my knuckles and circled in a pattern.

I forced myself to breathe. God, my heart was pounding. This touch was *nothing*, nothing in the grand scheme of touches or compared to the embrace we'd shared the other night, but his thumb...my skin...it was unparalleled. I couldn't remember ever feeling anything like this before.

How was that possible?

Just when I thought I felt a little push, a force to turn my hand and bring us palm to palm, the sky lit up and a loud *boom* shook the earth.

I wrenched my hand back when Marley's legs kicked out in surprise. She tipped her head up, eyes round as her fists clenched and her arms locked and trembled.

Sensing her fear, Nathan shifted her on his thigh and leaned forward, peering into her face.

"Is she okay?" he asked.

"Yeah. She likes it!" I held Marley's fist and wiggled it open so she could grip my finger. Another firework bloomed overhead. "Look, baby!" I pointed at the sky, and Marley grinned and giggled, falling back against Nathan. Her squeals poured into the night. Nathan wrapped his arms around her.

The twins cheered and chanted for more, eventually joining us on the blanket and sprawling out on their backs. Marley stayed in Nathan's lap. They were both smiling so big. I watched them more than the fireworks.

This would be an amazing memory for them. *For all of us*, I thought. My two would never forget it.

We left shortly after the fireworks ended.

Davis high-fived my kids and wrapped his arms around me, finding it hilarious when Nathan rushed him through the embrace. Marley was asleep on Nathan's shoulder before we made it to the truck, and she stayed asleep the entire drive home despite the constant conversation bouncing between Oliver and Olivia. Two hours of reliving every second of our evening didn't seem to bother her. It didn't seem to bother Nathan either.

He answered every "Remember when we did this, Nate?" and played along like he needed reminders.

I, on the other hand, would've killed for an interlude. I was dying to speak to Nathan alone. Or as alone as we could be with three children sitting behind us. So much had happened tonight. What was going on here? I had no idea. The only thing I knew for sure was it was pushing midnight and my children were wound up.

What the hell was in those Popsicles?

When Nathan pulled into the driveway, I couldn't thwart my disappointment. My body slumped against the seat.

Our evening was over. I never wanted it to end. What would happen the next time we saw each other?

"Do you want to come inside?" Nathan asked, cutting the engine.

I looked over at him and blinked. My heart began working double time.

It was crazy late. Marley was passed out. My kids needed to go to bed an hour ago. And Nathan wanted me to come inside?

"I do," Olivia answered before I could get a word out.

"Yeah, can we watch a movie or something?" Oliver asked.

"Sure," Nathan said, staring right at me.

There it was again—that serious, uncertain gaze. He'd taken his aviators off to drive and was back to wearing his prescription glasses.

"Do you want to watch a movie, Jenna?"

I heard his question. I also heard what he wasn't saying.

Come inside. I don't want to watch a movie.

"Sure. I'd love to." I smiled at him.

We could talk. We could figure out what was happening between us. Or, something else maybe? The way he was looking at me...

I threw the door open and stumbled out of the truck.

After gathering both bags, ignoring Nathan's protest about it, I trailed behind him and the kids and stepped inside the house. I dumped the bags near the front door as Nathan flipped on the lights. Marley was still asleep on his shoulder.

"Go sit down," I told my kids.

Oliver and Olivia rounded the couch and sprawled out on separate ends. They yawned and blinked tiredly at the TV.

"What movie do you want to watch?" I asked no one in particular. I stood in front of the couch and scrolled through Netflix at lightning speed. I could feel Nathan's stare on my profile.

"Here. This is good." I cued up *The BFG*. I knew Oliver and Olivia enjoyed that. Dropping the remote on the love seat, I looked between the two of them and said, "You guys stay here, okay?"

"Okay, Mom," they both mumbled, eyes heavy-lidded and glued to the screen.

I crossed the room and entered the kitchen, following Nathan up the stairs. He didn't ask me to follow him. In fact, he didn't say a word to me. My feet moved without prompting. I knew Nathan didn't want or need help putting Marley to bed. That wasn't why he'd waited, and it sure as hell wasn't why I'd suddenly become his shadow.

One, Marley was already asleep. And two, Nathan was perfectly capable of putting her to bed even if she were awake right now.

Come inside. I don't want to watch a movie.

Instead of following him into Marley's room, I stepped inside the bathroom across the hall, closing the door behind me and flicking on the light. After relieving myself, I washed my hands and stared at my reflection in the mirror.

My hair was still tied up in a knot, but it looked messier than usual, with several pieces falling around my neck and in front of my ears. I pulled the tie out of my hair and ran my fingers through the strands, smoothing them out. Then I rubbed at my nose and cheeks, trying to remove the excess lotion that hadn't been absorbed. My skin looked pink from the sun and my lips were cherry-Popsicle stained.

I quickly wiped at my mouth, which did absolutely nothing to the color; then I flicked the light off and opened the door, stepping out into the hallway.

Nathan was slouched against the opposite wall, and our eyes met instantly as I emerged, as if he'd been staring at the door. Waiting.

"Hey, sorry," I said, smiling at him. I pulled the door closed behind me. "Do you want to go downstairs?"

"The kids are asleep."

"Mine too?"

"Yeah. I checked. They're out cold."

"Oh."

We stared at each other across the small space. I could hear my breathing. I could hear *his*.

God, he looked so sexy. Relaxed and maybe a little tired. His hat and glasses removed now, hands shoved in his front pockets and head tipped back. The hallway lighting was dim above us, a soft amber glow, but it was enough. I could see him clearly.

I lowered my eyes to his neck. His Adam's apple was even more prominent, courtesy of his stance. If Nathan stayed there and remained still, I could've openly gazed at it for hours.

I wanted that, and I didn't. I could stare at him later. *After.* Right now I needed him to move.

There was only one reason we were both up here.

"They're heavy sleepers," I shared, my breath quickening.

"Um, my kids....so, if we wanted to talk or...anything, they wouldn't hear it."

I was provoking him. I wasn't sure if it was needed or not, but what if it was, just like earlier at the pool?

Jenna, I need you to ask me.

I wasn't typically this forward, but it came easily with him. Around Nathan, my shyness slipped away.

"Or anything," he repeated, testing out that option on his tongue. He tilted his head to the side. "You've become my favorite person to talk to. Did you know that?"

I smiled. *Wow*, that was sweet. "No, I didn't know that."

"I don't want to talk right now, Jenna."

I swallowed thickly. My fingers curled against my palms. "Honestly, me neither."

Nathan moved then, pushing away from the wall and stalking toward me.

My head tilted up and up, until our shoes bumped and his fingers brushed against mine. That touch, *my God*. I felt my pulse throbbing in my neck.

"I keep holding back with you. Can you tell?" Nathan bent his arm and braced it on the door above my head, his fingers slowly gliding over my hand, my wrist, the side of my elbow. "It's not because I don't want something to happen. There is *little* I've wanted more than this."

"I want it too." I reached out and held on to his waist. I had to. My legs were threatening to give out.

Nathan glanced down at my grip on his body. His chest was heaving now.

"It's okay if you need to hold back, and it's okay if you don't," I said. Our eyes locked. "I'm not going to stop you, Nathan."

His fingers had worked their way up my arm and were cur-

160

rently teasing the bikini string around my neck. He pulled it away from my collarbone.

"I don't think I could stop right now." He caught my eyes, bent lower, and floated his mouth over mine. "This fucking top," he growled. "You nearly killed me today."

I didn't move. I wasn't sure I wanted to. We were so fucking close, we shared breath. Him out, me in. Me out, him in. He hovered there, staring at me. If I tilted my head up, we'd kiss. I knew we would.

I didn't move a muscle. Neither did he. For seconds, we never touched, and it was the hottest tease of my life.

"How is *this* good?" he asked, head shaking ever so slightly in disbelief. "I could stay right here...*Fuck.*"

"I know." My hands flexed around his hips. "You really don't have to move."

"Oh, I'm going to move," he promised.

The beat of a second passed before he acted, sliding his hand around my neck and into my hair, forcing that tilt of my head I'd been so patiently refusing. I gasped as our lips pressed together, arching away from the door and wrapping my arms around his neck.

Nathan groaned and hauled me up his body, his fingers digging into my ass and his hard dick trapped between us.

The feel of him...*Holy shit.* Wetness pooled between my legs.

And good God, he could kiss.

Soon we were moving, him backward and me barely needing to lift my feet. I felt like I was floating. My hands were in his hair, tugging as I sucked grape Popsicle off his tongue. I moaned into his mouth.

"I want you. God, I want you." His voice was needy. Urgent. His hot mouth moved down my neck and sucked.

"Nathan." My entire body shook. "Get us in a room. *Please.*"

His back hit a door, and he blindly reached around to open it.

I squeaked when his hand returned to my ass and grabbed, fingers digging into denim and lifting. My legs wrapped around his waist.

He carried me inside the room. I reached over his shoulder and pushed the door closed. He locked it. I swiped the wall and turned on the light.

We toppled over onto the bed, kicking our sandals off. The sheets underneath my back bunching as he slid me higher toward the headboard. He was panting as he crawled over me. I fell back onto the pillow, my hands on his face as I kissed him.

I didn't want to stop. Just like out in the hallway, this was *so good*. Just this. His tongue inside my mouth. The way Nathan sucked on my lips. His dirty little noises, I could eat them for hours.

I whimpered when he sat back on his heels and forced us apart, until he reached over his shoulder and stripped off his shirt.

Right. Too many clothes. This could get so much better. *Move, Jenna.*

I quickly sat up and drew off my top, tossing it beside the bed to join his while I openly stared at his chest and carved-out abs. I fell back as Nathan reached for me. Our hands collided at my shorts.

I popped the button. He pulled down the zipper. I lifted my hips. He yanked the shorts down my legs.

"Teamwork," I said. I smiled when he smiled and slid my fingers underneath the ties at my hips.

"Leave that on for a minute." He sank back over me, bracing his weight on his elbows and dipping lower.

"Sure." I licked along his tongue.

Again, I was good with doing this for hours. He wanted a minute? No problem.

I rubbed my hands over his sides and back as we kissed. I gripped onto muscle. His skin was smooth and warm from the sun. When Nathan rocked his hips forward and pressed the head of his dick against me, I gasped and dug my nails into his skin. "God, *yes*."

"Yeah?"

I nodded fast, dropping my knees wider and gripping his trim waist. I drew him in.

Nathan peered down at me and moved, another surge between my legs. This one working into a glide and ending with a heavy press to my clit. His mouth dropped open through a moan.

I felt close to coming straight off the bed. I could feel everything. *Everything.*

His basketball shorts hugged the line of his thick dick. And my bathing suit did absolutely nothing in terms of being a barrier. If anything, our bottoms made the glide smoother.

"I haven't done this in years," he said, kissing my jaw, my neck. He pumped his hips.

I grasped at his body, moaning. "Me either."

Hell, I couldn't remember the last time I dry humped. And even though I knew incredible things existed beyond this, I began to wonder how it was possible to top what we were doing.

What was better than grinding one out? Absolutely nothing. I couldn't stop now if I tried.

"This feels so good," I panted. I spread my legs wider and clutched his ass through his shorts.

Nathan dipped closer. Our foreheads touched, our bodies building into a rhythm. He pushed down and up. I rode his glide, tipping my pelvis to meet him. His hand wiggled between us and squeezed my breast. We both moaned. My fingers slid to his mouth, and I whimpered when he sucked on the tips.

"Kiss me," I begged, grabbing him. I gripped handfuls of his hair.

Nathan crashed our mouths together, his hand staying between us. He slid the triangle aside and rolled my nipple to a stiff peak.

"Oh God," I gasped. "Don't stop."

"This?" he asked, his thumb teasing me.

"Everything. I'm close."

He kept torturing my nipple as his hips pistoned relentlessly. Soon his pace grew desperate.

"*Fuck*," he breathed. "Ah...holy shit." He harshly grabbed my breast.

I loved how unrestrained he became. I felt just as frantic.

This chase...I'd never experienced anything like it.

"I'm gonna come," he said. His body shook. His dick throbbed between my legs.

Oh my God, him saying that...I fell over the edge.

Fingers digging into his ass, I closed my eyes as my orgasm took hold. "Nathan," I groaned. "*Oh God...*"

He rode it out with me. He kept moving, grinding wildly against my clit. He moaned through it and begged my name. *"Jenna."*

And the noises leaving him...Jesus. Words spilled out of me. I couldn't help them.

"You're so sexy," I panted, my body still shuddering. "I'm so into you, you have no idea."

Nathan slowed the rock of his hips, watching me, his expression wrecked. Sweat beaded on his brow. "Come here," he said, bending to take my mouth. "Fuck, this is so good."

"Yeah." I melted inside our kiss.

My body went slack against the sheet as I came down, gathering my breath... only to lose it again when Nathan hunched over and tongued my nipple.

"Oh," I gasped, pushing my fingers through his messy hair. He sucked my flesh like a man starved. *"God..."*

I'd been expecting an intermission. Maybe a cuddle break. Honestly, I'd been hoping for one, only because I knew how amazing Nathan's arms felt around me and I'd been dying to feel them again.

But when he slid his hand into my bathing suit bottoms and pressed his finger against my sex, I quit wishing for anything besides *more*.

"Please...*please*." I reached down and tore my suit off. "Do you have a condom?" I asked. I guided his face to mine and kissed the word "yeah" as it left his mouth.

Nathan pushed back and over, kneeling beside my hip. He bent over me, two fingers inside now, and worked me over with his lips and tongue.

My hands flew to his head as it pressed between my legs. I both held him to me and attempted to push him off.

"Nathan." I gasped, writhing on the sheets. "N-N...Please, I—" I fumbled for words. I didn't know what to beg for.

Sex? More of his mouth and fingers? This was so good. I couldn't decide.

"I know. I had to," Nathan whispered against my clit. He pressed his lips there once more, sucking gently. Then he eased away and slid off the bed.

I untied my top and pulled it off, dropping it beside me. Then

165

I pressed my palms to my chest and felt the steady beat of my heart. "Wow," I whispered, turning my head on the pillow. My eyes widened at Nathan's bare ass.

Wow is right. He had muscle there too? Damn.

Nathan finished cleaning himself off with his T-shirt and tossed the garment across the room at the hamper in the corner. Then he sat on the edge of the bed and dug through the drawer in his nightstand. The muscles in his back flexed.

I rolled to my side as he retrieved something out of the drawer, a box of condoms by the sound of the paperboard flap popping open. I watched him reach back and rub at his neck, his head lowered. When his arm fell away, he remained in that position.

He didn't turn around. He didn't stand with a condom. He didn't move at all.

Shoulders hunched forward. Head down. The only sound I could hear was his breathing.

I was holding mine.

chapter twelve

NATHAN

"Nathan, are you okay?"

Jenna's soft voice lifted my gaze off the box in my hand. I peered back at her.

She was on her side now, pushed up on her elbow, her dark hair spilling over her shoulders and down her chest. She'd removed her top. Her full breasts heaved slowly.

"Yeah, I'm just checking for an expiration date." I cleared my throat and gazed into her eyes, watching them widen ever so slightly. *Right.* Confession time. "I haven't been with anyone since... These are pretty old. I don't know if they're still okay to use or not."

The paperboard bent in my hand. I forced my grip to ease.

Jenna could've reacted to the news of my bleak sex life with surprise. Her pretty green eyes could've rounded further. Her lips could've parted. Maybe her breathing would've hitched. I was watching her closely enough, I wouldn't have missed a damn thing she did right now. And I would've anticipated shock. When I thought about it perceptively, it was shocking to *me.* I expected no less from Jenna.

"I haven't been with anyone in four years," she revealed.

I stared at her.

She hadn't reacted to my admission. But there was no way in hell I wasn't reacting to hers.

I turned sideways to face her more. "*Excuse me*. How is that even possible?"

"What do you mean, *how*...?"

"You're *you*." I gestured at her.

A little smile tugged at her mouth. "With the kids, I don't really have a whole lot of time to date. The dates I have been on haven't worked out, and we never got to that step. Or the guys are only looking for a hookup. I can't do that, so—"

I cut her off, not knowing whether this needed to be said, but I couldn't risk Jenna getting hurt over this. We hadn't discussed what was happening between us. We hadn't talked at all, no thanks to me. I told her I didn't want that tonight. How did she interpret my request? Any conversing outside of what we said to each other while we fooled around was off-limits?

You dick. What the fuck?

"That's not what this is," I said. "I'm not just looking to hook up with you."

She smiled a little more. "I didn't think you were."

"We can talk. I know I said I didn't want to, but we can. I didn't mean...*Fuck*, I just..." I pushed my hand through my hair. "I've been fighting this with you. For *weeks* I've wanted to be here. I haven't felt that in...well..." I held up the box in my hand.

"I know we can talk," Jenna said, pushing up to her hip. "I know if I asked to stop right now, we would. I know what this *isn't*, Nathan. I'm not sure what it is yet, but if those aren't expired"— she pointed at the box—"I'd like to keep going, if you do."

"The only way I wouldn't want to keep going is if you didn't."

"Well, then, what's the verdict?" Her eyes slid to the box.

"I don't know yet." I turned away from her then and brought the box closer to my face. I squinted at the fine print.

"Can you even see that?" she asked, her voice wrapped around a chuckle.

"I'm trying to." I laughed with her. "I don't know why they make this shit so fucking small. Who isn't checking for an expiration date?"

The mattress shifted. "Where are your glasses?"

"Downstairs. I took them off after I checked on your kids."

While I paced the kitchen and stalled coming back upstairs, not knowing whether I should.

"Here. Let me see it." Jenna was kneeling at my shoulder now, one hand reaching while the other pressed against my back, keeping her balanced. She slid her hand up my spine to my neck, gripping there gently as I passed her the box. Then she pushed her fingers up into my hair.

"Mm." I groaned and dropped my head. My eyes slipped closed. "That feels good."

She kept it up, feathering over my scalp, her nails scratching gently. "Oh my God," she mumbled. Her hand froze.

"What?"

"Guess when these expired?"

I jerked my head around and glared at her. "You're fucking kidding."

Jenna laughed softly as she passed over the box. "I'd say see for yourself, but we both know you can't." She pressed a kiss to my cheek. "May."

"May?"

"Yep." She giggled. "It's funny, right? I mean, it could be worse. June would've been like a giant *ha ha, screw you.*"

"That's basically how this feels."

I threw the box across the room. It hit the wall and busted apart, condoms splattering to the floor. Jenna cracked up at my back.

"Enjoying yourself?" I asked, standing from the bed, only to plant my knee on the mattress and climb back on. I crawled toward her.

She was on her side again, cheek on the pillow, giggling sweetly. Her dark hair fell over her beautiful breasts. "Well, there's always things that don't involve condoms."

"Thank God for that."

She smiled and rolled over.

I stretched out beside her, bracing my weight on my elbow and hip. I bent over her and we kissed.

Her warm arms wrapped around my neck, and her hot little tongue licked along mine. *Fuck, her mouth is good.* I sucked on her.

"Shorty," I murmured, dragging my lips over her cheek. I watched her smile.

Her hand slid between us and wrapped around me, dragging a moan out of my throat.

Enough flirting, then.

I reached down and brushed my fingers between her legs, playing with the small patch of hair leading to her pussy before I dove in with my middle and fourth finger.

Her body gripped me. She was soaked and shaking.

I pressed my mouth against hers and moved my thumb over her clit.

Jenna shuddered and gasped against my tongue. "You're... *very good* with that left hand."

"You sound surprised."

"Well, you throw with your right."

"I'm ambidextrous." I looked down between her legs, curled my fingers inside her and pressed in, pumping them.

"Ugnh." She arched off the bed, breathless. "*Good,* that's... so good. Holy shit." She lifted her head and mouthed at my jaw while her hand frantically stroked me.

It was messy and methodless, jumping from firm to soft. Her hold tightening around my base, pulling to the tip, barely touching the head and then gripping me mid-shaft. I couldn't predict her next move. It was unfuckingreal.

I closed my eyes and fought the urge to hump into her grip.

"Too bad I'm not good with my left," she whispered against my cheek, kissing it. "Sorry."

"*Sorry?* Are you kidding?" I watched her sink back onto the pillow. "If you keep it up, I'm going to come all over you."

Her eyes widened. "Really?"

She was shocked. I got that. I just came minutes ago and here I was, confessing to getting off without any difficulty from a hand job.

But Jesus Christ, this hand job. This *woman*.

"Yeah." I bent down, brushing my lips against hers. "But you first."

I pumped my fingers fast into her pussy and rubbed her clit. She spread her knees wide and pulled her legs higher. Soon she was rocking against my palm. I rubbed her out while she rubbed me out, her hold on me tightening. Her body tightening.

"Nathan...*Nathan*." She held my hand still and rode it as she came.

I leaned away to watch her. She was shameless in her pleasure, and she looked right fucking at me. It drove me mad.

My resolve broke. I moaned through tiny thrusts of my hips. I couldn't hold back anymore. Not after that.

"Squeeze me harder," I begged.

She gripped at me clumsily, her breaths leaving her in desperate little pants. When she rocked toward me to slip her other hand between us and fondle my balls, I groaned deep and shot, my head falling to her shoulder.

I stopped moving and let her stroke me out. I kept my hand between her legs. I told her she dripped all over it.

"I like it," I said, kissing her hungrily.

I'd gone what, five minutes without her mouth? Ten? It felt like the first time. I'd nearly eaten her alive in the hallway.

"You're not much better," she said through a smile. Her cupped hand knocked against my ribs. "I need a towel."

We slid out of bed and cleaned up in the master bath.

I noticed Jenna's gaze lingering on the corner shower. It was new compared to everything else in the bathroom and didn't perfectly match the other fixtures. And when Jenna looked at me, I knew I didn't need to explain why that was.

She took my hand and led me into the bedroom.

Two orgasms down, my body fell heavy against the mattress. I pulled the sheet over us as Jenna curled against my side.

We stared at each other. I thought we might talk. I wanted to...

When fingers pushed through my hair, I closed my eyes and dozed.

* * *

I stirred awake, hand sweeping the mattress beside me, seeking her. I fisted the sheet.

"Jenna?" I called out. My eyes creaked open.

She stood beside the bed, dressing. She pulled her shorts up to her hips. Her top was already in place.

"Hey." I pushed up to my elbows. "What are you doing? How

long have I been asleep?" I peered over at the blurred numbers of the alarm clock. *Fuck, my glasses.* "What time is it?" I rubbed at my eyes.

"It's almost one. I need to get going."

I watched her round the bed. Her gaze barely lingered on me. *Is she in a rush to get out of here or something?*

"Stop. Why are you leaving?" I sat up and swung my legs over the side, bunching the sheet in my lap. "And why are you acting like that? What's wrong?"

Jenna stopped a foot away and blinked at me. She appeared almost sad. "How am I acting?"

"You're barely looking at me."

"I'm looking at you now."

I cocked my head. "Okay..." I raked a hand down my face. *We should've talked. Why the hell did I fall asleep?* I gripped the edge of the bed on either side of me. "I didn't ask you to leave, did I? You don't have to go."

"No, but... Nathan, my kids. Waking up here, me in your bed, it would confuse them. I shouldn't stay." Jenna kicked her sandals in front of her and slipped them on.

Well, she wasn't wrong there. I understood why that might be an issue.

"I'm sorry. I would've said goodbye before I left. I was just trying to let you sleep. You... seemed tired. You were dreaming." She gathered her hair off her neck like before at the party, securing it into a messy knot on top of her head.

"You were doing that thing with your fingers," I explained. "It felt too good. I didn't mean to fall asleep."

Jenna smiled, the lamp on the nightstand illuminating the side of her face. I reached out for her and caught her wrist, tugging her between my knees.

"Stay for another hour," I pleaded. I wrapped my arms around her waist and kissed the underside of her jaw.

"I can't. I'll pass out if I stay." She dropped her forehead to mine. Her fingers tickled my neck. "Thank you for inviting us to that party. Oliver and Olivia...they'll never forget it. Neither will I, Nathan. It was amazing."

"Yeah, I'm glad you guys got to go." I tipped my head up and kissed her.

She moaned against my mouth, her body melting. "Okay, I *really* need to leave," she said. She slid her nose along mine.

"Let me grab some shorts. I'll walk you down."

"No. Stay here."

"Just give me a second."

"Seriously, it's okay." Jenna pushed down on my shoulders when I tried to stand. "My kids might ask what we've been doing...why you're shirtless. They're nosy. Just stay here."

"I can grab a shirt," I argued.

She shook her head, smiling, and moved her fingers through my hair. "You look all sexed up and sleepy." When I moaned at her touch, a soft little laugh escaped her. She bent to kiss my cheek. "I'll lock up," she whispered.

I rubbed at my face, watching her back away. "I like walking you out," I grumbled.

"I know. And I like when you do." She touched the knob. "No Marley tomorrow, right? You took off?"

"Yeah." Marley. *Fuck, I almost forgot.* "Shit..." I scanned the room for my gym bag, then remembered Jenna carrying it inside for me. It was still by the door. "Wait a minute," I said, digging through my nightstand. "I might need to go downstairs with you anyway. I don't know how much I have in here." My hands curled around wrinkled bills.

"Nathan..." Jenna's voice was cautious.

"I can grab my wallet before you get them up. They won't see me," I explained, pulling out the cash and counting it. I had a little over two hundred dollars in there. "Never mind. We're good." I stuffed the extra cash away and then held out the rest for Jenna.

She stared at me, her eyes crinkling as she looked at the money. She began to fidget. "Yeah...I really wish you weren't doing this right now," she said, smoothing her hands around her neck. She huffed out a breath.

Doing this? Doing *what*?

I glanced at the cash. My stomach turned over. *Oh shit.*

"I'm sorry." My arm fell to my thigh. "Fuck, I'm so sorry. This isn't...I'm not paying you for what we did. You watched Marley today. That's what this is for." The bills crinkled in my hand.

Jesus Christ, this looked terrible.

"I know that. I know." Jenna covered her face and shook her head. "But it still feels...God, can you just not pay me?" Her eyes were pleading when she looked at me.

"Jenna, you can't watch Marley for free. I don't feel right about that." I smoothed out the bills on my thigh. Then I folded them in half, like that was actually going to help somehow. *Good job. This isn't shitty now at all.* "You know what?" I tossed the cash on the nightstand. "Forget this happened. I'll just pay you double the next time you're here."

Jenna looked down, remaining quiet, even though I could tell she wanted to argue this. Maybe she was thinking the same thing as me.

What if we do something the next time? Why wouldn't we? I knew I'd want to.

"I'd rather you not pay me at all, Nathan," she finally said.

I tried thinking about this, working it out another way in my head, even though I knew it wouldn't change a damn thing.

In terms of Marley, Jenna did too much for me. I knew what all I was taking from her. She was always there for my daughter, and for me, no questions. Would I be using her if we took this any further? What am I giving her in return if we do this?

"I'm sorry, Jenna. I'd have to pay you," I said.

"Yeah." Her shoulders lifted in defeat. "I know."

We stared at each other.

When her gaze fell away again, I pinched my eyes shut and rubbed at my face.

"There's gotta be something," I mumbled. This couldn't be *it*. No fucking way was this over. We just got started.

"Nathan, when you were dreaming you...you were calling out for Sadie, and you were holding me, and—"

I stopped her with a look. She *was* acting different with me. "I can explain that."

"You don't have to." Jenna shook her head, hands raised defensively as she crept closer. "I'm not mad about it. I under-stand—*God*, of course I do. I'm just, I'm wondering if maybe we should wait."

"Because of that? Jenna, that dream—"

"Because of *everything*, Nathan." She stopped a foot away. Her eyes drifted to the cash. "This entire night...This happened pretty fast, all things considered." Jenna looked at me. "I don't know, waiting a little more might not be so terrible. I'm only watching Marley through the summer—that's two months. Barely that. We could wait and see if what we're feeling is still there." She gave me a tight smile.

Two more months. That wasn't long, yet I knew how difficult

a delay like that would be. I barely lasted three weeks with this woman. She was asking me for eight more?

Did the amount of patience needed for this even exist? I wasn't so sure.

I exhaled heavily and raked my hand through my hair.

We had moved fast. She wasn't wrong. Maybe I should've thought about this longer before I acted on it. I went from acknowledging my feelings to learning my condoms had expired. I hadn't even considered how this could affect our working relationship. That complication aside, was I even ready for this with Jenna? For everything this could become?

Fuck. I couldn't answer that.

"Yeah...I think you're right," I said. "It's probably for the best that we wait."

"Probably."

When I smiled easily, she smiled back. "And, you know"—I gestured between us—"it won't be weird. We'll just go back to the way it was."

"Okay, good." Jenna's stance relaxed. "I'd like that." She retreated toward the door, smiling back at me when she reached it. "See ya."

"Yeah, later."

She slipped out into the hallway.

When the door latched shut, I collapsed onto the bed, my mind whirling.

Back to the way it was... heavy flirting and doing absolutely nothing beyond that.

I'd just agreed to two more months of torture.

chapter thirteen

JENNA

I didn't hear from Nathan at all the next day.

Which wouldn't have been strange—it was his day off—but lately he reached out to me in some way or another on the days I didn't keep Marley for him. We'd text a little. Sometimes he'd call. Maybe we'd end up getting together with the kids...

Nathan never reached out on Saturday. I wondered if he was at least thinking about me, because I couldn't stop thinking about him.

I remembered our night together. The wild hunger in his kiss. The way he gripped at my body. Our mutual grinding session and round two when we touched each other until we both came. It was difficult *not* thinking about it. I'd never experienced pleasure like that, not with anyone before. I kept replaying moments inside my head.

I thought about what happened after too. How quickly things got awkward and the agreement to put us on pause—that was also a memory I couldn't shake.

Sunday when we got to his house, Oliver and Olivia went hard at Nathan the moment we walked in the door. They couldn't stop talking about the Fourth and occupied all conversation while I got Marley set up with breakfast.

Nathan didn't act out of the ordinary at all with them. He

smiled at Olivia when she tugged playfully at his tie and reciprocated the little hug she gave him. And when Oliver showed off his football, as if he hadn't seen it before, Nathan matched my son's excitement over the signature.

Maybe I was worrying for nothing. They could've simply been busy yesterday. And it wasn't a requirement for Nathan to check in. Why was I acting like he had to? I was reading too much into this. If anyone was making things weird, it was me.

When it was time for him to leave, Nathan walked over to the kitchen table and kissed Marley goodbye. The twins had moved into the family room.

"What did you end up doing yesterday?" I asked him, grabbing hold of Marley's wrists so she wouldn't touch Nathan with her sticky syrup fingers.

"Nothing," he answered, straightening up. "We just hung around here."

Huh. Okay, not busy.

"Yeah, us too." I tucked my hair behind my ear. "I mean, we didn't do anything either. Just hung around."

He smiled at Marley, then slid his eyes to me, where I sat beside her. I waited for it—that warm, easy look we shared now, but it was as if we'd just met. There was nothing familiar in the way Nathan regarded me. He was being polite, nothing more.

He smoothed out his tie. "I gotta go. I'll see you around seven."

"Great."

I put my focus on Marley and helped her fork another triangle of pancake as Nathan's heavy footsteps took him out of the kitchen. The front door creaked open and closed.

I wasn't reading too much into the way Nathan was acting

with me. That wasn't normal. Maybe things weren't weird yet, but they were definitely different.

Great, indeed.

My morning with the kids played out typically. We stayed outside and ate chicken fingers and fries for lunch. Everyone was happy. Yet by nap time, I still felt off. When my phone beeped with an incoming text, I wondered if it was Nathan. Maybe our interaction from this morning was bothering him as much as it was bothering me and he wanted to reach out.

I palmed my phone and saw it was Travis texting me, and my initial reaction was surprise. Then I remembered our last conversation. I'd completely forgotten about our impending date.

Should we still go out? With everything that had happened with Nathan, I hesitated responding.

I needed to talk this out with someone.

After laying Marley in her crib, I rushed downstairs, phone in my hand and number waiting to be dialed. I swiped the baby monitor off the counter and peeked into the family room.

"Stay in here, okay?" I said to the kids. "I'm just going out on the deck."

They were stretched out on the couch and deep into their iPad time. Their eyes remained focused on their screens as they nodded in answer.

I stepped outside and called Sydney. Time for our weekly check-in.

"Hey, Jenna," she answered as I crossed the deck. "How are you? What's going on?"

"I fooled around with Nathan." The words tumbled out of my mouth. I held onto the rail, registering her breathless gasp. "So, uh, how was your Fourth?"

"U-um...it was good!" She cleared her throat. "Hold on one second."

I heard shuffling through the line, then my brother's deep, questioning voice. They must've both been off for the day. A heavy door closed. I pictured Sydney on her front porch and smiled when the glider made noise beneath her weight. It was old and had been left there by the previous owner.

"*How was my Fourth?*" Sydney hissed. "How was *yours* is the better question. What happened? Tell me everything."

I breezed through my recount of the holiday, leaving off heavy details but offering enough that she made little noises of approval in my ear. Until I got to the part when Nathan dug around in his nightstand for cash.

"Oh...wow. *Wow*. That's incredibly awkward." She groaned in discomfort for me. "Jeez, did he have any idea how bad that looked?"

"He caught on right away," I said. "He felt terrible for it. Apologized...a lot. I had to stop us though. I mean, I kind of work for him. There's no other way I can look at this."

"Well, yeah, you pretty much are an employee at this point. I can see that."

"And the thing is, I don't even need to be paid. I love spending time with Marley. This isn't a job to me." I frowned at the rail. "But he's adamant about paying me. I can't do things with Nathan and then accept money. Even if we worked it out to where he was somehow wiring me the cash, it's still *there*. And, like, God forbid, what if the transaction messed up and tripled? Do I pay him back? Do I just hold all the money? I'd be thinking about this while we were having sex. I know I would."

Sydney's laugh cut with a groan. "Ugh, Jenna...I'm sorry. That sucks."

"It really does."

"So, you two just called it off?"

"I suggested we wait until the summer is over and I'm no longer watching Marley for him. Nathan agreed. Honestly, I'm not sure he's even ready for something right now." My eyes fell to the baby monitor beside me on the rail. I watched the lights flicker in response to Marley's adorable sleeping noises.

Holy crap, I loved that little girl.

"Things just happened really fast," I said.

"Well, slowing down isn't the worst idea, then. I'm sure it's complicated for him. Not only because of Marley, but with Sadie…"

"Yeah."

"Two months isn't that long," Syd considered.

"It isn't, and it *is*…but we have to wait."

"If it's what you both agreed on, that's probably what needs to happen."

"Nathan said it was for the best. Of course, he also said it wouldn't be weird. But this morning when I got here—"

"Weird?"

"Pretty much."

She sighed. "I'm sorry, Jenna. Maybe it's just too soon, you know? It'll get better."

"I hope so. I love how it used to be."

We could still be us. I thought we could. Just the us we were before the party. I didn't think I could handle Nathan full-on flirting while we waited this out in the friend zone.

Talk about torture. Nathan flirted really well.

"There's another thing I wanted to talk to you about." I lifted my head and looked out at the beach, at the little sandcastle we made this morning. Marley loved building those. "Travis reached out to me today about our date. Remember I told you we spoke after seeing each other at Wax?"

"I completely forgot about that."

"So did I..."

"What did he say?"

"He wants to know if I have any free nights coming up, and I'm wondering if there is any reason why I shouldn't go out with him. Before the Fourth, I didn't really have one..."

"Well, you said Nathan might not be ready for anything right now, and you both agreed to put on the brakes. Honestly? I'm not sure you have a reason not to go out with Travis."

"Me either."

"It's just a date. It might not even lead to anything. Plus, Travis is really hot. I met him once."

"He's definitely hot."

"So is Nate though. They're both super fun to look at."

I laughed, keeping to myself how super fun Nathan was in every way. Naked ways especially.

"Don't think and answer me—do you want to go out with Travis, Jenna?"

"I think I do..."

"So do it. Dates are fun. And you're overdue for one."

"It has been a while." I leaned forward and braced my weight on my elbows. Syd was giving me the push I needed. I'd wanted to go out with Travis before. What was stopping me now? Nathan wasn't ready... "I'm going to do it," I said, voice steadier now. "I'm going to go out on a date with him."

"Awesome!"

"Mama, you're going on a date!"

I pushed off the rail and spun around. Olivia had her head poking through the slider and was currently beaming at me.

183

"Cool! When?" she shrieked, her voice carrying.

"Sweetheart, please go back inside," I requested, bringing a finger to my lips. "I'll be in in a minute."

"Okay! Woo! A date! A date!"

"Olivia, shh!"

I winced, looking back at the monitor as the slider pulled shut. The lights flickered typically, then all five dots lit up and held bright as Marley's cry came through the little speaker.

"Damn it," I whispered, grabbing the monitor off the rail.

"Aw, I hear the sweet girl," Sydney said. "Call me later, okay?"

"Yeah, okay. Bye, Syd."

"See ya!"

I ended the call and headed back inside the house.

* * *

I was upstairs getting Marley ready for bed when Nathan got home that night.

"Daddy's home," I said, smiling at her sweet face as it popped through the pajama shirt.

I could hear Oliver and Olivia greeting Nathan below me. The enthusiasm in their muffled voices was unmistakable. I wondered if they'd ever react differently to seeing Nathan.

Marley dropped the little book she was holding and grinned, her breathing excited now. She stood and tried squirming away from me.

"Hold on." I giggled, catching her around her waist. "Pants first."

We finished getting dressed. Then I took a small towel and rubbed her curls dry. They bounced around her face.

"You're so pretty," I said, kissing her cheek twice. She smelled like sweet lavender soap.

"Hey."

At Nathan's voice, I turned my head and peered behind me. He was standing in the bedroom doorway.

"Daddy!" Marley squealed. She tumbled over and pushed to her feet, rushing around me to get to him with the book in her hand.

"Hey," I said, smiling at the two of them. Nathan scooped her up. "How was work?"

"It was okay." He smiled at Marley and kissed her. She giggled against him.

I reached for the toy basket and began to clean up the mess around me. I dropped stuffed animals into the bin. "We built another sandcastle today. Marley is becoming a pro."

"Oh yeah?"

His tone made me pause. He sounded bored, like what I'd shared meant absolutely nothing to him, which was never the case with Nathan. He always absorbed every bit of information I shared about Marley and practically begged for more.

I lifted my head to figure out why.

Nathan was staring at me.

"Is everything okay?" I asked.

"Everything's fine. Tell me about this date you have coming up."

My mouth dropped open. *No, she did not.* I sighed and resumed the cleanup. "Olivia shouldn't have told you that. She was listening in on a conversation she shouldn't have heard." I shifted the basket aside and stood then, meeting his serious gaze.

Could things get any more awkward? I was worried we'd barely scratched the surface.

"Okay, I think we need to talk. And I'd rather do it here in front of her than downstairs in front of them, if I had the option."

"What do you want to talk about?"

"You being different with me." I crossed my arms under my chest. "You said things wouldn't be weird, and I think they're pretty weird."

"How am I being different with you?" He reached up and pulled at the knot in his tie, loosening it.

I cocked my head. "Come on, Nathan. You barely spoke to me this morning. And yesterday..." I trailed off, pinching my eyes shut.

Shit. I didn't want to sound needy. He was allowed to have a day to himself. *Why did I say that?*

A ragged breath left him. I opened my eyes to find Nathan's gaze suddenly gentled.

"You're right. I'm sorry," he said. "I *was* short with you this morning and I shouldn't have been. I guess I'm still trying to figure this out."

"I'm trying to figure it out too."

Nathan pressed his lips to Marley's temple and watched me.

"I haven't agreed to the date yet, but I am going to," I said, dropping my arms and inching closer. "I mean, unless there's a reason I shouldn't..."

Here I was, provoking him again. I couldn't help it though. I hadn't planned on telling Nathan about my date with Travis, but now I was oddly grateful for Olivia's eavesdropping. I needed to know how he felt about this. If we were waiting the two months solely because of the money issue, that was one thing. But I didn't think we were.

Nathan simply kept watching me. He remained silent.

"Um, did you hear what I said?"

His eyes narrowed playfully. "Yes. Surprisingly, I can hear you up here."

"Oh, ha ha." I lightly shoved his chest. "You're hilarious."

He smiled at me then. I felt heat burn across my face. I missed this—playing with each other. This was so easy. Why couldn't we keep doing it?

"Who's the guy? Do you know him?" Nathan asked.

"Yeah, I do, actually. He's Jamie's older brother...you know Jamie, Tori's fiancé."

"Surfer?"

"Yep." I nodded. "I haven't seen Travis in a long time. Our families used to live within five minutes of each other."

"Nice guy?"

"Uh...sure, he's nice."

"So, he's a family friend?"

"I guess so, yeah." I tilted my head, confused. "Why are you asking so many questions about him? Are *you* interested?"

"Oh yeah. He sounds cute."

I laughed. Nathan held my gaze for a moment, and then he looked down.

"What is it?" I asked.

"Nothing." He lifted his head and peered at me. "I was just thinking that there isn't any reason why you shouldn't go out with him."

"Right." I forced a smile, hiding the disappointment I couldn't help but feel.

Nathan shifted Marley to his other arm and turned toward the door. He took a step and then paused, looking back at me. "I'm really sorry about this morning, Jenna."

I didn't need to force my smile a second longer.

I turned off the light and followed them out of the room.

chapter fourteen

NATHAN

One Week Later

Hey. I'll probably be home close to 11 tonight. Got behind on a few things. Is that ok?

Yep, no problem!

Thanks

It was twenty after eleven when I finally pulled into the driveway.

I used my key to get into the house and secured the door behind me. The family room was dark, minus the glow emanating from the TV and the light spilling into the room from the kitchen.

I walked around the couch and peered down at Oliver and Olivia. They were at either end, heads on the pillows and eyes closed behind their glasses. Jenna was curled up on the love seat, lying on her side. She was asleep as well.

I turned the volume down on the TV, then moved into the kitchen and headed upstairs to check on Marley. I'd wake Jenna and her kids when I came back down. I didn't see any harm in waiting a few more minutes. They were obviously tired.

After turning on the hallway light, I stepped into Marley's room and walked over to her crib. She was asleep on her stomach with her knees tucked under her and her butt stuck up in the air, her cheek pressed to the mattress. I didn't know how she could be comfortable in that position, but she was. Marley slept like that a lot.

Bending down, I grabbed the blanket she'd thrown out of the crib and tucked the soft satin around her.

I decided to get changed before heading back downstairs and strode into my bedroom, tugging at my tie. I got undressed and pulled on a pair of shorts, tossing my clothes into the hamper against the wall. As my head pushed through the neck hole in my T-shirt, Marley began to cry.

"Damn," I whispered. I worried I'd woken her when I gave her the blanket. I should've left her alone. I couldn't help it though. What if she got cold in the middle of the night?

I pushed my arms through the sleeves, slid my glasses back on, and moved quickly down the hallway.

Marley was on her knees when I entered her bedroom, gripping the rails as she peered between them. Her crying grew louder and sharper. Tears streamed down her face. They glistened in the hallway light.

"Shh, it's okay. Come here." I lifted her out of the crib and drew her against me.

I figured I could rock her back to sleep in the chair, keeping the bedroom light off for that reason, but when my lips touched her forehead, I jerked back to peer into her face and remained on my feet. Her skin was on fire.

Panic quickened the pace of my heart. I forced myself to breathe. She definitely had a fever. *Fuck!* When was the last time she felt bad and what the hell did I do? My mind went blank.

I began aimlessly pacing in front of the crib as I tried to soothe my daughter with back rubs, which seemed to be doing absolutely nothing for her.

"Okay...shh, it's okay," I chanted.

Marley screamed and rubbed her face against my shirt. I began to feel nauseous.

"Baby, what do I do? What do you need?" I asked.

Jenna rushed into the room, staggering a little when she noticed me. "H-hey!" Her whisper was startled. "Sorry. I didn't mean to fall asleep. I heard her crying on the monitor in the kitchen."

Relief dipped my shoulders. Thank God she was here.

"She's burning up," I said.

"Oh no. Is she?"

Jenna walked over and felt Marley's face with her palms, and it was incredible how quickly her presence comforted me. Nearly half the worry I had been feeling slipped away.

"God, she is. She's been fine all day...Sweet girl, what's wrong?" Jenna frowned and rubbed Marley's back.

"What do we do?" I asked. "Should I take her to the hospital?"

The nearest one was twenty-five minutes away. I didn't know if I could stand her screaming like this for that long. I needed to do something for Marley now. She was obviously in pain.

"I don't know what's bothering her. She won't tell me," I said.

"Let's take her temperature and see how high it is first. We can get her cooled down."

"How?"

"Cold compresses. Or a bath if we need to." Jenna peered up at me. "Where's your thermometer?"

"I think it's in the bathroom."

Jenna followed me into the hallway bath. While I searched for the thermometer, she gathered washcloths out of the small linen closet while reassuring me everything was going to be okay.

How did she know I needed to hear that?

"Here." I pulled a basket out from underneath the sink and fished through wads of gauze and a collection of various sizes of Band-Aids. I pulled out the thermometer and passed it to her.

"Ooh, you have the good kind," Jenna said.

"I do?" *Fuck yes*, I had the good kind. Whatever the hell that meant.

"Yep. This one reads fast. Watch."

Jenna held down a button, waiting for it to beep. Then she swiped the rubber head of the thermometer just below Marley's hairline down to her temple while my daughter continued to wail. When the device beeped a second time, Jenna held it out so we both could read it.

My eyes jumped to her face. "A hundred and one is bad, right? That's high."

"It could be worse," she was quick to say. "My kids have had higher temperatures."

That news was oddly comforting.

"I wouldn't rush her to the hospital unless it keeps getting higher. Let's see if we can bring it down."

"Just tell me what to do. I'll do anything." I wiped tears from Marley's flushed cheeks. She wouldn't stop screaming.

Jesus Christ, what was worse than this? I felt completely helpless here.

Jenna put the thermometer away and moved the basket, freeing up room on the counter. "Okay. Is her medicine in here? Do you have children's Tylenol or ibuprofen?"

I opened the cabinet on the wall and scanned the row of

bottles and toiletries. "I have both." I grabbed them with one hand.

"Let's do Motrin first. It's a little more powerful," Jenna said.

"Can you...?" I held out the bottles, my other arm clutching Marley.

"Yep." Jenna checked the dosage, then measured out some of the thick pink liquid into the tiny cup provided and brought it to Marley's mouth. "It's cherry flavored. She should take it okay."

I held my breath. Marley kept crying until she got a taste of the medicine. Then she quieted down, only whimpers escaping her while she drank. Her little tongue licked at the plastic.

My shoulders dropped. "I was worried she wouldn't take it," I said, rubbing Marley's back and pulling her against me when she started crying again. "It's okay, baby. You did so good."

Jenna set the medicine aside, pulled her phone out of the back pocket of her shorts, and checked the time. "In four hours, she can get Tylenol if she needs it. You can alternate the two."

"Okay."

Jenna shoved her phone away. Then she grabbed the washcloths and separated them. "Get her shirt off. I'm going to get these wet. Let's try to get her body temperature down."

I did as instructed, getting Marley undressed from the waist up.

Jenna wrung out the rags, telling me, "You don't want them to be too cold. Cool is better. We don't want her to shiver."

"Okay."

"If this doesn't work, we can give her a bath. She needs fluids too. That's really important with a fever."

I absorbed everything Jenna said and committed it to memory.

"Here." She flattened one of the washcloths against Marley's back, guiding my hand on top of the damp rag. "Hold this on here. This one is for her head. Let's get her out of this harsh light so she can rest."

I carried Marley to her bedroom, shielding her eyes from the hallway light. I kissed her forehead. Instead of taking a seat in the rocking chair, I sat on the floor with her, pressing my back against the crib and stretching my legs out.

Marley straddled my lap. She sniffled and whined softly, her big eyes blinking the room into focus. Tears continued to roll down her cheeks.

Jenna folded the second cloth and bent over me to put it against Marley's head. I held it in place. When my daughter tipped forward, resting her cheek against my chest, Jenna smiled.

"There we go. Keep this one here."

"Okay," I said, not caring at all when my shirt became damp and clung to me. When Jenna didn't sit down, I almost told her my reason for getting on the floor. Only one of us could fit on the chair. And I didn't want her to leave yet.

"I'm going to grab her a drink. I'll be right back," she said before fleeing the room.

A heavy breath left me. I dropped my head against the crib rail and willed my heart to slow.

Jenna returned minutes later carrying one of Marley's cups. It had a lid she could easily drink from without spilling.

"Here you go, baby. Do you want some water?" Jenna knelt beside me and offered Marley the cup, holding it for her while she drank from it. "There. Are you feeling any better?" she asked quietly.

"I think she is," I said. "The rag must be helping already. She's not crying like she was."

Marley's little body hiccupped with her breaths as she whimpered.

"We'll check her temperature again in a little bit."

"We?" I asked, with unmistakable hope in my voice. I peered into Jenna's face. "You'll stay?"

She shifted beside me. "I want to make sure the medicine is working," she said. "If her fever spikes any higher, we should probably take her to the hospital. Hopefully, that won't happen."

"Thank you," I said in a rush. "I don't know what I'd do if you weren't here. I definitely wouldn't be doing this." I repositioned the rag on Marley's back after flipping it over, giving my daughter the cooler side.

"You could've called me. I would've helped you through it."

I watched Jenna offer Marley another drink.

She *would've* helped me through it—I knew that. I also knew it wouldn't matter how late it was. If I needed something and reached out to her in the middle of the night, she would answer. It was Jenna, down to her bones. I'd never met a kinder, more selfless person.

Did she know I'd do the same for her?

"I'd help you through anything," I told her. "I hope you know that."

She blinked, smiling softly.

"You're always here. You're always doing stuff for me...I'm not sure there's anything you would ever need me for, but if there was, I'd do it. I don't want you to think this doesn't go both ways."

"I don't think that."

"Good. So, if something comes up, I want you to tell me...although I doubt there's anything you couldn't do damn well on your own..." I tried to think of something. Anything. "Seriously, what can't you do?"

Jenna giggled, dropping her head back. "You only see me

around kids. I'm not good at everything. There are things I don't know how to do. And there are absolutely things I'm just flat-out terrible with."

"Until I see proof, I won't believe that."

"I can't change a tire to save my life," she said, sounding almost proud in her admission. "Don't remind my father if you ever meet him. I've been shown how to do it several times. No dice—I can't get it down. I always mess up. My brother is my go-to if I ever get a flat." She looked at me for a moment. "Would you like to be that guy for me? I could call you instead."

"I would love to be that guy."

This could've felt like the silliest thing compared to the countless ways Jenna was there for me. Yet somehow it didn't feel small or insignificant. The smile I received in return made that clear.

Before any more could be said, Marley sat up quickly and blinked at me, looking like she just now realized I was holding her. The rag from her head fell between us.

"Hey, sweetheart." I brushed damp curls out of her face. "Are you okay?"

My daughter looked from me to Jenna, then back to me. She yawned and rubbed at her eyes. Then she collapsed forward, hitting my chest with her full weight.

Jenna reached over and felt her cheek. "She doesn't feel as warm," she whispered. "Her eyes are still open, but she looks tired. She might fall asleep soon."

I resituated the rag on her head and shifted a little so the rails weren't digging into my back, crossing my feet at the ankles.

I was getting comfortable. I'd sit here until Marley fell asleep. Until I *knew* she was feeling better.

Jenna stretched her legs out then too and sighed, tipping her head back. The corner of her mouth lifted. "I haven't sat on the floor in front of a crib in so long. I kinda miss this."

"I can see why. This is, without a doubt, the most fun I've had in years."

She playfully nudged my side.

"Do you think you want more kids?" I asked.

"I absolutely want more kids." Jenna peered over at me, and there was this glow on her face from the hallway light, but I swore she would've looked that way even without it. The way she spoke, how happy she sounded, it radiated from her. "What about you?"

"I don't know," I answered honestly. "I actually never thought about it."

"So, think about it now."

"How about you ask me on a night when I'm not on the verge of a heart attack, caring for my sick kid."

Jenna laughed quietly. "It's terrifying, isn't it?"

"What?"

"Loving someone this much."

I peered down at the top of Marley's head and pressed my lips there.

Jenna and I stayed quiet after that. We watched Marley, waiting for her to fall asleep. We occasionally watched each other. And when Jenna's eyes slipped closed, I watched her until I couldn't. Without meaning to, I passed out sometime after Marley dozed off. I realized this the next morning when something nudged my foot, and I opened my eyes to Oliver and Olivia standing over me, smiling.

Over us. Jenna was still asleep with her head on my shoulder.

chapter fifteen

JENNA

Nathan decided to stay home with Marley the next day in case she started feeling bad again, which freed up our Sunday evening, giving the kids and me the opportunity to attend family dinner at my brother's house.

It had been more than a month since we last went. Family dinners were always a good time, in terms of company and food. You never knew who was going to show up. Attendance varied week to week, depending on everyone's work schedules. Before I started watching Marley, my Sundays were always free, meaning the kids and I always showed up at Brian's for dinner. So our recent absences had stood out a little more than anyone else's.

"We were beginning to forget what you guys looked like," Syd teased from where she stood at the oven.

"Yeah, Jenna. Way to ditch us," Jamie added. He leaned back in his chair and smirked.

I peered around the table. Brian, Jamie, and Cole were already seated. Cole worked with my brother and Jamie at Wax.

"Okay, Cole hasn't been to one of these in months," I pointed out. "I don't hear you ragging on him."

"Throw me under the bus, why don't you," Cole mumbled, acting offended, but I knew him well enough to know he was joking around.

"I'm just saying," I returned. "Tori misses. She's missing tonight, along with Shay, Stitch, Kali, who I understand couldn't make it last minute. Still, she isn't here. Jamie, you miss when you have a meet."

"When I'm kickin' ass at a meet is what you meant to say."

Oliver and Olivia snickered from their seats.

I glared across the table. "Language. Don't make me stab you with my fork."

My brother slid my utensils closer to me. Everyone, aside from Jamie, started laughing.

"We're only kidding, Jenna." Syd walked over to the table, carrying a large casserole dish. Steam wafted into the air. "We just missed you guys, that's all." She placed the dish in the center of the table. Enchiladas, by the looks of it.

"That smells amazing," I said.

Syd grinned proudly, taking a seat beside my brother. "Thank you."

Conversation came to a halt while everyone dished out helpings onto their plates and refilled their drinks, resuming once we began to eat.

"We should invite Nate to these," Syd proposed. "Him and Marley. Problem solved. We'd all be together then."

I smiled at her suggestion. I wanted them included in this too.

"Nate's the best," Olivia announced. "Right, Ollie?"

My son nodded through his bite. "Yeah, he's real cool."

"We spent the night at his house yesterday."

Syd gasped. Coughing started in the general direction of my brother. My fork hovered in the air an inch away from my face.

"Oh, really?" Jamie asked, sounding more than pleased to be on the receiving end of this information.

Great. Here we go. "It was not...how it sounds," I began to

explain. "We fell asleep by accident." I brought the fork to my mouth and pulled off the bite.

"Aw. I love accidental sleepovers," Syd said.

"Marley got sick," I added. "I didn't want to leave until her fever went down."

"Oh no. I hope she's okay."

"She felt better this morning. No fever."

"That's good."

"Nate's couch is super comfy," Olivia shared, lips smacking as she chewed. "It's like a big, fluffy cloud. Too bad we can't all fit. That's why Mama and Nate had to sleep in Marley's room."

"Together?" Brian asked.

I quickly shook my head as Oliver spoke up.

"Yep. We found them this morning."

"Again, not how it sounds—we were sitting with Marley and we both fell asleep. Everyone remained vertical."

I looked down at my children's plates, grabbed the serving spoon, and gave them each another enchilada when they were both nearly finished with their first.

"Do you guys want more?" I asked, but I wasn't waiting for an answer. And too bad if they didn't. Maybe if they had another helping, they'd quit oversharing.

"What's vertical mean?" Olivia asked.

"Up and down," Syd answered.

"Oh." My daughter nodded as she processed that. "Well, Mama, your head wasn't up and down. Not really."

I quickly looked at her. "Olivia, yes, it was."

"No, it wasn't. It was sideways."

"That's called horizontal," Oliver said.

"Yeah, it was horizontal!" Olivia punched the air. "I knew that."

"Anyone else picturin' what I'm picturin'?" Jamie asked.

"Jen." Brian's gaze was serious.

Okay, really? Were they all concluding the same thing here?

"My head was on his shoulder—that's how I fell asleep," I said. "Seriously, you guys?" I scowled around the table. Then I looked between my kids. "Both of you, eat. No more talking."

Olivia sank in her chair and pushed around the food with her fork. "But I like talking," she mumbled. Oliver didn't seem to mind the order of silence. He was enjoying his meal too much. His cheeks were already stuffed full as he tried fitting in another bite.

"Slow down, please," I said.

He pulled the fork back and breathed loudly through his nose as he chewed.

"Let's talk about something else," I suggested. "Like you two." I gestured between Syd and my brother with my fork, asking, "When's the wedding?"

Sydney immediately grinned, threw her arms around Brian's neck, and yanked him closer so she could kiss his cheek. "Yes, Trouble. When?"

Brian fought a smile as he glared at me.

I was able to successfully divert all conversation until after the meal was over and my kids had moved away from the table. Once they fled into the other room to play with Sir, Syd's adorable boxer pup, I sat back in my chair and relaxed. I didn't have any issues talking about Nate. I just didn't want to do it in front of Oliver and Olivia. The threat of it stressed me out a little.

"Sleepovers, huh?" Jamie draped his arms over the empty chairs flanking him. Cole had left right after the meal. It was just us four, not counting the kids.

"*And* you're going out with Travis this weekend? I didn't peg you as the type to juggle multiple guys, Jenna."

I slid my gaze over to Syd, who knew all about my plans this weekend. Funny thing was, I had not shared them with anyone else sitting at this table. And Travis didn't seem the type to brag, so Jamie knowing all about my plans came from one person and one person only.

My future sister in-law didn't hide her guilt well. She immediately looked behind her and scanned the room, like she was forgetting to do something.

"Did I turn off the oven?" she asked.

I seriously needed to stop confiding in other women.

"That's not at all what I'm doing," I spoke up.

"Yeah, Jamie." Syd sat forward and narrowed her eyes down the table. "She can't do anything with Nate until the end of summer. In the meantime, Jenna's dating around. That's not juggling two guys."

"I wouldn't say I'm dating around. This weekend—"

"All this time you and the kids are spending with Nate," Brian cut in, turning my head. "You think that's a good idea?"

"What do you mean?" I asked.

"I mean, you're with the guy practically every day, Jen. Oliver and Liv are gettin' attached. Anyone can see that."

"Okay. And?"

"What happens when this doesn't work out?"

I felt my body melt against the wood. "*When* it doesn't work out...because it won't work out. That's what you're telling me—you know it won't?"

"Why would you say that?" Sydney asked him, dropping her voice lower.

Brian kept his gaze laser-focused on me. "I don't know it

J. DANIELS

won't, but I'm wonderin' if you're even considerin' the possibility of this thing not pannin' out. That guy has some serious baggage. What's gonna happen to the kids if you two fall apart? Do you think they won't be affected by that?"

"He's got a point," Jamie added.

I ignored King Gossip and stared down my brother. "The kids would be around Nathan whether or not we dated, Brian." Was he completely forgetting the fact that I babysat Marley? *What the hell?* "It's not like I'm putting ideas into their heads or sharing how much I like this guy. I haven't said anything even remotely close to that. And you act like I wouldn't be careful once Nathan and I got together. Of course I'd think about Oliver and Olivia. I'm always thinking about them. What's the matter with you?"

"I'm just lookin' out."

"Well, you don't need to," I snapped. "I have and will always consider my kids when it comes to anything involving me. I always put them first. And you know what? Even though you don't seem to care enough to ask, let me fill you in on something— Nathan is great with them. Amazing, actually. Oliver and Olivia are so happy when they get to spend time with him. You should see them together..." I paused to clear my throat when my voice began to quiver.

Shit. Why am I getting so worked up right now? Keep it together, Jenna.

"And me, Brian. I'm so happy when I'm with him."

I could feel tears threatening to build. Syd was already wiping underneath her eyes as Brian pushed from the table, apparently finished with this conversation.

Good, I thought. Jamie mimicked him and stood too.

"I'm not tryin' to upset you, Jen. I'm just makin' sure you're bein' smart."

I looked up at my brother. There was nothing left to say to

him. I'd spoken my piece, so after holding his gaze for a solid second, I let mine drift, peering into the other room, where Oliver and Olivia chased Sir around the furniture.

Brian sighed while Jamie mumbled something I couldn't hear and gave fuck-all about anyway. He'd side with his best friend on this one. On anything. The two of them left the room.

"I'm sorry. I love him, but this is a total pot/kettle situation."

I turned back to Syd after she spoke. "A *what?*"

"He's pot, you're kettle, or reverse that. Whatever." She swiped her hand through the air. "He's being a hypocrite. Brian wants you to take it slow and be careful, but we basically fell in love over the phone before we even met each other, and when we *did meet*, he bought me a house practically the next day."

I laughed against my lips.

"I get him looking out for you, Jenna, but he needs to relax. Everyone takes a risk when they enter a relationship. Your heart is on the line. Or in your case, three hearts. What's that saying, you gotta play to win?"

"I think that refers to the lottery though."

"It refers to anything I want it to refer to," she countered. "And I'm full of wisdom, unlike your brother today. Don't listen to him."

I shook my head. "I'm not. He's talking like I'm already moving forward with Nathan. Did I blink and miss the rest of summer? Is it September already?"

God, I wish.

Sydney sat back in her chair. "He needs to let you do you and keep his mind on other things, like our wedding. Did you know my divorce is final in three weeks?"

I smiled. "I can't wait until you're a Savage."

The grin that took up Sydney's face...It didn't matter how pissed off I'd been at my brother. He had to see this.

"Brian!" I hollered.

"What?"

"Come here and look at your girl!"

Brian moved back into the kitchen, his gaze sliding from me to Syd. I watched a smile light him up.

"What's on your mind, Wild?"

Brian called Sydney Wild, giving her that nickname before they'd even met face-to-face.

"Just thinking about marrying you," she responded with a cute little head tilt. "Wanna think about it with me?"

My brother answered by moving at Syd and wasting zero time doing it. I swore he crossed the room before she even got out her question.

Brian bent down and held Sydney's face as he kissed her, and as I watched Syd get lifted into the air, her legs being guided around Brian's waist and her arms sliding around his neck, both of them smiling at each other between kisses, I thought about how amazing it would be to one day have someone do the same to me at family dinner.

I wanted someone to watch me, to watch us—me and one person in particular. I wanted someone to think, "I want that too," just like I was doing now.

* * *

By the time we got home that night, it was already after nine.

I got the kids put to bed after showers and a bedtime snack. When I turned off the lights and headed to my room, my phone began to ring. I stepped up to my nightstand and looked down at the device. Brian was calling me.

I wanted to ignore it. I didn't feel like getting into another discussion, because I knew Brian wasn't simply calling to say good night or to admit he'd overreacted. I knew the latter for certain.

My hand froze in the air an inch above the phone. *Come on, Jenna. Don't answer it.*

I wanted to relax. I was tired. I had several episodes of *Claws* recorded, a show I always laughed at. And I needed that. I wanted to veg out and have some me time.

When was the last time I'd done that? I couldn't remember.

The call went to voice mail when I didn't answer. And just like that, I was immediately flooded with guilt. The weight of it covered me like a cloak. I grunted at the ceiling.

I always answered when people called me, if I had the ability *to* answer. Was it wrong to want to turn off my phone and keep it off for the night? Or to at least silence it? I'd never turn it off completely. What if there was an emergency? God, what if Marley got sick again...?

No, I needed to be able to receive texts for that very reason, and if I turned off my phone, I couldn't do that.

Sometimes I missed living with my parents. I felt like I needed permission not to call Brian back and instead take some time to myself. How ridiculous was that?

I unplugged my phone from the charger and carried it into the living room.

I already had Brian's contact information pulled up and was a second away from calling him back, but my thoughts had drifted to Marley and were staying there. I hadn't checked on her since this morning. I wanted to make sure she was still feeling okay.

And maybe get a little help from Nathan, since taking a night off seemed to be something I couldn't do on my own.

Smiling, I collapsed onto the couch and dialed him up instead.

He answered on the second ring. "What are you doing, Shorty?" His voice was low and smooth. He was clearly smiling.

I closed my eyes and pictured it.

"Nothing," I said, knees drawn up. "Well, I want to be doing nothing, which I'll get to in a minute. Tell me how Marley is doing first." I looked down at my toes, at the plum-colored polish chipping off.

Mm. Another "me" thing I could absolutely get into tonight.

"She's good. No fever all day. I checked it every hour."

I bit the inside of my cheek. *Oh, Nathan.* "You were on it."

"Made that virus my bitch."

My head hit the back of the couch as I chuckled, hand to my mouth.

"You laugh so fucking pretty. I love listening to you."

I felt my face flush. "Thank you. I love laughing."

"Now what's this 'you want to be doing nothing,' shit? What's keeping you from doing nothing?"

"Me."

Nathan was silent for a long moment. "Okay."

He sounded completely perplexed. As well he should. I couldn't let myself do nothing? I was absurd.

"You see, my brother called and I didn't pick up because I just don't want to get roped into this long, drawn-out conversation right now. I just want to sit on my couch and watch episodes of *Claws*, possibly paint my nails—actually, not possibly. I really want to do that. They look bad—maybe snack a little, drink some wine...I don't know. Whatever. I just want to do whatever I want or nothing. Maybe just sit here and stare off until I fall asleep. But I feel guilty for not answering him and I'm having difficulty not feeling that way. It's bothering me. I'm very bothered right now, Nathan."

"I can tell."

"And you said to reach out to you if I ever found myself in a situation I couldn't handle on my own...I thought maybe you could help me with this. Tell me I can avoid everyone and everything tonight, except in cases of emergencies, of course. I'd never ignore someone if they truly needed me."

"You couldn't. That's not you."

"It's why I carry a spare phone charger with me at all times. You never know when the one might stop working, and then what if my phone dies? I can't risk that."

His laugh was quiet and sweet. "I am not at all surprised that you carry a backup phone charger."

"What's the point of having a big purse if I'm not stuffing that thing full, am I right?"

"I wouldn't know anything about that, but yeah, sure."

I heard movement through the phone. Quiet shuffling, the squeak of a mattress. Nathan was in bed. *Yum.*

"Just getting into position here," he shared. "Hold on, okay?"

"Take your time."

"No, Jenna." Nathan's tone grew harsh and demanding. "Don't tell me to *take my time.* Don't wait for me. This is something you need, right?"

"Yes."

"So tell me to hurry the fuck up with it."

"Uh." *What?* "O-okay..." I sat up a little taller. *This was odd, but what the hell?* "Move your ass, Nathan. Jesus."

"I'm just getting comfortable first."

"Why do you need to get comfortable to help me? Why is this

about you? I should be the one getting comfortable...Yes, I absolutely should. Let me do that."

I stood from the couch and moved into the kitchen, grabbing supplies, which included an already open bottle of wine and a bag of barbecue Lay's. Then I hurried to the bathroom to grab the little basket containing nail polish, remover, and cotton balls. With my arms full and the phone pinched between my ear and shoulder, I returned to the couch.

"Okay, I'm comfortable now," I said, popping the cork and taking a generous swig of wine straight out of the bottle. It was sweet and bubbled against my lips. When Nathan remained silent, I pressed him with a harsh, "*I'm waiting...*" I instantly regretted it. "Sorry...This is weird for me. I don't talk like this." I set the bottle on the coffee table and slumped against the back cushion. "I feel like I'm being mean."

"You're not being mean. This isn't about me. It's about you. Don't ever be afraid to take what you need."

"Okay, I won't, but...telling you to *move your ass*? That's not me, Nathan. I want you to do this for me, but I can wait five seconds while you fluff your pillow."

"That's not the point," he returned quickly. "Of course you'd wait five seconds if I asked you to—that's who you are, Jenna. You put everyone else first, no matter what. I'm not saying that's a bad thing. It's incredible, actually. I've never met anyone like you. I know you're not the kind of person to demand I stop everything I'm doing to help you out. I know telling me to *move my ass* isn't something you'd ever say unless I provoked you. That's not who you are. And that's okay, as long as you're doing what you want."

"So, that was a test..."

"If you want to look at it that way. I pushed you just now

because I wanted you to see that even if you told me to *move my ass*, you wouldn't be wrong saying it and you sure as hell wouldn't need to apologize. You're not hurting me. Does that make sense?"

"I think so."

"I realize I'm being extreme, and I know there are ways to get what you need without cussing someone out, but if you needed to yell at me or call me out for making you wait for something *you needed*, you're allowed to do that. This isn't about me. What do you want to do right now?"

"I want to watch TV and paint my nails." My teeth scraped along my bottom lip. "And... and I don't want to feel bad about not answering my brother."

"You don't owe anyone anything," Nathan said. "Was he calling because he's in the middle of an emergency?"

"I don't think so. He didn't leave a message."

"And if there were an emergency he probably would've, or he'd at least call back if it were something important, right?"

"Right."

"So why do you feel bad right now? You're not letting him down."

I dropped my head back and blinked at the ceiling. *I am not letting him down. I am not letting anyone down tonight.*

"I guess when I look at it that way, I'm not sure why I feel bad," I replied. A smile pulled at my mouth. "So I don't. I don't feel bad anymore. I'll call him back tomorrow."

"And what are you going to do tonight?"

"Exactly what I want to do." I sat forward, snagging the remote and the bag of chips off the coffee table. I cued up *Claws*, popping a chip in my mouth. Then I pulled the basket of polish into my lap. "You're good at this. I'm really glad I called you."

"I'm glad I could help."

"What about you? What do you need tonight?"

"*Jenna.*" Nathan sighed, laughing a little. "Jesus Christ! You can't stop yourself, can you?"

I chewed up another chip. "What?"

"This is not about *me.*"

"I'm not saying I'm going to help you!" I countered, giggling. "Awfully full of yourself, aren't we? *God...*"

Nathan's chuckle was soft in my ear.

"I was just curious. What do you need, Nathan?"

"Right now?"

"Right now."

He thought for a long moment. "Nothing."

chapter sixteen

NATHAN

Four Days Later

Marley came rushing at me from the kitchen the second I stepped inside the house. "Daddy! Daddy!"

I scooped her up and tickled her. She squealed against my neck, twisting her little body in my arms, but not pushing away. She loved being tickled. "How's my girl doing?" I asked, closing the door behind me.

"Daddy, pway?"

"What did you play today, baby?"

"Daddy, go side?"

"You went outside?"

"She's saying slide," Olivia said, popping her head up from behind the couch. Her braids were messy. "We went to the playground after lunch. It was *epic*."

I chuckled. "Did you have fun on the slide?" I kissed Marley's smiling cheek as she nodded, her fingers holding tight to my neck. Then I peered into the kitchen.

Jenna was standing at the counter talking on the phone. She was already smiling, but when our eyes locked, I swore it felt like I was the reason for it. The way she looked at me lately...

I wondered if it was how I looked at her.

I lifted my hand, greeting her. Then I rounded the couch and took a seat beside Olivia. I peered over at Oliver. "What's up, O? How was Scouts?"

Oliver was reclining on the love seat in his uniform, head on one end and bare feet on the other.

"Dumb," he mumbled, eyes glued to his DS screen.

"Really?" I thought he liked it.

"All we did was go over stuff happening at the campout. That's it."

I thought about last month—Oliver crying, how upset he was over this, followed by my conversation with Jenna outside on the deck. I decided not to pry any further.

"If you ever want to talk about it, I'm here, all right?"

He glanced over at me and nodded, looking like that meant something to him, hearing that from me. Then he got back to his game.

Marley knelt in my lap and grabbed the stuffed turtle beside my hip. She spoke softly to it and studied its legs sticking out of the shell.

"My mom's date is tomorrow night," Olivia said, keeping her voice quiet.

"Oh yeah?"

She looked up from her iPad and grinned. "Yep. And we get to have a sleepover at Uncle Brian's house. We haven't done that in forever."

My smile was so fucking forced right now, but I couldn't not smile at her. Shit, I smiled the other night when Olivia told me all about this date. She was excited about it then. As soon as I walked in the door, Olivia shared the news.

She was speaking fast and jumping around, grabbing on to me so I'd stand beside her and listen. She told me how much her mom loved dates, all kinds of dates, because all girls did, and how Jenna never got to go on them but when she did get to go on them, "You should see how happy she is, Nate, and how pretty she looks. She dresses up and does her hair all wavylike with accessories, and her makeup is so super fancy. You should see her. I can't wait for her to go on another one! You want her to go too, right, Nate? Don't you want her to go?"

What the hell was I supposed to say to that? Olivia was impossible to disappoint. If I made her sad by answering how I wanted to answer, I'd hate myself for it. I knew I would. So I lied, telling Olivia I wanted her mom going. That I couldn't wait either.

You should see how happy she is, Nate.

Fuck. And this shit was happening tomorrow.

I steadied Marley when she stood on my thighs. Then I looked over at Jenna. She was still smiling, listening to whoever she was on the phone with.

Shit, was it him? That motherfucking "family friend"?

"O'ver! O'ver!" Marley squirmed out of my hold. She climbed down and hurried over to the love seat with her turtle. Then she stood next to Oliver's shoulder and watched his screen.

I heard a rustling sound and looked beside me.

Olivia pulled that same notepad she was always bringing over out of her duffle. She shoved her iPad away, dropping her bag on the floor. Then she clicked a pen open and steadied it on a blank page, eyes finding mine and mouth opening, readying to fire a million questions at me.

She did this a lot. And I never had any issues answering her. Olivia's questions were harmless. It was more about my opinion on things, not anything personal. The questions were typically random too, jumping from topic to topic. Although, I had a pretty good idea what the theme was going to be tonight.

"Do you like going out on dates, Nate?"

I threw my arm behind her and rested it on the back of the couch. "Sure. Who doesn't like dates?"

"What kind of dates do you like?"

"Dinner. Maybe a movie. It depends."

She nodded thoughtfully and scribbled down her notes.

I kept my eyes from straining to the page. I figured if Olivia wanted me knowing what all she wrote down about me, she'd eventually share it.

"Depends on what the girl wants, right?" she asked. "My uncle Brian says boys should always do whatever the girl wants to do, even if they don't like it."

"That's true, they should." When she looked up at me, I asked, "What about your mom? What kind of dates does she like?" Might as well use this Q&A to my advantage. I could always store this information for later.

Olivia's eyes lit up. She pushed her glasses up her nose. "Oh, like, all kinds. She loves going out to dinner. But she doesn't like going to the movies."

"No?"

"No. She thinks they're gross. Everyone puts their heads on the seats and they might have lice. You could catch it."

I snorted. "Well, I think the risk of that happening is pretty slim."

"It happened to Oliver." Olivia nodded slowly when my eyes flickered wider. "We were six. Mom swears he got it from the movie theater. We had to wash *everything*. And she made us all put that special shampoo on our heads, not just Oliver. I had to do it too." She glanced down at the page. "Did you ever get lice when you were a little kid?"

"No." I gestured at the notepad as she scribbled my answer. "I don't currently have it either, if you'd like to make a note of that as well."

"I'm just going to put *no*, if that's okay."

"I guess that's fine."

"I think it is." Olivia finished writing and peered up at me. "Um, my mom..." She paused, thinking over her next words. Then she scooted closer on the cushion until she was pressed up against me. Her voice softened to a whisper. "My mom said Marley's mom died. So...who do you go out on dates with now?"

"Nobody."

"Oh." Her eyes filled with sadness.

I didn't want this upsetting her. We always had a good time doing this. She'd ask questions. I'd answer them. She'd always smile. I wanted Olivia smiling now. And, obviously, I'd do a lot to keep this girl happy. Like tell her how excited I was about some guy taking her mother out.

"How about we go out sometime?" I proposed, thinking Olivia might like that idea. "You can be my date."

She quickly nodded her head. She was back to grinning now. "Okay! We can go to the movies. That's where I'd want to go."

"Really? You're not afraid to get lice?"

"Nope. I like bugs."

I chuckled. When Marley moved down the couch again and tried climbing into my lap, I picked her up. She stood on my thighs and bounced her turtle in the air.

"Marley can go with us," Olivia suggested sweetly.

"Yeah?" I looked at my daughter. "Just me and my girls— what do you think, sweetheart? You in?"

Marley tossed her turtle at my face. She squealed when I pulled her closer.

"I'm not sure how to take that," I grumbled, kissing her cheek. I felt Olivia scoot away from me, and when I turned to look at her, she had her back pressed against the arm of the couch so she was sitting sideways now, her legs stretched out between us and her toes digging into my leg. She frantically flipped through the pages of her notepad, settled on one and smiled when she found it. Then she quickly jotted something down.

When she peered up at me, I narrowed my eyes and asked, "What are you writing?"

"Nothing!" she shrieked, flattening the notepad against her stomach.

She broke into laughter when I wrapped my hand around her knee and gently tugged her closer. I squeezed her side until she twisted and squealed. Marley crawled over her, the two of them giggling. It was really fucking cute.

"I'm going to go talk to your mom," I said, standing from the couch.

"Okay." Olivia closed her notepad and swapped it out for her iPad again. She climbed on the cushion beside Marley.

"Sit with Olivia, sweetheart," I said, kissing Marley's head.

I padded across the room and moved into the kitchen, heading for the fridge. Jenna was still on the phone. I grabbed a bottled water out of the door, twisted the cap off, and took a drink. When Jenna glanced over at me, I gestured, offering her a beverage.

She shook her head, a soft smile lifting her mouth, then spoke into the phone. "Okay, sounds good. I will. Love you too." She disconnected the call and set her phone on the counter. "Hey. Sorry. It was my parents."

"Do they ever try to get you to go back to Denver?" I asked, moving to stand across from her.

216

Jenna was wearing the yellow top she wore that first day in my office. She looked good in yellow. *She looks good in everything.* Her hair fell in a braid in front of her shoulder.

"Not really," she said. "I think they know they couldn't convince me even if they tried. I like it here too much."

"That's a relief."

"Oh, I'm sure you'd have no issues finding someone to watch Marley for you if you needed it."

"I'd hope not, but I'm not talking about that." I watched her above the bottle as I took another drink. A flush colored her cheeks. "So, this date—Olivia said it's happening tomorrow..."

"Yep."

"Where's he taking you?"

"I don't know yet. I just know he's picking me up at six. I didn't ask where we were going."

"And the kids are staying over at your brother's house for the night."

I squeezed the back of my neck, wincing through a head roll. I was tense as fuck just thinking about that. Jenna could go home with this guy. Maybe she'd invite him back to her place. There was no reason why this date couldn't last all night.

"Are you okay?" she asked, watching me carefully.

"Yeah, I'm fine." I dropped my arm.

"Are you sure? You seem...stressed."

"Why would I be stressed? I'm just tired," I lied. "Long day."

"What are your plans tomorrow? Are you and Marley doing anything?"

I glanced into the family room when my daughter laughed at something Olivia was doing. "Just going over to my parents' house," I said. "They haven't seen her in a while. She's spending the weekend with them."

217

"That'll be nice." Jenna smiled when our eyes met. "So you'll have some time to yourself."

"Looks like it."

"Mm. Maybe *you* should go out on a date."

My brows lifted. I watched the smile pull from Jenna's mouth and her hands slide off the counter. Her reaction was immediate, like she hadn't even considered her words until she heard them herself.

"I don't know why I said that," she rushed out. "I mean, you could if you wanted to...obviously. She better not try anything though." Jenna narrowed her eyes playfully.

Speaking of that...

"He better not try anything either."

"Travis?"

"If that's his name, yeah."

"Like what? What would he try?"

"Something you don't want." I set the bottle on the counter and flattened my hands on the granite. "You know you don't have to do anything with this guy, Jenna. There's no obligation here. You could eat and leave, and he better be grateful for that. If he tries anything you don't want to do—"

"Nathan," she cut me off before a threat slipped out of my mouth. Her pretty green eyes jumped between mine. "I know. And he wouldn't do that."

I pushed breath in and out of my nose. My chest was heaving now. *Get it together, Nathan. Jesus.* What the fuck was wrong with me?

I was jealous, and I had zero fucking right to react this way. Waiting the two months wasn't solely Jenna's idea—I'd agreed to it. Hell, I'd told her it was probably for the best. I didn't know if I was ready to start something with Jenna, and until I was, we couldn't go beyond friendship.

She deserved to go out and enjoy a nice time. And I couldn't say shit about it. I needed to back off.

"Sorry." I held her eyes. "Like I said—I'm just tired."

Jenna nodded like she was buying my excuse.

I walked them to the door after paying Jenna for the day. She gave Marley a kiss and told me she'd see me next week.

I wanted to see her tomorrow. I almost told her not to go through with this date.

I held Marley on the porch and watched the car drive down the street and disappear over the hill. Then I closed the door and dropped my head against it.

* * *

It was a little after eight thirty when I left my parents' house Friday night.

Even though Marley was excited to spend the night with her grandparents, I almost changed my mind and drove all the way back over there to get her. Marley was my only distraction. I knew there would be nothing stopping me from pacing my entire fucking house the rest of the night.

Jenna was two and a half hours into her date, which was no time at all if she was planning on spending the entire night with this guy.

I began to dissect her evening as I drove. I thought about everything—from where he'd taken her to what she wore. I was certain she looked incredible, and there was no way he wouldn't be into her. The only way this prick was staying friend-zoned was if she forced it or if one of them backed out of this thing at the last minute.

I began to consider that possibility. I turned it over in my mind. It became an obsession. *What if Jenna never went through with this date?*

Reaching out with a text would be an easy way to get the answer I was suddenly desperate for. And we *were* friends...I could simply be checking in.

At the next red light, I palmed my phone and typed out the message.

How's the date going?

My thumb hovered over the screen. *What the fuck am I doing?* I deleted the text and tossed my phone on the passenger seat.

Any way I tried to spin this, sending that text made me a douche bag. I wouldn't be checking in for friendly reasons. Fuck that. There was nothing friendly about what I wanted with Jenna. I needed to leave her alone tonight.

The light turned green, and I sped through the intersection.

chapter seventeen

JENNA

I don't know how you do it," I said, looking over at Travis as he drove. "I can barely handle it when my children get a scrape. I can't imagine operating on someone."

"Well, these aren't my kids I'm operating on. Besides, I started pretty young. I used to cut animals open when I was little."

"What?"

He smiled over at me. "Tell me you don't believe that..."

"I thought you were serious!" I laughed, dropping my head against the seat. "Our family dog went missing when I was seven. I was beginning to panic."

Travis chuckled as he pulled off the main road and into the parking lot surrounding my apartment complex. It was nearly eleven, though it didn't feel that late. I'd had a nice evening with Travis. He was easy to talk to, we got along well, and the restaurant had great food and an incredible view of the bay. Our evening flew by.

"Thanks again for tonight. I had a nice time," I said as he pulled into a space in front of my building.

"Yeah, me too. It was fun." He shifted into park and peered through the windshield. The corner of his eye crinkled. "Unless men typically sit out here waiting for you, I'm assuming that's the guy?"

"Huh?" I looked away from Travis and followed his gaze. My back straightened away from the seat.

Oh my God.

Nathan was seated on the steps leading to my apartment, hunched forward with his elbows resting on his knees and his hands clasped together. He was staring directly at us.

My breaths grew quicker. What was he doing here? I thought, but immediately wondered if I already knew the answer. In my heart I hoped I did.

"Um, yeah, that's him," I said, offering Travis a gentle smile he returned without hesitation.

He knew. I'd shared everything with Travis during the phone call when I accepted his invitation out tonight. It was one thing to take him up on an offer to hang out, but it was another thing entirely to lead him on.

Even though I'd originally wanted to go out with him, my heart wasn't in dating other people right now. Going out on the actual date hadn't changed my feelings either. I really did like Travis, but I knew I couldn't give him anything more. We'd agreed to go out as friends.

"I can still walk you to your door," he offered.

God, what a great guy. Some lucky woman was going to land herself a freaking catch with this one.

"That's okay. Thank you though." I reached out and squeezed his arm. "Good night."

"Good night, Jenna."

I opened the car door and stepped out, walking toward my building. My heels clicked against the pavement.

Nathan remained seated on the step, watching Travis's car as it pulled out of the parking lot. Then he turned his head and looked at me.

His dark eyes were serious and studied me as I approached, but his brows were relaxed. He wasn't clenching his jaw. His mouth wasn't tight. His shoulders weren't tense. I was anticipating one version of Nathan and staring at another. He looked almost embarrassed to be here, and in the same breath, relieved to see me.

I stopped right in front of him.

"I didn't know if you'd come home or not," he said.

"How long would you have waited here if I didn't?"

Nathan sat up a little and shook his head. The corner of his mouth twitched. Maybe he didn't want me knowing that answer. Maybe he didn't want to admit it to himself.

I reached for his hand as I climbed the steps. "Come on."

Nathan pushed to his feet. Our palms slid together, and we held on with equal pressure as we walked side by side up the five flights of stairs.

"How was your date?" he asked while I unlocked the door.

I pushed it open, stepped inside, and secured it behind us. I turned to him after I flicked on the lights and dropped my purse on the small table along the wall.

"Did you really come over here to ask me about my date, Nathan?"

Instead of answering, he slowly trailed his eyes down my body and back up, as if he were just now noticing what I was wearing. The baby-blue dress I'd chosen for tonight cinched at my waist and flared out around my thighs. It was strapless and light. The perfect summer dress.

"You're taller," Nathan observed.

I glanced down at my four-inch sandals. "Well, this guy I know likes to joke about how short I am. He even gave me a nickname for it." I peered up at him. "Because of that, I'm a little self-conscious about my height."

223

Nathan's eyes grew wider behind his glasses. "I hope you're joking. I never meant any of that as an insult."

"I know you didn't. And I am kidding. I like wearing heels."

"You look beautiful." His gaze moved all over me. "I thought I'd be prepared for this—Olivia warned me about how you dress up for dates, wear your makeup 'all fancy,' I believe were her words. And something about hair accessories…"

I smiled and ran my finger along the jeweled pin beside my temple. "She hooks me up. I'm pretty sure my daughter owns every hair accessory ever invented."

"All night, sitting out there, I've tried to picture this." Nathan shook his head, as if he were in a daze.

"Is that why you're here? So you could see what I looked like tonight?"

"I think you know why I'm here."

"And I think I'm going to need to hear you say it."

Nathan stood taller. His shoulders lifted as he pulled in a deep breath. "I can't stop thinking about you."

I approached him slowly. A difficult task when I wanted to run at him.

"I can't stop thinking about you either," I said, stopping when our shoes nearly touched. "I know this whole waiting thing was my idea, but you also said we should stop. You said it was for the best. And then when I told you about this date and wanted you to give me a reason why I shouldn't go through with it, you said there wasn't one."

"I have no right to tell you not to go out on dates, Jenna."

"But you can't stop thinking about me," I argued. "And you're here right now."

"I know."

"You had a reason to give me. Why didn't you just say it?"

"I couldn't," he said, sounding frustrated now. I could hear the sharp breaths leaving him. "I want you to be happy. You love dates. You get excited about them—Olivia told me you do. And I was still trying to work through how I feel...I didn't know if I was ready for this. And it's not just because you're the first woman I've wanted to be with since Sadie died. I'm not just talking about being attracted to you and wanting you physically. Jenna, I know what this could become. I wasn't sure I could do it yet. And if I wasn't sure, I couldn't tell you not to go through with this date. I couldn't tell you how it made me feel when I found out your kids were staying with your brother all night. I couldn't say shit about any of it."

"Are you still trying to work through it?"

"No." He reached out and gently held my waist, drifting closer but stopping before any other part of him touched any other part of me. "I wouldn't be here if I were."

I flattened my hands to his chest. His heart pounded against my palm. "It's a good thing I came home, then."

"I'm glad you did, but I would've waited out there all night—you have to know that."

Now my heart was pounding.

"Look, I don't really want to ask about your date, but I'm not going to lie to you—I need to know if you hit it off with this guy." His fingers tensed on my back. "If you're into him...or if you're not sure yet but you want to find out, tell me."

The worry in his voice was so honest and raw, it tore at me. "I went out with Travis as a friend. I'm not interested in anything more with him."

Nathan frowned instantly. "That was a friend date?"

"Yes."

"Is that why he didn't walk you to the door? Because he fucking should've."

I studied his eyes and the crease in his brow. "That really bothers you, doesn't it?"

"The way someone treats you? If they don't do it right—yes, it bothers me."

"Travis offered to walk me to my door. I told him not to."

"Why?"

"There was this guy sitting outside. You might've seen him. Glasses. Totally my type. Only thing missing was a backward hat. I'm such a sucker for those." I slid my arms around his neck and molded to his front. There was nothing but breath between us now. "If I had a choice, I wanted him walking me to my door tonight. Not Travis."

"What are you doing?" Nathan peered down between us, at our bodies pressing together. "What about the whole money issue?"

"You technically touched me first."

"I also kept space between us for a reason." His eyes lifted and locked onto mine. "Jenna, I can't wait and do *this* with you. I can't feel you again and then…"

"Maybe we shouldn't wait. Is it really what either of us wants?"

"Well, *I* sure as hell don't want it."

"Don't pay me, Nathan."

"Jenna." He sighed and shook his head. "You know how I feel about that…"

"Please don't pay me. *Please*," I begged, voice dropping to a whisper. I sounded desperate all of a sudden because I was. "You pay people who do a job for you, but Marley has never been a job to me," I explained. "I *want* to be around her, and on the days I'm not, I miss her, Nathan. I miss her like I miss my own kids. Being with her never feels like something I have to do. It's something I *want* to do. Don't pay me anymore. I don't want your money."

"I take so much from you. Your free time. Weekends...You should be spending them with your own kids, doing whatever you want."

"You haven't taken anything from me. I give it, Nathan. I could tell you no. You realize that, right? When you ask me to watch Marley—I have a choice. I *choose* to be with her. You're not taking anything from me when it comes to Marley. I love her."

His breathing paused.

"I really do. You don't see it?"

Nathan's eyes closed briefly in bliss when my fingers pushed through the hair at the base of his neck.

"I see you with her, how you've always been with her." He opened his eyes and looked at me then. "I didn't know that's what I was seeing. I should've though."

"I want to be around her as much as I can. She's impossible not to love."

He watched me, saying nothing for seconds that felt more like minutes.

"Please," I whispered. "Nathan..."

"I need to make sure I'm giving you something, Jenna. I can't ever have you feel like I'm using you."

"You do give me something. Do you have any idea how happy I am when I'm with you? I've dreamed of feeling this way my entire life."

His lips slowly parted.

"Oliver and Olivia too...They love being around you. And the fact that you spend time with them and make them feel important means more than anything you could ever give me."

Nathan stared deep into my eyes, pulling in a full breath before he responded. "Okay."

My heart squeezed. "Okay...like, *okay*, okay? You won't pay me anymore?"

"Not unless you tell me I need to."

"I'd never do that." I smiled up at him. My stomach was flipping around like crazy now. "Oh my God, *finally*."

"Why did we say we should wait again?"

"Seriously. Worst idea ever."

He chuckled, pressing the softest kiss to my forehead.

"I'm so glad you're here," I said, staring into his deep brown eyes. "Thank you for coming over and waiting for me."

"You say that like I had a choice. I assure you, I didn't."

"Choice or no choice, that meant a lot, Nathan. I was so happy to see you when we pulled up."

"Not as happy as I was to see you...trust me."

I smiled as his arms wrapped me up. My chin rested on his chest. Even in heels, I felt so small in his embrace.

"So," he said in this sexy, teasing way.

God, he was killing me.

"So."

"No kids, huh?"

"We have my entire apartment to ourselves." I leaned away and arched my brow.

"Mm. What to do..."

"Want a tour?"

"Of your bed? Absolutely."

I grinned.

Nathan glanced around behind him. "Or the couch. I'd love a tour of the couch. I'm also dying to see the kitchen." He turned his head and smirked. "Would you like to show me your counter space?"

Giggling, I stepped back and grabbed his hand. "Bed first." I started backing down the hallway, pulling him along, until Nathan stopped, grabbed me by the waist, and spun me around. His touch left my body. "What are you doing?" I asked, peering behind me. There was a foot between us.

His gaze lowered and locked on. "Sorry. I just really want to stare at your ass right now. You have such a hot ass."

My face heated.

"Could you...walk a little?"

I knew exactly what I looked like from behind in this dress. What girl doesn't do the look around in the mirror before leaving the house?

Knowing Nathan was watching me so intently right now didn't cause me to hesitate. I continued the walk down the hallway, nearly making it to my bedroom door before strong arms wrapped around me again. I gasped. Nathan pulled me against his chest and got us the rest of the way into the bedroom, his legs pushing mine to move.

"Good?" I asked, eyes closing when I felt his hot mouth on my shoulder.

"Do you really need me to answer that?" With his palm flat on my stomach, Nathan held me still while he ground his arousal against my hip. His other hand swept my hair over my shoulder, and he kissed his way to my tattoo. His mouth opened around it. "Fuck, this is sexy. Tell me about it."

I bit my lip when his fingers worked the zipper of my dress down my back.

"I got it after my kids were born. I wanted something to symbolize this significant change in my life...I think I became the person I was always meant to be after I had them."

My dress hit the floor. Nathan unclasped my bra and let that

229

drop as well. Then he cupped my breasts, lifting their weight and playing with my nipples.

I groaned, reaching back, and clutched at his body, digging my fingers into his ass. My head hit his chest. I was panting. "Can you get undressed, please?"

"Must I do everything? I'm a little busy."

I spun around, eager to get to work on his clothing removal when Nathan gave me a gentle push, sending me falling backward onto the bed. "Nathan!" I laughed, propping my weight on my elbows. "I was going to strip you."

"You can still strip me. I just want to play with you a little." He stepped between my legs, ran his hands up my thighs, and slipped his fingers under the string of my thong. "I barely ate your pussy the other night."

"Glad to see that bothered you as much as it bothered me."

A grin took up his face. "You're so fun...Does everyone tell you that? I laugh so much with you."

I smiled. *Wow. What a compliment.* "Ditto."

Nathan pulled off his shirt and tossed it onto the floor while I slipped off my heels. He resituated his glasses, then bent down and sucked my nipple into his mouth.

"Oh God." I arched away from the mattress and moaned.

"Turn over," he said, licking my other breast.

I held his head against me, fingers sliding through his thick hair. "What? No way."

"On your knees, shorty."

"You're staying right here." I gasped at the pressure of his mouth. God, I loved the way he sucked on me.

I felt Nathan grin. "I want to lick you from behind. Let me."

Looking down my body, our eyes met. "I've never done that before."

"Do you not want me to?"

"No, I do! I do...don't you?"

He cocked his head, forcing my hands to slide through his hair.

"Right. Obviously." I released his head and sat up, scooting back a little on the bed. My skin tingled all over. "I don't know why I'm nervous about it. I mean, I'm not *nervous* nervous...I just don't want you to not enjoy yourself. Sorry. Am I making this weird?"

Nathan smirked. "I'm not sure yet. Why wouldn't I enjoy myself?"

"Well, you're going to be right at my ass..."

"I know exactly where I'm going to be."

We stared at each other.

"Jenna."

"Mm?"

"There isn't a part of your body I'm not going to *enjoy myself* with, okay?"

I forced myself to relax and nodded quickly. "Okay. Sure."

Nathan smiled then and reached down to adjust himself through his shorts. "Will you get on your knees for me now?"

My eyes lowered. I stared at the outline of his dick.

I wanted what Nathan was offering to do to me, but I wanted something else too, maybe even a little more.

I slowly looked up and met his eyes again as I slid off the bed. "You're asking me so nicely, how could I not?"

I think he knew what I was planning before my knees hit the carpet. Maybe Nathan heard it in my voice. Maybe he could tell by the way I watched him.

Did I look hungry for it? I felt like I did. I'd never wanted to suck someone off so badly before. What did he taste like? How would he feel inside my mouth? I couldn't wait to find out.

Nathan was already shaking his head when I glanced up at him, but he didn't stop my hands as I slid his shorts and boxers down just enough to free his dick.

"This isn't what I meant," he said, mouth dropping open when I licked the crown, just a tease.

"So stop me."

He moaned and pushed my hair out of my face. "I can't."

God, I felt powerful doing this to him. He couldn't stop me...I couldn't stop myself. I held him at the base and sucked on the head. I took him as deep as I could.

Nathan watched my mouth move over his dick. His gaze was electric. His thumb caught a drop of saliva as it dribbled down my chin. "Fuck, look at you. Do you like that?" he asked, sounding breathless.

I smiled around him and pumped his shaft. I licked him from base to tip, swirled my tongue there and sucked him inside again. My lips hit my hand each time. I wanted to take all of him. I tried and gagged, coaxing the filthiest noises out of Nathan when he'd hit the back of my throat. My eyes watered. My lips burned as they stretched. I kept going.

"You're so good," he groaned. "Fuck...Jenna, let me...Is this okay?" He pushed his hips forward in little jerks. He was gentle and studied me so carefully while he did it. "Tell me I can do this," he begged.

I nodded. God, he was so big. He was throbbing now.

"*Good,*" he gasped. He pumped into me.

The muscles in his abs flexed and quivered. The veins in his arms bulged. I wanted to stare at his body, but his face—he looked wrecked. Nathan watched my mouth as if he'd never seen anything like it before. How he could make me feel cherished in this position was beyond me, but I did. I would've let him use me to get off for hours. I wanted to suck him dry.

Nathan cursed and pulled back, falling from my mouth, stopping this before he came. Saliva dripped off the end of his cock. He gathered a shaky breath and collected my spit in his hand, stroking himself with it as he helped me to my feet.

"Knees on the bed," he said against my ear.

I turned my head and gave him a shy smile. "You weren't specific before."

"I didn't think I had to be." He kissed my temple, took his glasses off, and set them on the nightstand. Then he urged me forward with his hand on my back.

I knelt on the bed, hands below my shoulders, and spread my legs a little more when I heard Nathan curse behind me. I felt the heat of his mouth on my right cheek. His finger smoothed down the string of my thong and dipped between my legs. His tongue followed.

I gasped and dropped my head, fingers curling into the mattress.

Nathan wasn't even licking my pussy yet. He kept his tongue on my thong. He wet it further, though I knew it was already soaked. He pulled the string away from my body and sucked my arousal off it.

"God." My arms shook. "You're so dirty."

I felt him smile against my ass.

"Ready?" His breath tickled my body as he held the string aside now.

I pushed back and wordlessly begged for this. I wasn't sure I knew how to speak anymore.

Nathan started slow, licking thoroughly between my lips, sucking on them. His fingers dug into my ass. He dragged his tongue all over me, pressing it flat against my clit, circling my pussy. He spread my cheeks and licked me higher.

"Oh my God." My arms stretched out. I turned my head and pressed my face into the mattress. I couldn't believe how good that felt.

Nathan groaned, licked down to my pussy again, and fucked me with his tongue. He slid my thong down to my thighs. He bit my ass, and then he was gone.

"What...?" I peered over my shoulder and watched Nathan lower to the floor.

He removed my thong, wiggling it underneath my knees. Then he sat with his back against the mattress and dropped his head between my legs. He stared up at my body. He slid his hand around my waist and urged me down.

"Come on," he said.

I'd never done this before—Nathan wanted me to grind myself on his face. Or maybe he just wanted me to sit on it and he would take care of everything. Inexperience aside, I was good with either of those options.

I pushed up so my weight was fully on my knees, spread them a little more, and slowly sank down.

"Holy shit." I gasped when I felt his mouth there. I looked down my body. Nathan was already watching me. He winked. *God*...I felt my heart skip. "You kill me, you know that?"

He gave me a long, slow lick in answer.

I fisted his hair and began to move with him. I chased after his tongue.

We did this together.

He licked and sucked. I circled my hips and humped his face. At one point, I thought I was smothering him and lifted away from his mouth, but Nathan followed me, head jerking off the mattress so he could bury his face between my legs again. I gasped and gripped handfuls of his hair. He pulled me down and held me in place with his strong arm across my thighs, his other hand guiding mine to cup and squeeze my breast. He ate at me roughly then.

I took his cue and played with myself while he tongue-fucked me. My legs felt lifeless. I couldn't catch my breath. I pinched and tugged on my nipples as he took me there, and when I came, I dripped onto his face.

Nathan went wild for it. He moaned loudly as he lapped at me. I could feel my arousal running down my thighs.

"Not fair," I gasped, falling sideways onto the bed when my orgasm moved through me. I panted against the mattress. "You wouldn't let me make you come...and you...That's so not fair." I rolled onto my back, watching Nathan stretch to his feet.

"You made me come," he said, turning to face me. He peered down at his chest and abs. They glistened with his arousal. "I didn't even touch myself. Jesus Christ."

My mouth dropped open. I pushed up to my hands and watched Nathan grab a few tissues from the nightstand and wipe himself off. "You came just from...You didn't touch yourself at all?"

Whoa. Really?

"Nope." He chuckled and shook his head, balling up the tissue and tossing it into the wastebasket against the wall. "I mean, I was close from the blow job, but *shit*." He smiled at me.

I beamed. Best compliment ever. "That good, huh?"

"Mm." Nathan nodded and wiped at his mouth. Then he pushed his shorts and boxers down, stepping out of them, and dug through his pocket, pulling out his wallet and thumbing through it. "Probably for the best though. I most likely would've embarrassed myself sinking inside you the first time. You know how long it's been for me."

"And you know how long it's been for me," I countered. Our eyes met. "There wouldn't be any reason to be embarrassed. I'll probably come again as soon as you push in."

"That would be awesome. Please do that."

I dropped my head back, laughing. "God, you make me feel..." When I looked at Nathan again, I bit my lip and shook my head. *Could I admit this?*

"What?" he asked.

"I don't know." I sat up fully and drew my knees against my chest. "I'm not old—I'm only twenty-seven—but you make me feel like I'm fifteen or something. Like I've never done anything before this. I'm so excited right now. You should feel my heart."

"You should feel mine."

I huffed out a breath, holding his gaze until he broke it to dig a condom out of his wallet. Then I turned my head. I watched myself in the tall mirror on the wall across the room. I expected to look different.

I was falling in love for the first time. I shouldn't recognize myself.

chapter eighteen

NATHAN

I knew exactly what Jenna meant, because I felt the same way.

I wasn't inexperienced. I'd been with Sadie for nine years and plenty of women before that. Most weren't memorable in any way, which wasn't an insult to them. I just fucked around a lot growing up. I was practiced at foreplay. I knew how this should feel.

But with Jenna it was different.

I kissed her like I didn't know what the fuck I was doing, just that I needed to be doing it. I couldn't get enough. I touched her body like I'd never felt a woman's shape before. Like I could touch her and do nothing else for hours, and Jenna let me. She didn't rush me along when I settled beside her, dick harder than steel. She let me drag this out.

I thought I was wild when I ate her pussy, but playing with Jenna's body...I grabbed at her desperately. I moved her how I wanted. I worried I was being too rough.

I wasn't.

Jenna got off on everything I was doing.

When I squeezed her breasts and sucked on them, she wrapped her arms around my shoulders and begged me not to stop. When I stretched her with two fingers inside and dared to press a third to her ass, she pushed against me, inviting me in, and smiled into the crook of my neck when I merely rubbed her. She came again, clawing at my back and moaning in my ear. My mouth and hands left marks all over her. Her soft body glistened with sweat.

Jenna played with me too. She crawled over me and stroked my dick. She slid it between her breasts. She let me fuck them, her hot tongue lapping at the head. She sucked me into her mouth, licked my balls, and pumped my shaft. Then she kissed her way up my body.

I wanted to close my eyes—her mouth felt too good—but I watched her, my head on the pillow and my hands in her hair. I couldn't miss this.

She kissed my abs and my chest. She stroked her hands up to my shoulders and down my arms, wrapping her grip around my muscles. When she straddled my waist and leaned down, I thought she was going to kiss me and couldn't fucking wait for it, but Jenna put her hand on my chin and tipped my head back. She licked my throat.

"You have the sexiest neck I've ever seen," she whispered, pressing her lips there, sucking a little. "When you get home from work and you unbutton your collar and I get to see it…I nearly die every time."

"Yeah? That gets you going?"

"Oh yeah. Among other things. The rolled-up sleeves is a hit with me too. Your arms are incredible."

God, it felt good knowing how I got to her. "Thank you," I said, a little smugly.

Jenna smiled as she sat up. She glanced over at the nightstand and reached for the condom. "When did you buy new ones?"

"The day after we realized the others had expired."

She peered down at me. The foil pressed against my chest. "Staying ahead of those two months, huh?"

"I think we both knew we'd never make it that long." I held her waist as I sat up, shifting her over so she was beside me on the bed. Getting to my knees, I tore the wrapper open with my teeth.

Jenna stretched out on her back. She bent her leg and dropped it to the side, opening herself to me as I rolled on the condom.

"Thanks for the view."

She blushed. "No problem."

We were both smiling and laughing when I settled over her, and then, immediately, we weren't. We looked at each other, mouths open, chests heaving with our breaths, as I dropped to my elbow and slid my other hand between us.

Jenna cupped my face. She kept staring at me. She never closed her eyes once as I slid inside. As I stretched her.

Pleasure wrapped around my body. My muscles burned. *Holy fuck, this woman.*

"*Nathan,*" she gasped. Her heels dug into my back.

I shifted forward, moving in, in, in, her body gripping me. I pumped my hips gently until I was fully inside.

"Are you okay?" I asked. It had been four years for her. I didn't want this to hurt.

Jenna nodded, breathing sharply against my mouth.

Now we could fuck. *Finally.* But I didn't move. I couldn't. I stared at Jenna, and she stared at me. And there it was again— that feeling of discovering something for the first time. I couldn't remember wanting something so badly before.

And God, I wanted to make this good for her.

I bent down and kissed her, licking inside her mouth. Jenna moaned against my tongue, and hearing that, I couldn't *not* move. I shifted my hips, reared back, grabbed her knees, and held her open. I pumped into her.

Now we were fucking.

"*God*...oh my God." Jenna gasped, hands stretching above her and bracing on the headboard. *"Nathan."*

I stared between us. I groaned, bit my lip, and rubbed her pussy with my thumb so I could feel myself enter her.

"Fuck, Jenna...*Fuck*, you're so good. This feels—" I lost my breath. My mind shortly after. I thought I had the words to describe how this felt, but I didn't.

"Tell me," she urged, reaching down and pressing her fingers against mine. "How does it feel? Tell me."

I looked at her, crawled closer, and guided her legs around my waist. I braced my hands beside her head and drove in, making her gasp.

"It feels too good."

She smiled a little. "How could anything be too good?"

"I don't know." I dropped lower and we kissed. My hips surged forward. I groaned, resting my forehead against hers as I pumped into her slowly. "Tell me I'm wrong...Tell me this isn't too good. I want to hear you say it."

She smiled through a moan. "I can't." Her fingers pushed through my hair, gripped, and urged me down. We kissed. "Don't stop," she begged.

Don't stop kissing her? Don't stop fucking her? I didn't ask. I also didn't need clarification, since I couldn't seem to stop doing both without any difficulty.

Until I wanted to take Jenna from behind. On her knees, with her hair wrapped tight in my hand, kissing became a little tricky, but we managed.

Our mouths touched and opened together as I fucked her. Her little breathless noises drove me wild. I ate her gasps. I licked her jaw and sucked wildly at her neck. I bit the tattoo on her

240

shoulder and laughed through a groan when she started singing that fucking song that drove me crazy that day in my office.

"Trying to concentrate here." I pulled out, flipped her onto her back, and slid inside again. We moaned together. "I don't think I've ever laughed during sex before."

She smiled. "Me either. Maybe we're not doing it right."

"Maybe we never were until now."

Jenna wrapped her arms around my neck, our lips close. "Maybe," she whispered. She stared into my eyes as I moved inside her. When her breaths grew quicker and needier, I slid my hand down her body and rubbed her clit.

"God, I can't wait to feel you," I moaned, kissing my way to her ear. "Come on. You're right there...Do it with me."

"*Please*," she begged, like I wasn't asking for this. Jenna reached down and squeezed my thighs, grinding her hips against me. Her body began to shake. She sucked and licked my neck. I felt her teeth. "*Oh God*...Nathan. *Nathan.*"

Jesus, my name on her lips—was there anything better? I slid my grip to her waist and pounded into her. Pressure rolled down my spine. I blinked the sweat from my eyes. I couldn't stop. I wanted to chase after this feeling forever. I never wanted it to end.

"Fuck, Jenna...fuckkkk. Ah, *God.*"

My spine burned as I filled the condom, slowing my strokes, dragging this out too. With one final thrust, my body sagged forward.

"Don't stop," Jenna demanded. She wiggled against me. "I'm...Oh shit, oh shit."

Was she...again? Already?

I pulled out of her and slid my fingers inside. Her pussy clamped down.

Holy fuck, she was.

Jenna tugged on my neck.

I bent over her and we kissed, hard and hungry, as I pumped into her. I sucked on her tongue. She dripped all over my hand.

"Wow." Her body trembled as she came down. She clung to me, gasping against my cheek. "Holy shit."

"Holy shit is right." I slid my fingers out, kissing her jaw, her mouth. "I think that was the hottest thing I've ever seen." I pushed back to my knees and looked at her.

Jenna slowly drew her legs in, pressing them together, and rolled to her side. "Thanks," she said, smiling, still a little breathless.

I smiled back. "No, thank *you*. I know exactly what I'll be thinking about next time I jerk off." I pushed damp hair off my forehead.

Jenna bit her lip and blushed.

"Look who's all shy now," I teased.

"I'm picturing you doing that."

"Yeah? I'll show you sometime." I stood from the bed, carefully tugging off the condom. "Bathroom?"

She pointed at the door closest to the bed. I assumed the other on the opposite wall led to a closet.

I stepped inside, disposed of the condom, and cleaned up at the sink. With damp hands, I slicked my hair back. Then I lifted my chin at the mirror.

"You gave me a hickey," I called out, turning my head to the side. The vein in my neck bulged under a reddish mouth-shaped mark. "I haven't had one of these in, like, fifteen years."

"Did you give me any?"

I turned the bathroom light off and walked out into the bedroom.

Jenna flipped onto her back and pressed her head into the pillow, showing me her neck as I climbed onto the bed. I settled beside her.

She smiled as I inspected her. Her breaths sounded hurried—a little excited. "Well?" she asked.

"None." I kissed her jaw. "Well, none visible. You have some here." My hand brushed over her right breast. I gave it a little squeeze.

"Damn it," she mumbled.

"You want a hickey?"

"I've never had one."

I stared at her. "Well, I don't understand *that* at all. You're way too sweet not to suck on." I bent lower. "Shall I?"

She giggled and tipped her head back again. "Please."

I slid my lips over her skin, barely touching her. "How visible are we wanting this hickey?"

"We should probably keep it PG."

"A PG hickey? I'm not sure what that is." I kissed around to the back of her neck. "How about here? Your hair will cover it."

"Sold."

"Permission to suck?"

She giggled again. "Yes, please." Her hand moved over my hip, and as my mouth latched on to her skin, Jenna dug her fingers into me. "Unh." She gasped, her legs sliding against the sheets. Soon she was panting. "Do we match yet?"

"Almost." I slid my mouth over her again and darkened the bruise, smiling against her when she made the faintest little moan. "Do you mind?"

"What?" She laughed.

"Don't tempt me with those sounds. I could cover you in these."

"I can't really help it."

I kissed the mark once more. Then I pulled back and loomed over her, resting my head in my hand. "Wanna go check it out?"

She grinned and shot up, crawling over me to scramble off the bed. She knocked me onto my back.

"Jesus, woman."

"I'm excited!" Jenna dashed into the bathroom. I heard her suck in a breath. "Oh my God, you animal."

"What?" I barked out a laugh, sitting up to catch her when she flew out of the bathroom and jumped on the bed. She wrapped her limbs around me. "That's a very PG hickey," I told her. "You act like I went all nasty on you."

"I look like I got attacked by a vacuum." She wiggled in my lap and kissed my cheek. "I love it. Thanks for popping my hickey cherry."

"I should be thanked. What a hardship that was."

Jenna laughed, and we kissed, starting fast and then moving impossibly slowly.

God, I could kiss her for hours.

When she reached between us and wrapped her hand around my hard dick, she smiled again. "Hi there."

"Hey."

We kept kissing as we tumbled over together, untangling our bodies to lie side by side on the pillow.

I humped a little into her grip, and when she whispered, "Show me how you do it," I took over, stroking myself.

Jenna stared at me in wonder, studying the way I jerked off.

Even this felt new. Having her watch me made everything hypersensitive. I was close before I wanted to be.

"Keep going," she urged when I squeezed the base of my dick, holding myself off.

I gasped and kept stroking. Within seconds, I was there. "*Fuck,*" I groaned.

Jenna slid closer, holding on to me, and smiled against my mouth as I shot all over her stomach.

"Jesus Christ." I panted, sagging against the bed. I laughed into her shoulder when she pointed out how nasty I got all over her—using my words from before.

We cleaned up together in the bathroom that time, then returned to bed. We talked and touched, because the two seemed to go hand in hand. Jenna curled against me, pointing out how snuggly and comfy I really was, remembering our day at the Arctic Circle. I laughed and kissed her.

She asked me to stay the night. I told her I never even considered leaving and tucked the covers around us. We fell asleep together.

I woke sometime later with her hands exploring my body. I had no idea what time it was and I didn't care to check. I lost my mind when Jenna sucked my dick into her mouth and grumbled something about this being a dream.

"It feels like it is," she whispered.

I grabbed another condom out of my wallet, rolled it on, and encouraged her to get on top. I watched Jenna ride me.

Head on the pillow, I stared at her body as it moved. Her breasts, the soft curve of her waist, her strong thighs as they gripped my hips. I sat up to suck on her nipples. I told her this was my favorite way to wake up, and she smiled against my mouth.

When Jenna was breathless, I flipped us and finished between her legs, our hands linked together beside her head. Her eyes watered through her orgasm. She looked beautiful—moaning my name, her hair messy on the pillow.

I cleaned up alone and fell into bed, pulling her against me. Jenna grumbled how sleepy she was now. I agreed, but neither one of us could stop talking and laughing and touching.

We stretched our night as long as we could.

chapter nineteen

JENNA

A quiet banging in the distance roused me awake. I blinked against my pillow, trying to distinguish the sound, as the heavy arm around me threatened to pull me back into slumber.

God, Nathan's body felt good. Behind me, over me, beside me. I never wanted to move.

The banging grew louder and quicker, splitting into two fast-pounding knocks that echoed each other and rivaled in elevation. I faintly heard voices calling out.

My eyes flew to the clock on my nightstand.

"*Shit*," I whispered, squirming out from under Nathan's arm and scooting out of bed. "Shit! Wake up! My kids are home." I spun around and gripped Nathan's shoulder, giving him a shove while keeping my voice low and urgent. "*Nathan!*"

"Mm?" His eyes remained closed. He grabbed my pillow and pulled it against his chest, grumbling incoherently.

"Really?" I ripped it away from him, tossed it off the bed, and tugged on his arm as the banging on the door continued. He was deadweight. "My kid are here. Kids. *Here*."

Nathan's eyes flashed open.

"I didn't realize it was this late . . . Brian said he'd drop them off by ten. God, I feel like we just fell asleep."

"Probably because we did." Nathan yawned and rolled to his back, stretching his long body. He rubbed at his face.

I stared at his chest, lower to his abs and then lower still. He was barely covered by the sheet.

Damn, he looks incredible.

I searched the floor around me, grabbing my bra and panties and slipping them on. The laundry basket next to the nightstand was filled with clothes waiting to be folded. I found a pair of pajama shorts and pulled those on as well.

"They can't see you...Can you sneak out?" I asked.

Nathan sat up and swung his legs out of bed. He squinted at me. "You're on the fifth floor. What would you like me to do? Jump?"

"I don't know!" I picked up the T-shirt next to the basket and pulled it over my head, slipping my arms through the sleeves as the pounding at the door continued. The hem touched my thighs and covered my shorts completely. "What are we saying if they see you?" I asked, pulling the jeweled pin out of my hair when I felt it digging into my scalp. I tossed it on the nightstand. "God, this is going to be so confusing for them, after my *date* last night? Should we tell them anything? Are we telling *anybody* anything? We really should've had this conversation before the sex."

"Which time?"

"Oh, ha ha."

Nathan cocked his head, a sleepy smile tugging at his mouth. His hair was a mess and stuck out in sharp pieces. He looked so fucking adorable right now, and sexy. *God*, he was sexy.

"Jenna?"

"Mm?"

"You're staring at me." His brows ticked up. "Not that I don't appreciate it, but shouldn't you be answering the door?"

"Shouldn't you be getting dressed?" I gestured at him.

His eyes skimmed my body. "Sure. I'll get right on that."

"Yeah. How about some hustle?"

He laughed. "I never see you like this—you're hot all worked up and worried." Nathan was full-on grinning now.

The severity of this situation aside, that was really nice to hear. I should look manic more often.

"Thanks. But seriously, what are you going to do? You can't just hide in here."

"Relax. I'll handle it." He pushed out of bed, swiping at his boxers as he stood and stepping into them.

"You'll handle it how?" I crossed my arms under my chest as I pictured Nathan shimmying down the side of my building. "Okay, I know you're tall, but you can't be seriously considering any other way out of here besides the front door. You'll hurt yourself."

"Just get the kids in the kitchen," he said, the band of his boxers snapping against his stomach. "I'll take care of the rest."

"Okay. I trust you."

His chest shook with a laugh.

"How are you finding any of this funny?"

"It's not hard." Nathan slid his glasses on, then glanced down at the front of me again. He gestured at the door. "*Let's go.* How about some hustle?"

"Oh my God." I tucked my hair behind my ears and spun around, hurrying out of the room.

My bare feet beat against the hallway flooring. I skidded to a stop at the front door, quickly sliding the locks open. "I'm coming!" I hollered. I turned the knob and opened the door. "Sorry! I'm sorry, guys."

"Jeez, Mom. We've been out here forever," Oliver said, typing quickly on his iPad. "I'm telling Uncle Brian he can go now. *Finally*."

"I'm sorry. I overslept."

"You never sleep this late, Mama," Olivia pointed out, following her brother inside.

"Well, I guess I was just really tired. Here. Come on." I closed the door and put my arms around them both, urging the kids to move while I glanced over my shoulder. "Let's go into the kitchen."

I didn't see any sign of Nathan. I couldn't hear him either. *What in the world does he have planned?*

"We already ate breakfast at Uncle Brian's, Mom," Oliver said. "He made us eggs."

"There's more than just food in the kitchen. Let's just…sit in here and talk." I guided them toward the table. "You guys can tell me all about your night. What did you do?"

"Played games. Watched movies," Olivia said. "It was super fun."

"Syd cooked lasagna. It was real good," Oliver shared.

"I'm sure it was. She's such a good cook."

The kids slung their duffle bags up onto the table just as the door sounded behind us, latching shut again.

"Morning," Nathan called out, turning our heads.

He stood in the small foyer wearing his basketball shorts and sneakers. He was shirtless.

I glared at this bare chest. *Really?*

"Nate!" Olivia shrieked, bouncing on her toes beside me. "Hi! What are you doing here?"

"I was out for a jog and got hungry. I thought I'd have breakfast with you guys." He walked toward us, smiling. "You didn't eat yet, did you?"

"We did, but I could totally eat again. If you're hungry, I mean," Oliver was quick to say.

I slowly looked over at my son, who I was sure would've turned down a second breakfast, or hell, a snack in general, had I been the one offering it.

"Me too," Olivia added. "I'm actually still pretty hungry."

"I was in the mood for some pancakes. Do you guys like pancakes?"

"We love pancakes! I'll get the mix." Olivia rushed around the small island to get to the cabinets. "Help me, Ollie! *Come on.*"

"Yeah, okay. I got the milk." Oliver shoved his iPad into his duffle and hurried to join her just as Nathan stopped in front of me.

"Good morning," he said.

A smile took up my face. I didn't even try to fight it. "Morning."

"How was your evening? Anything memorable happen?"

"Stop it," I whispered, leaning in close. "Aren't you forgetting something? Where is your shirt?"

He leaned in even closer, brushing his mouth against my hair. "You're wearing it."

"What?" I jerked back and peered down at my front. "Oh my God." I tugged the material away from my body. *No wonder this fits me like a dress.* "Why didn't you say anything?" I demanded, scowling at his stupid, smiling face, which wasn't stupid at all. It was perfect.

"What's the problem? It's not like it says 'Property of Nathan' on the back."

My heart skipped. I felt my entire body tense up. *Oh man. I was totally wishing it said that. Is that weird?*

Nathan's smile turned to 100 percent pure mischief. "I'm sorry. I'll make sure to wear that shirt next time."

"I mean, whatever." My shoulders lifted in a quick jerk. "Wear what you want."

He laughed quietly.

"Mom, where's that rectangle thing?" Oliver asked. I heard pots and pans clanging together.

"The griddle?" I stepped up to the island. "Bottom cabinet, I think. Next to the fridge."

"Oh, right. Hey, Nate," Oliver called out as he searched. "When we're done eating, do you wanna see my room? I got all this cool football stuff I've been wanting to show you."

"Yeah, absolutely." Nathan walked over, getting beside me. He yawned, lifting his glasses to rub at his eyes.

I stared at his profile. His hair still stuck up a bit. He needed to shave, though he also absolutely did not need to shave. Nathan looked amazing with a little scruff. How was it possible to look this good on barely any sleep? I felt like a zombie right now.

Olivia finished carrying over ingredients and spread everything out on the island. She grabbed a large mixing bowl and the serving spoon we used for batter and neatly set them beside the griddle as Oliver plugged it in.

"Hey, where's Marley?" Olivia peered up at Nate.

"At her grandparents' house," he answered. "She spent the night over there."

"Aw. Everyone had a sleepover."

I nearly choked on my own spit.

Nathan pressed against my side, mumbling, "Get ahold of yourself please," and laughing under his breath.

Seriously. If anyone was going to blow our cover, it was going to be me.

"What's that on your neck?" Oliver asked, pointing at Nathan.

I sucked in a breath and held it. *Oh God, no.*

"Vacuum," Nathan mumbled without missing a beat. He glanced over at me.

I took action and quickly smoothed down my hair in the back. Thank God I hadn't pulled it up yet this morning. I hadn't thought about wearing a ponytail when Nathan picked that spot.

"That's crazy!" Olivia giggled.

"A *vacuum* did that to you?" Oliver asked, not finding this amusing like his sister in the least. My son looked concerned. He also looked ready to pick this lie apart.

"Yeah. Weird, right? Are we ready to make pancakes?" Nathan must've sensed the impending interrogation. He moved quickly around the island, holding out his fist, and seeing that, Oliver forgot all about strange vacuum attacks, smiled big, and bumped it. "Where are we at on the ingredients, Liv?"

"We're ready," my daughter said, rubbing her palms together. "What should we do first?"

I pulled out one of the stools and took a seat as Nathan stepped between Oliver and Olivia, giving out instructions. Chin propped on my hand, I watched the three of them.

Olivia dumped the mix into the bowl and cracked one egg while her brother cracked the other. Holding the measuring cup together, the kids added the milk Nathan poured, then took turns stirring while he got the griddle ready.

"Can you make them look like footballs?" Oliver asked.

"Ooh. Or a flower? I want a flower," Olivia said.

"I think I can knock that out."

"Really?" I asked, intrigued.

Nathan ladled some of the batter. The griddle sizzled and smoked as he formed the shape.

"I have this girl living with me who refuses to eat traditionally shaped pancakes, even though I know she eats them for everyone else. I've seen her do it." He glanced up. "I've had to get creative so she doesn't starve."

Olivia giggled, covering her mouth. "He's talking about Marley," she whispered.

"Duh, Livvy." Oliver side-eyed his sister, then stood on his toes to watch Nathan flip the pancake. "Can you show me how you do that, Nate?"

"Yeah, it's easy. Come here."

Nathan made another football, this time letting Oliver hold the ladle with him. The next pancake he made was for Olivia, and he picked her up when she requested so she could watch him form the flower petals.

"How's that?" he asked her.

Olivia held tight to his neck and grinned at his creation. "Really good."

We moved to the table when all the pancakes were finished. Nathan took the seat beside me so we both sat across from the twins. We talked and ate, getting five minutes into the conversation before Olivia brought up my night with Travis.

I was surprised she'd made it that long.

"Are you going out on a second date?" she asked, grinning with syrup-covered lips.

I wiped at my mouth with a napkin. "No, sweetie. We had a nice time, but we're just going to be friends."

"Oh." Olivia pouted at her plate and forked another bite.

I looked down when I felt Nathan's touch on my knee.

Slipping my hand underneath the table, I gently squeezed his thumb, smiling when he turned his palm over and pushed his fingers between mine. My skin tingled all over.

How could I keep something that felt this amazing a secret

for long? I couldn't. I didn't even want to. I vowed to give this a week. Or, who was I kidding, at least a couple of days. Maybe that would be enough time for my kids to understand. I had no idea how they would react to Nathan and me when I'd just gone out with another man the night before. What was the correct way to navigate this?

When we finished eating, the kids cleared the table, showering Nathan with pancake compliments. Apparently they'd never tasted so good.

"Must've been the fancy shapes," I said, getting to my feet.

"Must've been." Nathan stood behind his chair and yawned beside me, rubbing harshly at his face. He looked ready to drop.

I felt the same way. The only difference was, I had the entire day off and Nathan didn't.

"How are you going to get through work tonight?" I asked him, smiling at the kids when they returned to the table.

Nathan didn't speak. I felt his touch move across my lower back and barely registered the two pairs of eyes widening behind glasses before my face was being turned.

Nathan kept one hand on my hip, slid his other over my cheek, and bent down, gently kissing me.

What the fuck! I froze against his mouth.

"Jenna," he murmured, his voice sleep heavy. He pressed his lips against mine once more. "Come on..."

I felt that "come on" *everywhere*. My toes curled against the kitchen floor.

"Oh my gosh," Olivia whispered excitedly. "Ollie, look!"

"*Nathan*," I grumbled, pulling away from his mouth and gripping his waist. "What are you doing?"

"Yeah, what are you doing?" Oliver asked, sounding a little grossed out.

"Nate, you *totally* just kissed my mom!" Olivia shrieked.

Nathan blinked at me. His eyes focused on my face. Then he blinked again and quickly turned us so his back was to the table and the kids and I were being completely shielded by his body.

"I am so sorry," he whispered, still holding my face and hip. His gaze was now mildly panicked. "I think I'm still asleep."

"How are you still asleep? You just made pancakes. *And* ate them."

"I'm so tired...I closed my eyes for like an hour last night. I think my brain just shut off for a minute." He did this thing where he tried to look back at the kids without turning his head.

I cracked up then. I couldn't help it. "Oh my God." I laughed.

"Do you think they saw anything?" Nathan asked loudly on purpose. He was smiling now.

"We saw *everything*!" Olivia answered.

I shook my head at him. "You're unbelievable."

Screw waiting a couple of days. We'd barely made it a couple of hours.

I held his arms and peered around him. Both the kids were smiling now. *Maybe this isn't the big deal I thought it was going to be.*

"Do you guys want to sit down and talk?" I asked.

"Are you boyfriend and girlfriend or something?" Oliver studied me.

"Yeah!" Olivia giggled. "Are you? Say yes! Say yes!"

"Uh—" My breath caught when Nathan pulled me against his chest and pressed his mouth to my hair.

"Whatever you want to say right now, I'll back you," he mumbled for only me to hear. "I'm fine with this. They can know."

I lifted my head and peered into his face. "Um, I'm not really sure what to tell them," I whispered.

Nathan kept his voice lowered when he answered me. "You could say we're dating…"

"So, that's what we're doing, then?" My heart began to race. *Oh God, please say yes…*

He stared at me for a long moment. "Isn't it?"

We are dating. Oh my God. We are dating and telling people. Yes! Yes! Yes!

I nodded quickly.

Nathan smiled. "Okay. What's the problem, then?"

"Nothing. Just making sure we're on the same page."

"Mama, is this why you and Travis are just being friends?" Olivia asked. "Because you like Nate *more* than him?"

Nathan quickly looked behind him. "That's exactly why."

"Okay." I laughed, giving him a shove so he'd turn around and step beside me. "Nathan and I are dating," I announced.

Olivia covered her mouth and squealed. Oliver smiled at his sister, then looked at Nathan.

"How do you guys feel about that?" I glanced between the kids. My question barely left my mouth before Olivia was rushing around the table and wrapping her arms around Nathan and me.

She squeezed us tight, saying, "I was hoping this would happen!"

I rubbed her back and smiled at Nathan when he reciprocated the hug. Then I turned my head and looked at Oliver. "What do you think, sweetheart?"

Nathan peered over at him too, asking, "You good with this, bud? You wanna talk about it?"

That meant a lot to me. But aside from being caught off guard, I didn't think Oliver would have a problem with this. He adored Nathan. And he had been smiling a minute ago.

Why wasn't he anymore?

My son nodded. "Can we talk? Just us?" he said to Nathan.

I pressed my lips together, keeping my expression stoic. A difficult task, considering how concerned I'd suddenly become. *Crap. Does Oliver have a problem with this?*

"Yeah, of course." Nathan stepped out of Olivia's grasp and moved around the table.

"I really like Nate, Mama," Olivia whispered, wrapping both arms around me now. Her chin hit my chest. "So, so much. These feelings feel too big for me."

My daughter and I shared the same heart.

I cupped her cheek. "Me too, baby."

She beamed at me. I brushed her soft hair out of her face, then turned my head, watching the boys walk side by side through the family room. They disappeared down the hallway.

"Why don't you go watch some TV?" I suggested to Olivia.

"Okay." She hurried out of the kitchen and scrambled onto the couch.

I really wanted to take a shower, or at least get dressed, but when I peeked down the hallway, I saw Oliver's bedroom door was open. I could faintly hear him and Nathan speaking. I didn't want my son thinking I was creeping down the hallway to listen in on their conversation. Even though that was *exactly* what I wanted to do.

Worry tightened my chest and coiled my stomach. I forced myself back into the kitchen.

Fifteen minutes later, Oliver returned by himself.

He heaved his duffel bag off the floor, set it on one of the stools, and started searching through it.

"Hey, sweetheart." I left the remaining dishes in the sink and dried my hands off, tossing the towel on the counter. I stood across from him. "Is everything okay?"

"Yeah," he said, taking out his iPad and showing it to me. "Can I play this?"

Oliver seemed completely fine. He didn't look any different than he had when he first got home this morning, or any different from how he typically looked. This was good...

"Sure." I smiled at him.

"Cool. Thanks, Mom."

I watched my son leave the room and join his sister on the couch. When I stepped over and peered down the hallway, I saw Nathan standing there, admiring a picture I had hanging on the wall. I quickly walked over to him.

"What's going on?" I whispered. "He seems...good. He's good, right?"

"Yeah." Nathan smiled at the photo of the kids at their first birthday party. They were covered in cake. I was squatting between their high chairs and smiling at the camera. "Cute picture."

"Thanks. Could you maybe elaborate a little for me?"

"*Really* cute picture?" Nathan turned to face me then. He was smirking now. "We didn't talk much about me and you, but he doesn't have a problem with it, if you're worried about that."

Tension released from my shoulders. "I was, yeah."

"He's good with us dating. He thinks it's cool."

That made me seriously happy. I began to grin, then lost it a little when my curiosity got the best of me. "What did you two talk about, then?"

"The campout. He asked if I could go."

My eyes widened. For a good five seconds, I completely forgot how to form a coherent thought and just stared up at Nathan.

"Are you okay?" he asked, the corner of his mouth lifting.

"That's . . . Sorry. He . . ." I waved my hands in front of myself. "I'll talk to him. He knows my brother will take him if he's still wanting to go."

Nathan lost the smirk and tipped his head, gesturing for me to follow him down the hallway. We entered my bedroom.

He pushed the door closed behind us, then faced me, crossing his arms over his chest. "Those little shitheads are going to make fun of Oliver if he goes with your brother."

I rubbed at my eyes, trying to ignore that very worry. It seemed impossible. "They might not."

"He's scared they will. He asked me to go instead. They'll leave him alone if he's with someone they don't know."

"I'm sorry he put you in that position, Nathan. I wish he would've said something to me first."

"What position? I don't mind going . . ."

I blinked up at him. "Did you tell him you'd go?"

"Yeah."

Oh my God. *"Really?"*

He cocked his head. "Yeah, really. He should get to go, Jenna. He wants to . . . This way those kids can't make fun of him."

"They might ask who you are. I know they called out Brian the first time he went."

"So? Let them call me out. That doesn't mean I'm going to give them an answer. They can think what they want."

My lips parted. "Nathan." I stepped closer, forcing my arms to remain at my sides when the only thing I wanted to do was wrap them around him. I couldn't believe what he was offering to do. "We just started seeing each other," I reminded him. "Like, *a minute ago*. What you're trying to do right now is so unbelievably sweet and I want to say okay—I do—but this is a big deal. Are you sure you want to do this?"

"I wouldn't have said yes if I wasn't sure," he replied. "And a *minute*? Where are you getting that? I would say we've been together since the Fourth, at least."

"But then we agreed to wait…and even if we hadn't—"

"Jenna." Nathan's tone grew serious. "This isn't a big deal to me. If Oliver wants to tell them I'm his mom's boyfriend, he can. If he doesn't want to give them an answer, I'm fine with that too. I don't care. My entire reason for being there is to make sure he has a good time—I don't give a fuck about any other kid or what they have to say. I only care about Oliver."

Breath rushed past my lips. I knew Nathan had just said a lot right now, and I absolutely heard and felt everything he was telling me, but only one thing began circling inside my mind. I couldn't let go of it.

"So you're my boyfriend, then?" I asked shyly, placing my hands on his hips and stepping even closer. I couldn't hold back from touching him anymore. And holy crap, when had I ever felt this happy? I couldn't remember.

Nathan's smile was warm and sweet. "We're dating…What else would I be?"

"I guess that makes me your girlfriend, then."

"That's typically how it works." He let his arms drop and fall around me, linking his hands behind my lower back. "I'm thirty years old," he said. "Am I doing this wrong? Should I be asking you out, like, officially? Do you want me to? I feel like I was very *official* with you last night."

"You were."

"Several times."

"You could still ask. I couldn't tell you the last time I was asked."

Nathan's expression hardened. "What the fuck, Jenna? Who are the men you've been hanging around?"

"Um...like, lately? You. My brother. Travis..."

"Stop. Forget I asked that." He sighed in frustration, then bent lower until our foreheads touched. "It's been a while for me...I might word this wrong."

"You could never word this wrong. I promise." I fidgeted on my feet, shifting my weight around. "I'm so excited," I whispered.

Nathan chuckled. "I can tell." He stared deep into my eyes. "I want to be with you so fucking badly. Will you be my girlfriend, Jenna?"

"OhmyGodIwouldlovetoyes," I answered in a one-breath rush, smiling so big, my cheeks ached. He grinned and we kissed.

"Thank you for telling Oliver you'd go with him," I said. "That means a lot to him, and to me."

"I'm happy to do it. Honestly, it's not a big deal." Nathan's phone beeped twice from his pocket.

I let go of him so he could get to it. I yawned and rubbed at my face. "God, I'm so amped up and tired at the same time. I feel like I could run a marathon but also pass out at any second."

"You and me both," he said, looking at his phone. He immediately began to smile, reacting to whatever message he was reading.

"What is it?" I asked.

"It's my dad...Marley misses me." Nathan studied the screen in disbelief, his forehead wrinkling in confusion.

"Of course she does. Why do you seem surprised?"

"I don't know—Marley's close with my parents. Closest, actually."

"Maybe she used to be, but would you really say that now?

Look at the two of you... I'd argue you're the person she's closest with."

"No, she unfortunately has more history with my parents than she does with me." He lowered his phone and looked at me then. "You should've seen her. She couldn't wait to go over there last night. She didn't mind me leaving her either."

"And now even though she has them, she misses you."

Nathan nodded tightly, like he couldn't fully believe what was happening. "My dad said she's been asking to come home since she got up. She keeps watching for me out the window. I..." His neck worked with a swallow. "I wasn't expecting that at all. I figured she'd fight me when I went to pick her up on Monday."

I reached out and took his free hand in mine. This meant something huge to Nathan. I could see it. And God, I couldn't be happier for him.

I smiled. "What are you going to do?"

His answer came without the slightest hesitation. "I think I'm going to skip work and go pick her up." He looked at his phone again, rereading the text. "She actually misses me," he said.

"So, don't make her miss you another second."

Nathan nodded at my suggestion and shoved away his phone. He patted his pockets, making sure he had everything he came with, then lowered his gaze to my shirt—his shirt. "I have an extra one in the truck," he said, grabbing my face and kissing me.

I was beyond happy not to part with his shirt. It had this clean, masculine scent that was so purely him. If it had once smelled like soap or laundry detergent, it didn't any longer. It smelled like Nathan, my boyfriend.

Oh my God. He's my boyfriend. Oh my God.

I walked behind Nathan to the door, where he surprised me

by pressing his lips against mine again. I figured the kiss we'd shared in the bedroom had been our goodbye kiss.

Olivia gasped behind me. "They're doing it again, Ollie," she whispered from her seat on the couch.

"Let me know when they're *not* doing it."

I laughed against Nathan's mouth.

He pulled away, smiling, and lifted his hand to wave at the kids.

"Bye!" they both yelled.

"If you guys aren't busy later, maybe we could meet up for dinner or something?" Nathan opened the door and stepped outside.

I leaned my shoulder against the doorframe, fighting the smile of my life. "We've never met up for dinner before... Would this be a date?"

He grinned, answering quietly, "You bet your sweet fucking ass it's a date. Do you have any idea how badly I've been wanting to take you out? Seriously, Jenna, I plan on dating you so much, you're going to get sick of it."

"Doubt it." I winked at him.

His hands flew dramatically to his chest. "Is that what it feels like to be winked at?"

"Every time."

"Damn." Nathan looked back at me as he walked to the stairs. He disappeared to the floor below. "I just winked!" he yelled.

"I felt it!"

"Yeah, you did!"

I closed the door and laughed into my apartment.

chapter twenty

NATHAN

I stayed true to my word and took Jenna on a date every chance I got. We hit nearly every restaurant in Dogwood Beach (excluding my own, since I wouldn't be paying for a meal there). And on the evenings I worked late—when she couldn't hold off on making something to eat for her and the kids—we went somewhere for dessert.

She was happy, so fucking happy—even though the kids tagged along on our dates. We never went out just the two of us. We couldn't. I felt like every moment I had with her was being chaperoned.

Not that I didn't like us all being together. I did. I liked Oliver and Olivia a lot, but I wanted to be alone with Jenna. *Needed* to be alone. Two weeks of practically zero intimacy aside from what could be done in front of our kids led to a substantial amount of daydreaming on my part, and I did that shit everywhere.

At work. Driving around. At home, with Jenna five feet away from me...

"Are you listening to me? Nathan..."

I lifted my head, dragging my gaze off the granite countertop I had zoned out on, and met Jenna's curious stare. She stood right across from me. "Mm? Of course I was listening. I always listen."

"Yeah?" Her brow lifted in challenge. "What did I just say?"

"Something about the kids..." I was guessing.

"What *specifically* about them?"

I tugged at the knot in my tie, loosening it as I glanced into the family room. The three of them were huddled together on the couch, watching something on TV. They hadn't moved since I got home—however long ago that was. I'd completely lost track of time, and my focus.

In my head I was trying to remember how Jenna moved beneath me.

"You have no idea what I was saying. Just admit it."

Jenna was smiling when I looked at her again. Her hair had been in two braids this morning before I left for work, but it wasn't now. It fell past her shoulders in thick, dark curls.

"I like your hair like that," I said.

"Thank you."

"You're too far away from me. Come here."

She walked around the counter, watching me closely as she moved. "Do I need to be over here next to you to get that admission?" she asked, stopping in front of me.

"I'm not admitting to anything, aside from wanting you over here." I gently held her waist with one hand. Two and I'd pull her against me. I couldn't do that. I wouldn't bet on my own restraint at this point.

"You know, I can tell when you're thinking about other things. It's okay if you weren't listening." Jenna popped the top button of my shirt, flicked my collar open, and sighed as her fingertip grazed my throat. "I miss you," she whispered. "So much, Nathan. God, how long has it been?"

I pinched my eyes shut and groaned. "We're on day thirteen."

"It feels longer than that."

"Tell me about it." My eyes flashed open, and I grabbed her wrist when I felt her touch move down my chest and reach my stomach. "Don't," I said. "I'll admit to anything right now. Just please, keep your hands above my waist."

Jenna laughed. "I wasn't going to go any lower than your belt." Her green eyes narrowed, and in the quietest voice she said, "Admit you want me to go lower."

My voice echoed hers in volume. "I want you to go lower."

"Admit you thought about me at work today and got hard."

I cocked my head.

She cocked hers, losing most of her smile when I remained silent. "Okay, I totally wish I wouldn't have said that now . . . sorry."

"I thought about you at work today and got hard." When she grinned up at me, I added, "More than once."

"I think about you constantly," Jenna admitted, sounding a little shy all of a sudden. "Especially when I'm trying to get something done. I was reviewing this document today for my boss and I completely lost my focus. I had to restart the same paragraph six times. It was so frustrating."

"I need to be alone with you, Jenna."

"*I know.* Trust me, I know." She gripped my shirt, rolled up onto her toes, and kissed me. "I'm working on it," she said against my mouth.

I watched her sink back onto her heels. "Yeah?" I asked. Hope quickened the pace of my heart.

She nodded, peering out into the family room. "Just give me two more weeks . . ."

"*What?*" My vision vibrated. I blinked her into focus. *Is she insane?* "Jenna, I can't . . . I won't make it that long. I know I won't. Please tell me you're joking."

"I'm joking." Her smile was full and satisfying. "You were so panicked." She giggled, throwing her arms around my neck.

I fake glared at her. "Well, guess who wasn't listening to you *at all* earlier? Me. I have no idea what you said."

She dropped her head against my chest and laughed. Her entire body shook. "You're my favorite," she said. She was slow to peer up at me.

"Yeah?"

She nodded. "I mean that in a lot of ways...not just favorite person to talk to, like you said about me. I've never laughed so much with anyone before. I want to be around you all the time, Nathan. If I had to choose one person to do something with, it would be you." Her teeth scraped across her bottom lip. "Say something."

I said the only thing I wanted to tell her in that moment, aside from giving her a flat "ditto" in response, which would've covered how I felt and fallen short in the same breath.

"I think you're my best friend."

When did this woman become so important to me? I didn't just desire Jenna physically. Yes, of course that played a huge role in this longing to be near her all the time, but it went beyond that. I wanted to be the first person she thought of at any given moment, because she was quickly becoming mine. I wanted to know her better than anyone else, and I wanted people aware of it—everyone. I wanted it recognized that I had that privilege and they didn't. This relationship stretched into new territory for me. Again I felt completely unprepared for what this was turning into or, let's be honest, what it already was, which didn't make any sense.

I had been married to Sadie for four years. I took my relationship with her farther than anyone else I'd ever been with. I'd shared a life with her...

So how could this feel bigger?

Jenna pressed her body against mine, slid her arms around my waist, and pulled me into a hug. "You're my best friend too," she mumbled against my chest.

I dropped my head and held her.

I expected to feel terrified, or at the very least, hesitant. I'd never felt this way about anyone before. I waited for uncertainty to pull me away from Jenna, one worrying thought, something, anything to slow us down.

It never came.

* * *

Two days later, I was passing the time coloring with Marley while we waited for Jenna and her kids. I was off today. Last night we'd talked about possibly heading down to the beach and getting in the water if the weather was nice.

I didn't know whether that was still the plan, so I hadn't mentioned anything to Marley about it. Right now she was just eager for Jenna, Oliver, and Olivia to get here. She always was.

"Daddy, where awre they?" she asked for the fourth time in the past five minutes. Maybe less than that. Her fist holding the purple crayon moved furiously over the page.

"They're coming. They'll be here soon." I held her steady on my lap with one hand and leaned over, swiping a crayon off the floor. "Here." I showed it to her. "You want to throw some pink in there?"

"'Kay." Marley dropped the purple crayon and grabbed the one I was holding. She scribbled in sharp lines. "Daddy, they here now?"

I smiled and kissed the side of her head. "Almost."

The doorbell rang. Marley gasped and wiggled out of my lap, crawling underneath the table and popping up to stand once she cleared it. "They're here!" she hollered, her little legs carrying her quickly into the family room.

I scooped her up before she could reach the door and smiled against her cheek when she squealed in surprise. "Ready?"

"Ready!" she answered, wrapping her arms around my neck.

I pulled the door open, eyes lowered to greet the twins, since they typically barged in first, but Jenna stood alone on the porch.

"Hey," I said, lifting my gaze.

She was wearing this shirt/shorts combo thing. It was one solid piece, navy blue, and sleeveless. A tie cinched the waist.

I didn't know how the fuck she got it on, but she looked good wearing it. Even in clothing I did not fucking understand, she looked good.

"Jenna!" Marley reached out with both arms, tipping forward.

Jenna smiled at me, then gave it all to Marley as she took her, balancing my daughter in the crook of her arm. "Hey, sweet girl." She kissed her cheek.

"Where are your kids?" I asked, getting her attention.

"Remember that thing I was *working on* . . ."

My brows lifted. *Holy fuck. Did she get a sitter for today?*

"Oliver is at a friend's house. They're bringing him home later tonight," she said, stepping back a little on the porch and turning sideways to face the driveway. "And Shay has generously offered to take the girls to get their nails painted."

I stepped out of the house and peered over at the car parked behind Jenna's.

Shay and Olivia both waved at me through the windshield.

"They could be gone for close to two hours, depending on how picky the girls are about their colors."

I looked over at Jenna after she spoke. "Two hours, no kids?"

"If you're okay with Shay taking Marley..."

"I'll grab the car seat out of your car. It'll be faster than getting to mine."

A smile stretched across Jenna's mouth. She turned her attention to Marley, asking, "What do you think, princess? Do you want to get your nails painted super pretty?"

The second my daughter started nodding her head, I stepped down off the porch and crossed the yard. I wasn't wasting any more time. We were already on day fifteen, half a fucking month, and that car seat could be the biggest pain in my ass. I needed to move.

"Hey, Nate!" Olivia leaned across Shay's lap and waved at me out the driver's-side window.

"Hey, sweetheart." I stopped at Jenna's back seat and smiled at Shay. "Hey. Thanks for offering to do this."

"Desperate times," she replied coyly.

"What?"

"Nothing." She dropped her sunglasses in front of her eyes.

Jenna walked over with Marley and jumped into conversation with the girls. I got to work on the car seat, nearly snapping one of the belts in half in the process of getting it out of the car. *This shit should not be that difficult.* I paused with it at Shay's hood when she leaned out the window, hollering.

"No need! I got two back here for Sean's girls. The youngest is still in that stage." She gestured with a flick of her hand. "We're good!"

My face hardened. "You couldn't have mentioned something *before* I pulled it out?"

Jenna laughed, and I turned my head.

"God, I could make the best joke right now," Shay said.

I stalked back over to Jenna's car. Securing the car seat took twice as long as removing it. By the time I was finished, sweat beaded on my forehead and the back of my shirt was damp.

"Your car is like an oven," I said, stopping beside Jenna. I waved at the girls as they backed out of the driveway, then used the hem of my tee to wipe my face.

Jenna groaned, looking at my abs. "Please refrain from any more of *that* until they turn off your street. We're almost in the clear."

I let go of my shirt, laughing. "Shay knows this whole scheme is just us buying time to have sex all over my house, correct?"

The car pulled away.

"Well, I left out the 'all over your house' part, but yes. She knows we wanted a little privacy."

Was it weird having one of my employees help me out in this situation? Yes. Was it weird enough that I wouldn't capitalize on this opportunity? Absolutely not.

I stared at Jenna's profile until she slowly turned to look at me. "What?" she asked.

"I'm about to fuck the shit out of you."

Her eyes widened. *Damn. Was that too blunt?*

"Romantically, of course," I quickly added, just in case. "Also, you look really pretty today. Have I told you that?" I adjusted my glasses.

Laughter burst out of Jenna's mouth. She grabbed my hand and pulled me across the yard, backing up toward the house. "Can I make a request before we begin all this romantic fucking?"

"Go for it."

"Leave your glasses on for me."

When Jenna reached the porch, I stepped toward her and

bent down, gripping her thighs and guiding her legs around my waist.

She gasped and held on to my neck, breathing sharply against my mouth. "Please," she whispered.

"You got it."

I smiled, kissing her, and carried her inside.

* * *

"Oh my God, you should've seen your face!" Jenna rolled onto her stomach beside me and dug her elbows into the mattress, propping herself up. Her breasts billowed against the sheet. "You looked so angry at my romper. I thought you were going to rip it to shreds."

"I almost did when it refused to come off. What the fuck?" I tucked messy strands behind her ear, getting them out of her face. "That was the most confusing piece of clothing I've ever seen. Never wear that again."

"You figured it out." She leaned over, pressing her lips to my abs and then resting her cheek there. She sighed in content. "That was some top-notch romantic fucking. Well done, Mr. Bell."

I smiled at her.

"I saw the new billboard today. It looks really good."

"Yeah, I thought so too. Tori did a great job with it."

I was kicking myself for not giving Tori a management position a long time ago. I could've been spending more time with Marley. With Sadie...I pushed that guilt out of my head. I didn't want to think about what-ifs right now.

"What made you want to own your own restaurant? Did you always want to do that?" Jenna asked.

"No." I bent my arm and slid it behind my head, raising myself up higher. "Not until college. Sadie came up with the idea. We met working at this restaurant on campus."

"I don't know that story. Tell it to me."

"There really isn't a story. We were both servers..."

"Who made the first move?"

"I guess I did." I chuckled at the memory. "She, uh... This place we worked at, you had to write your name backward and upside down on these paper tablecloths when you first introduced yourself, before going over specials and shit."

"That sounds difficult. Backward *and* upside down?" Jenna lifted her hand and slowly traced her finger in the air. "I don't think I could do it."

"It was hard, but I got good at it. Sadie was terrible. She couldn't get it down. So I started watching out and when people got seated in her section, I'd go over there first and write her name for her."

Jenna smiled against me. "That's sweet. I love a good meet-cute."

My brow furrowed. "A good *what?*"

"How a couple meets for the first time... a meet-cute."

"Did you just make that up?"

"No. People use it."

"Who are these people besides *you*? Did my daughter teach you this phrase? This sounds like something Marley would say when she first started forming sentences."

"Shut up." Jenna giggled, and I laughed with her. "So you got together and talked about owning your own restaurant?"

"Eventually it came up. I majored in business to cover my ass. I didn't have one fucking clue what I'd end up doing. During one of our shifts together, Sadie mentioned something about owning our own place and everything we'd do better than the management we were working under. We'd throw out ideas, trying to top the other person. Closer to graduation, I thought more seriously about it. Then it became something I had to do. I wanted it."

"Did Sadie ever work at Whitecaps?"

"Not like I do or how you're thinking. She was a financial examiner—that was her actual job—so yeah, she did stuff on that end...I mean, Whitecaps was ours. We were in that together, but she also worked a lot on her own. There were weeks where she'd work more than I did. Until she had Marley..."

I thought about how different Sadie became after that. Going from a woman who barely spent any time at home to one who hardly ever left the house. I remembered our conversation about her wanting to cut short her maternity leave.

"You were both workaholics," Jenna concluded.

"Can we talk about something else?" I asked. She nodded immediately. "Sorry, I just...That's basically the whole story anyway. There's not much else to say about it." That wasn't entirely a lie. At least I'd given Jenna what she'd asked for.

"What do you want to talk about?" she said.

"You." Her one visible cheek deepened in color with her flush. "Where did you go to school? I don't think you ever told me."

"I probably didn't. I went to this little community college out in Denver. You wouldn't know it." Her gaze fell between us to a spot on the sheet. The corner of her mouth twitched.

"What are you thinking about right now?" I asked.

"I'm not thinking about anything."

"And I'm not borderline obsessed with your rack."

Jenna looked into my face and smiled. When my phone began to ring, she lifted her head and peered over at the nightstand. "Do you need to get that?"

I reached over and checked the caller. "It's just my parents. I'll call them back," I said, hitting ignore. "They're probably calling to talk to Marley anyway." I settled against the pillow again. "Go ahead. Tell me what you were thinking."

Jenna sighed, dropping her cheek against me. "I'm not sure I want to admit this, or if it's even something I should *think* without anyone else knowing about it..."

"Well, now you absolutely have to tell me," I said, pushing my frames up my nose. "I kept the glasses on for you, didn't I?"

"Oh, I hadn't realized your sight was something only *I* cared about."

"Jenna." I forced a serious tone. "Why are you such a liar?"

Her mouth dropped open. "How am I a liar?"

"You wanted me wearing my glasses because you like how I look in them. Your request had jack shit to do with my vision."

I could see fine without my glasses, as long as I wasn't trying to read something. She knew it too. I'd shared that information with Jenna before. And I knew exactly how she looked at me when I wore them, compared to when I didn't. The difference was subtle, but it was there.

Jenna lifted her head and fought a smile. "I care very much about whether you can see properly. Even during intimate moments."

"I was thinking about changing frames."

"You better not."

"No? Are you saying you prefer these? I thought it was *all about my vision*..." I grinned at her then.

She huffed out a breath and rolled her eyes. "Fine... but I do care about your sight, Nathan."

"That's sweet."

"Thank you. It is, isn't it? You're welcome for that."

We were both laughing now.

"Damn, you're fun," I said, stroking her cheek.

A warm look passed over her face. "So are you."

"What were you thinking about before? You can tell me."

Jenna bit her lip and shook her head.

"Come on…" I rubbed her side. "I want to know."

Shit, I felt like I *needed* to know. Had any thought ever been this important?

"I wish you'd been the boy in my freshman psych class," she blurted. Her eyes closed and pinched shut. "Um…yeah, I totally said that."

I stared at her. I couldn't blink. Breathe. I didn't dare move.

"I just…I wish there was some way I could have everything I have right now." She looked at me then. "And you could have everything you have, minus…I wouldn't want the bad things too. I'd never want that…What I mean is, if there were a way it could've been you instead, but obviously I wouldn't want to take away what you had with Sadie. That's not what I mean."

Jenna flinched and sat up, kneeling beside my hip. She quickly gathered the sheet in front of herself, tucking it underneath her arms and around her thighs so she was covered.

"See, this is why I didn't want to admit this—I know exactly what I'm trying to say and it's coming out all wrong…" She started rushing through the rest. "What I meant to say was, if there were a way to keep things how they are now, with the kids, but change how it happened…for *me*." Her hand flattened to her chest. "Change it for me, not you. I don't mean you, Nathan. I'm not saying—"

I jerked upright and kissed her.

Jenna moaned when our lips touched. Her breath was quick

against my mouth. "I'm sorry...I know how that sounded. I shouldn't have said that."

"Stop." My hand slid from her cheek to the back of her neck. I guided her down to her side, pulling the sheet away and rolling Jenna onto her back.

She stared up at me, expecting me to say more, and I couldn't. I couldn't think to speak. My heart was pounding too loud. I could barely hear Jenna's quiet begging voice when I began to kiss my way down her body, let alone the thoughts I was trying to grasp at.

I didn't dare move before. I couldn't stop myself now.

I kissed her breasts, her ribs, the sweet dip in her stomach and lower. I hovered my mouth between her legs and watched her eyes roll closed as I breathed in and out, right fucking there.

"Nathan." She gasped, spreading her thighs wider. Urging me.

I nuzzled my mouth against her pussy.

Jenna whimpered and pushed her hand into my hair. She held me still when I tongued her clit like she never wanted me to move, but when I licked lower between the folds of her sex, she jerked her hips up and pressed herself against my mouth. She rocked into the pleasure.

"God...oh God, *please*," she begged. Her stomach quivered underneath my hand.

I slid my touch up her body and squeezed her breast. I worked her with my tongue, licking where she grew wettest, and sucked on her clit until she trembled against the bed. And when she arched her back and shook against my mouth, I didn't dare close my eyes.

Jenna panted and writhed as she came, gripping my hair and tugging, her pretty voice crying out.

Again, *still*, I couldn't speak. I could only move.

Her legs fell heavy against the mattress as I slid them from my shoulders and then curled around my waist when I crawled up her body. I sank over her.

We kissed long and deep. Jenna moaned when she felt how hard I was, trapped between our bodies. She tried peering down to see it. Her hand sought me out and cupped the tip.

"I want you," she said.

Move, I thought.

I pushed up, straightening my arms, and reached for the nightstand to grab another condom.

On my knees between her bent legs, I rolled the rubber down my shaft, then covered Jenna's body with mine again and pushed inside her.

Finally, *finally*, words flooded my mouth. I chased after my thoughts, sharing every single one as they came to me. I couldn't stop giving them to her.

I told Jenna how amazing she was. How again, this was too good. *How is this real? Tell me.* I said she made my favorite sounds. And after I came seconds before she did, I pressed my mouth to her ear and told her how hard I was again already. How I'd never been this into someone before.

I said everything short of admitting I felt the same way she did, that I wished it had been me in her psych class too. That I knew exactly what she had been trying to say and how she said it perfectly to me. No one could've said it better. I didn't think those words were needed. She had to know...

I was out of my mind for this woman. How could she not see it?

chapter twenty-one

JENNA

After Shay dropped the girls off with freshly painted nails, Nathan offered to make us dinner. A gesture I was beyond excited about—no man had ever made me dinner before. Not one I was dating anyway. He also insisted on handling all preparations and forced me over to the table after I kept grabbing ingredients to rinse, chop, and/or dice, even after he told me not to.

"I said I'll do it. Do I need to tie you down?" Nathan asked low in my ear, pulling out one of the kitchen chairs and guiding me to sit.

"I'm sorry! I can't help it." I laughed. "I'm just used to doing everything. It's weird when I don't. And it isn't like I mind lending you a hand..."

"I know you don't mind. That's not the point." Nathan moved around the kitchen. "I'm not great at this. I can cook three things really well and spaghetti is one of them. That's why I suggested we have spaghetti." He stopped in front of the cutting board, admiring the prep I'd completed. "Jenna..."

"What?" I giggled at his solemn expression.

"I'm trying to show off a little here," he said, lifting his gaze. "How am I supposed to do that if you dice the onion better than me?"

Every muscle in my body tightened in delight. "I didn't know you were trying to show off."

"For you? When am I not?"

Nathan studied me for a moment like I was insane to think anything different than what he'd just shared, then gathered the cut-up veggies and walked over to the stove, dumping them in the sauce.

I looked down at my lap and bit my lower lip. I couldn't stop smiling. He was trying to impress me. How could I not feel so happy I could burst?

No one had made an effort like this for me before. No one had come close.

Earlier, I had been terrified to share what had been on my mind, not only in that moment, but recently, for at least the past few weeks. I had no idea how Nathan would react to hearing me say I wished it would've been him and not Derek nine years ago. I knew exactly how that admission sounded and the implications it would lead to. Revealing that was a huge risk. Even worse, I'd gone on trying to explain myself and had failed miserably in my clarification.

I should've felt embarrassed, and for long, uncomfortable seconds, I did. I wanted to take it all back. *Way to show your inexperience with relationships, Jenna.* I'd said too much. I was moving us too fast. Nathan would pull back and slow us down. His apprehension would be obvious. I waited for it.

He kissed me instead. And the way we came together after, the look in Nathan's eyes and every moaned word he spoke, his desperate grip on my body...I'd never felt so sure of my feelings for someone before. Any worry I'd had, any regret that I had misspoken and overstepped, it slipped away.

Falling in love was overwhelmingly scary. It was also becoming the easiest thing I had ever done.

The girls giggled from the family room, getting my attention off my lap. I leaned over to peer at them around the table.

Olivia was on her hands and knees, stacking dominoes behind the couch in a slithering snake pattern. Marley sat beside her, watching closely while clutching the bucket of tiles in her lap.

I stood, heading for the stairs. I'd left my phone on Nathan's nightstand, forgetting to grab it after we hastily dressed.

"What are you doing?" he asked, his back to me. "I swear to God, Jenna, if you touch that garlic bread..."

I laughed loudly, and hearing me, Nathan looked over his shoulder and grinned.

"I'm just getting my phone," I told him, pausing at the corner of the island. "The girls look so sweet. I want to take a picture of them before they move."

"Here." Nathan kept stirring the sauce with one hand and with the other, dug his phone out of his pocket. He stretched his arm out and held it above the counter. "Take pictures with mine. By the time you come back down, they'll be doing something else."

He was right about that.

"Thanks." I hurried over, reaching across the island, and took Nathan's phone.

"The password is 0502."

I blushed, meeting his eyes.

"Surprised I told you that?" he asked.

"No..."

"You sure? You look surprised." Nathan turned back to the sauce.

Surprised wasn't the word I'd use for what I was feeling. I was happy. This was another first for me. I'd never been serious enough with anyone to be in the "sharing passwords" stage. Mm. I really liked this stage.

"Mine is 1387," I announced as I moved out of the kitchen. When I glanced back at Nathan, our eyes met.

He'd already been looking at me. And he was looking at me in a way that told me he liked this stage as much as I did.

In that moment, another piece of my heart became his.

I stopped in the family room a few feet away from the girls and clicked the home button. Several notifications appeared on the screen.

Nathan had two missed calls now, both from his parents' house. His ringer must've been off, because the last call was made two minutes ago. There was also an unread text from his dad.

Checking in. Call me please.

"Hey, did you know your parents called you again?" I asked, peering behind me. Nathan was carrying the large pot over to the sink. Steam wafted into the air as he dumped the water and noodles into a strainer. "Your dad texted you too. He says to call him. Do you want to do it now?"

"No. I'll call them after dinner. I'm sure they just want to talk to Marley. They haven't in a few days."

"Okay." I entered the passcode and pulled up the camera mode, turning the phone sideways to get the shot. "Girls, smile!"

Olivia and Marley whipped their heads around. Both of them grinned. "Cheese!" they said in unison.

I took three quick photos, catching the two of them as their heads drifted closer together. "So cute!" I crooned.

I spun around and drifted back into the kitchen, nearly reaching the island when Nathan's phone vibrated in my hand. I glanced at the screen. It was a text from Davis.

Don't read it. This isn't for you, I thought as my eyes automatically scanned the message. I stopped frozen, a foot away from the counter, and read the message again.

Your dad just called. Says he's been trying to reach you. I know today is 2 years. U ok?

I lifted my head and looked at Nathan.

He was standing at the oven, adding more seasoning to the sauce. He gave it a stir and then tasted it as today's date flashed in my mind.

It was July 29.

A date that had absolutely no meaning to me before this very moment. Now I knew it as the day Sadie took her own life.

"It's almost ready," Nathan said, pushing bottles around the spice cabinet he was searching through. "Am I out of red pepper flakes? I can't find any."

My breathing slowed and grew louder as a single, worrying thought circled inside my head. Nathan could not have spent the afternoon with me, doing everything we did and saying everything he said without forgetting what today was. I didn't think this sweet, thoughtful man would be cooking us dinner and making me feel so incredibly important to him without overlooking the reason I could be here right now.

"Nathan?" My voice hitched and was too quiet for him to hear, but God, I didn't know if I had it in me to speak any louder.

I didn't want to do this. I didn't know if I *could* do this. I just knew I had to. I couldn't know and let him forget.

I moved closer, close enough I wouldn't need to raise my

voice. Close enough I could hold his hand or wrap my arms around him if I needed to.

"Nathan," I repeated at his back.

He closed the cabinet door and stirred the sauce. "It's fine. I don't need it. It's good without the added heat."

"Can you stop for a second?"

"It's almost ready. Let me just put the garlic bread in..."

I wrapped my hand around Nathan's elbow and held on to him when he attempted to step around me. "Nathan, *stop*," I pleaded. "Please..."

He looked at me then. At my eyes as they watered. Then at my hand on his arm. My grip was severe.

"What?" he asked, lifting his gaze. "What is it? What's wrong?"

"Your phone...Davis texted you." I pressed the device into his hand. "I think you need to call your dad, Nathan."

"I'll call him later—I'm busy." His eyes jumped between mine. "What's going on? Why do you look like you're about to cry? What the hell did Davis say?"

"It's July twenty-ninth," I whispered.

He stared at me for a long moment. "Okay...so it's July twenty-ninth." He shook his head, laughing a little. He was lost. He didn't know... "Is that all he said? It's also Thursday. I'm not sure why that's something he thought I—"

Nathan blinked once, and then rapidly in succession, as if someone had just given him a hard shake. His lips parted as he gulped in a breath. There was suddenly so much shock and hurt in his eyes. And his breathing...It was labored now and so much louder than mine could have ever been.

"How do you know?" he asked quietly.

"Davis. His text... Your dad reached out to him. He was worried when you didn't answer your phone." I watched Nathan raise the device between us and pull up his messages. "I'm sorry I read it. It just popped up on the screen. I…What do you need right now? Do you need me to do something?"

"Like what?"

"I can call your parents, if you want. I don't know…" My eyes burned with the threat of tears. "I don't know what you need, Nathan. What can I do for you?"

"Nothing." His voice was gruff, thick with emotion, as he stuffed his phone into the pocket of his shorts. "I don't need you to do anything. I just—" He peered over my head at the island. "Um, let me just…get this garlic bread in."

I planted my hands on his chest. "Nathan, dinner can wait."

"No, it can't." He spoke with finality, and he was holding on to my wrists now and tugging, lowering my arms between us. "Let me do this, Jenna. Everything else is ready."

"Don't you want to talk first?"

"No." He moved past me then. "No, I don't want to talk. I want to finish making you dinner. That's the only thing I want to do right now."

I plastered myself against the counter as Nathan slid the tray of garlic bread into the oven and set the timer for five minutes. He stayed facing away. He took the sauce off the heat, wiped the counter down with a towel, and stacked our plates.

I watched him move on autopilot. That had to be what he was doing…Nothing else explained how he was staying so focused right now. And I wanted to make him stop. I wanted to reach out and hold on to him so badly, but I didn't.

Finally he had nothing left to do and stood still, flattening his hands on the granite. His back to me and his head lowered.

I moved to him then, hugging him from behind. "Nathan."

His body went stiff the moment my arms linked around his waist. A reaction he couldn't help or hide from me. We both felt it. Before I could ask or Nathan could explain, the oven timer sounded.

"Let me get that," he said, slipping away from me.

I wrapped my arms around my stomach as Nathan pulled the sheet tray from the oven and set it on the stovetop. The edges of the bread were brown and crisp. He turned the oven off, then glanced at the sauce and the plates stacked on the counter as he tugged out his phone.

"I need to give my parents a call. You can start eating."

"We can wait for you."

Nathan shook his head as he brought the phone to his ear. "I don't know how long I'll be," he said, moving past me.

"Of course."

He wouldn't rush this phone call. He *shouldn't* rush it.

I felt helpless as I watched Nathan ascend the stairs. I would've done anything for him in that moment, anything he needed, and even though eating the meal Nathan had prepared seemed incredibly unimportant in the grand scheme of things, I knew I could at least get the girls fed. Taking care of Marley was something I could absolutely do for him.

After making their plates and getting them set up with drinks, I padded into the family room.

I smiled when they smiled and talked about how delicious the meal looked as we cleaned up their mess. Their joy was easy to latch on to. Especially Marley's. I hugged her a little tighter on our walk to the kitchen.

"I love spaghetti," Olivia announced, climbing into her chair. "Hey, where's Nate?"

"He'll be down soon. Napkin in your lap, please." I got

Marley buckled in her booster chair and handed her the cup she always used. "Let's eat before it gets cold." I took a seat beside her.

Olivia didn't waste any time, twirling noodles on her fork and stuffing her mouth. She chewed loudly and licked sauce off her lip. "Mm."

"Good?" I asked, helping Marley with her bite. She slurped a noodle, giggling at herself.

"So good," Olivia said, concentrating hard as she spun her fork, getting her next bite ready. "Aren't you eating too?"

Marley reached for her plate I was holding, wanting more.

"Of course I am," I said.

After helping Marley with her next bite, breaking off a piece of garlic bread and giving that to her as well, I slid the small portion I'd plated for myself in front of me and picked up my fork. Zero appetite aside, I was going to eat the dinner Nathan had prepared. He'd worked hard on it. I alternated taking bites for myself and assisting Marley with hers, and Olivia had been right. It was *so good*. The sauce was full of flavor.

As I ate, I watched the stairs, waiting for Nathan to return. I wanted him to see how much we were enjoying his meal. But he didn't come back down. And we finished eating without him.

After cleanup, which including wiping off Marley, who had a face covered in sauce, and putting the leftovers into the fridge, I grabbed the bucket of dominoes from the family room and returned to the table with them.

"Olivia, I want you to play right here, okay?"

I handed Marley a couple of blocks. She was still in her booster seat, and I wanted her to stay there for now—she was safely confined and content.

"Stack them on the table. Try to make a snake again." I set

287

the bucket in front of Olivia. "I need to go upstairs and I'm not sure how long I'm going to be up there. If Marley wants to get down, come get me, okay?"

"Okay." Olivia stood from her seat and dug around the bucket. "Is Nate coming back?"

"That's what I'm going to find out."

"Is he sick?"

"Sweetheart, please...just play with your dominoes."

"Okay, okay. That's what I'm doing."

Olivia began stacking the blocks in front of Marley. Kids occupied and self-control stretched thin, I gave in to the overwhelming urge I'd been battling against during our meal and finally slipped upstairs. The hallway was quiet as I walked past Marley's nursery. I strained to listen.

Nathan's bedroom door was open and the light was on. If he was still on the phone with his dad or someone else, I wouldn't eavesdrop. I'd let him know I was there to talk if he wanted, and then I'd leave him to his call.

But I didn't hear his voice. I didn't hear a sound.

Nathan was seated on the bed, hunched forward with his elbows on his knees and his head lowered as he studied a spot on the carpet. The phone was beside him on the mattress.

"Hey," I said softly, hovering in the doorway.

He didn't look at me. "Did you eat?"

"Yes. The girls loved it. They both had seconds."

"And you?"

God, he was so caught up in this meal. Why was this so important right now?

Nathan looked over at me when I didn't answer. "Jenna, please, if you didn't eat yet—"

"I ate. It was delicious, Nathan." I took a small step forward. "Can I come in?"

He nodded. His dark, serious eyes followed me as I took a seat beside him on the bed. "I'm glad you liked it."

"It was probably the best spaghetti I've ever had. Didn't even need those red pepper flakes." I gave him a smile he didn't return. "Thank you for making me dinner."

"I've wanted to do it for a while..."

"I wish we could've enjoyed it together." I placed my hand on his thigh, and when Nathan looked away and resumed staring at the carpet, I asked the question eating away at my mind. "Are you okay?"

Breath moved through his body, lifting his chest and shoulders. He shook his head.

"What can I do for you?"

"Nothing."

"Do you want to talk about it?" When he didn't give me an answer, I pulsed my hand on his leg. "Nathan..."

"No, I...I'm sorry. I don't want to talk about this with you."

I flinched, involuntarily squeezing his thigh again before I pulled away.

"I'm sorry, Jenna," he rushed out. "I know how that sounded. That's not...I don't mean—"

"It's okay." Hurt filled my voice. I dropped my hands together in my lap. "I'm sorry for prying."

"You're not prying."

"Do you want me to go back downstairs?"

"I don't know," he mumbled. He stood from the bed.

"Nathan, just be honest with me—if you want me to go, I'll go."

A heavy sigh left him as he pushed his hand through his hair. God, he seemed so conflicted right now. Why?

"Nathan." I stood then too, getting in front of him. "Talk to me. Please...I can't tell what you want me to do." I cupped his face. "What are you thinking? What's going through your head? Tell me..."

His neck rolled with a swallow. Reaching up, Nathan held on to my wrists and pulled my hands away from his face. "I don't want you here right now."

"Okay. I'll go back downstairs."

"I don't mean *here*..."

My breath caught, the hand of rejection slamming me in the chest as his meaning became clear. He wanted me to *leave* leave?

"O-okay," I stammered, shuffling back to separate us. I crossed my arms and then lowered them a second later. I stared at the carpet.

My discomfort was obvious, but how could I hide it? I wanted so badly to be here for Nathan, to help him, and he didn't want me to be.

"Thank you again for dinner," I said, my voice surprisingly steady. "I'll just grab my phone and then I'll go."

When I tried to move around him to get to the nightstand on the far side of the bed, Nathan's arm shot out and caught me around the waist. He turned to me and fit us together.

"I'm sorry," he said, grabbing my face now and tilting it up so I would look at him. His voice was pained. "I'm not trying to hurt you."

"It's fine." I stared into his eyes, my lips trembling. "It's fine, Nathan, r-really. It's...I'll go. You want me to go."

"I don't want you to go, okay?" He leaned down, putting his face closer to mine. "If you're asking me what I *want*, it's not that. It would never be that. Jesus Christ...I couldn't want you with me more, Jenna. I want you next to me all the time. You're never close enough...I just can't do this right now. You don't understand."

"So, help me understand. Talk to me."

He just needed to let me in. We'd work through this together. I could help him...I knew I could.

"I know how this must look, how *I* must look to you."

"What do you mean?" I pulled back to see him better. His arms dropped. "Nathan." I placed my hand on his chest. "I'm not judging you...Is that what you're talking about?"

No...How could he think that?

"I forgot." His voice deepened and shook. "*You know* I forgot...you were the one who had to tell me." Nathan read my thoughts and continued before I could correct him. "Through Davis—I know, but it was you who told me, Jenna. It shouldn't have been you."

The text? *Really?* Didn't I already apologize for that?

"I'm sorry I read your text. I really wasn't trying to..."

Nathan shook his head and sighed. He was obviously getting frustrated. "This is why I asked you to go. I knew if we did this now, you wouldn't understand..."

"I'm trying to understand." I spoke slowly, my voice pitching louder. "You're not making it easy, Nathan. I still don't know if you want me to apologize for reading your text or not."

"I don't give a shit about you reading my texts."

"Then what is it?"

"I could've dealt with this on my own!"

I stormed around him to close the door. "The girls..."

"Fuck. Sorry...I'm sorry."

"It's fine. I don't think they heard you." I spun around to face him and moved closer, urging him with my hand. "Keep going.

You could've dealt with this on your own. Okay. And with me here, you can't?" *What does that mean?*

Nathan looked down. I could hear his breathing.

"Come on, Nathan. How am I supposed to understand if you don't tell me?" I stopped right in front of him.

He lifted his head. *Here we go.*

"It's fucked up, okay?" he nearly growled. "I know it is. *I know how this looks.* Who the fuck forgets the day their wife committed suicide? Who needs a reminder of the worst day of their life? I never should've had you here today, Jenna. I didn't need you telling me Sadie died two years ago. That shouldn't have been you!"

Heat burned across my face. I suddenly felt cornered, blamed for Nathan's distress and the anger he was feeling.

"I don't know what you would've wanted me to do...just hand you your phone back and act like I didn't know? I couldn't do that."

His nostrils flared. I wasn't the only one getting irritated with this exchange.

"If you weren't here, it wouldn't have happened. It wouldn't have been you telling me."

"Okay. Coming over today was a mistake. It shouldn't have happened."

He shook his head as if to argue.

"*What?* Nathan, that's what you *just said...*"

"That's not what I meant. I don't regret what happened four hours ago in this room or how I felt...I don't regret any of that. Do you?"

"No, of course not. I didn't mean it like that. I'm not saying *that* was a mistake."

"Then what are you saying?" he asked.

"I'm still trying to understand why you're mad at me for this."

"I'm not mad at you. *Jesus Christ.*" He gripped his hair. "How could you think I'm mad at you?"

"How could I not? You keep saying it's *me. I* shouldn't have been here. *I* shouldn't have told you..."

"I'm not mad at you for telling me. I'm angry that it was *you who told me*, okay? It's—" He paused, his jaw tight. "Fuck, this is frustrating..."

"It is."

He wanted me here. He didn't. He wasn't mad at me. He was absolutely mad—that was certain. My head was spinning.

"I don't know how else to say it. I can't explain this to you..."

"You're not really trying to explain it though."

He stared at me. "What? Yes, I am."

"You just keep repeating the same thing, Nathan. That's not explaining."

"Because I don't know how else to tell you! It shouldn't have been you, Jenna! *That's it!* And if you weren't here right now, it *wouldn't* have been you."

"Well, maybe if you would've remembered..."

Nathan blinked, jerking back as if I'd slapped him. I might as well have.

My mouth immediately dropped open, which I quickly covered with my hand. *Oh my God. How could I say that?* I shook my head, gearing up for the apology of my life. I didn't mean that at all...

"I'm so sorry," I rushed out, my hand sliding down my neck. "I don't know why I said that. I don't feel that way, Nathan. I swear."

God, how did this conversation get so out of control?

"No, you're right," he said somberly. "This is on me. I mean,

293

I should've remembered..." He looked down and rubbed the back of his neck. "I should've done a lot of things..." His voice trailed off.

"I don't know where that came from. I think it's just, we're having difficulty understanding each other and we're both getting frustrated...We were bound to say something we didn't mean."

"This is why I didn't want to get into this tonight."

He hadn't, and he'd made that known. This was on me.

"I pushed you. It's my fault."

"I'm too angry with myself. I never should've raised my voice to you." He lifted his head, and there was so much sadness and regret in his eyes now, it stole my breath.

I went to move closer. I wanted to hold on to Nathan so badly, I felt like I needed it, but he gestured at the door with his hand, halting me where I stood.

"I should go downstairs and get Marley," he said. He left off *and you should leave*, but I still heard it. *How could I not?*

Our conversation might've been a string of misunderstandings and misspoken words, but Nathan was clear on one thing. He didn't want me here right now. He didn't want to do this tonight, with me.

I was the factor.

"Thank you for taking care of her while I was on the phone. I think I forgot to thank you for that," he said.

"Of course. No thanks needed."

I walked around him to grab my phone and keys and followed Nathan to the door, but I ended up leading him down the hallway and stairs when he stepped back, urging me to go ahead. We were silent as we walked. We'd said so much to each other minutes ago, and now I felt like I couldn't speak.

The girls were still playing dominoes at the table when we got to the kitchen, giving no indication of either one of them hearing any parts of the conversation Nathan and I just had.

"Nate!" Olivia jumped out of her chair. "Check out this pattern. Isn't it cool?"

Nathan unbuckled Marley and pulled her into his arms. "Yeah, it is. Good job."

"Wanna build with us?"

I guided Olivia away from the table. "Go pack up your things, please. We need to go."

Her face fell. "But we're playing…"

"We need to be home before your brother gets there."

Thank God for that. I knew Olivia would prolong this goodbye if I didn't give her a reason to hurry.

"Fine." My daughter dropped her head back and sighed, pouting into the family room and stepping in front of the couch. She packed up her duffle.

Like he always did, Nathan walked us to the door. I hit the button on the key fob once I stepped out onto the porch, unlocking the car for Olivia.

"Bye, guys!" she hollered, sprinting across the yard, her duffle bouncing against her hip.

I faced Nathan when he stepped outside and considered what I wanted to say to him. I still felt caught in this weird state of shock. I replayed our conversation, obsessing over it as words stuck to my tongue. Why was it suddenly so difficult to talk to the one person I never had any difficulty speaking to?

"You don't need to keep Marley for me on Saturday," Nathan said, saving us from the awkward silence we were being swallowed up in. "I'm going to take off work for a few days. Maybe more, I don't know. I just need some time with her."

I nodded tightly. "Sure. Of course."

I couldn't help feeling disappointed. I wanted to help him. Not just in terms of watching Marley. I wanted to help him through *this*. Despite how things transpired tonight.

"Nathan, I know tonight was…difficult and didn't…I mean, I know it didn't help, but you can always talk to me."

He tilted his head. I didn't know if he was about to turn down my offer or ask me to stop talking altogether at this point, but I kept going. I had to get this out.

"You can talk to me about anything. I just need you to know that, okay? I don't want you thinking you need to go through this alone, or anything alone. I'm here. I'll always be here. What I said upstairs—I didn't mean that. I would never mean that. Ever. I—I…" My voice broke. "I'm so, so sorry. I hate that I said that to you."

Tears pricked at my eyes and spilled onto my cheeks. I couldn't help my emotions. I felt raw and exposed, like I'd been split open. That conversation had kicked the shit out of me.

Nathan didn't contest what I was saying. He didn't speak at all. He stepped in, wrapped his free arm around my shoulders, and pulled me against his chest. His breath pushed through my hair.

"I'm sorry," I whispered.

His arm tightened around me.

I molded to him, gripping his shirt and back. I'd never hugged him so tight, and I wanted to stretch this out, but he wanted me to go. When I anticipated the end of our embrace and tried to pull back, Nathan shocked me by holding on, prolonging our hug.

I clung to him before. I could've sworn he was the one doing it now.

"Nathan." I peered up at his jaw. "I can stay. I don't have to go yet." I held my breath. *Please ask me to stay.*

He shook his head and let his arm drop. "I'll call you."

"Okay." My heart took another hit.

Stepping back, I regarded him. I felt like I was suddenly wearing a mask, hiding my disappointment and the hurt filling me. It took everything inside of me to pretend I was okay with leaving, when in reality I felt the furthest from it.

"Jenna, wook. See?" Marley held out her hand, showing off her nails.

It was hard to believe that was how today had started—Shay taking the girls to get manicures. The hours with Nathan I had that followed and everything we'd shared. How loved I'd felt and how in love with him I'd fallen.

Our day together felt like a lifetime ago.

chapter twenty-two

NATHAN

I stood on the porch until Jenna's car disappeared. Then I carried Marley inside and fought every urge I had to pull the phone from my pocket and call Jenna to come back.

But I couldn't. It was bad enough forgetting the anniversary of my wife's death, but having Jenna *know* I'd forgotten? Having her be the one to remind me? I'd never felt shame like this, and I'd felt it on an unbelievable level when it came to Sadie.

I didn't want to see anyone tonight. I didn't want to speak to anyone either. My parents had offered to come over when I returned my dad's call earlier. Davis had as well. I'd declined everyone.

The only person I could be around right now was Marley. I carried her upstairs and sat with her in the rocker, reading story after story until she pulled me to the floor. Marley collected toys and dropped them in my lap. She smiled and giggled as we played.

For a moment, I think we both forgot how badly I continued to let her down.

That night, I barely slept. I sat in Marley's room long after she'd fallen asleep. I didn't want to leave her. And I didn't want to close my eyes anyway. I was certain of the dream I would have, but when I drifted off, seated in the rocker, it was Marley I dreamed about.

I saw my daughter years from now. Older and able to understand what today was. I pictured her grief and the overwhelming anger she would feel. I watched her grow up and go through it alone, because in this nightmare I continued to forget.

Fear became my motivation. I stirred awake at four in the morning and lifted Marley out of her crib. I spoke promises to her as she slept. I told her how sorry I was for not making today about her and shared memories of Sadie as the sun came up.

Marley woke hours later with my voice in her ear. She rubbed her sleepy face against my chest, then wiggled out of my hold and guided me to play.

I should've felt relieved. She wasn't angry with me or sad. She didn't act disappointed, and over the next few days we became closer. Inseparable. I spent every waking moment with my daughter and prolonged our time together until sleep became a necessity. I cut off everyone but her. I ignored every call and text. I got coverage for work and made arrangements so I didn't need to leave her. I did what I should've been doing all along...I made Marley my life. So I didn't understand why I still felt like I was messing up. I couldn't shake my failure. I held on to it.

Why shouldn't I?

It was mine to bear and mine alone.

* * *

It was Wednesday afternoon when a knock sounded at the door.

I stood from the couch with Marley asleep on my chest. We'd given up on naps in her crib two days ago. They were pointless anyway. As of recently, I wouldn't let her out of my arms for long.

I wasn't expecting anyone today, so I had no idea who I was about to come face-to-face with.

I pictured Jenna on my porch and wanted it to be her so fucking badly, even though I hadn't reached out yet—I wasn't ready to—but it wasn't Jenna staring back at me when I opened the door. It was my father, and he was alone.

He never came here alone.

"Son," he said, dropping his head into a nod. His gaze slid to Marley where she remained asleep, her head on my shoulder. "Now, that's a sight I wasn't sure I'd ever see three months ago."

"What are you doing here?" I asked.

"Well, I wasn't about to be ignored much longer, Nathan. Five days is my limit." He stepped forward and paused to inquire, "May I come in?" even though we both knew he wasn't waiting for permission.

I stepped aside and closed the door behind him.

"Let's sit down," he suggested, gesturing at the kitchen table before walking toward it. He pulled out two chairs that were side by side, letting me know without words where he wanted me to sit. "Would you like me to take her for a while?"

"No. She's fine." I hugged Marley against my chest as I sank into the chair. No way was I giving her up.

My father gazed over at me and smiled. "You been doing much besides that the past few days?"

"Not really." There was no point in lying about it. I sighed into Marley's hair. "I'm sorry I haven't called or answered you. I'm just..." My chest grew impossibly tight. "I don't know what I'm doing, Dad. I keep messing up."

"What are you messing up, Nathan?"

"I forgot," I whispered. I turned my head and looked over at him. "How could I forget? What's wrong with me?"

"Hey." Dad leaned over and held onto the back of my neck. "There's nothing wrong with you. Nothing, okay? Things happen. You're finally living your life after two years of not doing that, and you just got caught up. Look how close the two of you are now. Don't regret what you've done to get here."

"I should've remembered...I keep letting her down. She'll hate me eventually."

"Who will?"

"*Marley.* I'm failing her, Dad."

His mouth twitched. "I hate to tell you this, but you will constantly feel that way, son. It's part of being a parent." He gave my neck a squeeze before releasing me and sitting back. "You don't think I have regrets when it comes to you?"

"Like what?" He was only saying that to make me feel better. How could my father have any regrets? I respected the hell out of him.

"Most recently, the past two years..."

When my eyes flared with confusion, Dad went on to explain.

"You were hurting, Nathan. I knew you were, and I sat back and watched you. I should've stepped in sooner. No matter how you chose to grieve or how long you needed to do it, I should've been there, at your side. I know that now."

"But you and Mom...you took care of Marley when I couldn't. How could you think you needed to do more?"

"Because I'm your father," he stated simply. "And there will never come a time when I'll think I've done enough when it comes to you."

I swallowed the lump forming in my throat. Fuck, I wanted to cry.

"I shouldn't have abandoned you the way I did before Memorial Day. I'm sorry about that too. At the time, I hadn't seen another way to force you to change, but I should've done it differently." He held my eyes. "I hope you can forgive me for that."

Is he serious? "Dad, if you hadn't done that, I wouldn't have *this*." I tipped my head down, gesturing at Marley. "Please stop apologizing to me."

"Okay, then," he said. "What about this woman you've been seeing? The one with the kids of her own. I'm surprised she isn't here." He glanced around the room. I stared at the table. "Son."

"I need to call her."

"Is there a reason you haven't?"

"She knows I forgot. She was here on Thursday."

"I see." Dad was silent for a moment. "You don't want her thinking you're the kind of man to forget something like that."

"That's not all I'm worried about," I said.

"Okay. What else is stopping you from calling her?"

I dropped my head and buried my face in Marley's hair. Tears built in my eyes as my father laid a comforting hand on my shoulder. I couldn't do this right now, but fuck, I wanted to. I wanted to get past this.

"What I feel for her—it's more than I've felt for anyone, including Sadie."

"And you don't think you should feel that?"

"I don't understand how I *could* feel it. I loved Sadie, Dad. I married her . . . What the hell am I feeling for Jenna if it's already more than that?" *And what will it become?*

My father dropped his hand and turned in his chair to face me. "Nathan, I'm going to say a few things, and I want you to let me finish before you step in, okay? Can you give me that?"

"Yeah."

Shit. That was all he was asking for? Momentary silence? He could have it. I owed him a lot more.

"You and Sadie loved each other, there was no doubt about that, but I'm not sure either one of you ever really *needed* the other. I don't think you allowed yourself to feel that for her, and I don't think she did either. Or maybe you simply couldn't. What-ever the case, I never saw a dependency there. You were solid with her and you were solid on your own. I think she was the same, until she wasn't."

Anger burned in my blood. I was solid without her? *What the fuck did that mean?*

I quickly looked over at him, ready to question whatever the hell this bullshit was he was trying to say, but I bit my tongue when I remembered the request to let him finish.

"I'm not saying that was necessarily a bad thing." He paused in thought. "I'm not saying it wasn't either. None of us know what Sadie was going through, but I refuse to put any blame on her and I sure as hell won't put it on you, so I'm going to move on and say that it's okay to need other people, Nathan. It is okay to let yourself rely on someone so they can help you through this life that can sure as hell be a real kick in the ass sometimes. I think what you're feeling for this woman is just that—you need her. And I hope I don't have to explain myself and clarify that I do not mean you *need her* in terms of watching Marley..."

"No, I know what you mean."

"This feels different to you because it is different," Dad went on. "It's bigger. When you move past loving someone to needing them—they become a necessity to your own survival. You no longer get to decide whether you can be without this person. You can't. It's decided for you. I think you're having difficulty understanding this because you've never felt it before. I also think maybe you're a little scared of it for the same reason."

I considered his explanation. I stepped outside of my own re-action to look at it more clearly, and fuck, he was right. How did I not see what this was? I did need Jenna. From the very begin-ning, I was better with her. Being together, simply listening to her voice and the things she would say to me, her encouragement, *everything.* Around Jenna I was who I wanted to be.

And even though it was strange and somewhat difficult to an-alyze my relationship with Sadie now, with her gone, I couldn't deny the truth. We hadn't been dependent on each other. We worked just as well together as we did on our own. We didn't rely on the other person for anything. That wasn't us.

"Why didn't I need Sadie?" I asked. "Why didn't I get there with her?"

My father was shaking his head before I finished speaking. "I don't have the answer to that, Nathan. I don't know if there is one...but I want to be clear on one thing: It doesn't matter if that guilt is yours and something only you can understand—it's okay to let someone help you through it. In fact, I think it's vital. Don't fight this."

"I'm not."

"Nathan."

My nostrils flared as I pulled in a breath. I wiped wetness from my eyes. "Dad, come on..."

"Don't *come on* me. I know you. I know there's things we haven't talked about and maybe you'll never talk about them with me, and I'll deal with that as long as I know you're going to give that woman everything you're feeling. Promise me you'll do that, son. Hey." He gripped my neck when I looked away and leaned in, gently forcing me to do the same. Our foreheads

304

touched. "Promise me," he begged, his voice tight. "You gotta have help with this, Nathan. We all lost Sadie. We are not losing you."

I could barely see him through the tears in my eyes. "How did you know?"

He stroked my neck, smiling a little as he sat back. "Do you think I don't see your guilt? That's another thing about being a parent—no one knows your child better than you do."

"I'm sorry... *fuck*." I pulled my glasses off and wiped my forearm across my face. "I know I should've talked about it. It's just hard."

"I know it is. I can only imagine the weight you carry around with you. There are things I've told your mother that have been difficult to share, but I don't hold back with her. She gets it all. And that's not just for me, Nathan. When I let her in like that, that's for her too. Do you understand what I'm saying?"

"Yeah."

"I'm sure that woman wanted to be here..."

"Her name is Jenna."

"Sorry. I'm sure Jenna wanted to be here..."

"I wanted her here. I always do. It's just..." I looked down, gritting my teeth. "I was embarrassed. The whole thing, it messed me up. It's *still* messing me up. I never would've told her I forgot about Sadie. I wouldn't want her thinking I could do that."

"Well, I'm going to tell you right now—that would've gotten you into trouble."

"What would've?" I lifted my gaze.

"Not sharing something like that," he explained. "Letting that eat away at you..."

"I'd rather Jenna not know about it than have her look at me any different."

"Nathan." My father shook his head and sighed through his nose.

"I can't lose her, Dad."

"You're going to lose her if you don't let her in." We stared at each other for a moment. "You can't worry about what-ifs, Nathan. That's no way to live." He brought his arms across his chest. "Your fear will make you miss out on a lot of things if you let it. Don't forget how close you were to missing out on her." He tipped his chin at Marley.

I pressed my mouth to her soft hair as I tried to imagine not knowing my daughter the way I did now. I couldn't even fathom it.

And Jenna...the best parts of me were a tribute to her. What was I without her?

"I'm worried I'll always be scared of this," I said. "Not enough to keep me from being with Jenna though. There's nothing that could stop me from that."

"The risk is what you're afraid of—how much you have to lose. I'd worry more if you weren't scared of it, to be honest."

I breathed a laugh, meeting his eyes. "You say that like you know how I feel."

My father slowly smiled. "The moment I think I'm okay with the possibility of being without your mother is the moment I'll need to reevaluate my entire life. I'm scared every day, son. Of loving her, of losing her. That's how I know it's right."

Marley stirred awake in my arms then and lifted her head off my chest. She rubbed at her eye, then peered behind her at my dad.

"There's my angel." Dad sat forward, arms outstretched, and took her from me.

"TaTa!" Marley crawled into his lap and hugged him.

I watched the goofiest grin take up my father's face, and I laughed. "I thought you hated that nickname."

My father was supposed to be Pop Pop, but Marley had difficulty pronouncing that early on. TaTa stuck with her. You couldn't get her to call him anything else.

"Oh, it isn't so bad," he said, rubbing her back. He watched me over the top of her head and smiled with emotion in his eyes. "Take the risk, Nathan. It's scary, but it's worth it."

"I will. I want to." God, did I want to.

I pulled out my phone, but paused before I made the call, and looked at him again. My intention must've been written all over my face, because I didn't even need to ask the favor. He knew.

Dad got to his feet, holding Marley. "Your mother was wanting to visit, but she had some appointments she couldn't move around. How about I take this one home with me and you can pick her up later?"

I stood then too. "That would be great. Thanks." I leaned in and kissed Marley's temple. Then I looked at my dad.

Fuck, I owed him. I owed him more than I could ever give back.

"There's no need for any more words right now. Just give me a hug, son." He held out his arm.

I stepped in, reciprocating the embrace.

After Dad drove off with Marley, I went upstairs and got showered and dressed, then drove over to Jenna's apartment.

I knocked on her door. No one answered.

chapter twenty-three

JENNA

Nathan had said he would call, so I waited for it. I didn't reach out to him. I had pushed enough.

On Friday, the kids wondered why we weren't hanging out with him and Marley, since we typically spent his days off together. On Saturday, they questioned why we weren't going to his house like we normally would.

"Nathan has some things going on right now. He took the day off," I told them.

Fortunately, the kids didn't press any further. Until Sunday, when again, our routine was disrupted. We should've been with Marley.

"What's going on with Nate, Mom?" Oliver asked.

The kids were seated together on the couch, sharing Olivia's iPad since Oliver's needed to charge. I took a seat on the edge of the coffee table and looked between them.

"Is he sick?" Olivia wondered. "We can still be around Marley if he's sick. We probably should be...She might catch it. We should just bring her over here and let her stay with us."

"No, he isn't sick."

I hadn't planned on explaining what was going on with Nathan to either one of them. It was his business and not mine to share. However, both Oliver and Olivia knew what had happened to Sadie. And even though I didn't think they understood it fully, they were understanding of it. Sensitive and sympathetic to Nathan and Marley both. And because of that, I felt comfortable giving them a partial explanation.

I told them it had been the anniversary of Sadie's death and that Nathan needed some time with Marley so that they could think about her. I said Marley should be with her dad right now and explained how the two of them could help each other through this.

I expected Oliver and Olivia's agreement and acceptance. I think they tried for it. But even though I knew them better than I knew anyone, I forgot—they were still only eight-year-old kids. They felt everything on a deeper, personal level. They wouldn't always understand reasoning that wasn't their own. And their emotions were unflinching and uncontrollable more often than not.

"But why can't *we* help them?" Olivia asked as she blinked rapidly behind her glasses to ward off tears. "Why can't we all be together? We're supposed to be . . ." Her bottom lip trembled.

"Sweetheart, I'm sorry. Nathan just wanted it to be him and Marley right now."

Olivia flinched, as if my words physically hurt her. That killed me.

"That's not fair." She sniffled and wiped at her nose with the back of her hand, then looked over at her brother as he slid off the couch.

"Hey. Come here." I reached for him, but he pulled back and slipped around me. "Oliver . . ."

My son's disappointment came in the form of silence. He sulked to his bedroom without saying a word and slammed the door shut behind him.

"Can I call him?" Olivia asked.

"No, not right now."

"Okay. When? Tomorrow?" Her eyes were pleading.

"I don't know, sweetheart."

I didn't know what else to say to her. I couldn't promise her tomorrow when I had no idea when Nathan would reach out.

I opted for distraction. "Why don't we do something fun this afternoon?" I suggested. "Anything you guys want. And then don't forget, tonight is family dinner."

I knew they would both be looking forward to that. They always were.

Olivia lifted her head and glared at me as she scooted off the couch. "I don't want to go to *family dinner*. I'm staying here." She scooped up her iPad and stormed off.

"Olivia."

For the second time that day, I was ignored. Oliver's door opened, slamming behind Olivia after she disappeared behind it. I sighed, hunching forward and digging my fingers into my temples.

I could picture them seated together on Oliver's bed, comforting each other with words neither of them believed. I wanted to be in there with them, but I gave them their space and busied myself with work instead.

But I couldn't distract myself completely. I thought about Nathan. How could I not?

It was bad during the day with Oliver and Olivia around, but it was the worst late at night. Surrounded by silence in my bedroom, I worried and wondered. I fought the urge to call. I grew sadder when he didn't.

On Monday, another day I would have normally watched Marley, I packed our afternoon with activities to keep us occupied. We went to the park and ate a picnic lunch, and then I surprised the kids with tickets to the aquarium. We hadn't been in more than a year.

"Marley would like this," Olivia mumbled as she and Oliver admired one of the large tanks filled with brightly colored fish. She gently tapped on the glass. "Right, Ollie?"

Oliver tugged on his sister's hand. "Come on. Let's go," he said, leading her away.

I searched through my bag as I followed them, checking my phone for any notifications I might've missed. August in the aquarium was packed with families. Even the noise was noisy. I had a text from Brian saying he missed seeing us yesterday at dinner, and nothing else.

I hid my disappointment behind a smile when the kids looked back.

Later that night, I was sitting on the bed folding laundry when my phone rang.

I shot to my feet and swiped the device off my nightstand, knowing it was Nathan—I was sure of it. And when it wasn't, I wanted to rip my hopeful heart out of my chest and throw it outside, five stories down. I hated my unyielding optimism.

And worse, I hated feeling disappointment to see Sydney was calling me.

"Hey, Syd," I answered, plopping down on the edge of the bed. I picked at the hem of my top.

"Hey! How are you?"

"Good." *Good?* I was so far from good it wasn't even funny. "How are you?"

"I'm great! You know, the same really. Not, like, great because of other reasons or anything...Nothing's going on."

I could vaguely hear my brother's voice in the distance.

Then Sydney spoke away from the phone. Her voice was muffled.

"Anyway," she said, clear in my ear again. "I was wondering if you were supposed to watch Marley on Wednesday because, if *not*, I thought maybe you'd like to come over for lunch. I'm off for the day."

Wednesday was another Marley day for me. Tomorrow was as well, and even though Nathan still had hours left to call before my plans for the next two days became obvious, somewhere in my mind, where awareness flowered from fear to a fact I could no longer ignore, I already knew I wouldn't see Marley.

"No. I'm free," I answered. "I just have some work I'll need to do in the morning, and then I can come over with the kids."

"Awesome. Want to do one o'clock? I'm taking Sir to the dog park to meet up with some of his furry friends at eleven. We should be home by then."

"Yeah, that works. Do you want me to bring anything?"

"I don't think so. I got it."

"Okay. I'll see you Wednesday at one."

"Hey, Jenna?"

"Mm?"

"Is everything okay? You seem a little off…"

I wanted to tell Sydney what was going on. I could've used another opinion, but I also felt like this was a discussion we could save and have face-to-face. I didn't know if I was up for it tonight.

Hope whispered in the back of my mind. *And maybe he'll call tomorrow. The discussion won't even be needed.* I squeezed my eyes shut and blocked it out.

"Shut up, Ollie!" Olivia yelled from the hallway. "You don't know that!"

I frowned at the door.

"Yes, I do! I know it for a fact!"

"No, you don't, idiot!"

"*You're* an idiot!"

A door slammed, followed by another. I heard something hit the wall behind my bed.

I quickly got to my feet. "Sorry, I gotta go, Syd. The kids are fighting for some reason."

"Okay, no problem. See you Wednesday!"

"See ya."

I dropped the phone on the bed after ending the call, then hurried down the hallway and stopped at Olivia's door. I opened it without knocking. Privacy didn't exist when objects were being chucked at my walls.

"What was that?" I asked, stepping inside her room. "And why are you two yelling at each other?"

Olivia was on her bed, lying on her side so I couldn't see her face. The notebook she always carried around was open on the floor in front of her dresser. The pages were bent up under its weight. I knew that was the object she'd thrown.

I picked up the notebook and carried it over to the bed, taking a seat behind her. "Olivia, what's going on?"

"Ollie said you and Nate broke up." Her voice was quiet and sad. "He said that's why we aren't going over there anymore. But he's wrong." Olivia sniffled and peered over her shoulder at me. "He's wrong, right, Mama? That's not true..." Tears glistened in her eyes.

For a moment I didn't answer her, mainly because I couldn't answer her. I knew the reason for Nathan's silence, but I couldn't deny how it felt on day four. This felt like a breakup.

"Mom." Olivia whimpered. She began to cry.

"Baby, I'm sorry." I placed my hand on her hip and fought

tears of my own. "Things are just complicated right now...I know this is hard to understand."

"What happened? Everything was so good!"

"Nothing happened."

"Then why isn't Nate here? Why isn't he here, Mom! And why can't we go over to his house? We should be there with him! He wants us to be. I know it! I know he does! We're supposed to be together!"

"Hey, shh." I leaned over Olivia and pulled her glasses off, setting them on the small table beside her bed. Then I wiped away her tears. "It's going to be okay, I promise," I said, kissing her shoulder. I pushed strands of hair back off her forehead. "We're always okay, right? Me, you, and your brother—"

"No! We're not okay, Mom! We need Nate!" She turned her face into the pillow and sobbed. "We're not going to be okay. I know we won't!"

My heart ached so badly, I wanted to tear it out of my chest. Olivia really believed we weren't going to be okay, and it was my fault that she did.

"Baby, I need you to listen to me," I began, resting my hand on her arm. "You know, Mommy has always dreamed of finding the perfect dad for you and your brother because I wanted this version of a complete family so badly, but we're already a family. We're the best I could ever want—just us. We don't need anything more than what we have to be happy, and I am so sorry for making you think we do."

God, all those dates and the wishing I did aloud. No wonder Olivia felt this way.

"We're going to be okay. I promise."

Olivia sniffled and stared at the wall. "What about *my* dream?"

314

"Honey, it's okay to dream still…It's okay to want more. We just don't need it. Do you understand the difference?"

"I don't want it to be just *us* anymore, Mama. I'm sick of it."

"Sweetheart…"

"I want Nate!" She glared back at me. "That's my dream. You just said I could have it!" She jerked her arm, pulling out of my grasp, and cried into her pillow.

I closed my eyes through a breath. Then I looked down into my lap at Olivia's notebook. Some of the pages were still turned in and bent. I opened the book to fix the paper for her, unfolding one of the corners and moving on to the next. After I fixed it, I stared at the page and at the list I had never seen before.

In Olivia's large, careful handwriting, she'd written:

Reasons Why Nate Makes the Best Dad Ever
by Olivia Savage

1. He's 30. That's older than my mom. She likes that.

2. HE WEARS GLASSES!! His hair is dark like ours. He's tall. I think I'm tall for 8.

3. Knows how to make smores. I can't wait to try them.

4. Likes games like us.

5. Holds my hand.

6. Talks to me a lot.

7. Called me and Marley his girls!! BOTH OF US!!

8. So funny.

9. Makes the best pancake shapes.

Olivia drew a giant arrow indicating a page turn, and on the back of the paper, she'd continued.

10. We already look like a family.

Below number ten she had taped the Fourth of July picture of us. I wiped tears from my eyes and skimmed the rest of the list.

11. Wanted me on his Putt-Putt team.
12. Plays with me.
13. GLASSES! I'm writing glasses twice. I think it's so cool how we match.

Olivia's explanations were random and each one just as important to her as the previous—I knew that in my heart. She wrote down things I didn't know about, like Nathan telling her she looked pretty in a dress she wore one day and a confession Oliver revealed—*My brother said he wished our last name was Bell. ME TOO!* Her list ended with reasons seventeen and eighteen.

17. Smiles at me & Ollie.
18. Smiles at my mom.

Tears fell onto my cheeks and rolled down my neck.

I kept my agony silent while Olivia revealed hers to me, to Oliver in the next room, and to anyone living in the apartments above and below us. She was loud in her heartbreak. Her cries couldn't be absorbed into the pillow.

I left the room feeling responsible for the pain she was feeling. For Oliver's, which I saw when I pushed his door open and found him on the floor, plucking at the string of his coiled sleeping bag.

He was already packed and ready for the camping trip on Friday.

I almost told him it could still happen. I wanted to tell him it *would*. I'd give anything to promise that, because I couldn't stand to see the little tremble in his bottom lip he thought he hid from me when he turned away and glared at the wall the second I peeked into his room.

"Can you ask Olivia to stop crying like that? She's bothering me." With a quick hand, Oliver wiped underneath his glasses. His small shoulders trembled in little jerks.

He could cry in silence if he tried hard enough. I'd seen him do it before.

"I don't want to talk right now, okay?" Oliver said, keeping his focus on the wall.

"Okay, sweetheart."

I left him, pulling the door closed, and walked back to my room. I didn't tell Olivia anything. I knew Oliver wasn't really bothered by her. He sympathized. He felt what she felt, and that had absolutely nothing to do with the two of them being twins.

That was it. I was sick of waiting. I palmed my phone and carried it to the farthest corner of my apartment. I didn't want the kids to hear me.

I steadied my breaths as the phone rang and rang, and when Nathan's voice mail picked up, I shook my head and cursed. I hated leaving this in a message. I wouldn't get the answers I needed.

"Hey, it's me," I said, keeping my voice low. "I wanted to know if you were still planning to take Oliver on the campout or if I needed to ask Brian... If I don't hear from you, I'm going to assume you aren't going." I looked in the direction of the hallway. I pictured my son's face. "I wasn't going to tell you how disappointed Oliver will be if you bail on him, but I think you should know. And Olivia too..." Tears spilled onto my cheeks. I quickly wiped them away. "Um, anyway, that's why I'm calling. And I wanted to make sure you were okay. I hope you are." I almost hung up, adding my last words on a whisper. "Please call me, Nathan."

* * *

Sydney prepared a favorite for the kids at lunch on Wednesday afternoon: Mexican chicken. Oliver and Olivia loved the crunch of the Doritos she sprinkled on top of the dish. They scarfed down seconds, then asked permission to go out back with Sir, Syd's dog. They loved chasing him around the yard.

I had never been more grateful for an animal before in my life. Maybe Sir could get a smile out of the kids.

As soon as they slipped outside, Sydney inquired about the overall mood the three of us had difficulty hiding, and I broke down at the table. I told her about everything—Thursday at Nathan's, his promise to call, the fact that he hadn't, and Olivia's list. That one killed me to share. I told her how responsible I felt and how Brian had been right to warn me weeks ago.

When the front door opened and my brother strolled in, questioning my tears the second he saw me, I shared that last part again. He stood behind Sydney's chair and listened with his arms crossed over his chest.

"What happened on Thursday?" he asked.

"Nothing. I don't know, we just had a fight." I picked at my napkin. "Well, not really a fight. More like a really emotional discussion."

"About what?"

I glanced at Syd, telling her with my eyes that I did not want Brian knowing all of Nathan's business, that it wasn't mine to tell, and that the only reason why I told her in the first place was because I needed to confide in someone. She was the someone I chose. I said a lot in that glance, and miraculously, Syd picked up on it.

"They just got into it," she said, turning sideways to look back at him. "You know, when you argue and it's not really about anything—we do that."

Brian peered down at her, brow cocked. "No, we don't."

"Yes, we do. All couples do." She glared at him.

"Why are you lookin' at me like that?"

"I'm not looking at you like *anything*." Syd kept glaring.

"Wild."

"Trouble."

"Is there somethin' wrong with you?"

I knew the direction this was headed. If I didn't intervene, Syd would blurt out all of Nathan's business. My future sister-in-law did not do well under pressure.

"It was about his wife," I said, getting Sydney's attention first, and then Brian's when his head slowly came up. "That's all I want to say about it though, okay?"

My brother's face relaxed. He tipped his head at the glass slider, suggesting, "Why don't we step outside on the deck? I wanna say hi to the kids before I head back to work."

"Sure. Okay." I stood from my chair, and Syd did the same.

"I'll put the food away, and then I'll join you guys," she said, spinning around and giving Brian a kiss before she started clearing the table.

I followed my brother outside and peered out into the yard as he hugged Olivia and then Oliver.

He spoke to them both as he petted Sir. Then Brian climbed the stairs and walked over to where I stood, stopping beside me.

"They're missing him. No doubt about that."

My eyes stung. I peered out over the deck. "They can't understand what's going on."

"They'll be all right." He sounded so sure.

"I have a favor to ask," I said, watching the kids. "It's last minute, and if you already have plans on Friday, don't change them. I'll figure something out—"

"You know I'll take him, Jen."

I turned my head and met his eyes. "Oliver might not want to go now...He won't talk about it yet, but I think he knows Nathan isn't taking him."

"You sure he isn't takin' him?"

"He hasn't called me, Brian. He said he would call...I even left him a message, asking him to let me know if he was planning on going or not." I squeezed the wooden rail until my palms ached. "I should've listened to you. I never should've let the kids get attached."

My brother threw his arm over my shoulders and pulled me close, a heavy breath leaving him. "If Oliver wants to go, I'll be there."

"Thank you."

"Same meeting place as last time?"

I nodded. Warm breath pushed against the top of my head.

"I ain't always right, Jen," Brian told me.

I knew that was his way of saying he hoped he wasn't right and that he still might not be. I blinked wet lashes and burrowed into his side.

When Syd came out to join us, Brian and I separated, allowing her to step in between. She leaned back against Brian's chest and held on to his arms when he wrapped them around her. They looked happy. They always did.

I smiled at the two of them, and then my brother mentioned

needing to leave soon. "Aren't you going to eat anything?" I asked. "Isn't that why you came home?"

"Already ate at Wax. Just wanted to see you and the kids for a minute."

"Oh." That made my heart warm. "That was nice."

He shrugged, dropping his head on top of Syd's. "Wild," he urged, giving her a squeeze.

"Right." She grinned at me. "August fourteenth is a Friday. Do you and the kids have plans that night?"

"I don't think so."

"Great. Because we're throwing a massive party."

"Okay."

"At Jamie's house."

"Why there?"

Her eyes went round. "Huh?"

I laughed at her confusion. "Why are you having it there and not here? What's wrong with here?" Their house was nice and plenty big enough to host a party.

"Nothing's wrong with here," Syd was quick to answer. "We just...wanted a bigger space. Plus, Jamie's view. You can't beat it."

"Oh." Well, that made sense. Jamie's house was beachfront.

So is Nathan's, I thought.

My shoulders dropped. "Cool. Sounds fun."

"It's going to be *amazing.*" Syd grinned. "You have to be there. No dates that night." We stared at each other.

Syd frowned. "I'm an idiot. Sorry."

"It's okay."

"Nate's even closing Whitecaps early so none of the girls will have to miss it."

"Really?" Closing up for a *party?* That seemed strange. But I was more surprised to hear he knew about this party before I did.

"When did he tell you he'd close Whitecaps?"

"Yesterday when we spoke on the phone."

What? "You spoke to him yesterday?"

Sydney blinked. Her lips slowly parted. "Y-yes, but really briefly, Jenna. Super brief. He called work to talk to Tori and I basically just stole the phone from her. I'm sorry I didn't mention it. We didn't talk long or about you, obviously... I mean, not obviously like he wouldn't *want* to talk about you..."

My brother mumbled a curse, dropping his arms from around her and stepping back.

"I just mean I would've told her if he had said something." Syd snapped her eyes to mine again. "I was literally on the phone with him for two seconds, Jenna. That's it."

"How was he? How did he sound?"

Sydney shook her head, shrugged, glanced back at Brian, who didn't offer any assistance since he'd preoccupied himself by watching the kids, and then she met my gaze again. "Okay?" She winced.

She looked uncomfortable giving the answer. It was more uncomfortable to hear. I didn't want Nathan *not* to be okay. I would never want that. But he *was* okay. He was okay and talking on the phone.

He just wasn't talking on the phone to *me*.

I had been frustrated with Nathan because of his silence. Hurt too. Now I was pissed off.

Day six felt official.

* * *

It was just after five o'clock when I pulled into the apartment complex.

After learning of Syd's conversation with Nathan, I had wanted to leave right along with my brother when he headed out, but the kids had asked for more time with Sir and Syd had asked for more time with me, so we stayed. It didn't take much convincing.

If there was ever a time for my children to push for a puppy of their own, now was it. I was shocked they weren't going there yet.

After leaving Syd, we swung by my office so I could hand in the documents I had been working on. I collected new forms, filings that needed proofing, and spoke briefly to my boss—one of the partners at the firm—then I took us home.

"Any thoughts on dinner?" I asked, driving through the lot.

"No," Oliver mumbled over Olivia's, "I don't care."

My attitude echoed hers as I pulled into a space and shifted into park. If it weren't for the kids, I doubt I would've cooked anything that night. I had zero desire to eat.

"Mom, look!" Olivia shrieked, startling me. She pointed over my shoulder.

Heart racing and hands gripping the wheel, I focused through the windshield.

Nathan was seated on the steps.

chapter twenty-four

NATHAN

I got to my feet as the kids fled the car, Olivia pushing past Oliver and jumping up onto the sidewalk. She ran at me, smiling and yelling my name.

"Nate! Nate!"

Oliver walked behind her with his head lowered. He wouldn't meet my eyes. Jenna stood frozen beside the car. I wasn't sure whose reaction I had been expecting more.

I met Olivia at the bottom of the steps.

"I *knew* you'd come over! I knew it!"

She launched herself at me, wrapping her arms around my neck when I lifted her off her feet and held on with all the strength she had. The pounding of her heart mirrored mine. I was so fucking happy to see them. I rubbed Olivia's back as we hugged, keeping my eyes on Oliver as he slowly made his way over. He stopped in front of me and stared at the sidewalk.

"Hey, bud."

"Hey," he mumbled.

I held out my fist. Oliver glanced up and looked at it for a moment, then quickly bumped his knuckles against mine.

He was feeling something—anger or dejection, maybe both. Maybe a lot of things, and even though he could've been reacting to something that had nothing to do with me, I knew it had *every-*

thing to do with me. I had a lot to fix, to explain. I'd known that coming over here.

"I want to talk to you," I said, getting Oliver's attention. "To both of you." I looked at Olivia when she leaned back. "But I need to talk to your mom first, okay?"

"That's probably a good idea," Olivia said.

"Yeah, she's been crying," Oliver said sharply. "Like, a lot."

My gut twisted. I snapped my gaze to Jenna, who was still stuck on the pavement, watching me, watching *us*, but seemed to realize she hadn't moved the moment our eyes met.

She blinked, looking down at her keys, then locked her car and stormed over. She was wearing a sleeveless maroon top and those faded cutoff shorts she favored. Her hair fell in thick, dark curls. I imagined it braided earlier like Olivia's was now. Jenna reached me quickly, her sandals smacking the sidewalk.

"Hi," I said.

Jesus, was there ever a more loaded word? That *hi* was so many things. *I'm sorry. I missed you. I love you. I need you.*

Jenna avoided my stare and glanced between the kids. "Can you guys go inside, please? I need to talk to Nathan."

"Yeah," Oliver answered.

Olivia wiggled down. "We already knew that," she said, giving me a secret thumbs-up against her chest her mother couldn't see. I smiled at her.

"Here, Oliver." Jenna handed him the keys.

They climbed the steps together, both of them peering back at me before they reached the door. They disappeared inside the building.

I looked at Jenna. She was already watching me.

"I'm sorry," I said, needing to get that out first. *Fuck, that needed to be said days ago.* "I should've called you. I wanted to, Jenna. Please don't think I didn't."

She pulled in a breath through her nose. Her chest heaved. "Are you okay?"

"No." I rubbed at my face. "I don't know. Not really." I took a seat on the steps. "Can you sit with me?"

Jenna blinked, sending a tear down her cheek.

Hand on the cement, I was pushing off to stand, to go to her, when she walked over and sat down on the step. She left space between us, two bodies' worth. Way too much space for me.

"Why are you here right now, Nathan?" she asked. Her eyes were tear-filled. "Why didn't you call me or come over? *Anything.* It's been six days…"

"I know. I wanted to see you."

"Don't tell me what you *wanted* to do," she bit out. "You should've done something about it. Do you have any idea what that did to them?" Jenna didn't point or gesture behind her and she didn't need to. I knew who she meant. "You disappeared. You dropped them, Nathan, after seeing you practically every day for two and a half months."

"Jenna, that shit I was going through…and what I'm still going through, it fucked me up. Thursday—"

"Of course, I get it." She jabbed at her chest. "I know how difficult Thursday was for you. *I* understand. I will always understand, but *they can't*, Nathan. My kids will never understand why you don't want to be around them."

"It wasn't them, Jenna."

"Who was it, then? *Me?*" Her bottom lip began to tremble. "Because you didn't want me with you while you went through that. You made that very clear…"

"*No.*" I moved closer, reaching out, and took her sweet face

326

between my hands. "Fuck, no, it wasn't you," I rasped. "It wasn't anyone. I wanted you there. I *always* want you there...You have no idea what I feel for you."

"You asked me to leave." She grabbed my wrists and pulled my hands down. "What could you possibly feel for me if you could do that?" I watched big tears roll down her cheeks. "I needed you to need me," she whispered. "I wanted it so bad..."

"I do need you."

"Stop, Nathan." She pulled back when I wiped her face.

"I can't. I can't see you like this and do nothing." I slid even closer until her knees pushed into my leg and held on to her hands. We stared at each other.

I had to let her in. Now. I had to tell her.

"I messed up a lot with Sadie, Jenna." I felt her hand tense in mine. "I missed things. I know I did. She could've been asking me for help and I didn't see it. I don't know how I could do that. I loved her...But there are things I know I overlooked. When she wanted to go back to work weeks before her maternity leave was up, I didn't know that was her way of telling me she was having a hard time. Now I know it was."

"You don't know that for sure." Jenna spoke softly. Sweetly. Her hand held on to mine now. She was trying to make me feel better, despite how massively I had fucked things up.

And God, I loved her for that.

"No, I do. I know it for sure," I argued. "Sadie loved her job, but she was so fucking excited for Marley. We both were."

Jenna looked at me. She didn't argue it now. She couldn't.

"I have this dream about her sometimes." My chest moved deeply as I breathed. "That night me and you were together, that first night when I called out for Sadie...I always dream the same thing. Not every night, but enough. It scares the shit out of me when I have it."

"What do you dream?"

"I wake up. She wakes me up." I smiled a little at the memory. "It's our last day together. I can remember it clearly. It plays out just like it happened, but after I leave for work, I'm still there with her. In my dream I can see her...I follow her around and she's struggling. She's wishing I'd stayed and she wants me there. And I think it's the fact that I don't know what happened that fucks me up so bad. I don't know what she was feeling and I don't know if she hesitated taking those pills, if she was waiting for me...I don't know. I'll never fucking know."

"Have you talked to anyone about it?"

"No. Only you."

"Nathan, you should probably talk to someone—"

"I only want to talk to you about it. I should've already." I lifted my glasses to wipe wetness from my eyes. "Thursday would've been difficult to handle if I'd simply forgotten, but I have guilt already when it comes to Sadie—I always will. I didn't see her when she was alive, Jenna, and I have no problem seeing you. I will never have that problem." She blinked at me. "I messed up. I'm sorry I told you to leave. I'm sorry I acted like I didn't want you there...I did. I should've called. I should've been here sooner. I'm sorry. I'm so fucking sorry." I stroked my thumb along her cheek, leaning closer. "I can't lose you."

"Nathan..."

"You were right."

She studied me. "About what?"

"How scary it is to love someone this much. It is completely terrifying."

Her pink lips slowly parted. She inhaled sharply and pulled

back, letting my hand fall away. "I don't think we should do this," she whispered.

I stared at her mouth. I waited for the words, to hear them again. I must've misunderstood her. *We shouldn't do this?*

"What?" I asked.

Jenna moved my hands out of her lap, depositing them into my own, then pushed to her feet and stood on the sidewalk. She clutched at the strap across her body with both hands, like she needed something to hold, and if it wasn't that, it might've been me, and she couldn't let it be me.

"Why shouldn't we do this?" I pressed her, getting to my feet then as well. I stood in front of her. "What are you talking about?"

"I don't think you're ready."

"To move on?" *How can she think that?* "Jenna, I am ready. I want to be with you."

She quickly shook her head. "No, see? It's not just me, Nathan. You can't just want to be with *me.* And maybe this is my fault. Maybe I should've said something before we started anything. Then my kids wouldn't have gotten hurt...I let them get attached to you. God, I *wished* for it. I wanted this to work so badly. It's the only thing I've ever wanted...I want a family."

Her tears fell, streaking down her face. She let them. She didn't wipe them away, and when I stepped closer, needing to do it for her, Jenna took a step back.

"Jenna." Her name was a plea on my lips.

"No. Please, don't. I can't do this. I'm not just looking for someone for me, you know? And maybe you're ready to move on and date. That's one thing, Nathan. But I don't think you're ready for me and my kids. You have no idea how deep into this they are already. Oliver worships you. I see the way he looks at you. He wants to be your son. He wants to throw like you and be as tall as you are. And Olivia, oh my God, she made this list in her little notebook. She wrote down all the reasons why you would be the best dad for her. She's so in love with you, Nathan. They both are. And for six days you let them think you didn't feel the same about them. You're not ready."

"Yes, I am." I stepped closer, grateful when she didn't move back. "I am ready."

"They needed you, Nathan."

"I need them. I need all three of you." I hovered my hand above her cheek. "God, please, let me...I messed up, Jenna. I'm sorry. Let me fix this."

She stared into my eyes as she wiped her own tears away. She wouldn't let me do it. I lowered my arms and looked at her. My heartbeat pounded in my ears.

"Brian is going to take Oliver camping on Friday. I already asked him to."

My muscles tensed. I suddenly couldn't breathe.

"No," I rasped. I wanted to scream it. "Let me take him."

"I called you two days ago." Her voice vibrated. "I asked you to let me know if you were going to take him or not and you didn't. I should've stopped you when you agreed to do it and said it wasn't a big deal, because it is a big deal. To Oliver and to me."

"I didn't mean it like that, come on."

"How could you mean it, Nathan?" Her tone was incredulous. "You were literally saying it wasn't a big deal..."

"I only said it like that because I wanted you to let me take him. Do you think I didn't see what that meant to you? I knew you weren't sure about it, and I wanted you to be sure, of me. I want to take him, Jenna. Let me take him."

She thought for all of a second and shook her head. "It's not a good idea."

"Why?"

"I already told you why. You aren't ready for this."

"And I already told you—I am ready. I wouldn't push this if I wasn't. I would never purposely hurt those kids."

When more tears streamed down Jenna's face, I went to reach for her, but she held me back with her hand on my chest.

I grunted. "This is killing me. I want to hold you."

"I wanted you to hold me yesterday. Where were you then?"

I pressed my lips together. Fair point. "Listen to me, okay?" I said. "I made a mistake, and I'm probably going to make more. Maybe a lot more. I'm not perfect, Jenna. And that family you want, the one I'm going to give you, it won't be perfect either, but I swear to God, it's going to be everything."

Her breath caught and started hiccupping. "Nathan, please don't make promises to me like that."

I held her face with both hands, and she didn't stop me that time.

"I love you and I love those kids, and I will fix this." I stared deep into her eyes. "I'm not going anywhere. You're going to see how much I need all three of you. You won't question it again." I wiped her tears away with my thumbs. She let me.

Progress.

"I can't," she whispered. "I'm still not sure."

Slight setback. I could handle it.

"So I'll get you there."

"It might take me a while…or forever. I don't know. You really hurt us, Nathan." She pulled my hands away. "I think you should just go. I can't talk about this any more tonight."

"I need to say something to them. Can I come in first?"

"Um…I don't know."

"Jenna, I just want to apologize. That's it. I won't tell them

331

I'm in love with you." I paused when her head snapped up. "And I won't tell them I love them, even though I really fucking love them. It's a three-way tie with Marley at this point. Nobody's in the lead. That could change though, once I see this list Olivia made…"

"Nathan." Her eyes flared with panic.

"I won't say any of that, just apologies. I promise." I smiled at her. She did not smile back.

Holy shit, I loved this woman.

"This isn't funny," she said, her tone sharp.

"I didn't think it was."

"You're joking around though."

"No, I'm not. I meant every word I just said to you."

She blinked, not expecting to hear that. Then she pulled in a slow, deep breath through her nose. She was back to gripping the strap across her body. I was hoping that meant she wanted to hug me and was fighting against it.

"Okay," she said. "You can apologize, but then you need to go."

"Agreed."

"And you need to make it clear that we aren't together anymore." I gave her a look. She gave it right back. "I'm serious. I don't want them getting their hopes up."

"Am I allowed to make it sound like I *want* us to be together?"

"No."

Fuck. "Okay." I scratched at my jaw, thinking. "What about alluding to the probability of us getting back together once I fix this…?"

"That would absolutely get their hopes up, Nathan. No."

"Jenna, you know those kids. They're going to ask what's going on. I'll be lucky if I can get an apology out before they fire a million questions at me. And I don't want to make it sound like I'm no longer in their lives. That will fucking kill me to say and it'll hurt them to hear it. You know it will. I'll tell them we aren't together right now if that's what you want, but if Olivia asks me if I'm fixing this, I want to tell her I am. Same goes with Oliver— if he asks me if I'm still going on Friday, I want to tell him I'll be there, that I would never fucking miss it. I'll be honest with them, I swear, but my honesty has hope in us. I know we end up together."

Jenna stared at me for the longest moment. "Okay, that's...fine, I guess. I don't want them getting hurt either." She went to turn away but doubled back, adding, "You can hope for things, but you can't guarantee them. No promises."

"I need you to be more specific on that, because I can guarantee I'm doing everything I can to get you back. I can promise that, Jenna."

"No promises we're getting back together. You can't tell them that."

"Fine."

Jenna hurried past me then and climbed the steps. I trailed behind, catching up to her, and skidded to a stop when she abruptly spun around at the door.

"Also, this really kills me, but I don't think it's a good idea for me to watch Marley anymore." She looked up at me then, and I could see the pain in her eyes. Jenna hated to do this. "I don't think the kids should see you every day. We can't just go back to the way things were."

I was absolutely not in agreement on this, and my views had nothing to do with Jenna helping me out with Marley, but I understood her reluctance. I'd hurt her. I'd hurt her kids. She was worried I'd do it again.

"Okay. I'll make arrangements." What exactly those arrangements would be, I had no idea.

"Good. How is she? God, I miss her so much..."

I tilted my head, smiling. "She's good. Happy right now, I'm sure. She's with my parents." I went to tuck a strand of hair behind Jenna's ear, but she slowly leaned back.

"Stop that."

"Sorry. Habit." I lowered my arm and followed Jenna inside the building. We were silent as we climbed the steps side by side. I couldn't help but remember. "Last time I sat out there waiting for you, you held my hand doing this."

"Well, you had waited for a while."

"That wasn't the only reason you did it..."

"No, it wasn't." She side-eyed me. "Of course, I had my own motives—I wanted to. Not that I don't want to now." Her grip on the strap tightened. "Things were just different."

"I know."

"I was just saying, that was part of it. Knowing you waited for me, that you would've waited longer... How long did you sit outside tonight?"

I peered into my pocket, checking the time on my phone. "Four hours. Maybe four and a half. I can't remember what time I got here." I halted two steps above Jenna and looked back.

She gaped at me. "You've been here for *four hours*?"

"Maybe four and a half," I repeated.

"Why didn't you call me? God, I could've been gone longer than that, Nathan. What if I had been?"

"Then I would've waited longer." I smiled and kept climbing, reaching her door and pausing there. I watched her ascend the remaining steps, and she watched me. Shocked to hear that. Happy to have heard it.

I followed Jenna inside her apartment.

"Hey, guys!" Olivia ran around the couch and stopped in

front of me. She was breathless. "Hi, Nate. I've been waiting for you to come in."

I imagined her scaling the furniture. Olivia was too excited to sit still.

Oliver padded down the hallway from the direction of the bedrooms, halting a few feet away. "Hey."

"Hey, bud. Can we talk?"

He nodded and stuffed his hands into his pockets.

"Me too?" Olivia asked, stretching to her toes and fighting the urge to bounce on them.

"Yeah, of course. Unless you want to wait and have it just be me and you…"

"Uh." She thought on this, shifting her weight from foot to foot as she looked from me to Jenna, then back to me. "I don't know. Can I do both?"

"I want to talk to Nate alone," Oliver announced. "I have some things to say." He lifted his chin at his sister.

"Duh, Ollie. So do I," she returned. "I have *things*."

I put my hand on Olivia's shoulder. "Let me go talk to your brother, and then me and you can go talk. Okay?"

"Okay." She smiled up at me.

Jenna pulled off her bag and carried it to the couch, dropping it over the side. "Come on, Olivia. You can help me with dinner." She held out her hand.

Olivia rushed over, taking it, and the two of them walked together into the kitchen.

"You coming?" Oliver asked.

"Yeah." I turned away from my girls, two out of the three, and shadowed Oliver down the hallway and into his bedroom.

He took a seat on the bed while I grabbed the desk chair, wheeling it into the center of the room. I leaned forward in it, bracing my elbows on my knees, and watched Oliver pick at his laces.

"I'm sorry I haven't been around the past few days," I told him. He peered up at me. "I should've called. I had some stuff I was dealing with, but that's no excuse. I should've talked to you and your sister and I didn't, but it was nothing you guys did, okay?"

"Okay." His voice was quiet.

"There's nothing you could ever do to make me not want to be around you guys."

Oliver looked down briefly to blink a couple times. He pushed up his glasses. "Did you and my mom break up?"

"Yeah."

"Why?"

"I messed up. I didn't talk to her when I should've, and it hurt her feelings."

"So, you're talking to her now, right? Are you getting back together?"

"I'd like to. It's a little complicated, but I'm going to do everything I can to make it better. I just want your mom to be happy."

"So do I." He held my stare.

I smiled. God, I loved this kid.

"She's happy when you talk to her, so . . . like, really happy. So just talk to her." His shoulders jerked. "That should be all you gotta do."

"I'm afraid there's a little more to it than that, but whatever it takes, I'm going to do it, okay?"

"Yeah." Oliver cleared his throat when his voice cracked and scooted to the edge of the bed, letting his feet dangle off. "Thanks."

"You don't need to thank me, O. I want us to be together. All of us."

He stared at me.

I tipped my head at the camping gear stacked and packed in the corner of his room. "Friday, if you still want me to go with you, I'll go. What do you want to do?"

Oliver sat up as tall as he could. "I want you to go."

"Yeah?"

He nodded fast.

"Are you excited? It's supposed to be nice weather."

"I am. I'm really excited." He cracked his knuckles. "Are you excited?"

"Absolutely." I smiled at him, then looked over at the doorway when Olivia peeked her head around it. "Hey."

"Are you guys done having your *alone time* yet?" she asked. "I want mine. Mom's making me wash lettuce. That's dumb."

My chest rattled with a laugh. I looked at Oliver, and he gave me a thumbs-up.

"I'll say goodbye before I leave, okay?" I stood from the chair and held out my fist.

"Yeah." He bumped it. "I'll probably be in here. No way am I washing lettuce."

"Oliver!" Jenna hollered. Her voice carrying down the hallway.

"Oh man." Oliver hung his head and crept out of the room. I followed Olivia across the hall.

"Come in. You can sit here." She tugged on my hand, pulling me to the bed and patting the quilted bedspread. "Just don't put your shoes on the bed. Mom will fah-reak."

I chuckled, taking a seat beside her. "Got it."

Olivia kicked off her sneakers. Then she crossed her legs like a pretzel and smiled at me.

"You know, I'm really, really sad that I made you sad," I told her, and her smile fell away. "I don't want you or your brother getting hurt. It bothers me, Liv."

Her head was lowered now, so she had to peer at me above her glasses. "Because you love us, right?"

Damn. I knew I promised not to say this, but technically, I wouldn't be saying it. I'd be agreeing...And there was no fucking way I could ever let this girl think I didn't love her.

"Right," I said.

Olivia looked up and blinked at me behind her frames. "We love you too, you know? That's why we like you so much."

I grinned. "You like me because you love me?"

"Yes."

"I like your logic."

"What's logic?"

"Your reason for thinking something. Why it makes sense to you..."

She shrugged. "It's just how I feel. I don't know."

I chuckled, placing my hand on top of the one she had resting on her knee. "Listen, Liv, I'm really sorry I made you sad, okay?"

"Okay."

"And I'm sorry if you thought I didn't want to see you or your brother. I always want to see you guys, no matter what."

"I wanted to call you, but Mom said I couldn't."

"Well, she had reason to say that and you were smart for listening to her, but I want you to know you can always call me." I gave her hand a squeeze. "Even if it's just to say hi. If you want to call me, I want you to. You just need to make sure it's okay with your mom."

Olivia stared at me for a moment, her expression somber. "Oliver said you and Mom broke up."

"We did."

She pulled her hand out from under mine. "So you're never going to be together ever again?" Her voice was panicked.

"I didn't say that."

"But you're not together now, right?"

I shook my head. "No, we're not together."

Olivia scooted back to put space between us. She crossed her arms over her chest and pouted at her lap.

"Hey."

"What?" she mumbled.

"Can you look at me?"

Olivia lifted her head.

"You know you're one of my favorite girls, right?"

She slowly smiled.

"I like you being a little mad at me right now," I told her.

"You do?"

"Yeah, I do. Do you wanna know why?"

"Why?"

"Because when you get older, like your mom's age, and some stupid guy messes up and does something to upset you, I want you to stay a little mad at him for a while. Don't forgive him right away, even if he's so, so sorry he can't even stand it." I tugged gently on one of her braids. "Make him work for it, okay?"

"Work for what?"

"For you."

"Oh." Her smile was lopsided. She lowered her arms to her stomach and uncrossed them. "Are you going to try to get back together with my mom?" she asked.

"Are s'mores the best snack ever?"

Olivia sat up tall. "Yes." She grinned and punched the air. "That means yes! *Yes!*" She threw her arms around my neck, pulling me into a hug. Her heart was racing. "Thanks, Nate."

We held hands on the walk to the kitchen.

"Hey, bud, I'm leaving," I announced, getting Oliver's attention off the table he was setting. Jenna was at the stove, stirring soup by the looks of it. I hugged Olivia goodbye. Then I bumped fists with Oliver when he walked over.

"Can't you stay for dinner?" he asked.

I met Jenna's eyes when she glanced back at me.

"Not tonight. I gotta go pick up Marley."

"When will we see you next?" Olivia asked. She had climbed onto one of the bar stools.

"Olivia, go wash your hands. Dinner is almost ready." Jenna turned away from the stove and motioned at the door. "I'll walk you out," she said to me.

I glanced between the kids. "I'll see you guys soon, okay?"

Oliver nodded and resumed setting the table. Olivia gave me a small hug again. "Bye, Nate," she whispered. Then she ran down the hallway.

I stepped outside Jenna's apartment and watched her stand in the doorway.

"Can I see you guys tomorrow?" I asked.

She leaned against the frame and dropped her head closer to her shoulder. "I said we shouldn't do this every day, remember?"

Right. That agreement I wasn't behind. I wondered if Jenna was really behind it, or if she was just scared and protecting herself.

"What about every other day?" I asked, studying her closely.

A faint smile played at her lips. "Nathan..."

"I love you."

Her mouth went slack.

I backed away from the door. "Good night, Jenna."

She was slow to respond. "Good night," she said, watching me descend the stairs.

chapter twenty-five

JENNA

I squinted, shielding my eyes from the sun, as the large Greyhound bus pulled up in front of Dogwood Beach Community Center. Oliver's Boy Scout troop was lined up along the sidewalk, fathers and sons loaded up with gear. Everyone was ready for the camping trip.

"Bus leaves in ten!" one of the troop leaders announced.

Families shuffled about, taking pictures. Nearly every mother had her phone out.

I glanced around the parking lot. *Come on. Please...*

"Do you wanna get in line?" Brian asked Oliver.

We stood a few feet away from the group with all of Oliver's gear at our feet.

"Not yet." Oliver checked the compass watch my brother had given him, then peered around me. He adjusted his hat, lifting the brim to see a little better.

"Maybe you should grab your stuff," I said quietly to Brian, but not quietly enough.

Oliver glared at me as he straightened up. "He's coming, Mom. He said he's coming."

"He's still got time," my brother mumbled from beside me.

I slowly peered up at him, shocked to hear those words come out of his mouth. I'd asked Brian to be our backup tonight, just in case. My brother was in no way 100 percent positive Nathan was showing up. I could tell when we spoke about it over the phone. Now he was holding out hope right along with my son?

Okay. Weird.

I hadn't seen Nathan since Wednesday night, but I had spoken to him. He'd texted and called throughout the day. He'd spoken to the kids. He'd told me repeatedly how much he wanted to see us, knowing I needed the reminder without me having to say it.

My heart was cautious now, but it was still my heart.

Nathan had assured me yesterday and this morning that he would be here. He'd sent me a text two hours ago, letting me know he was dropping Marley off with his parents and then he'd be on his way. He'd given me every guarantee.

I was terrified to see him. I was even more terrified he wouldn't show up.

Gravel popped and cracked loudly behind me. Someone was pulling into the lot.

"Nate!" Oliver stepped over so he could be seen and waved his arm in the air. He wore the biggest smile on this face.

Peering over my shoulder, I watched Nathan park his truck.

"Bet traffic was bad," Brian said. "It is Friday night."

Again, I slowly peered up at my brother.

Arms pulled across his chest, he smirked at me. "I'm just sayin'."

I felt my forehead wrinkle. *What the hell is happening right now?*

"See, Mom? I told you he'd be here. I *told you*." Oliver stepped around his gear and got beside me. "Nate! Do you need any help?" he yelled.

"Nah, bud, I got it!"

I turned sideways and watched Nathan walk across the lot, carrying a coiled sleeping bag and the large black duffle he had

342

with him on the Fourth. He wore military-green cargo shorts and a white Fighting Irish shirt that looked well loved. The writing and logo were faded. I wondered if he'd had it since college. I pictured Nathan wearing it after practice or a game. His muscles and abs covered in sweat... the material clinging.

Oh my God, Jenna. Stop it.

"Hey." Nathan greeted the group when he reached us, his gaze lingering on me. "Sorry. Two of my servers called in sick right when I was about to leave. I got Tori to handle it, and then I hit the worst traffic."

"Told you," Brian mumbled under his breath.

I barely heard him. I was too busy focusing on the fact that Nathan had a work issue and still made sure he could be here. No matter what, he wouldn't have missed this.

"You're not late or anything," Oliver was quick to say.

Nathan set his duffle next to the gear and bumped fists with Oliver before extending a hand to Brian. "How's it going?"

"Good. You?"

"Good." Nathan's eyes slid to mine as their handshake ended. He gently smiled at me. "Didn't think I'd show?"

I shrugged and was about to tell him I wholeheartedly feared it—what did I care if he knew?—but Brian spoke up first.

"I wanted to drop off that watch for him." My brother tipped his chin at Oliver.

"Check it out. It's got a compass." Oliver stood in front of Nathan and tapped the face. "It's cool, right?"

"Yeah. It's very cool." Nathan looked over at me. I looked over at Brian. Brian smirked.

What the hell? Is he in love with Nathan now too?

The Scout leader hollered above the crowd, advising everyone to load up onto the bus.

"Come on, Nate. Hurry. We gotta go." Oliver grabbed his gear, carrying as much as he could over to the sidewalk while Nathan bent down and unzipped his duffle.

He pulled out his hat and slid it on. Backward, of course.

I refused to look at him. Fully, anyway. I did, however, have one helluva peripheral view.

Nathan carried the rest of Oliver's stuff, a backpack and two canteens, and stood with him in line. I walked over with my phone, the camera mode ready, and bit my lip when Oliver turned his hat around to match Nathan. The line moved up and up as people loaded.

"Get together," I instructed. "One quick picture before you guys go."

Nathan stood next to Oliver with his hand on his shoulder and the gear at their feet. Their smiles matched now too.

I took the picture. "Want to do one more?"

"Mom, we gotta go," Oliver said, hurrying to snatch up his gear.

I walked along the curb beside them, rattling off reminders to Oliver, mainly things about safety, which I was sure were being ignored and were probably unnecessary anyway, but I couldn't help it. Before he hopped onto the bus, I pulled him into a hug and kissed him.

"Mom!" He groaned, leaning away.

"Sorry." I laughed. "I love you. Have a great time, okay?"

Oliver hustled onto the bus. He dragged his backpack up the steps.

"Do I get a send-off like that? Because I want one." Nathan paused at the door. He looked so fucking good—the eyes, the jaw, that neck of his. Ugh.

I fought a smile, along with my heart's desire to hug him and hold on. "Thank you for taking him."

344

"Thank you for letting me."

"Come on, Nate!" Oliver yelled out a window.

I waved at him as he stepped onto the bus, and then I walked away. I almost told him to call me and check in later, but Oliver would be fine. He would be more than fine.

I stood beside my brother and watched the bus pull out of the parking lot and drive down the street. I was feeling all kinds of things I could easily acknowledge and other things I couldn't yet name.

"How long are you gonna fight this guy?" Brian asked.

"You warned me about moving too fast and you questioned all the time I let the kids spend with him. Since when are you pro-Nathan?"

Brian looked over at me. "Since he showed up for your son."

* * *

It was just after eleven that night when my phone rang.

I rolled over and untangled my arm from the satin sheet. I held the lit screen above me, smiling at the caller. I had been hoping to hear from him.

"Hey."

"Hey. Did I wake you?" Nathan asked.

Behind his voice, I could hear a cricket chirp. I pictured him surrounded by woods and the darkened sky above sprinkled with stars.

"No. I wasn't asleep yet. It usually takes me a while when nobody's here."

"Olivia isn't there?"

"She's at a friend's house." I boosted my pillow higher underneath my head and pulled the sheet up to my neck. "She was jealous of your campout, so I told her she could have a sleepover tonight. I think she's still jealous though. She's dying to make s'mores with you."

"Well, I am pretty awesome at it."

"How's Oliver? Is he having fun?"

"Oh yeah. He's having a blast. He's asleep right now." I heard sticks snapping. "I just left him in the tent. He made me promise we'd stay up all night and then he passed out about five minutes after saying that."

I laughed quietly. "What all did you guys do? Did you do the archery stuff? Oliver was looking forward to that."

"Yeah, that was cool. He's really good at it too. We showed up this kid and his dad who were next to us. They both sucked." Nathan laughed. "Uh, besides that, we learned how to kill a bear."

"What?"

"Nah, I'm kidding. That would've been cool though. We went out in canoes for a while and fished. Then some guy showed us how to start a fire without matches, which is something I already knew how to do. Oliver made sure everyone here was very aware of that fact. I think he even reminded them after dinner."

I smiled and flexed my calves against the sheet. "Has anyone asked who you are to him?"

"No." Nathan sounded disappointed admitting that. "But I am getting looks, which is weird. Like, who gives a fuck? I'm ready though. Nobody better say a damn thing to Oliver. I'll throw all of their shit into the lake."

I cracked up, hand to my mouth. I couldn't help it.

Muffled voices came through the line. "Oh. Sorry, man," Nathan said. "My bad. I thought everyone was asleep."

"You're going to get banned from future campouts," I warned. I was grinning now.

"Probably." He chuckled, his voice growing soft. "I hope not. Oliver's really into this."

He was, but Nathan was having a good time too. I could tell. He could've said *he* was really into it and he chose not to. Nathan made it about my son.

I closed my eyes and breathed.

"I should get off here before I get him thrown out of Scouts," he said.

"Okay." I stared at my bedroom ceiling. "Thanks for calling me."

"Do you need anything?"

"Like what?"

"I don't know—you're alone. I know you don't like it."

"How do you know that?"

"Because I know *you*. And I can tell...I'll stay on the line with you if you want. I could walk farther into the woods so I'm not around anybody. I'll probably get murdered, but—"

"Oh God." I rolled my eyes and giggled.

"I'll just get back in the tent, but seriously, Jenna, I can drain my battery. Do you want me to stay on the line? What do you need?"

What do you need, Nathan? The memory echoed inside my head.

"Déjà vu. Remember?" I smiled.

"What are you talking about?"

"On the phone that night when I wanted you to give me permission to ignore my brother, you said you didn't need anything when I asked you."

Nathan was silent for a moment.

"I didn't—I was talking to you."

"Ask me again."

"What do you need, Jenna?"

I pictured Oliver in the tent fast asleep and gave my answer.

"Right now? Nothing."

chapter twenty-six

NATHAN

Six Days Later

"Daddy, I get 'nother one?"

"Yep." I stood from my desk, tearing free another Post-it note, and took it over to Marley, who was seated in the middle of the office with her play gate around her.

Marley took the neon yellow paper and stuck it on her foot, giggling.

Hair. Face. Arms. Legs. She was covered in fluorescent squares.

I didn't give a shit. Marley could go through every Post-it note I had in here if she wanted to.

She was smiling, and I knew most of that happiness came from her contentment to stay in the same room with me for longer than two minutes now and not for my office supplies. Marley wanted to be around me. She liked coming here. She didn't get to do it often.

Since Jenna stopped watching her, my parents had picked up two days a week. They never minded helping out, as long as that was all they were doing. I was with Marley the most. I wasn't working nearly as much now, thanks to Tori, so I got a lot of time with her at home. I wanted to be with her as much as I could.

Marley was happy, but she missed Jenna and the kids. She asked about them constantly. She hadn't seen them since that Thursday. That was two weeks ago.

I was still trying to fix things with Jenna, and I saw her and her kids as much as she allowed, but I hadn't involved Marley in that yet. I didn't know if it would look like I was trying to use my daughter as a pawn, since I knew Jenna loved her. Maybe I was worrying for nothing, but it was important to me that Jenna knew where my dependence on her stemmed from.

I needed her for *me*. My daughter needed her for her. There was a difference.

It was getting difficult keeping them apart though. Marley's happiness meant more than my own. I hated denying it.

"Daddy, more? I get some?"

I tore off another square and took it to her, returning to my desk just as my cell rang. I accepted the call without looking at the screen. I was too busy looking at Marley.

"Yeah, this is Nathan."

"Hi, Nate."

Olivia's voice in my ear spread warmth throughout my chest and down my limbs. This was her first time calling me.

"Hey, sweetheart." I lowered myself into the chair. "How are you?"

"Good."

"How's your brother?"

"He's good. We're going to the movies tonight."

"Oh yeah?"

I wondered how much Oliver and Olivia had to beg for Jenna to take them, but then I stopped wondering because I knew Jenna. I doubt she made them beg much at all.

"That sounds fun," I told her.

"It's going to be, for sure. But"—her voice grew quiet—"remember when you said you'd take me out on a date, and then *I* said we could go to the movies? Remember that?"

I smiled, catching my head in my hand. "Yes, I remember."

"Well, could this be our date?" Olivia was whispering now. "Can you come with Marley? You can meet us there. Mom said we're leaving in one hour. Can you leave in one hour too?"

Olivia was keeping her voice down because she didn't want Jenna knowing what she was asking me. That was obvious. She was worried her mom would tell her no, and I wanted to tell her yes. I could swing getting there in an hour, no problem. I was finishing up for the night anyway.

"Liv, we should probably ask your mom if I can come," I said. "Can you ask her?"

I sat forward then, hunching over the desk. The muscles in my back went rigid. Now *I* was suddenly worried. My plans for the night were set, in my opinion. I wanted to go with them. I wanted us all to be together.

"She likes surprises, Nate. Let's just surprise her."

"She might not like *this* surprise."

"No, she will. I know she will. She wants to see Marley. She told me that when I asked her why she was so sad yesterday..."

My hand tightened around the phone. "She was sad yesterday?"

"Uh-huh. And she was super quiet. I knew something was up."

I hung my head and rubbed at my neck, my eyes closing as I inhaled. *Fuck*, that bothered me. Jenna needed this—she needed to be around my daughter. And maybe she would eventually ask to see Marley while she still made up her mind about me, but I couldn't wait for that.

I wouldn't make *her* wait for it.

* * *

I finished up at work and drove straight to the theater.

I wanted to beat Jenna there. Olivia had told me what they were seeing before she briskly disconnected the call, too excited to stay on the phone any longer.

After I purchased the tickets, I waited with Marley and watched the doors.

The kids walked inside first, spotting us right away and waving, hurrying over.

Marley pushed against me until I let her down. She shouted for Oliver and Olivia and made little squeals of excitement. She hugged them both, clinging to Oliver's leg and making him laugh. And when Jenna walked inside, Marley ran at her.

Jenna looked shocked to see us for all of a solid second, and for that second it was me she looked at. Then it was Marley and only Marley who made her move nearer, drawing her away from the doors and farther inside the building. It was Marley who put the smile on Jenna's face and the tears in her eyes I noticed when I got close enough.

"Surprise!" Olivia yelled, giggling with her hands on her cheeks.

Jenna heard her. I knew she did—Olivia was loud and the lobby wasn't that busy—but Jenna was caught up. She was holding Marley and kissing her face, telling her how much she missed her and how big she looked. How pretty. She hugged her like it had been longer since they'd last hugged. Jenna didn't react at first to Olivia or to Oliver when he asked her if she was surprised. She didn't even react to me when I told them I'd already purchased everyone's tickets, which was something she most likely would have disputed.

In her eyes, we still weren't together. She'd fight me on passing this off like it was a date. Especially with her kids here.

Little did she know, Olivia saw this as exactly that.

But Jenna was in her moment with Marley, so she couldn't react. And that was something she needed right now. They both did. My daughter wouldn't let her go.

"Let's get our snacks," Olivia suggested, tugging on my hand.

I walked with her and her brother to the concession stand and bought popcorn, candy, and drinks: soda for the rest of us and a juice box for Marley. Jenna waited by the kid who took our tickets. She watched us, looking at me like I'd just given her something.

"Hey," she said when I walked over.

"Hi." *I'm sorry. I missed you. I love you. I need you.*

We smiled at each other.

If Jenna was thinking this wasn't a good idea yet, she didn't let that on. She followed the kids down the hallway, passing the theaters, and kept at my side. She didn't question what I was doing here. Maybe she couldn't while she held on to Marley. I knew what I wanted to believe. That despite her own reservations and her worry, she wanted us together right now.

She wanted us together.

I held the tub of popcorn in the crook of my arm to free up my hand. Then I pulled the hat out of my back pocket, flicked it open to fix the brim, and handed it over to Jenna before we entered the theater. The twins were already inside.

"What's this for?" Jenna asked suspiciously.

"Lice."

Her eyes widened as she pulled her lips between her teeth.

"Oh, I know all about your phobia, you big weirdo."

She laughed loudly, head tipping back. "I'm assuming Olivia

told you about that since Oliver was too embarrassed. I would like to add, this is not the theater we went to that one time."

"Still, I'm surprised you're not prepared."

"Honestly? I wasn't planning to sit back at all."

"Edge of the seat for two hours?" My brow cocked. "Sounds uncomfortable."

"Or I would've stood. I was still debating."

I chuckled and tipped my chin at the hat. "Now you can sit with her."

Jenna pressed her lips to Marley's temple and cupped the back of her head. "I'm going to put you down for two seconds, okay? Maybe three. Can you count for me?" She set Marley on her feet.

"Oneee," Marley dragged out slowly with her finger raised in front of her face.

"Keep going," Jenna encouraged. She tucked her hair into the hat and pulled the brim over her eyes before Marley got to three. "Good job counting, baby." Jenna picked her up again and kissed her.

"You look good," I said, admiring the hat. It was too big for her and hung over her ears, but she looked cute.

Jenna gazed at me after I spoke like she wanted to say something in return. Then she moved quickly inside the theater.

"Not as good as you do."

Her compliment stopped me mid-stride. I grinned in the doorway. "What was that?" I called out at her back before breaking into a quick pace. I reached her before she turned the corner to the rows of seating and whispered against her ear, "I love you."

Jenna's step faltered, but she recovered without a word or a glance back and rounded the corner, climbing the levels and squeezing down the row. She took her seat next to Oliver. Marley relaxed in her lap.

I sat beside Olivia when she patted the seat on the end.

"Hey," she said.

"Hey. Ready for our date?"

She nodded fast and beamed at me.

We divvied up drinks out of the carrier and passed the bucket of popcorn back and forth down the row. The lights dimmed for previews, and when the movie started and the theater darkened even more, Jenna looked over at me.

I knew because I was already looking.

The movie kept the twins engaged throughout and Marley for close to half. An hour in, she was passed out on Jenna's chest and stirred awake only when the lights came back on and the crowd stretched and spoke.

I waited for Jenna while Oliver and Olivia walked ahead, giving their opinions of the movie to each other and discussing the plot. From what I gathered, they both enjoyed it.

Jenna met me at the door with Marley sound asleep again. Head on her shoulder and eyes closed.

"Do you want me to take her?" I asked. We walked down the hallway together.

Jenna hugged Marley against her chest. "Not yet."

Not yet. *Not ever*, I thought. I wondered if she thought that too.

"Guys! Check out this rain!" Olivia waved us over to where she and Oliver stood at the entrance doors. "It's a monsoon!"

Jenna and I glanced at each other and then at the people around us, the ones who had just arrived for their show and stood in line to purchase tickets. Water dripped down their faces and nearly soaked their hair. Their clothing clung. Everyone chatted about how suddenly the storm had hit.

"It came out of nowhere!" one woman proclaimed. "We left our umbrellas at home. We had no idea it was supposed to rain."

"Same with us!" the lady in front of her said.

I stepped up to the glass front and peered outside. Jenna got up beside me.

"Oh my God," she muttered.

The rain was heavy and thick. It pounded against the pavement and puddled in areas like it had been coming down for hours. A steady stream flowed in front of the sidewalk and curled around a bend.

"This is crazy," Jenna said. She jolted when thunder cracked above the building. A streak of lightning lit up the sky.

"It's a monsoon, right?" Olivia asked.

"It's just a storm," I said.

"I bet it's a tornado." Oliver had his hands cupped to the glass and was peering between them. "Probably suck us up."

Olivia's eyes snapped to him. "What?" She looked panicked.

"*Oliver*," Jenna said in a warning tone.

"It could be, Mom. Tornados suck people up. It's what they do."

"It's not a tornado." I got beside Olivia and rubbed her shoulder. "It's just a storm. We can wait it out."

"That could be a while," Oliver said. "It's not stopping *or* slowing down. And that river is getting bigger." He pressed his finger to the glass and pointed at the stream.

I looked over at Jenna. "What do you want to do?"

She bit her lip, thinking. "Mm. I'm not sure. I'm a little worried the roads will just get worse with standing water if we don't leave soon."

"Your drive home shouldn't be bad," I said, thinking of her route. "It's all major highways. No back roads or anything that could flood."

"Yeah." Her gaze moved to the glass.

Jenna's hesitation was obvious. She watched the rain like she really was anticipating getting sucked up into the sky.

"Why don't you let me drive you home?" I suggested. "Just leave your car here for the night."

"Or we can *all* go to Nate's house." Olivia slowly grinned.

Nice.

"No, we should really get home," Jenna was quick to say. She slid her gaze to mine and softened her dismissal of Olivia's suggestion with a smile. "Could you drop us off? That would be great."

"Yeah, of course. No problem." I dug out my keys. "Let me pull the truck up."

I opened one of the doors and stepped outside.

The rain was cold and pelted against my head and shoulders on my run to the truck. I slid in the driver's seat and wiped water from my face, removing my glasses and keeping them off for now. I pulled off my tie, tossed it up onto the dash, and slicked my hair back. Then I started the truck and pulled up to the curb. The twins ran outside and laughed into the night as the rain hit them.

I met them at the door, taking Marley from Jenna so she could get in the truck herself. Marley roused awake and whined a little. I shielded her face, got her secured in her seat, and gave Olivia a boost after Oliver got in on his own. The back of my shirt was drenched by the time I got around to the driver's side.

"Nate, you look like you've been swimming." Olivia giggled.

"Yeah?" I peered at her in the rearview. Water dripped down my face. "I feel like it."

"Thanks to you, my hair is mostly dry." Jenna pulled off the hat, smiling at me as her dark hair toppled down her back and over her shoulder. "And lice free," she murmured.

I chuckled, slipping the hat on myself, and began to unbutton my shirt. I stripped it off and tossed it in the back, leaving on the white shirt I wore underneath. It was barely damp. I looked over at Jenna when I was finished.

She blinked and looked ahead as if something had suddenly grabbed her attention. Following her lead, I peered out the rain-splattered windshield. Even with my headlights on, nothing stood out.

Something outside hadn't grabbed her attention. I'd had it. Jenna wanted to look at me and look longer than she would allow. I felt us moving closer to being us again, and I was smiling as I pulled away from the curb.

We talked on the drive—me, Jenna, and the twins—as I carefully navigated the roads. Marley had fallen asleep soon after we turned out of the theater parking lot. The conversation lingered on the film and I had fuck-all to add. I'd watched Jenna through most of the movie. I couldn't help myself.

Everyone was laughing at something I had said when I parked in front of Jenna's apartment building. If someone had asked me to repeat myself, I wouldn't have been able to. I suddenly couldn't remember details of our discussion.

We were here, and our evening was over.

Something that felt close to panic moved inside my chest. I didn't want this to be done yet. We'd had a great time together tonight. I wanted to stay with them or for them to stay with me. I wanted to bottle up their sounds. In a minute, I would no longer have them.

"Here, Oliver." Jenna handed him her keys. "You guys need to run for it. I'll be up in a minute."

Olivia was giggling, excited for the opportunity to run out in the rain again. "Come on, Ollie." She opened her door.

"Bye, Nate," Oliver said.

"Bye!" his sister echoed as she climbed out of the truck.

I blinked when two doors slammed, snapping out of it, and watched them through the windshield.

Oliver and Olivia dashed under the rain and up the stairs. They disappeared inside the building.

That panic moved again, spreading itself out underneath my ribs.

"Thank you for paying for everything tonight. You didn't need to do that, Nathan."

I peered over at Jenna after she spoke.

I wanted to tell her how I was feeling, but I couldn't quite describe what it was. It felt like everything and nothing.

I knew I'd see her and the kids tomorrow night at that party her brother was having. I felt shitty right now for no real reason. Jenna loved her surprise tonight. I was fixing this.

"Jenna."

It was too dark in the truck to see her eyes, but I didn't miss the little part in her lips when I said her name. Maybe it was the way I had said it that had her touching my arm and leaning over the center console to kiss me. Or maybe it was a culmination of things. It had to be anything but how I was looking at her, because if I couldn't see her eyes, how could she see the fucking misery in mine?

The kiss was meant to feel like we were starting over and getting somewhere. It should've felt like I was getting Jenna back, because I was. I *knew* I was. She was kissing me, for fuck's sake. But that strange sensation underneath my bones spread out and out and out. It unnerved me. Our kiss began to feel desperate. I held Jenna's face and pressed firmer against her mouth. I kissed her deeper. Longer. I moaned against her tongue.

I kissed her like I didn't want this to end, yet no matter what I did, it was ending.

Then Jenna put her hand on my chest and pulled away from me before we took it too far or too fast. She shyly dipped her head as she sank against the leather, and then she was telling me good night and fleeing the truck.

I drove home surrounded by silence, to a house that was too quiet to endure. I laid Marley in her crib and then I paced. I felt tense and unsettled. I couldn't shake this feeling.

I wanted to drive back to Jenna's. I wanted her here. I didn't understand why I couldn't deal with this shit tonight. I was fine waiting this out, waiting her out. *So what the fuck?*

I pulled out my phone as I took a seat on the couch and dialed her number. The rain barely made a sound outside. The storm was passing.

"Hey," Jenna answered on the second ring. "What are you doing?"

"I need to talk to you."

She must've heard something in my voice, because hers rose with concern. "Is everything okay?"

"No." My answer poured out of my mouth.

"Is it Marley? Is she sick?"

"No. It's me." Hunched over, I rubbed at my neck. "I'm sorry. I'm just having a hard time right now . . . I don't know."

"Was it that dream? Did you have it again?"

"No." I brusquely laughed. "I couldn't sleep right now if I tried."

A door quietly latched shut. "What is it, then? What's going on?"

"Jenna, I did not want to say goodbye to you guys tonight."

For a moment it was only her breath in my ear. And then she told me, "Okay," but I heard her encouragement. *Keep going.*

"It fucked with me...I don't know why. I just hated coming home without you."

Again, she paused. I worried she misinterpreted my motive.

"Look, I don't want you to think I'm telling you this to try to rush you—I'm not. I know we're taking this slow and you're still feeling me out..."

"That doesn't matter."

"Yes, it does. I'm not pushing you." I spoke clearer and louder, my voice loosening.

"Telling me how you're feeling wouldn't push me, Nathan. I want you to share things with me."

"I am. That's what I'm doing." Holy shit, it was. And it was simple. I blinked and let her in.

My head pressed into the cushion when I sank back. I stared at the ceiling. "I needed you to know how I felt. That's why I called."

"I'm really happy you did. I'm glad you told me."

I knew she needed this. I didn't hesitate to call for that very reason, when weeks ago, I would've. But the threat of losing Jenna that motivated me now was twofold. It was significant, and I didn't think she understood that yet. How could she? I hadn't told her.

"Are you going to be okay?" she asked.

"I'm scared out of my fucking mind of losing you," I said as my answer.

I heard a mattress squeak and pictured Jenna sitting on her bed. "You say that like you don't know we end up together. I thought you did?"

"That's not what I mean."

I knew the moment it all clicked for her—the impact of her understanding—it shuddered her breath.

"Nathan, you wouldn't lose me," she said quietly.

"You can't say that. I don't need you to say that—I'm okay with being scared. I just needed you to know...Being with you, it became something I've never felt before. I couldn't understand it at first. I didn't know it could be like this. But it's you, and it's your kids...it's us together, all of us. I need it."

"*God*, Nathan..."

"Listen, I can wait. I want you to be sure of this, Jenna, because I am so fucking sure of it. But I don't want to be without you and those kids tonight. Or tomorrow night. And that's something I'm going to continue to feel right along with being terrified of losing you."

Quiet sniffles came through the line.

"Are you okay?" I asked.

"Oh my God, I'm so angry right now," she whispered. "You have no idea."

Angry? "Why?"

"This stupid storm. If I had my car, I would come over there..."

I lifted my head off the back of the couch. "You would?"

"*Yes*. And now I can't because of this weather. *And* because you're this amazing man. You drove me home and now I'm fucked."

I laughed. Jenna rarely cursed.

"Could you come here?" she asked in the sweetest fucking voice, like it would kill her if I couldn't.

I dropped my head back again. "*Fuck*," I rasped. "Marley is out cold. I'd have to wake her."

"Oh, don't do that. Let her sleep."

"I can't believe you're telling me you'd come over."

Her response was immediate. "You need us, Nathan. Why wouldn't I?"

361

I closed my eyes. *Jesus, that felt good to hear.* "I'm really glad I called you."

"Me too," she quietly replied. "Do you want to talk more?"

"Yeah."

"Pretend I'm there and talk to me."

"I don't know if I'll fall asleep anytime soon," I responded. I could talk to her all night. She would need to be the one to end this call.

"Talk to me, Nathan."

With her voice in my ear, I did. And again, it was so fucking simple.

I blinked and let her in.

chapter twenty-seven

JENNA

My heart had become its own protector. It let me love, but it held me back. It hoped, just like it always did, but it wouldn't believe anymore in the certainty of what I was feeling. With every wish it allowed, it whispered caution behind it. *Be careful. You know how I can break.*

Now I could feel my locked heart unlocking. It reached out again for love without restraint, and after all the things Nathan was doing to prove he was ready to be with me, all the ways he was fixing it, after everything he shared last night—how could I not be sure of this?

And if I was sure, then what was I waiting for?

I thought back to that morning in my kitchen when he kissed me in front of Oliver and Olivia for the first time. "Come on," he'd spoken against my lips.

I'm coming, I promised.

Butterflies danced in my stomach as I parked in front of Jamie and Tori's house the following night. The anticipation of seeing Nathan here sent a thrill through my body. We'd texted earlier while he was at work, and it had killed me not to tell him then how I was feeling, but I knew doing it in person would feel so much better.

I wanted to see him and say it.

Vehicles lined the driveway and filled in parts of the grass in front of the large beach house Jamie owned and lived in with Tori, but I didn't see Nathan's truck anywhere yet. I wondered what time he was closing Whitecaps for this. I hadn't asked.

Closing Whitecaps for a party…so strange.

After I parked, the kids bounded up the lawn and into the house without knocking.

Jamie had an open-door policy, and even if he didn't, we used to live here with Brian when we first moved to Dogwood Beach, and in the eyes of my children, this was still their second home. Good luck keeping them out.

Tori greeted me as I stepped through the front door.

"Hey, girl!" She wrapped me up in a hug that smelled like sweet, floral perfume.

"Hey! How are you?"

"Good." She wore a yellow sundress and had a flower behind her ear. Her makeup was pretty, sun-kissed with a red lip. "This is for you," she said, holding up a near-identical flower to the one she wore. She stuck it behind my ear, explaining, "Theme of the party. All the girls are wearing them."

"Oh." I smiled and touched the soft petals. "That's cute. It's really dressing up my outfit."

I glanced down at my black tank and washed-out cutoffs. My toes wiggled in my gladiator sandals. I suddenly felt way under-dressed for this.

"You look perfect. Let's go." Tori grabbed my hand and pulled me farther into the house.

There was soft music playing and chatter all around me. I recognized some of the crowd hanging in the foyer and waved at Shay and Stitch. They were seated on the staircase. J.R., the other cook at Whitecaps, greeted me with a chin-lift. He was against the wall talking to Jamie's sister, Quinn. I heard she had moved here recently and took up as a waitress at Whitecaps. Tori had hired her. I waved to her as well. I hadn't seen her in years.

"Hey, Jenna!" She squeezed my arm as I passed.

Once we stepped inside the great room, I spotted Kali and Cole sitting together on the large sectional sofa. Oliver and Olivia were seated there as well and already fighting over the remote to the TV.

The crowd was heavier in here. There were a lot of faces I didn't recognize, and I considered Sydney's job at the hospital. Maybe she had invited a lot of her colleagues. Jamie stood near the slider, talking with Travis. I waved when they noticed me.

"Wow. Everyone's here, huh?" I said to Tori, following her farther into the room toward the kitchen.

Tori shrugged. "Usual crowd."

Usual crowd? *Travis?*

I weaved around tall, round tables covered in white cloth and decorated with tiny tea-light candles. "What kind of party is this? This seems...elaborate."

"I wouldn't say that," she replied.

I stopped at the long granite island and stared at the arrangement of finger foods. There were trays of mini cucumber and chicken salad sandwiches, bruschetta, pecan and chocolate tartlets, and a three-tiered tower of pastel macarons.

Huh.

"I know Jamie has thrown a lot of parties here in the past, but I seriously doubt he ever put out hors d'oeuvres, Tori. And the tables? This is definitely fancy."

She smiled, carrying over a tray of mini hot dogs wrapped in crescent rolls and stacked them together on a plate. "He'd probably just stick out boxes of Pop-Tarts for people. Or tell them to fuck off if they were hungry."

"Where are my brother and Syd?"

"They're coming." She stuck the tray on the stovetop and removed the oven mitt.

"They aren't here yet?" I frowned at her back. "It's their party, isn't it?"

"They'll be here. Don't worry." Tori waved a dismissive hand, her attention gliding around the room as if she were searching for something but couldn't remember what it was she was searching for.

Oliver came running over. "Are those pigs in blankets? I love those!" He stood on his toes and reached across the island.

"Oh, let's wait, buddy. Okay?" Tori asked him. She slid the plate farther down the counter. "Give it a couple more minutes. They're really hot."

"Oh, man," he grumbled.

"They just came out of the oven, Oliver," I added. "You'll burn your tongue."

"Fine. I'll starve, then." He sulked back over to the couch.

I laughed, expecting Tori to do the same. I was sure she had heard him. But when I looked at her again, she was messing with her phone.

She picked it up, set it on the counter, hit the home button when the screen went dark. Then hit it again.

"Is everything okay?" I asked. "You seem anxious."

Tori lifted her head and slid her eyes over my shoulder, holding there for a breath. Then she looked at me and smiled. "So what's going on with Nate? Any progress? Have you told him you're *crazy* in love with him yet?"

I scoffed. "I doubt I need to. I'm sure that's been obvious for weeks."

"I'm sure it hasn't."

Nathan's deep voice at my back nearly made me jump out of my sandals. I scowled at Tori, the fucking sneak, who looked to the ceiling and tapped her chin.

"I feel like I left my straightener on..." she mused before skirting away.

Nathan chuckled under his breath.

I slowly swiveled to face him and tipped my head back. Lord, he was tall when I wore flats. And his smile right now, sheesh. Nathan was more than pleased to have overheard that conversation.

"Hey," I said shyly.

I was slightly mortified. Even though I did think my feelings for Nathan were obvious and had been for a while, despite everything that had happened between us, saying those words out loud evoked all kinds of emotions from me. Fear. Excitement. Apprehension.

Outside of my family, I'd never said them to anyone before.

"Hi," Nathan returned. He was still in his work clothes. Dark slacks and a striped button-up. He hadn't even loosened his tie yet.

I was very okay with that. Nathan looked incredible right now. This was one of the things I'd missed since I'd stopped watching Marley for him, besides watching Marley, which was the greatest thing I'd missed. I hardly ever got to see Nathan dressed up anymore.

The fact that he hadn't loosened his tie yet made me reconsider my outfit for a second time tonight. I tugged on the hem of my shorts and adjusted, then readjusted my top, as if there were a way to make a simple tank elegant.

Nathan followed my movements. "What's this you're doing? I

feel like at any second you're about to strip." His brow playfully arched. "I'd like a heads-up, if that's the case. There's no way I wouldn't react to that and there are children present. Yours specifically."

I laughed against my lips. "Where's yours? I was hoping I would see her."

"With my parents. I wasn't sure how late this would go."

That made sense. It was already close to Marley's bedtime.

"Oh, well…I miss her." I tucked the front of my top into my shorts, then second-guessed that decision and pulled it free.

Again Nathan watched me. "She misses you. What are you doing?"

"I'm feeling like I should've worn something a little nicer. This party is way more than I thought it was going to be."

"Stop. You look amazing."

"Says the man in the tie."

He stared at me. Then he reached up and loosened the knot, pulling the tie over his head. I bit back a smile when he draped it around my neck.

"Is that better for you?" he asked, but before I could respond, Nathan raised a finger, saying, "Wait a second," and unbuttoned his collar, flicking it open so I could see his throat. "That's your sweet spot, right? Now you'll be too distracted to worry about what you're wearing."

"Oh, man," I mumbled, looking away. I was fighting that smile hard now.

Nathan laughed. "So, 'crazy in love,' huh?"

I side-eyed him and nodded. My heartbeat quickened and skipped.

"Was I getting us close to you sharing that with me?" There was no longer any trace of humor in his voice.

"You got us there," I said.

I turned fully to gaze at him and that sweet, suddenly surprised look on his face, but I had only a second to notice it before my eyes were being drawn over Nathan's shoulder, lured by the commotion coming from the front of the house.

People cheered and clapped. A sharp whistle cut through the air.

Everyone grew quiet when Tori stepped inside the room. She had tears in her eyes. "It is my absolute pleasure to present after way too damn long, Mr. and Mrs. Brian Savage!"

I gasped, hand to my mouth. "Oh my God. What?"

Holy shit.

Holy shit!

The room erupted as Brian and Sydney walked in together holding hands, dressed for their wedding day.

Brian wore a dark gray suit and had a clean-shaven face. He looked handsome and happier than I'd ever seen him. Syd's dress was white lace, long and bohemian-style, with a halter neckline and a short train in the back. Her red hair fell in elegant waves. She looked stunning and smiled directly at me before throwing her hand in the air.

"Welcome to our reception!" she bellowed.

Everyone was on their feet, applauding and shouting their praise. Even Oliver and Olivia. They had pushed their way to the front of the crowd. A crowd that included all of our closest friends. Everyone was here. We were never able to be together like this. Work wouldn't allow it.

I peered over at Nathan and slid nearer so he could hear me above the noise. Our arms touched.

"You knew they were getting married today, didn't you? That's why you closed Whitecaps early. So everyone could be here for this..."

He smiled down at me. *Now* it made sense.

Brian and Sydney made their way around the room, greeting their guests. Everyone flooded in from other parts of the house. The floor was packed now.

"I'm kind of mad at you for not saying anything," I said to Nathan.

He limply shrugged. "Wasn't my surprise to share."

"I'm at my brother's wedding reception and I'm wearing *shorts*. With *rips* in them." I fake glared at him and he chuckled. "You're lucky I'm so crazy in love with you."

He blinked, and his lips parted. His chest swelled with the breath he inhaled.

"Come here," he said. Nathan drew his arm over my shoulder and pulled me against his side. He pressed his mouth to the top of my head.

I hugged him back with my arms around his waist, then beckoned him lower with my finger and cupped his cheek when his face got closer to mine. I stood on my toes and spoke against his ear.

"I am so, so sure of this." Of him. Of us. He knew what I meant.

Nathan pulled back to look at me. "Yeah?"

"Yeah."

He smiled, ducking his head to kiss me.

When the newlyweds made their way over to where Nathan and I stood, I couldn't decide who I wanted to hug first and settled on throwing an arm around each of them.

"I'm so happy for you guys! This is *amazing*." We squeezed and let go. "I can't believe you didn't tell me though."

"We just wanted it to be a surprise," Syd explained while Nathan and Brian shook hands and conversed.

"I am surprised. I can't believe you went to a courthouse for this."

"I've done the whole big wedding thing and look how that marriage ended," Syd said. "I didn't need anything more than what we did. I didn't need anything other than him." She looked up at Brian when he slid his arm around her.

"Was anyone there besides you two?" I asked.

"Just my mom. Your parents couldn't make it out since we basically gave them zero notice, so we Face-Timed so they could watch. It was cute." She looked at Nate. "Hey, best boss ever. Thank you so much for letting everyone be here." They hugged, Nathan offering his congratulations. He was quick to brush off his role in this.

"It's still appreciated," Brian told him.

He nodded then, accepting the thank-you. Tori hurried over to our group just as Brian and Sydney were moving away to greet more of their guests.

"First-dance time!" she announced. "You can say hi to everyone later. Come on. I have the song cued up." She ushered them into the center of the room and directed everyone else to give them some space. "Work with me, people. This is the dance floor. Spread out! Move!"

Some guests roamed about, floating in and out of the great room, but mostly everyone hung around and formed a large circle around Brian and Syd. The song began playing overhead.

They'd chosen "Can't Help Falling in Love" by Elvis Presley.

Nathan and I moved closer to watch.

Brian dipped Sydney, making her shriek in surprise, and I smiled and laughed with my fingers to my lips. They swayed back and forth. Sydney sang along to the lyrics, directing every word at Brian. He couldn't stop watching her, and I couldn't stop watching them.

Their love. Their joy.

I no longer needed to wish for something similar.

"Hey, Nate," I heard Oliver say.

"What's up, bud? Pretty great surprise, huh?"

"Yeah, it's cool. Mom, can I get some of those little hot dog things now?" Oliver tugged on my arm when I didn't respond. *"Mom."*

I watched my brother and Sydney kiss, and answered, "Sure, baby, go ahead."

Oliver squeezed around me. The song began playing again when Sydney loudly requested, "One more time! I've been waiting *too long* for this!"

Brian laughed and spun her around. They kissed. The crowd swooned and sighed.

"Oliver! OLIVER!"

I jolted at Nathan's voice. It pierced through the air as he tore through the crowd.

"Move!" he shouted.

For a moment my vision blurred. I blinked. I gasped in air and held it. Someone bumped into my shoulder as the crowd pushed around me in panic.

The music cut off.

"Oh my God!" someone yelled.

I frantically shoved my way to a clear spot, and that was when I saw Nathan standing behind Oliver near a table with his arms around his waist. He was thrusting his fist against Oliver's stomach.

I stopped breathing.

My son was choking. His eyes were open, but he wasn't looking at anything. He clawed at his throat with rigid fingers. His lips were turning blue.

"Oliver!" I screamed, lunging forward. "Oh my God," I rasped. "Oh my God." I elbowed people out of my way and pushed to the front. I reached out. Strong arms caught me around the waist and jerked me back.

"Jen, wait," my brother said in my ear. "Nate's got him. He knows what he's doing."

I didn't fight Brian's hold. He was right, after all. Nathan appeared to know the steps, the method.

Unlike me. What would I have done?

"I'm calling 911!" I heard Tori yell.

Nathan switched to back blows and began alternating between the two. He kept talking to Oliver, telling him to cough it up and spit it out. Travis was beside him giving instruction.

When Olivia ran over to me, wailing, I gathered her into my arms. Brian held on to us both.

"Mama! What's the matter with Ollie?" Olivia cried.

"It's okay. He's okay," I said. I didn't know what else to tell her. I didn't know what to do. I couldn't do anything besides stare at Oliver's face and wait.

I felt helpless.

Everyone was gathered around, inching closer. Jamie, Stitch, and Cole hovered around Nathan. Their girls flanked my side.

The crowd stirred in distress when Nathan laid Oliver on his back.

"Oh my God." My heart crawled up into my throat. I reached around and grabbed at Brian. "Oliver!"

His eyes were closed now. He looked lifeless.

I collapsed onto my knees and screamed so loud, it terrified

Olivia. She clung to me and wept. Sydney collapsed at my side and held on to us.

Travis bent down and said something to Nathan, but Nathan pushed him off and roared, "I got him! I know!" He began chest compressions, thirty of them. He breathed twice into Oliver's mouth.

Nothing. Oliver didn't respond.

"Ollie!" Olivia cried.

"Oh no," someone said behind me. They were already at the end. They had given up.

Nathan wouldn't. I knew he wouldn't.

"Come on, baby. Come on," he begged. "COME ON!" He hit thirty. He breathed. He positioned his hands again on Oliver's chest.

Oliver coughed harshly and wheezed, his eyes shooting open. His limbs kicking out with life.

The room breathed in relief.

"Oh my God, thank God!" I shifted Olivia off my lap and crawled across the floor as Oliver coughed and gasped for air.

Nathan rolled him onto his side and scooped a finger into his mouth, fishing out the obstruction—a barely chewed crescent-wrapped hot dog. He wiped off Oliver's face, and when he began to cry, Nathan picked him up and hugged him. They clung to each other.

"Baby, come here. Come here." I reached them on my knees and pulled Oliver into my arms and against my chest. I was shaking. We both were.

"Mom!" he wailed against my neck.

I kissed him and cried. "You're okay. Shh, you're okay now." I rubbed his back.

We were swarmed then by our friends and family. Olivia

pushed her way through the group and latched on to her brother. I hugged them both, and then I passed Oliver off to Brian when my brother urgently requested it. I'd never seen Brian look so worried before.

I wiped my face as I got to my feet and fielded hugs from Tori, Syd, Shay, and Kali. I smiled at the kind words given by Cole and Stitch and from the strangers who filled the room. Everyone was happy Oliver was okay. They were grateful.

"Travis needs to check him out, Jen," Brian said.

Jamie stood beside my brother with shock and worry in his eyes. He wasn't relieved yet. "He's just gettin' his stuff out of the car. The ambulance just got here too."

"Okay." Of course he would need a doctor to look at him. He'd just had CPR performed. Oliver seemed okay now, but was he?

"I want Nate," Oliver said. He wasn't crying nearly as hard anymore.

I looked around and then behind me. Nathan was still seated on the floor several feet away beside the table, hunched forward with his arms draped over his bent knees and his head bowed. His glasses in his hand.

"God," Syd whispered at my back. "I'll never forget how he screamed for Oliver. How he sounded…"

"I'll never forget how he saved him," Shay said.

I stared at Nathan, waiting for that same wonder other people felt when they looked at him to hit me, and it didn't. Even my friends who knew of our relationship still saw only a man saving a boy. Some of the other people here had expected Nathan to accept what was happening, and I knew he wouldn't. I had been sure about it. When it's your child, you don't give up. You never give up. You can't.

I saw a man saving his son.

I walked over and knelt beside him, picking up Oliver's discarded glasses.

"Nathan." I cupped his cheek.

He immediately lifted his head. There were tears in his eyes, and fear. So much fear.

"Our son wants you."

His gaze sharpened and snapped over my shoulder after I spoke, then came just as quickly back to mine. He pulled in a breath through his nose, got to his feet, and walked over, taking Oliver into his arms again. They hugged each other.

When Travis came back inside with the paramedics, Nathan sat with Oliver on the couch to make the examination easier, but he kept his hold. Everyone had to work around him. Around them. Oliver wasn't letting go of Nathan either.

After we were assured a hospital visit wasn't necessary tonight, I declined my brother's offer to stay, congratulating him and Sydney again, and insisted the party continue without us.

There was no reason why it shouldn't—everyone was okay. I just couldn't stay any longer. I felt rattled.

Nathan met me at the door. He still held Oliver, who had his head on Nathan's shoulder and his eyes closed. Olivia stood beside them, holding on to Nathan's hand.

"I need you to come home with me," Nathan said when I reached him.

Oliver lifted his head and blinked awake behind his frames. "Can we, Mom? I wanna stay with Nate."

"Me too," Olivia added. "Can we go?"

"Of course we can." I looked up at Nathan. "We'll need to grab some stuff for the night. Do you want me to take them with me?"

"No."

"Okay." I smiled. I'd had a feeling he would say that.

Nathan didn't smile back. He still looked so worried.

We walked outside together. I followed Nathan to his truck instead of walking toward my car and caught his arm before he opened the driver's-side door. The kids had already piled inside it.

"Hey. Come here," I said, guiding his face down with my hand on his cheek. "He's okay."

Nathan panted a breath and circled his arms around me. "Fuck, Jenna." He sounded in pain.

"I know. I was scared too. But he's okay." I hugged him tighter, my cheek turned on his chest. "Because of you, Nathan. You were watching him when I wasn't. You saved him."

"I couldn't lose him. I never would've stopped."

Tears welled up in my eyes.

We held each other until something sharp knocked repeatedly on the glass at Nathan's shoulder.

"Can we go!" Oliver yelled, his voice muffled. "It's getting stuffy in here! I already almost died *once* tonight…"

I jerked back and glared around Nathan. "*Oliver!*" I snapped. "That isn't funny. Don't talk like that."

"I'm just kidding!"

"Well, don't."

"I'm still hungry. Can we go get some hot dogs?"

My eyes bulged in their sockets. *What!*

"I'm kidding again!" Oliver giggled hysterically, his cheek smashed against the glass.

"Good one, Ollie!" Olivia yelled.

"Oh my God." I rubbed at my temples. That boy…

Nathan's deep chuckle turned my head. He leaned his back

against the driver's door and smiled at me. "I strangely feel a lot better now."

"Yeah." I rolled my eyes, laughing a little. "Me too."

"He's morbid."

"Clearly he takes after you," I joked.

Nathan's smile gentled, and even with the night sky above us, I could see the emotion in his eyes. "Come on. Ride with me."

"What about my car?"

"Leave it." He reached out and took my hand. "Let's get Marley and go home."

* * *

I held Marley against my chest as I rocked her in the chair.

She'd fallen asleep on the ride home and could've easily been laid down, but I needed to hold her. And while Nathan and the kids cued up a movie, I'd brought Marley upstairs and sat with her in her room. I spoke softly to her as I smelled her sweet, lavender-scented skin and felt the soft curls around her face. I told her how much I loved her.

I imagined getting to do this every day, and the thought filled me with incredible happiness, when I was already so full of it. My heart overflowed.

"Hey." Nathan spoke softly from the doorway.

"Hi," I whispered.

"You've been up here awhile." He leaned his shoulder against the frame. "Are you ever going to put her down?"

"Probably not." I smiled at him. "But I guess since I get to do this tomorrow, and the next day, and the day after that…"

"Forever," he said.

All of this, our family—forever.

I stood with Marley and laid her in her crib, covering her up with the blanket. Then I walked over to Nathan. "That sounds like an amazing life."

"What does?"

"Forever with you and her. With all of us."

He smiled in the moonlight.

I gripped his shirt and kissed him. "Did you finish the movie?"

It wouldn't surprise me if they had. I really had been up here awhile.

With his hand on my back, Nathan began to lead me down the hallway toward the bedroom. "They fell asleep before it ended. And you know your kids...heavy sleepers." He looked at me with his brow raised suggestively.

Flashbacks from our first night together entered my mind. This hallway. This exact same conversation. We could talk or do anything, and I knew when we stepped inside the bedroom, we wouldn't talk.

"*Our* kids, you mean," I corrected.

Nathan stopped walking when we'd nearly reached the door.

I did the same, spinning around to face him. "What? What is it?"

Was he surprised I'd said that? He shouldn't be. I'd already called Oliver his.

Nathan stared at me intently. "You asked me weeks ago if I wanted more kids and I didn't know the answer to that. I know it now."

My heart began to race.

"Would you have more kids with me?" he asked.

"Yes." My answer was instant.

Nathan smiled and stepped closer. "Would you move in with me?"

"Yes. Absolutely." I was grinning now as I reached for him,

taking his hand. "Of course. Why wouldn't I? If we have more kids—"

"Would you marry me?"

I stopped grinning, and my breath caught.

"Yes. I would marry you," I said steadily. "But—"

"*But?*" Nathan's arms circled my waist. He wore the most perfect smirk. "That might be the meanest thing you've ever said to me."

"It's a good 'but.'" I held on to his neck, smiling. *God, I am so in love with this man.* "I would love to marry you, *but* it's not up to me...and even though I think the kids would be more than okay with it, I would need to talk to them about it first. It affects them in a very big way."

His eyes crinkled as he studied me. He stepped back, taking my hand. "Come on."

Nathan led me back down the hallway.

"Um, I'm confused." I laughed quietly as we passed Marley's bedroom. "Where are we going?" I whispered. "I thought, you know...kids. Asleep..." I held on to Nathan's arm as we descended the stairs.

He flicked on the lights, pulling me through the kitchen and into the family room. He didn't explain his actions.

The TV was still on. I peered at the couch when we got in front of it and at Oliver and Olivia fast asleep at either end.

Nathan released my hand and dropped to his knee. He gently woke the kids, rubbing their shoulders until they roused.

Oliver blinked awake first and stretched his arms.

Olivia sat up in a daze. Her braids were messy. "Huh?" She squinted at me. "We're not leaving, are we? I thought we were staying the night."

I looked at Nathan instead of answering. I had no idea what was going on.

"No, you're not leaving," he said, guiding Oliver to a sitting position. He reached for their glasses, which had been discarded on the end table, and handed them over.

The kids both yawned and pushed the frames up their noses.

"You can go back to sleep in a minute. Your mom wanted to know what we talked about earlier while she was upstairs. Can you guys tell her?"

My gaze jumped from Nathan to the kids. *What?* Oliver and Olivia looked at each other with matching grins.

"Mom, you're gonna marry Nate," Oliver said. "I mean, if you want to. Then we can get our last names changed to Bell. All of us. We really wanna do that."

"Nate said we could. You just gotta say yes." Olivia held her hands in front of her face like she was praying. "Please say yes! *Please!*"

"We wanna be a family, Mom."

"We want you to marry Nate!"

"Mom."

I bounced my gaze to Oliver as he scooted to the edge of the couch. I'd never seen him look more serious before.

"We're good with this," he said. "I know you gotta hear that. You know now, so do it. Marry Nate."

Olivia slid to the edge now too and nodded at me. "Please?"

I exhaled a shaky breath. They were all asking me to marry him. All three of them.

"I'll wake up Marley if I need to," Nathan said, determination in his eyes. "I've talked to her about it. I'm not sure she understands it yet, but she loves you. And them. I know this is what she wants."

"We can be a family, Mama. Just like our dream." Olivia got to her feet and moved beside Nathan. She took hold of his hand. "See? Like this."

Oliver stood then too and put his arm around Nathan's neck. The three of them stared at me, and my God, they looked so much alike, it shouldn't have been possible, it couldn't have been, but it was.

"What do I need to do?" Nathan asked. "I'll do anything for this."

My heart started beating faster. He would. There was no doubt in my mind.

Nathan had hope in us. He'd known we belonged together back when I could only wish for it. He loved me. He loved my kids. He never would've stopped trying to save Oliver.

My answer was the easiest one of my life. And I gave it to him, after I dashed upstairs, got Marley out of her crib, and returned with her asleep in my arms. An action everyone except me found amusing at first.

Once we were all together and surrounded by our kids, I told Nathan I would marry him, and then he stopped questioning what I'd done, the kids stopped laughing at me for needing to do it, and we embraced, all of us.

Our family.

epilogue

NATHAN

Three Years Later

W*ake up, Nathan."*
            I jerked awake and blinked against my pillow. My eyes
were slow to focus as fingers softly feathered through my hair,
pushing strands off my forehead.

"Hey." Jenna's gentle voice slid over me.

She was sitting up in bed, her back against the headboard
and the lamp on the table beside her turned on, casting a soft
glow around her and shadows on the wall. She had a book in
her lap.

"Are you okay?" she asked.

I nodded, turning my face into her hand when she cupped my
cheek. "Yeah." I kissed her palm.

"You haven't had one in a while."

She was right about that. My dreams had become much less
frequent. It was rare to have one now. A lot of that had to do with
the therapy Marley and I started going to together when she began to have questions that I wasn't sure how to answer. Talking
it out helped us both. And that was something we'd continue to
do for as long as we both needed it, which might be forever. And
if it was, that was okay.

But I knew the biggest reason for the scarcity of my dreams and how I felt overall about Sadie's death was Jenna.

We talked a lot about the guilt I had. Why I carried it around and why I shouldn't. There wasn't any shame or judgment. I let Jenna in completely. I never held back anything I felt anymore. And it was good, sharing with her. I needed to do it as much as she needed it to happen. She was significant to me and she never doubted it.

We were working through it together, all of us.

"What are you doing up this late?" I asked. I rose to check the time, then collapsed onto my side again. It was nearly two in the morning.

Jenna felt the top of her protruding belly just below her breast. The ring I gave her caught in the light and sparkled. "I think your boy has decided to practice his right hooks tonight. He's killing my ribs." She winced and shifted her hips on the bed before relaxing back again.

"What's his problem? Do I need to have a talk with him?" I rubbed her stomach, smoothing down the shirt of mine she was wearing so it looked like she was hiding a basketball underneath. I spread out my fingers and pretended to palm it. "How much bigger do you think you're going to get?"

"A lot. Double this, maybe? I still have four months to go." She smiled and rested her hand on top of mine. Then she gave me a pat, letting me know she was getting up before she took her time swinging her legs out of bed.

"Let me get them," she said.

"I'm fine. You don't need to." I felt the heat of her body on the sheets.

"You're such a liar."

Her voice was sweet and teasing, but there was seriousness in it too. I knew better than to argue with her right now. She'd win. She always did.

When I'd had my first dream with everyone in the house, Jenna had stirred awake and talked me through it. It had helped. Then she'd gotten up and, after ignoring my protests, brought all of the kids into the bedroom so I could be surrounded by them. She wanted me to have all of their love around me. She'd known I needed it even before I did.

Even on nights when I thought I was fine, Jenna still got them up. And every single time, I felt better because of it.

After placing the book she was reading on the table, Jenna held her stomach as she moved toward the door.

I rolled onto my back so my eyes could follow and blinked at the ceiling when she stepped out of the room, leaving me alone. For a moment the house was still and quiet the way it used to be and the way I hated, but that didn't last. It couldn't anymore.

Muffled voices floated down the hallway, followed by footsteps—bare feet against the wood. I heard Jenna speak softly in the distance as Oliver moved into the bedroom first.

He was tall for eleven and letting his hair grow out. A decision he'd made once he saw a few of my old team photos. Strands covered his ears and fell into his eyes. Jenna tried not to hate it.

"Hey, Dad." Oliver leaned over me so I could hug him. He squeezed my shoulder. "Love you."

"Love you too, bud."

As he was climbing into the bed on Jenna's side, Olivia padded into the room.

She was Jenna's twin now, in personality and in looks. Her freckles had remained while Oliver's had faded. And she favored her hair down as opposed to braids.

"I like you," she said as we hugged.

I smiled and kissed her temple. She loved me because she liked me. That was her logic.

"I love you too."

Olivia walked around the bed and climbed on beside Oliver, who had scooted over near the center. He left a small gap between us, but not because Oliver didn't want to be next to me. He just knew his sister.

Marley dragged the baby blanket she still slept with into the room and climbed up over my legs, crawling into the space her brother had left for her.

Blond curls spilled over her shoulders and back. Her eyes were still the bluest blue. She favored Sadie in every way.

Her warm arms wound around my neck.

"It's okay, Daddy." Her voice was sleep heavy and slow. "It wasn't your fault," she whispered.

It didn't matter how much younger she was than her siblings. Marley knew what I dreamed. We talked about it in therapy.

I held her tight. "I love you."

"Love you too." She kissed my cheek, and then she pulled the covers up and wiggled underneath them, rolling onto her side. She snuggled close to Oliver.

When Jenna returned to the room, I adjusted my pillow so it pushed my shoulders off the mattress and boosted me up a little higher in bed.

I never liked lying completely flat with our son.

"How's that?" Jenna asked, watching me settle Matthew against my chest.

He was long limbed already. He'd just turned one last month.

I cupped the back of his head, which was covered in thick, dark hair and curly like Marley's.

He looked like the perfect combination of all four of us—it was wild.

"Good," I murmured, smelling him, my hand on his back so I could feel him breathe.

"Just good?"

I looked over at her and shook my head.

She'd asked, but she knew I could never be *just good* getting what I needed. Just like she could never deny giving it to me.

Jenna bent down and we kissed. Then she got into bed beside Olivia and rolled to her side. She watched me above sleepy heads.

I knew, because I was already watching her.

"We're getting a little crowded in here," she said quietly, looking like that fact didn't bother her at all, and she was more stating it out of curiosity for me, wondering how I felt about it. "We might need a bigger bed when these two come along." She placed her hand on her stomach.

We'd found out we were expecting twins four months ago, and two months after that, their genders. A boy and a girl.

I couldn't fucking wait. None of us could. Oliver and Olivia were especially excited.

"We'll be fine," I told her.

"I'll remember you said that when you're complaining about not having any room."

"I'd never say that."

"What about the noise…three under the age of two?"

I grinned at her.

She giggled back. "You love that, don't you? You can't wait."

"I don't want it quiet in here. You know that."

"They'll all eventually grow up and move away…It won't always be like this."

Jenna was right. It wouldn't. Everything was temporary. I was scared of losing this. I always would be. And I was fine with that.

I would be fine with it until the day I stopped being scared.

"We have years until that happens," I said, voice breaking with a yawn. I hugged Matthew closer.

"What do you need, Nathan?"

My mouth twitched.

We still asked each other that question, and most of the time, our answers were the same.

I looked over at Jenna. "Right now?"

"Right now."

Between us, our family dozed.

"Nothing."

acknowledgments

My very last acknowledgments for this series, and I'm so sad to write them! What a ride this has been. I feel so lucky to have gone on this journey. So grateful.

Thank you to Kimberly Brower, agent extraordinaire. Your guidance throughout this series has been my lifeline. Thank you for always having my back and for your constant encouragement. You're the best. I don't tell you that enough.

To Leah and the Forever team, thank you! I'm so happy we teamed up for this. To Danielle Sanchez and the InkSlinger family, thank you for all of your hard work and for helping me reach new readers. To all of the amazing bloggers who have supported me and this series, I can't express my gratitude enough.

To Beth Cranford, Tiffany Ly, Yvette Truijillo, Lisa Jayne, and Sarah Symonds. I appreciate you all so much. Thank you for loving this series and for your friendship.

To the author friends I've made along the way, you know who you are. Special thanks to my reader's group. You guys are amazing. Thank you for being the best cheering squad I could ask for. And to my incredible readers, wow. I am so, so lucky to have you. Thank you.

Lastly, to my husband—my main squeeze. Aw man, you're the best permanent boyfriend/baby daddy ever. Thank you for loving me and for our sweet, sweet babies. Look how good we did, B.

about the author

J. Daniels is the *New York Times* and *USA Today* bestselling author of the Alabama Summer, Dirty Deeds, and Sweet Addiction series.

Best known for her sexy, small-town romances, her debut novel, *Sweet Addiction*, was first published in 2014 and went on to become an international bestseller. Since then, she has published more than ten novels, including the Dirty Deeds series with Forever Romance.

Daniels grew up in Baltimore and currently lives in Maryland with her husband and two kids. A former full-time radiologic technologist, she began writing romance after college and quickly discovered a passion for it. You'll still catch her in scrubs every now and then, but most of her time these days is spent writing—a career she is eternally grateful for.

Always an avid reader, Daniels enjoys books of all kinds but favors romance (of course) and fantasy. She loves hiking, traveling, going to the mountains for the weekend, and spending time with her family.

To receive an email when she releases a new book, sign up for her newsletter! http://bit.ly/jdaniels_newsletter

She loves meeting and interacting with her readers. Visit her website to see where you can find her! www.authorjdaniels.com

About the Author

SOCIAL MEDIA:

Facebook: http://bit.ly/jdaniels_facebook
Instagram: http://bit.ly/jdaniels_instagram
Twitter: http://bit.ly/jdaniels_twitter
Reader's group: http://bit.ly/jdaniels_readersgroup
Goodreads: http://bit.ly/jdaniels_goodreads